Arthur Howard Gelton

English prose

From Maundevile to Thackeray

Arthur Howard Gelton

English prose
From Maundevile to Thackeray

ISBN/EAN: 9783337282424

Printed in Europe, USA, Canada, Australia, Japan

Cover: Foto ©Andreas Hilbeck / pixelio.de

More available books at **www.hansebooks.com**

The Camelot Series

EDITED BY ERNEST RHYS

ENGLISH PROSE.

ENGLISH PROSE,
FROM MAUNDEVILE
TO THACKERAY; CHOSEN
AND EDITED BY ARTHUR
GALTON.

LONDON
WALTER SCOTT, 24 WARWICK LANE
NEW YORK: THOMAS WHITTAKER
TORONTO: W. J. GAGE & CO.
1888

INDEX.

INDEX.

INDEX.

PREFACE.

THE purpose of this book is to give specimens of English prose; it is not meant to supply a catalogue of English writers, nor to be a criticism of English literature, or a commentary on English history, or a guide-book to philology. I have, therefore, not felt obliged to include all those writers who are usually held to have been the best models of style by posterity, or the finest examples of the manner of their own centuries. Nor did I feel called upon to add a certain number of more obscure writers; either to create an impression of wide reading, or for any other of the less apparent reasons which have influenced several compilers of prose extracts, and too many critics of standard works. Since my object, then, was not to accumulate a list of names, but to give fair specimens of English prose as it has been written during the last five hundred years, I was not forced, by an array of names, to spoil and mutilate the several extracts. It was impossible, from the nature of the case, to give many unabridged extracts, for that could only be done with some of the Essayists; but I have tried, in every instance, to make each extract intelligible and interesting in itself. For this reason, I have observed no common uniformity of length, an attempt which has lessened the value and the pleasure of many books of selections; I preferred, rather, to aim at a common uniformity of completeness and interest.

As my volume is not designed for an historical commentary, and as I have kept almost entirely to names that are well known, I have not ventured to doubt the knowledge, or to outrage the intelligence, of my readers; and so I have given no information about the authors quoted, except their date. If the less minute details of their lives are not already familiar, they cannot be satisfactorily conveyed in short notices; and still less, if their works are not known, can such notices give an adequate, or even an useful, criticism of their style and matter. In an enterprise like the Camelot Series, it seems desirable to have a single aim, and that aim quite simple. The aim is, usually, to give the text of some famous author in a correct, a convenient, and an accessible form; with a sufficient explanation of the author and his work to make them intelligible to every reader. Beyond this, the less irrelevant matter that is added the better; for the editor's industry, and the intelligence of the reader, can be so far more usefully occupied with the text. In this volume, the aim is not to exhibit any special author, but to show what English prose was like in the various centuries from which examples have been chosen; it would, therefore, have been aimless and superfluous to have entered upon any criticism of the individual writers. In one case only have I added a few facts, it is in the case of Robert Southwell, an interesting Jesuit who died in the reign of Queen Elizabeth; his life and writings, at any rate his prose writings, are perhaps not so generally known as the lives and writings of the other authors from whom I have selected. And as this volume is distinctly not a work upon philology, I have added no notes about the vocabulary, about the meaning of words. In the earlier writers, a few words may appear strange at first sight, but more from the ancient spelling than from anything else; and it surely would have been impertinent to have written notes about a thing so obvious as a variation in spelling. Besides, in these days of ours every-one who cares for literature should resist the ambitious and mischievous encroachments of philology upon the domain of letters. It is clear that philology is not literature, because many excellent writers have been quite innocent of that, and of all other science; while the most learned philologists, like most other men of science, usually write an execrable style.

I have begun my selections with Sir John Maundevile; because to begin with Anglo-Saxon is pedantic; only a pedant, or a specialist, can fancy that Anglo-Saxon is English; to begin with Norman-French is also to mistake what English is; and to begin a volume of selections, as Mr. Saintsbury does, with the invention of printing, is ignoble: it is to confuse literature with a mere mechanical process, with the accidental manner of its reproduction. Such a confusion panders to our modern belief that trade is the standard of all things; and it supports Macaulay's vicious opinion that the English literature of the last three centuries is, by itself, more valuable than the literature produced by the whole world before the birth of Knox and Calvin. The extracts go down to Thackeray; partly because the limits of my space would not allow me to go much beyond his date; and partly because of the difficulties of copyright, and the invidiousness of choosing, in the case of more recent, or of living authors. I have no theory to offer to my readers, because it is far more profitable to study prose in concrete examples, than to hold vague and general theories about style, or about the development of prose. Perhaps prose has developed; it is not so certain that it has improved. Our spelling has changed a great deal; our vocabulary has altered considerably, and possibly not always for the better; but in other matters, even in the cast of the sentence itself, there has not been so much change as divers critics have tried to prove. One of the great uses of a book of selections is to remind us that, in all ages, the really great writers have differed very little from one another; all good prose has the same qualities of directness, plainness, and simplicity. And good prose can still be written whenever a writer condescends to think clearly, to stick to the point, and to express his ideas in the plainest, the simplest, the most direct and unpretentious way.

The compiler of a book of selections can never hope to please all his readers, or to please many of them entirely; for he cannot even please himself. His readers will always complain that this author, or that passage, is not given; may I beg my readers to be indulgent with me in this matter, because I share their feelings, and sympathise with them. My thanks are due to Messrs. Frederick Warne & Co. for their free permission to use an extract from Napier's Peninsular War; and to Messrs. A. & C. Black for their permission to use the extract from De Quincey. In conclusion, I must thank Miss Beatrice Horne for the immense care which she has bestowed upon all the . earlier texts; that they have been copied from the best editions, is entirely due to her devoted labours. It is only fair to Miss Horne to add that Mr. Walter Scott's proof-readers are wholly responsible for the final revisions of the printed text.

New College, Oxford,
    June 1888.

ENGLISH PROSE.

—◆—

SIR JOHN MAUNDEVILE.

1322–1388.

*Of the Hilles of Gold, that Pissemyres kepen: and of the
4 Flodes, that comen from Paradys terrestre.*

TOWARD the Est partye of Prestre Johnes Lond, is an Yle gode
and gret, that men clepen Taprobane, that is fulle noble and fulle
fructuous: and the Kyng thereof is fulle ryche, and is undre
the obeyssance of Prestre John. And alle weys there thei
make hire Kyng be Eleccyoun. In that Ile ben 2 Someres
and 2 Wyntres; and men hervesten the Corn twyes a Zeer.
And in alle the Cesouns of the Zeer ben the Gardynes florisht.
There dwellen gode folk and resonable, and manye Cristene
men amonges hem, that ben so riche, that thei wyte not what to
done with hire Godes. Of olde tyme, whan men passed from
the Lond of Prestre John unto that Yle, men maden ordynance
for to passe by Schippe, 23 dayes or more: but now men passen
by Schippe in 7 dayes. And men may see the botme of the
See in many places: for it is not fulle depe.
' Besyde that Yle, toward the Est, ben 2 other Yles: and men
clepen that on Orille, and that other Argyte; of the whiche alle
the Lond is Myne of Gold and Sylver. And tho Yles ben right
where that the rede See departethe fro the See Occean. And
in tho Yles men seen ther no Sterres so clerly as in other
places: for there apperen no Sterres, but only o clere Sterre,
that men clepen Canapos. And there is not the Mone seyn in
alle the Lunacioun, saf only the seconde quarteroun. In the
Yle also of this Taprobane, ben grete Hilles of Gold, that

(1)

Pissemyres kepen fulle diligently. And thei fynen the pured
Gold, and casten away the unpured. And theise Pissemyres
ben grete as Houndes : so that no man dar come to tho Hilles :
for the Pissemyres wolde assaylen hem and devouren hem
anon ; so that no man may gete of that gold, but be gret
sleighte. And therefore whan it is gret hete, the Pissemyres
resten hem in the Erthe, from pryme of the Day in to Noon :
and than the folk of the Contree taken Camayles, Dromedaries
and Hors and other Bestes, and gon thidre, and chargen hem in
alle haste that thei may. And aftre that they fleen awey, in
alle haste that the Bestes may go, or the Pissemyres comen
out of the Erthe. And in other tymes, whan it is not so hote,
and that the Pissemyres ne resten hem not in the Erthe, than
thei geten Gold be this Sotyltee ; Thei taken Mares, that han
zonge Coltes or Foles, and leyn upon the Mares voyde Vesselles
made therfore ; and thei ben alle open aboven, and hangynge
lowe to the Erthe : and thanne thei sende forth tho Mares, for to
pasturen about tho Hilles, and with holden the Foles with hem
at home. And whan the Pissemyres sen tho Vesselles, thei
lepen in anon, and thei han this kynde, that thei lete no
thing ben empty among hem, but anon thei fillen it, be it what
maner of thing that it be : and so thei fillen tho Vesselles with
gold. And whan that the folk supposen, that the Vesselle ben
fulle, thei putten forthe anon the zonge Foles, and maken hem
to nyzen aftre hire Dames ; and than anon the Mares retornen
towardes hire Foles, with hire charges of Gold ; and than men
dischargen hem, and geten Gold y now be this sotyltee. For
the Pissemyres wole suffren Bestes to gon and pasturen
amonges hem ; but no man in no wyse.

And bezonde the Lond and the Yles and the Desertes of
Prestre Johnes Lordschipe, in goynge streyght toward the
Est, men fynde nothing but Mountaynes and Roches fulle grete :
and there is the derke Regyoun, where no man may see,
nouther be day ne be nyght, as thei of the Contree seyn. And
that Desert, and that place of Derknesse, duren fro this Cost
unto Paradys terrestre ; where that Adam oure foremest Fader,
and Eve weren putt, that dwelleden there but lytylle while ;
and that is towards the Est, at the begynnynge of the Erthe.
But that is not that Est, that wee clep oure Est, on this half,
where the Sonne risethe to us : for whenne the Sonne is Est in
tho partyes, toward Paradys terrestre, it is thanne mydnyght in
our parties o this half, for the rowndenesse of the Erthe, of the
whiche I have towched to zou before. For oure Lord God made
the Erthe alle round, in the mydde place of the Firmament.

And there as Mountaynes and Hilles ben, and Valeyes, that
is not but only of Noes Flode, that wasted the softe ground
and the tendre, and felle doun into Valeyes : and the harde
Erthe, and the Roche abyden Mountaynes, whan the soft
Erthe and tendre wax nessche, throghe the Water, and felle
and becamen Valeyes.

Of Paradys ne can not I speken propurly : for I was not
there. It is fer bezonde ; and that forthinkethe me : and also
I was not worthi. But as I have herd seye of wyse men
beyonde, I schalle telle zou with gode Wille. Paradys terrestre,
as wise men seyn, is the highest place of Erthe, that is in alle
the World : and it is so highe, that it touchethe nyghe to the
cercle of the Mone, there as the Mone makethe hire torn. For
sche is so highe, that the Flode of Noe ne myght not come to
hire, that wolde have covered alle the Erthe of the World alle
aboute, and aboven and benethen, saf Paradys only allone.
And this Paradys is enclosed alle aboute with a Walle ; and men
wyte not whereof it is. For the Walles ben covered all over
with Mosse ; as it semethe: And it semethe not that the
Walle is Ston of Nature. And that Walle strecchethe fro the
Southe to the Northe ; and it hathe not but on entree, that is
closed with Fyre brennynge ; so that no man, that is mortalle,
ne dar not entren. And in the moste highe place of Paradys,
evene in the myddel place, is a Welle, that castethe out the 4
Flodes, that rennen be dyverse Londes : of the whiche, the first
is clept Phison or Ganges, that is alle on ; and it rennethe
throghe out Ynde or Emlak : in the whiche Ryvere ben manye
preciouse Stones, and mochel of Lignū Aloes, and moche
gravelle of gold. And that other Ryvere is clept Nilus or
Gyson, that gothe be Ethiope, and aftre be Egypt. And that
other is clept Tigris, that rennethe be Assirye and be Armenye
the grete. And that other is clept Eufrate, that rennethe also
be Medee and be Armonye and be Persye. And men there
bezonde seyn, that all the swete Watres of the World aboven and
benethen, take hire begynnynge of the Welle of Paradys : and
out of that Welle, all Watres comen and gon. The firste Ryvere
is clept Phison, that is to seyne in hire langage, Assemblee :
For manye othere Ryveres meten heren there, and gon in to
that Ryvere. And sum men clepen it Ganges ; for a Kyng
that was in Ynde, that highte Gangeres, and that it ran thorge out
his Lond. And that Water is in sum place clere, and in sum
place trouble ; in sum place hoot, and in sum place cole. The
seconde Ryvere is clept Nilus or Gyson : for it is alle weye
trouble : and Gyson, in the langage of Ethiope, is to seye

trouble ; and in the langage of Egipt also. The thridde Ryvere, that is clept Tigris, is as moche for to seye as faste rennynge : for he rennethe more faste than ony of the tother. And also there is a Best, that is cleped Tigris, that is faste rennynge. The fourthe Ryvere is clept Eufrates, that is to seyne, wel berynge : for there growen manye Godes upon that Ryvere, as Cornes, Frutes, and othere Godes y nowe plentee.

And zee schulle undirstonde, that no man that is mortelle, ne may not approchen to that Paradys. For be Londe no man may go for wylde bestes, that ben in the Desertes, and for the highe Mountaynes and gret huge Roches, that no man may passe by, for the derke places that ben there, and that manye : And be the Ryveres may no man go ; for the water rennethe so rudely and so scharply, because that it comethe doun so outrageously from the highe places aboven, that it rennethe in so grete Wawes, that no Schipp may not rowe ne seyle azenes it : and the Watre rorethe so, and makethe so huge noyse, and so gret tempest, that no man may here other in the Schipp, thoughe he cryede with alle the craft that he cowde, in the hyeste voys that he myghte. Many grete Lordes han assayed with grete wille many tymes for to passen be the Ryveres toward Paradys, with fulle grete Companyes : but thei myghte not speden in hire Viage ; and manye dyeden for werynesse of rowynge azenst the stronge Wawes ; and many of hem becamen blynde, and manye deve, for the noyse of the Water; and sūme weren perrisscht and loste, with inne the Wawes : So that no mortelle man may approche to that place, with outen specyalle grace of God : so that of that place I can seye zou no more. And therefore I schalle holde me stille, and retornen to that that I have seen.

The Voiage and Travaile.

SIR THOMAS MALORY.

FLR. 1450.

THE HOLY GRAIL.

Now sayth the history that whan launcelot was come to the water of Mortoyse as hit is reherced before, he was in grete perylle, and soo he leyd hym doune and slepte, and toke the aduenture that god wold sende hym.

Soo whan he was a slepe, there came a vysyon vnto hym and said Launcelot aryse vp & take thyn armour, and entre in to the first ship that thow shalt fynde. And when he herd these wordes he starte vp and saw grete clerenes about him. And thenne he lyfte vp his hande and blessid hym and so toke his armes and made hym redy, and soo by aduenture he came by a stronde, & founde a shyp, the which was withoute sayle or ore. And as soone as he was within the shyp there he felte the moost swetnes that euer he felt, and he was fulfylled with alle thinge that he thought on or desyred. Thenne he sayd, Fair swete fader Jhesu Cryst I wote not in what joye I am, For this joye passeth all erthely joyes that euer I was in. And soo in this ioye he leyd hymn doune to the shyps' borde, & slepte tyl day. And when he awoke, he fonde there a fayre bed & therin lyenge a gentylwoman dede, the whiche was syr percyuales syster. And as launcelot deuysed her, he aspyed in hir ryght hand a wrytte, the which he redde, the whiche told hym all the aduentures that ye haue herd tofore, and of what lygnage she was come. Soo with this gentylwoman syr launcelot was a moneth and more. yf ye wold aske me how he lyued, he that fedde the peple of Israel with manna in deserte, soo was he fedde. For euery day when he had sayd his prayers, he was susteyned with the grace of the holy ghoost. So on a nyghte he wente to playe hym by the water syde, for he was somewhat wery of the shyp. And thenne he lystned and herd an hors come, And one rydynge vpon hym. And whanne he cam nygh he semed a knyghte. And soo he lete hym passe, and went there as the shyp was, and there he alyghte, and toke the sadel and the bridel and putte the hors from hym, and went in to the ship. And thenne Launcelot dressid vnto hym and said ye be welcome, and he ansuerd and salewed hym ageyne, & asked hym what is your name, for moche my hert gyueth vnto yow. Truly sayd he my name is launcelot du lake, sir saide he, thēne be ye welcome, for ye were the begynner of me in this world. A sayd he aꝛ ye Galahad, ye forsothe sayd he, and so he kneled doune and asked hym his blessynge, and after toke of his helme and kyssed hym. And there was grete joye bitwene them, for there is no tonge can telle the joy that they made eyther of other, and many a frendely word spoken bitwene, as kynde wold, the whiche is no nede here to be reherced. And there eueryche told other of theire adventures and merueils that were befallen to them in many journeyes sythe that they departed from the courte. Anone as Galahad sawe the gentilwoman dede in the bed, he knewe her wel ynough, & told grete worship of her that she was the best mayde lyuyng and hit was grete pyte of her dethe. But whanne Launcelot herd how the merucylous swerd was goten, and who made hit, and alle the merueyls reherced afore, Thenne he prayd galahad his sone that he wold shewe hym the suerd, and so he dyd, and anone he kyssed the pomel and the hyltes and the scaubard. Truly sayd launcelot neuer erst knewe I of so hyhe aduentures done and so merueyllous & straunge. So dwellid Launcelot and Galahad within that shyp half a yere, and seured god dayly and nyghtly with alle their power, and often they aryued in yles ferre from folke, where there repayred none but wylde beestes, and ther they fond many straunge aduentures and peryllous whiche they broughte to an ende, but for tho aduentures were with wylde beestes, and not in the quest of the Sancgreal, therfor the tale maketh here no mencyon therof, for it wolde be to longe to telle of alle tho aduentures that befelle them.

Soo after on a mondaye hit befelle that they aryued in the edge of a foreste to fore a crosse, and thenne sawe they a knyghte armed al in whyte and was rychely horsed, and ledde in his ryght hand a whyte hors, and soo he cam to the shyp and salewed the two knyghtes on the hyghe lordes behalf, and sayd Galahad syr ye haue ben longe ynough with your fader, come oute of the ship, and starte vpon this hors, & goo where the aduentures shall lede the in the quest of the sancgreal. thenne

he wente to his fader and kyst hym swetely and sayd, Fair swete
fader I wote not whan I shal see you more tyl I see the body
of Jhesu Cryst. I praye yow sayd launcelot praye ye to the
hyghe fader that he hold me in his seruyse & soo he took his
hors, & ther they herd a voyce that sayd thynke for to doo
wel, for the one shal neuer see the other before the dredeful day
of dome. Now sone galahad said laūcelot syn we shal departe,
& neuer see other, I pray te ye hyz fader to conserue me and
yow bothe. Sire said Galahad noo prayer auaylleth soo moche
as yours. And there with Galahad entryd in to the foreste.
And the wynde aroos and drofe Launcelot more than a moneth
thurgh oute the see where he slepte but lytel but prayed to
god that he myghte see some tydynges of the Sancgreal. Soo
hit befelle on a nyghte at mydnyghte he aryued afore a Castel on
the bak syde whiche was ryche and fayre, & there was a
posterne opened toward the see, and was open withoute ony
kepynge, sauf two lyons kept the entre, and the moone shone
clere. Anone sir launcelot herd a voyce that sayd Launcelot
goo oute of this shyp, and entre into the Castel, where thou shalt
see a grete parte of thy desyre. Thenne he ran to his armes
and soo armed hym, and soo wente to the gate and sawe the
lyons. Thenne sette he hand to his suerd & drewe hit.
Thenne ther came a dwerf sodenly and smote hym on the
harme so sore that the suerd felle oute of his hand. Thenne
herd he a voyce say O man of euylle feyth and poure byleue
wherefor trowest thow more on thy harneis than in thy maker,
for he myghte more auayle the than thyn armour in whose
seruyse that thou arte sette. Thenne said launcelot, fayr fader
ihesu Cryste I thanke the of thy grete mercy that thou repreuest
me of my mysdede. Now see I wel that ye hold me for youre
seruaunte. thenne toke he ageyne his suerd and putte it vp in his
shethe and made a crosse in his forhede, and came to the lyons,
and they made semblaunt to doo hym harme. Notwith-
standynge he passed by hem withoute hurte and entryed in to the
castel to the chyef fortresse, and there were they al at rest,
thenne Launcelot entryd in so armed, for he fond noo gate nor
dore but it was open. And at the last he fond a chamber
wherof the dore was shytte, and he sette his hand therto to haue
opened hit, but he myghte not.

Thenne he enforced hym mykel to vndoo the dore, thenne he
lystned and herd a voyce whiche sange so swetely that it semed
none erthely thynge, and hym thoughte the voyce said Joye
and honour be to the fader of heuen. Thenne Launcelot
kneled doun to fore the chamber, for wel wyst he that there

was the Sancgreal within that chamber. Thenne sayd he Fair
swete fader Jhesu Cryst yf euer I dyd thyng that pleasyd the
lord, for thy pyte ne haue me not in despyte for my synnes
done afore tyme, and that thou shewe me some thynge of that
I seke. And with that he sawe the chamber dore open and
there came oute a grete clerenes, that the hows was as bryghte
as all the torches of the world had ben there. So cam he to
the chamber dore, and wold haue entryd. And anon a voyce
said to hym, Flee launcelot, and entre not, for thou oughtest
not to doo hit. And yf thou entre, thou shalt forthynke hit.
Thenne he withdrewe hym abak ryght heuy. Then looked he
vp in the myddes of the chamber, and sawe a table of sylver
and the holy vessel couerd with reed samyte, and many angels
aboute hit, whereof one helde a candel of wax brennying and
the other held a crosse and the ornementys of an aulter. And
bifore the holy vessel he sawe a good man clothed as a preest.
And it semed that he was at the sacrynge of the masse. And
it seemed to Launcelot that aboue the preestes handes were
thre men whereof the two putte the yongest by lykenes bitwene
the preestes handes, and soo he lyfte hit vp ryghte hyhe, & it
semed to shewe so to the peple. And thenne launcelot
merueyled not a lytel. For hym thouzt the preest was so
gretely charged of the fygure that hym semed that he sholde falle
to the erthe. And whan he sawe none aboute hym that wolde
helpe hym, Thenne came he to the dore a grete paas and sayd,
Faire fader Jhesu Cryst ne take hit for no synne though I
helpe the good man which hath grete nede of help. Ryghte
soo entryd he in to the chamber and cam toward the table of
syluer, and whanne he came nyghe he felte a brethe that hym
thoughte hit was entremedled with fyre whiche smote hym so
sore in the vysage that hym thoughte it brente his vysage, and
there with he felle to the erthe and had no power to aryse, as
he that was soo araged that had loste the power of his body
and his herynge and seynge.

Thenne felte he many handes aboute hym whiche tooke hym
vp, and bare hym oute of the chamber dore, withoute ony
amendynge of his swonne, and lefte hym there semyng dede to
al peple. Soo vpon the morowe whan it was fayre day they
with in were arysen, and fonde Launcelot lyenge afore the
chamber dore. Alle they merueylled how that he cam in, and so
they looked vpon hym and felte his pouse to wyte whether there
were ony lyf in hym, and soo they fond lyf in hym, but he
myghte not stande nor stere no membre that he had, and soo
they tooke hym by euery part of the body, and bare hym in to a

chambre and leyd hym in a ryche bedde ferre from alle folke, and soo he lay four dayes. Thenne the one sayd he was on lyue, and the other sayd Nay. In the name of god sayd an old man, for I doo yow veryly to wete, he is not dede, but he is soo fulle of lyf as the myghtyest of yow alle, and therfor I counceylle yow that he be wel kepte tyl god send hym lyf ageyne.

Morte D'Arthur.

HUGH LATIMER.

1470–1555.

SERMON OF THE PLOUGH.

From A notable Sermon of ye reuerende father Maister Hughe Latimer, whiche he preached in ye Shrouds at paules churche in London, on the xviii. daye of Jannarye. The yere of our Loorde MDXLVIII.

NOWE what shall we saye of these ryche citizens of London? What shall I saye of them? shal I cal them proude men of London, malicious men of London, mercylesse men of London. No, no, I may not saie so, they wil be offended wyth me than. Yet must I speake. For is there not reygning in London, as much pride, as much couetousnes, as much crueltie, as much opprission, as much supersticion, as was in Nebo? Yes, I thynke and muche more to. Therefore I say, repente O London. Repent, repente. Thou heareste thy faultes tolde the, amend them amend them. I thinke if Nebo had had the preachynge yat thou haste: they wold haue conuerted. And you rulers and officers be wise and circumspect, loke to your charge and see you do your dueties and rather be glad to amend your yll liuyng then to be angrye when you are warned or tolde of your faulte. What a do was there made in London at a certein man because he sayd, and in dede at that time on a iust cause. Burgesses quod he, nay butterflies. Lord what a do there was for yat worde. And yet would God they were no worse then butterflies. Butterflyes do but theyrē nature, the butterflye is not couetouse, is not gredye of other mens goodes, is not ful of envy and hatered, is not malicious, is not cruel, is not mercilesse. The butterflye gloriethe not in hyr owne dedes, nor preferreth the tradicions of men before Gods worde; it committeth not idolatry nor worshyppeth false goddes. But London can not abyde to be rebuked suche is the nature of man. If they be prycked, they will kycke. If they be rubbed on the gale: they wil wynce. But yet they wyll not amende theyr faultes, they wyl not be yl spoken of. But howe shal I speake well of them. If they could be contente to receyue and folowe the worde of god and fauoure good preachers, if you coulde beare to be toulde of your faultes, if you coulde amende when you heare of them: if you woulde be gladde to reforme that is a misse: if I mighte se anie suche inclinacion in you, that leaue to be mercilesse and begynne to be charytable I would then hope wel of you, I woulde then speake well of you. But London was neuer so yll as it is now. In tymes past men were full of pytie and compassion but nowe there is no pitie, for in London their brother shal die in the streetes for colde, he shall lye sycke at theyr door betwene stocke and stocke. I can not tel what to call it, and peryshe there for hunger, was there any more vnmercifulnes in Nebo? I thynke not. In tymes paste when any ryche man dyed in London, they were wonte to healp the pore scholers of the vniuersitye wyth exhibition. When any man dyed, they woulde bequeth greate summes of money towarde the releue of the pore. When I was a scholer in Cambrydge my selfe, I harde verye good reporte of London and knewe manie that had releue of the rytche men of London, but nowe I can heare no such good reporte, and yet I inquyre of it, and herken for it, but nowe charitie is waxed colde, none helpeth the scholer nor yet the pore. And in those dayes what dyd they whan they helped the scholers? Mary they maynteyned and gaue them liuynges that were verye papists and professed the popes doctrine and nowe that the knowledge of Gods word is brought to lyght, and many earnestelye studye and laboure to set it forth now almost no man healpeth to maynteyne them. Oh London London, repente repente, for I thynke God is more displeased wyth London then euer he was with the citie of Nebo. Repente therfore repent London and remembre that the same God liueth nowe yat punyshed Nebo, euen the same god and none other, and he will punyshe synne as well nowe as he dyd then, and he wyl punishe the iniquitie of London as well as he did then of Nebo. Amende therfore and ye that be prelates loke well to your office, for right prelatynge is busye labourynge and not lordyng. Therfore preache and teach and let your ploughe be doynge, ye lordes I saye that liue lyke loyterers, loke wel to your office, the ploughe is your office and charge. If you lyue idle and loyter, you do not your duetie, you folowe not youre vocation, let your plough therfore be going and not cease, that the ground maye brynge foorth fruite. . . .

For they that be lordes wyll yll go to plough. It is no mete office for them. It is not semyng for their state. Thus came vp lordyng loyterers. Thus crept in vnprechinge prelates, and so haue they longe continued.

For howe many vnlearned prelates haue we now at this day? And no meruel. For if ye plough men yat now be, were made lordes they woulde cleane gyu ouer plouginge, they woulde leaue of theyr labour and fall to lordyng outright, and let the plough stand. And then bothe ploughes not walkyng nothyng shoulde be in the common weale but honger. For euer sence the Prelates were made Loordes and nobles, the ploughe standeth, there is no worke done, the people sterue.

They hauke, thei hunt, thei card, they dyce, they pastyme in theyr prelacies with galaunte gentlemen, with theyr daunsinge minyons, and with theyr freshe companions, so that ploughinge is set a syde. And by the lording and loytryng, preachynge and ploughinge is cleane gone. And thus if the ploughemen of the countrey, were as negligente in theyr office, as prelates be, we should not longe lyue for lacke of sustinaunce. . . .

. . . . And nowe I would aske a straung question. Who is the most diligent bishoppe and prelate in al England, that passeth al the reste in doinge his office I can tel, for 1 knowe him, who it is I knowe hym well. But nowe I thynke I se you lysting and hearkening, that I shoulde name him. There is one that passeth al the other, and is the most diligent prelate and preacher in al England. And w[y]l ye knowe who it is? I wyl tel you. It is the Deuyl. He is the moste dyligent preacher of al other, he is neuer out of his dioces, he is neuer from his cure, ye shal neuer fynde him vnoccupyed, he is euer in his parishe, he keepeth residence at al tymes, ye shall never fynde hym out of the waye, cal for him when you wyl, he is ever at home, the diligenteste preacher in all the Realme, he is euer at his ploughe, no lordyng nor loytringe can hynder hym, he is euer appliynge his busynes, ye shal never fynde hym idle I warraunte you. And his office is to hinder religion, to mayntayne supersticion, to set vp Idolatrie, to teach al kynde of popetrie, he is readye as can be wished, for to sette forthe his ploughe, to deuise as manye wayes as can be to deface and obscure Godes glory. Where the Deuyl is residente and hath his ploughe goinge : there away with bokes, and vp with can-delles, awaye wyth Bibles and vp with beades, awaye with the lygte of the Gospel, and vp with the lyghte of candlles, yea at

noone dayes. Where the Deuyll is residente, that he maye pre-
uaile, vp wyth al superstition and Idolatrie, sensing, peintynge
of ymages, candles, palmes, asshes, holye water, and newe
seruice of menes inuenting, as though man could inuent a better
waye to honoure God wyth then God him selfe hath apointed.
Downe with Christes crosse, vp with purgatory picke purse vp
wyth hym, the popish pourgatorie I mean. Awaye wyth clothinge
the naked, the pore and impotent, vp wyth deckynge of ymages
and gaye garnishinge of stockes and stones, vp wyth mannes
traditions and his lawes, Downe wyth Gods traditions and hys
most holy worde, Downe wyth the olde honoure dewe to God,
and vp wyth the new gods honour, let al things be done in
latine. There muste be nothynge but latine, not as much as
Memento homo quod cinis es, et in cinerem reuerteris. Remembre man that thou arte asshes, and into asshes thou shalte
returne. Whiche be the wordes that the minister speaketh to
the ignoraunte people, when he gyueth them asshes vpon asshe
wensdaye, but it muste be spoken in latine. Goddes worde
may in no wyse be translated into englyshe. Oh that our prelates woulde be as diligente to sowe the corne of good doctrine
as Sathan is, to sowe cockel and darnel. And this is the deuil-
yshe ploughinge, the which worcketh to haue things in latine,
and letteth the fruteful edification. But here some man will
saie to me, what sir are ye to priuie of the deuils counsell that
ye know al this to be true? Truli I know I know him to wel,
and haue obeyed him a little to much in condesce[n]tinge to
some follies. And I knowe him as other men do, yea, that he
is euer occupied and euer busie in folowinge his plough. I
know bi saint Peter which saieth of him. *Sicut leo rugiens circuit querens quem deuoret.* He goeth aboute lyke a roaringe
lyon seekinge whom he maye deuoure. I woulde haue this
texte wel vewed and examined euerye worde of it. *Circuit,* he
goeth aboute in euerye corner of his dioces. He goeth on visita-
cion daylye. He leaueth no place of hys cure care vnuisited.
He walketh round aboute from place to place and ceaseth not,
Sicut leo, as a Lyon that is strongly, boldly, and proudlye
straytelye and fiercelye with haute lookes, wyth hys proude coun-
tenuances wyth hys stately braggynges. *Rugiens,* roaringe, for
he letteth not slippe any occasion to speake or to roare out
when he seeth his tyme. *Querens,* he goeth about seekyng and
not sleepyng, as oure bishoppes do, but he seketh diligently, he
searcheth diligently al corners, wheras he may haue his pray,
he roueth abrode in eueri place of his dioces, he standeth
not styl, he is neuer at reste, but euer in hande wyth his

plough that it may go forwarde.   But there was neuer shuch a preacher in England as he is.   Who is able to tel his diligente preaching ? whiche euery daye and euery houre laboreth to sowe cockel and darnel, that he may bryng oute of forme and out of estimation and roume, th[e] institution of the Lordes supper and Christes crosse, for there he lost his ryghte, for Christe saied.   *Nunc iudicium est mundi, princeps seculi hujus ciicietur foras, et sicut exaltauit Moises serpentem in deserto, ita exaltari oportet filium hominis, et cum exaltatus fuero, a terra, omnia traham ad meipsum.*   Nowe is the iudgemente of thys worlde and the Prynce of thys worlde shall be caste oute.   And as Moyses dyd lyfte vp the serpente in the wyldernesse, so muste the sonne of manne be lyfte vp.   And when I shall be lyfte vp from the earthe, I wyl drawe all thynges vnto my selfe.   For the Deuyll was dysapoynted of hys purpose, for he thoughte all to be hys owne.

And when he had once broughte Christe to the crosse, he thoughte all cocke sure.

FIRST SERMON BEFORE EDWARD VI.

The fyrste Sermon of Mayster Hughe Latimer, whiche he preached before the Kynges Maiest. wythin his graces palayce at Westmynster MDXLIX. the viii. of Marche.

.... My father was a Yoman, and had no landes of his owne, onlye he had a farme of .iii. or iiii. pound by yere at the vttermost, and here vpon he tilled so much as kept halfe a dosen men.   He had walke for a hundred shepe, and my mother mylked .xxx. kyne, He was able and did find the king a harnesse, wyth hym selfe, and hys horsse, whyle he came to ye place that he should receyue the kynges wages.   I can remembre, yat I buckled hys harnes, when he went vnto Blacke heeath felde.   He kept me to schole, or elles I had not bene able to haue preached before the kinges maiestie nowe.   He maryed . my systers with v. pounde or .xx. nobles a pece, so that he broughte them vp in godlines, and feare of God.

He kept hospitalitie for his pore neighbours.   And sum almess he gaue to the poore, and all thys did he of the sayd farme.   Wher he that now hath it, paieth .xvi. pounde by yere or more, and is not able to do any thing for his Prynce, for himselfe, nor for his children, or geue a cup of drincke to the pore.   Thus al the enhansinge and rearing goth to your priuate commoditie and wealth.   So that where ye had a single to much, you haue that : and syns the same, ye haue enhansed the rente, and so haue encreased an other to much.   So now ye haue doble to muche, whyche is to to muche.   But let the preacher preach til his tong be worne to the stompes, nothing is amended.   We haue good statutes made for the commen welth as touching comeners, enclosers, many metings and Sessions, but in the end of the matter there cometh nothing forth.   Wel, well, thys is one thynge I will saye from whens it commeth I knowe, euen, from the deuill.   I know his intent in it.   For if ye bryng it to passe, that the yo manry be not able to put their sonnes to schole (as in dede vniuersities do wonderously decaye all redy) and that they be not able to mary their daughters to the auoidyng of whoredom, I say ye plucke saluation from the people and vtterly distroy the realme.   For by yomans sonnes, the fayth of Christ is, and hath bene mayntained chefely. Is this realme taught by rich mens sonnes.   No, no, reade the Cronicles ye shall fynde sumtime noble mennes sonnes, which haue bene vnpreaching byshoppes and prelates, but ye, shall finde none of them learned men.   But verilye, they that should loke to the redresse of these things, be the greatest against them. In thys realme are a great meany of folkes, and amongest many, I knowe but one of tender zeale.   at the mocion of his poore tennauntes, hath let downe his landes to the olde rentes for their reliefe.   For goddes loue, let not him be a Phenix, let him not be alone, Let hym not be an Hermite closed in a wall, sum good man follow him and do as he geueth example. Suruciers there be, yat gredyly gorge vp their couetous, guttes hande makers, I meane (honest men I touch not) but al suche as suruci thei make vp their mouthes but the commens be vtterlye vndone by them.   Whose bitter cry ascendyng vp to the eares of the god of Sabaoth, the gredy pyt of hel burning fire (without great repentaunce) do tary and loke for them.   A redresse God graunt.   For suerly, suerly, but yat ii. thynges do comfort me I wold despaire of the redresse in these maters.   One is, that the kinges maiestie whan he commeth to age : wyll se a redresse of these thinges so out of frame.   Geuing example by letting doune his owne landes first and then enioyne hys subiects to folowe him.   The second hope I haue is, I beleue that the general accomptyng daye is at hande, the dreadfull daye of iudgement I meane, whiche shall make an end of al these calamities and miseries.

SIR THOMAS MORE.

1480-1535.

THE DEATH OF HASTINGS.

WHEREUPON sone after, that is to wit, on the Friday the——day of——many Lordes assembled in the Tower, and there sat in counsaile, deuising the honorable solempnite of the kinges coronacion, of which the time appointed then so nere approched, that the pageauntes and suttelties were in making day and night at Westminster, and much vitaile killed therfore, that afterward was cast away. These lordes so sytting togyther comoning of thys matter, the protectour came in among them, fyrst aboute ix. of the clock, saluting them curtesly, and excusyng hymself that he had ben from them so long, saieng merely that he had bene a slepe that day. And after a little talking with them, he sayd vnto the Bishop of Elye : My lord you haue very good strawberies at your gardayne in Holberne, I require you let vs haue a messe of them. Gladly my lord, quod he, woulde God I had some better thing as redy to your pleasure as that. And therwith in al the hast he sent hys seruant for a messe of strauberies. The protectour sette the lordes fast in comoning, and thereupon prayeng them to spare hym for a little while departed thence. And sone, after one hower, betwene .x. and .xi. he returned into the chamber among them, al changed, with a wonderful soure angrye countenaunce, knitting the browes, frowning and froting and knawing on hys lippes, and so sat him downe in hys place ; al the lordes much dismaied and sore merueiling of this maner of sodain chaunge, and what thing should him aile. Then when he had sitten still a while, thus he began : What were they worthy to haue, that compasse and ymagine the distruccion of me, being so nere of blood vnto the king and protectour of his riall person and his realme ? At this question, al the lordes sat sore astonied, musyng much by whome thys question should be ment, of

which euery man wyst himselfe clere.   Then the lord
chamberlen, as he that for the loue betwene them thoughte he
might be boldest with him, aunswered and sayd, that thei wer
worthye to bee punished as heighnous traitors, whatsoeuer they
were.   And al the other affirmed the same.   That is (quod he)
yonder sorceres my brothers wife and other with her, meaning
the quene.   At these wordes many of the other Lordes were
gretly abashed that fauoured her.   But the lord Hastinges was
in his minde better content, that it was moued by her, then by
any other whom he loued better.   Albeit hys harte somewhat
grudged, that he was not afore made of counsell in this matter,
as he was of the taking of her kynred, and of their putting to
death, which were by his assent before deuised to bee
byhedded at Pountfreit, this selfe same day, in which he was
not ware that it was by other deuised, that himself should the
same day be behedded at London.   Then said the protectour ;
ye shal al se in what wise that sorceres and that other witch of
her counsel, Shoris wife, with their affynite, haue by their sorcery
and witchcraft wasted my body.   And therwith he plucked vp
hys doublet sleue to his elbow vpon his left arme, where he
shewed a werish withered arme and small, as it was neuer other.
And thereupon euery mannes mind sore misgaue them, well
persceiuing that this matter was but a quarel.   For wel thei
wist, that the quene was to wise to go aboute any such folye.
And also if she would, yet wold she of all folke leste make
Shoris wife of counsaile, whom of al women she most hated, as
that concubine whom the king her husband had most loued.
And also no man was there present, but wel knew that his
harme was euer such since his birth.   Natheles the lorde
Chamberlen aunswered and sayd : certainly my lorde if they
haue so heinously done, thei be worthy heinous punishment.
What, quod the protectour, thou seruest me, I wene, with iffes
and with andes, I tel the thei haue so done, and that I will
make good on thy body, traitour.   And therwith as in a great
anger, he clapped his fist vpon the borde a great rappe.   At
which token giuen, one cried treason without the c[h]ambre.
Therewith a dore clapped, and in come there rushing men in
harneys as many as the chambre might hold.   And anon the
protectour sayd to the lorde Hastinges : I arest the, traitour.
What, me, my Lorde ? quod he.   Yea the, traitour, quod the
protectour.   And another let flee at the Lorde Standley which
shronke at the stroke and fel vnder the table, or els his hed had
ben clefte to the tethe : for as shortely as he shranke, yet ranne
the blood aboute hys eares.   Then were they al quickly bestowed

in diuerse chambres except the lorde Chamberlen, whom the protectour bade spede and shryue hym apace, for by saynt Poule (quod he) I wil not to dinner til I se thy hed of. It boted him not to aske why, but heuely he toke a priest at aduenture, and made a short shrift, for a longer would not be suffered, the protectour made so much hast to dyner; which he might not go to til this wer done for sauing of his othe. So was he brought forth into the grene beside the chappel within the Tower, and his head laid vpon a long log of timbre, and there stricken of, and afterward his body with the hed entred at Windsore beside the body of kinge Edward, whose both soules our Lord pardon.

A merueilouse case is it to here, either the warninges of that he shoulde haue voided, or the tokens of that he could not voide. For the self night next before his death, the lord Standley sent a trustie secret messenger vnto him at midnight in al the hast, requiring him to rise and ryde away with hym, for he was disposed vtterly no lenger to bide; he had so fereful a dreme, in which him thoughte that a bore with his tuskes so raced them both bi the heddes, that the blood ranne aboute both their shoulders. And forasmuch as the protector gaue the bore for his cognisaunce, this dreme made so fereful an impression in his hart, that he was throughly determined no lenger to tary, but had his horse redy, if the lord Hastinges wold go with him to ride as far yet the same night, that thei shold be out of danger ere dai. Ey, good lord, quod the lord Hastinges to his messenger, leneth mi lord thi master to such trifles, and hath such faith in dremes, which either his own fere fantasieth or do rise in the nightes rest by reason of his daye thoughtes? Tel him it is plaine witchcraft to beleue in suche dremes; which if they wer tokens of thinges to come, why thinketh he not that we might be as likely to make them true by our going if we were caught and brought back (as frendes fayle fleers), for then had the bore a cause likely to race vs with his tuskes, as folke that fled for some falshed, wherfore either is there no peryl; nor none there is in dede; or if any be, it is rather in going then biding. And if we should, nedes cost, fall in perill one way or other; yet had I leuer that men should se it wer by other mens falshed, then thinke it were either our owne faulte or faint hart. And therfore go to thy master, man, and commende me to him, and pray him be mery and haue no fere: for I ensure hym I am as sure of the man that he woteth of, as I am of my own hand. God sende grace, sir, quod the messenger, and went his way.

Certain is it also, that in the riding toward the Tower, the same morning in which he was behedded, his hors twise or thrice stumbled with him almost to the falling ; which thing albeit eche man wote wel daily happeneth to them to whom no such mischaunce is toward, yet hath it ben, of an olde rite and custome, obserued as a token often times notably foregoing some great misfortune. Now this that foloweth was no warning, but an enemious scorne. The same morning ere he were vp, came a knight vnto him, as it were of curtesy to accompany hym to the counsaile, but of trouth sent by the protector to hast him thitherward, wyth whom he was of secret confederacy in that purpose, a meane man at that time, and now of gret auctorite. This knight when it happed the lord Chamberlen by the way to stay his horse, and comen a while with a priest whome he met in the Tower strete, brake his tale and said merely to him : What, my lord, I pray you come on, whereto talke you so long with that priest, you haue no need of a pri[e]st yet ; and therewith he laughed vpon him, as though he would say, ye shal haue sone. But so litle wist that tother what he ment, and so little mistrusted, that he was neuer merier nor neuer so full of good hope in his life ; which self thing is often sene a signe of chaunge. But I shall rather let anye thinge passe me, then the vain sureti of mans mind so nere his deth. Vpon the very Tower wharfe, so nere the place where his hed was of so sone after, there met he with one Hastinges, a perseuant of his own name. And of their meting in that place, he was put in remembrance of an other time, in which it had happened them before to mete in like maner togither in the same place. At which other tyme the lord Chamberlen had been accused vnto king Edward, by the lord Riuers the quenes brother, in such wise that he was for the while (but it lasted not long) farre fallen into the kinges indignacion, and stode in great fere of himselfe. And for asmuch as he nowe met this perseuant in the same place, that jupardy so wel passed, it gaue him great pleasure to talke with him thereof with whom he had before talked thereof in the same place while he was therein. And therefore he said : Ah Hastinges, art thou remembred when I met thee here ones with an heuy hart? Yea, my lord, (quod he) that remembre I wel : and thanked be God they gate no good, nor ye none harme thereby Thou wouldest say so, quod he, if thou knewest as much as I know, which few know els as yet and moe shall shortly. That ment he by the lordes of the quenes kindred that were taken before, and should that day be behedded at Pounfreit : which he wel

wyst, but nothing ware that the axe hang ouer his own hed.
In faith, man, quod he, I was neuer so sory, nor neuer stode in
so great dread in my life, as I did when thou and I met here.
And lo, how the world is turned, now stand mine enemies in the
daunger (as thou maist hap to here more hereafter) and I neuer
in my life so mery nor neuer in so great suerty.　O good God,
the blindnes of our mortall nature, when he most feared, he was
in good suerty : when he rekened him self surest, he lost his
life, and that within two houres after.　Thus ended this
honorable man, a good knight and a gentle, of gret aucthorite
with his prince, of liuing somewhat dessolate, plaine and open
to his enemy, and secret to his frend : eth to begile, as he that
of good hart and corage forestudied no perilles.　A louing man
and passing wel beloued.　Very faithful, and trusty ynough,
trusting to much.

The Historie of Kyng Rycharde the Thirde.

JOHN FOXE.

1517–1587.

A PRAYER FOR THE CHURCH, AND ALL THE STATES THEREOF.

LORD JESUS CHRIST, Son of the living God, who wast crucified for our sins, and didst rise again for our justification, and, ascending up to heaven, reignest now at the right hand of the Father, with full power and authority, ruling and disposing all things according to thine own gracious and glorious purpose: we, sinful creatures, and yet servants and members of thy church, do prostrate ourselves and our prayers before thy imperial majesty, having no other patron nor advocate to speed our suits, or to resort unto, but thee alone, beseeching thee to be good to thy poor church militant here in this wretched earth; sometime a rich church, a large church, an universal church, spread far and wide, through the whole compass of the earth; now driven into a narrow corner of the world, and hath much need of thy gracious help.

First, the Turk with his sword, what lands, what nations, and countries, what empires, kingdoms, and provinces, with cities innumerable, hath he won, not from us, but from thee. Where thy name was wont to be invocated, thy word preached, thy sacraments administered, there now remaineth barbarous Mahumet, with his filthy Alcoran. The flourishing churches in Asia, the learned churches of Grecia, the manifold churches in Africa, which were wont to serve thee, now are gone from thee. The seven churches of Asia with their candlesticks (whom thou didst so well forewarn) are now removed. All the churches, where thy diligent apostle St. Paul, thy apostles Peter and John, and other apostles, so laboriously travailed, preaching and writing to plant thy gospel, are now gone from thy gospel. In all the kingdom of Syria, Palestina, Arabia, Persia, in all

Armenia, and the empire of Cappadocia, through the whole
compass of Asia, with Egypt, and with Africa also (unless
among the far Ethiopians some old steps of Christianity peradventure do yet remain), either else in all Asia and Africa thy
church hath not one foot of free land, but is all turned either to
infidelity or to captivity, whatsoever pertaineth to thee. And if
Asia and Africa only were decayed, the decay were great, but
yet the defection were not so universal.

Now of Europa a great part also is shrunk from thy church.
All Thracia, with the empire of Constantinople, all Grecia,
Epirus, Illyricum, and now of late all the kingdom almost of
Hungaria, with much of Austria, with lamentable slaughter of
Christian blood, is wasted, and all become Turks. Only a
little angle of the West parts yet remaineth in some profession
of thy name.

But here (alack) cometh another mischief, as great, or greater
than the other. For the Turk with his sword is not so cruel,
but the bishop of Rome on the other side is more fierce and
bitter against us ; stirring up his bishops to burn us, his confederates to conspire our destruction, setting kings against their
subjects, and subjects disloyally to rebel against their princes,
and all for thy name.

Such dissension and hostility Sathan hath sent among us,
that Turks be not more enemies to Christians, than Christians
to Christians, papists to protestants : yea, protestants with protestants do not agree, but fall out for trifles. So that the poor
little flock of thy church, distressed on every side, hath neither
rest without, nor peace within, nor place almost in the world,
where to abide, but may cry now from the earth, even as thine
own reverence cried once from the cross : My God, my God,
why hast thou forsaken me ?

Amongst us Englishmen here in England, after so great
storms of persecution and cruel murther of so many martyrs, it
hath pleased thy grace to give us these Alcyon days, which
yet we enjoy, and beseech thy merciful goodness still they may
continue.

But here also (alack) what should we say ? so many enemies
we have, that envy us this rest and tranquillity, and do what
they can to disturb it. They which be friends and lovers of the
bishop of Rome, although they eat the fat of the land, and have
the best preferments and offices, and live most at ease, and ail
nothing, yet are they not therewith content. They grudge,
they mutter and murmur, they conspire and take on against us.
It fretteth them, that we live by them, or with them, and cannot

abide, that we should draw the bare breathing of the air, when they have all the most liberty of the land.

And albeit thy singular goodness hath given them a Queen so calm, so patient, so merciful, more like a natural mother than a princess, to govern over them, such as neither they nor their ancestors ever read of in the stories of this land before : yet all this will not calm them, their unquiet spirit is not yet content ; they repine and rebel, and needs would have, with the frogs of Æsop, a Ciconia,* an Italian stranger, the bishop of Rome, to play Rex over them, and care not, if all the world were set a fire, so that they, with their Italian lord, might reign alone. So fond are we Englishmen of strange and foreign things : so unnatural to ourselves, so greedy of newfangle novelties, never contented with any state long to continue, be it never so good ; and, furthermore, so cruel one to another, that we think our life not quiet, unless it be seasoned with the blood of other. For that is their hope, that is all their gaping and looking, that is their golden day, their day of Jubilee, which they thirst for so much : not to have the Lord to come in the clouds, but to have our blood, and to spill our lives. That, that is it, which they would have, and long since would have had their wills upon us, had not thy gracious pity and mercy raised up to us this our merciful Queen, thy servant Elizabeth, somewhat to stay their fury : for whom as we most condignly give thee thanks, so likewise we beseech thy heavenly majesty, that, as thou hast given her unto us, and hast from so manifold dangers preserved her, before she was queen, so now, in her royal estate, she may continually be preserved not only from the hands, but from all malignant devices wrought, attempted, or conceived, of enemies, both ghostly and bodily, against her.

In this her government be her governor, we beseech thee, so shall her majesty well govern us, if first she be governed by thee. Multiply her reign with many days, and her years with much felicity, with abundance of peace and life ghostly : that, as she hath now doubled the years of her sister and brother, so (if it be thy pleasure) she may overgrow in reigning the reign of her father.

And because no government can long stand without good counsel, neither can any counsel be good, except it be prospered by thee : bless, therefore, we beseech thee, both her majesty, and her honourable council, that both they rightly understand what is to be done, and she accordingly may accomplish that

---

* A stork.

they do counsel, to thy glory, and furtherance of the gospel, and public wealth of this realm.

Furthermore, we beseech thee, Lord Jesu, who with the majesty of thy generation dost drown all nobility, being the only Son of God, heir and Lord of all things, bless the nobility of this realm, and of other Christian realms, so as they (Christianly agreeing among themselves) may submit their nobility to serve thee ; or else let them feel, O Lord, what a frivolous thing is the nobility, which is without thee.

Likewise, to all magistrates, such as be advanced to authority, or placed in office, by what name or title soever, give, we beseech thee, a careful conscience uprightly to discharge their duty ; that, as they be public persons to serve the common wealth, so they abuse not their office to their private gain, nor private revenge of their own affections, but that, justice being administered without bribery, and equity balanced without cruelty or partiality, things that be amiss may be reformed, vice abandoned, truth supported, innocency relieved, God's glory maintained, and the commonwealth truly served.

But especially, to thy spiritual ministers, bishops, and pastors of thy church, grant, we beseech thee, O Lord, Prince of all pastors, that they, following the steps of thee, of thy apostles, and holy martyrs, may seek those things which be not their own, but only which be thine, not caring how many benefices nor what great bishopricks they have, but how well they can guide those they have. Give them such zeal of thy church, as may devour them, and grant them such salt, wherewith the whole people may be seasoned, and which may never be unsavoury, but quickened daily by thy Holy Spirit, whereby thy flock by them may be preserved.

In general, give to all the people, and the whole state of this realm, such brotherly unity in knowledge of thy truth, and such obedience to their superiors, as they neither provoke the scourge of God against them, nor their prince's sword to be drawn against her will out of the scabbard of long sufferance, where it hath been long hid. Especially, give thy gospel long continuance amongst us. And, if our sins have deserved the contrary, grant us, we beseech thee, with an earnest repentance of that which is past, to join a hearty purpose of amendment to come.

And forasmuch as the bishop of Rome is wont on every Good Friday to accurse us, [as] damned heretics, we curse not him, but pray for him, that he with all his partakers either may be turned to a better truth ; or else, we pray thee, gracious

Lord, that we never agree with him in doctrine, and that he may so curse us still, and never bless us more, as he blessed us in queen Mary's time. God, of thy mercy keep away that blessing from us.

Finally, instead of the pope's blessing give us thy blessing, Lord, we beseech thee, and conserve the peace of thy church, and course of thy blessed gospel. Help them that be needy and afflicted. Comfort them that labour and be heavy laden. And, above all things, continue and increase our faith.

And forasmuch as thy poor little flock can scarce have any place or rest in this world, come, Lord, we beseech thee, with thy *factum est*, and make an end, that this world may have no more time nor place here, and that thy church may have rest for ever.

For these, and all other necessities requisite to be begged and prayed for, asking in thy Christ's name, and as he hath taught us, we say : Our Father, which art in heaven, etc.

Private Prayers of Queen Elizabeth.

QUEEN ELIZABETH.

BORN 1533, REIGNED 1558-1603.

SPEECH TO THE ARMY AT TILBURY, 1588.

The Authentic Speech of Queen Elizabeth to her Army encamped at Tilbury, under the command of the Earl of Leicester, in the year 1588, when these Kingdoms were threatened with an Invasion from Spain.

MY LOVING PEOPLE—We have been perswaded by some that are careful of our safety, to take heed how we commit ourselves to armed multitudes, for fear of treachery ; but I assure you, I do not desier to live to distrust my faithful and loving people.

Let tyrants fear ; I have always so behaved myself, that, under God, I have placed my chiefest strength and safeguard in the loyal hearts and good will of my subjects, and therefore I am come amongst you, as you see, at this time, not for my recreation and disport, but being resolved in the midst and heat of the battle, to live or die amongst you all, to lay down for my God, and for my Kingdoms, and for my people, my honour and my blood, even in the dust.

I know I have the body but of a weak and feeble woman ; but I have the heart and stomach of a King, *and of a King of England too ;* and think foul scorn that Parma or Spain, or any prince of Europe should dare to invade the borders of my realm ; to which rather than any dishonour should grow by me, I myself will take up arms, I myself will be your general, judge, and rewarder of every one of your virtues in the field.

I know already, for your forwardness you have deserved rewards and crowns ; and we do assure you in the word of a prince, they shall be duly paid you.   In the meantime my lieutenant-general shall be in my stead, than whom never prince commanded a more noble or worthy subject ; not doubting but by your obedience to my general, by your concord in the camp, and your valour in the field, we shall shortly have a famous victory over those enemies of my God, of my Kingdoms, and of my people.

THE GOLDEN SPEECH

Of Queen Elizabeth to her last Parliament, November the 30th, Anno Domini 1601.

MR. SPEAKER—We perceive your coming is to present thanks unto us. Know I accept them with no less joy than your loves can desire to offer such a present, and do more esteem it than any treasure, or riches ; for those we know how to prize, but loyalty, love, and thanks, I account them invaluable ; and though God hath raised me high, yet this I account the glory of my crown, that I have reigned with your loves. This makes that I do not so much rejoice that God hath made me to be a queen, as to be a queen over so thankful a people, and to be the means under God to conserve you in safety, and preserve you from danger, yea to be the instrument to deliver you from dishonour, from shame, and from infamy, to keep you from out of servitude, and from slavery under our enemies, and cruel tyranny, and vile oppression intended against us ; for the better withstanding whereof, we take very acceptable their intended helps, and chiefly in that it manifesteth your loves and largeness of hearts to your soverign. Of myself I must say this, I never was any greedy scraping grasper, nor a strict fasting-holding prince, nor yet a waster, my heart was never set upon any worldly goods, but only for my subjects good. What you do bestow on me I will not hoard up, but receive it to bestow on you again ; yea mine own properties I account yours to be expended for your good, and your eyes shall see the bestowing of it for your wellfare.

Mr. Speaker, I would wish you and the rest to stand up, for I fear I shall yet trouble you with longer speech.

Mr. Speaker, you give me thanks, but I am more to thank you, and I charge you thank them of the Lower House from me ; for had I not received knowledge from you, I might a' fallen into the lapse of an error, only for want of true information.

Since I was queen, yet did I never put my pen to any grant but upon pretext and semblance made me, that it was for the good and avail of my subjects generally, though a private profit to some of my ancient servants, who have deserved well ; but that my grants shall be made grievances to my people, and oppressions, to be privileged under colour of our patents, our princely dignity shall not suffer it.

When I heard it, I could give no rest unto my thoughts until I had reformed it, and those varlets, lewd persons, abusers of my bounty, shall know I will not suffer it. And, Mr. Speaker, tell the House from me, I take it exceeding grateful, that the knowledge of these things are come unto me from them. And tho' amongst them the principal members are such as are not touched in private, and therefore need not speak from any feeling of the grief, yet we have heard that other gentlemen also of the House, who stand as free, have spoken freely in it ; which gives us to know, that no respects or interests have moved them other than the minds they bear to suffer no diminution of our honour and our subjects love unto us. The zeal of which affection tending to ease my people, and knit their hearts unto us, I embrace with a princely care far above all earthly treasures. I esteem my people's love, more than which I desire not to merit : and God, that gave me here to sit, and placed me over you, knows, that I never respected myself, but as your good was conserved in me ; yet what dangers, what practices, what perils I have passed, some, if not all of you know ; but none of these things do move me, or ever made me fear, but it's God that hath delivered me.

And in my governing this land, I have ever set the last judgment day before mine eyes, and so to rule as I shall be judged and answer before a higher Judge, to whose judgment seat I do appeal : in that thought was never cherished in my heart that tended not to my peoples good.

And if my princely bounty have been abused ; and my grants turned to the hurt of my people contrary to my will and meaning, or if any in authority under me have neglected, or converted what I have committed unto them, I hope God will not lay their culps to my charge.

To be a king, and wear a crown, is a thing more glorious to them that see it than its pleasant to them that bear it : for myself, I never was so much enticed with the glorious name of a king, or the royal authority of a queen, as delighted that God hath made me his instrument to maintain his truth and glory, and to defend this kingdom from dishonour, dammage, tyranny, and oppression.   But should I ascribe any of these things to myself or my sexly weakness, I were not worthy to live, and of all most unworthy of the mercies I have received at God's hands, but to God only and wholly all is given and ascribed.

The cares and troubles of a crown I cannot more fitly resemble than to the drugs of a learned phisitian, perfumed with some aromatical savour, or to bitter pills gilded over, by which they are made more acceptable or less offensive, which indeed are bitter and unpleasant to take ; and for my own part, were it not for conscience sake to discharge the duty that God hath lay'd upon me, and to maintain his glory, and keep you in safety, in mine own disposition I should be willing to resign the place I hold to any other, and glad to be freed of the glory with the labours, for it is not my desire to live nor to reign, longer than my life and reign shall be for your good.   And though you have had and may have many mightier and wiser princes sitting in this seat, yet you never had nor shall have any that will love you better.

This, Mr. Speaker, I commend me to your loyal loves, and yours to my best care and your further councils ; and I pray you Mr. Controubrand Mr. Secretary, and you of my council, that before these gentlemen depart into their countrys, you bring them all to kiss my hand.

EDMUND SPENSER.

1552-1599.

A VEUE OF THE PRESENT STATE OF IRELAND.

Discoursed by way of a dialogue betwene Eudoxus and Irenius.

Eudoxus. But if that country of Ireland, whence you lately came, be so goodly and commodious a soyle as you report, I wounder that no course is taken for the tourning therof to good uses, and reducing that salvage nation to better government and civillity.

Irenius. Mary, so ther have bin divers good plotts devised, and wise counsells cast aledy about reformation of that realme; but they say it is the fatall destiny of that land, that no purposes, whatsoever are ment for her good, wil prosper and take good effect: which, whether it proceede from the very genius of the soyle, or influence of the starrs, or that Almighty god hath not yet appoynted the time of her reformacion, or that he reserveth her in this unquiet state still, for some secret scourge, which shall by her come unto England, it is hard to be knowne, but yet much to be feared.

Eudox. Surely I suppose this but a vaine conceipt of simple men, which judge things by ther effects, and not by ther causes; for I would rather thinck the cause of this evel, which hangeth upon that country, to proccede rather upon the unsoundnesse of the counsell, and plotts, which you say have bin oftentimes layd for her reformacion, or of fayntnesse in following and effecting the same, then of any such fatall course or appoyntment of god, as you misdeme; but it is the manner of men, that when they are fallen into any absurdity, or theyre actions succeede not as they would, they are ready alwayes to impute the blame therof unto the heavens, so to excuse their own folly and imperfections : so have I also heard it often wished, (even of some whos great wisedome in [my] opinion should seme to judg more soundly of so weighty a consideracon) that all that land weare a sea-poole : which kind of speach, is the manner rather of desperate men far driven, to wish the utter ruine of that which they cannot redresse, then of grave counsellors, which ought to thinck nothing so hard, but that through wisdome, it may be maistered and subdued ; since the poet sayth, that the wiseman shall rule even over the starrs, much more over the earth : for weare it not the part of a desperate phisition to wish his diseased patient dead, rather then to imploy the best indevours of his skill for his recovery : but since we are so far entred, let us I pray you, devise of those evills, by which that country is held in this wretched case, that it cannot, as you say, be recured. And if it be not painfull to you, to tell us what things during your late continuance ther, you observed, to be most offensive, and impeachfull, unto the good rule and government thereof.

. . . . *Iren.* I will then according to your advisement, begin to declare the evills which seme to be most hurtfull to the comon-weale of that land : and first, those which I sayd were most ancient and long growne : and they are also of 3 kinds ; the first in the lawes, the second in customes, the last in religion.

Eudox. Why, Irenius, can there be anie evill in the lawes? can things which are ordayned for the safetie and good of all, turne to the evill and hurt of them? This well I wote both in that state and in all other, that were they not contayned in doutie with fear of lawe which restrayneth offences, and inflicteth sharpe punishment to misdoers, no man should enjoy anie thing, everie mans hand would be against another. Therfore in finding fault with the lawes I doubt me you shall much over-shote your selfe, and make me the more dislike your other dislikes of that government.

Iren. The lawes Eudox., I doe not blame for them selves, knowing that all lawes are ordayned for the good of the common weal and for repressing of licensiousnesse and vice : but it falleth out in lawes, no otherwise then it doth in Phisick, which was at first devized, and is yet dayly ment* and ministred for the health of the patient : but neverthelesse we often se that either through ignorance of the disease, or unreasonablenesse

* Ment, from menge=to mix.

of the time, or other accidents comming betwene, in stead of good it worketh hurt, and out of one evill, throweth the patient into many miseries : so the lawes were at first intended for the reformacon of abuses, and peaceable continuance of the subjects : but are since either disanulled or quite prevaricated through chang and alteration of times, yet are they good still in them selves : but to that common wealth which is ruled by them they worke not that good which they should, and sometimes also perhaps that evill which they would not.

. . . . For lawes ought to be fashioned unto the manners and condicons of the people, to whom they are ment, and not to be imposed upon them according to the simple rule of right : for then, as I sayd, in stead of good they may worke ill, and pervert justice to extreame injustice : ffor he that would transfer the lawes of the Lacedemonians to the people of Athens should find a great absurdity and inconvenience : for those lawes of Lacedemon were devised by Licurgus, as most proper and best agreeing with that people, whom he knew to be inclined altogether to warrs, and therefore wholy trayned them up even from ther cradles in armes and military exercises, cleane contrary to the institution of Solon, who, in his lawes to the Athenians labored by all means to temper ther warlike courages with swete delights of learning and sciences, so that as much as the one excelled in armes, the other exceded in knowledg : the like regard and moderation ought to be had in tempering and menaging of this stubburn nation of the Irish, to bring them from their delight of licensious barbarisme unto the love of goodnesse and civillity.

Eudox. I cannot se how that may better be then by the discipline of the lawes of England : for the English were, at first, as stout and war like a people as ever were the Irish, and yet ye se are now brought to that civillity, that no nacon in the world excelleth them in all godly conversacon, and all the studies of knowledg and humanity.

Iren. What they now be, both you and I se very well, but by how many thorny and hard wayes they are come therunto, by how many civill broyles, by how many tumultuous rebellions, that even hazard[ed] often times the whole safety of the kingdome, may easily be considered : all which they neverthelesse fairely overcame, by reason of the continewall presence of the King, whos onely person is oftentimes in stead of an army, to contayne the unruly people from a thousand evill occasions, which that wretched kingdome, is for want thereof daily carried into.

. . . *Eudox.* Truly Irenius, what with the prayses of your countrie, and what with the lamentable Dysolucon thereof made by those ragtailes in Scotland, you have fylled me with a greate compassion of theire calamaties, that I doe moch pittie that sweet land, to be subject to so many evills, as everie daie I see more and more throwen upon her, and doe halfe begynne to thinke, that it is, as you said at the begynnynge, her fatall misfortune, above all countries that I knowe, to be thus miserablie tossed and turmoiled with theis variable stormes of afflictions : But synce wee are thus far entred into the consideracon of her mishappes, tell me, have there ben any more such tempestes, as you terme them, wherein she hath thus wretchedlie ben wracked ?

. . . . *Iren.* All these which you have named, and many more besides, often tymes have I right well knowne, to kyndle greatcly fyres of tumultuous troubles in the countries bordering uppon them. All which to rehearse should rather be to Chronicle tymes, then to searche into the reformacon of abuses in that Realme : and yet veric nedefull it wilbe to consider them, and the evills which they have stirred upp, that some redresse thereof, and prevencon of the evills to come, may thereby rather be devysed. But I suppose wee shall have a fitter oportunity for the same, when wee shall speake of the particular abuses and enormities of the government, which wilbe next after these generall defectes and inconveniences, which I sai were in the lawes, customes, and religion.

Eudox. Goe to them in gods name, and followe the course which yee have purposed to your selfe, for yt fitteth best I must confesse with the purpose of our discorse. Declare your opynion, as you begon, about the lawes of the Realme, what incomoditie you have conceived to be in them, chiefly in the comõn lawe, which I would have thought most free from all such dislike.

Iren. The comon lawe is, as I before said, of it selfe most rightfull and verie convenient, I suppose, for the kingdom for which it was first devized ; for this I thinke, as yt seemes reasonable, that out of the manners of the people, and abuses of the countrie, for which they were invented, they tooke theire first begynninge, for else they should be most unjust : for no lawes of man, according to the straight rule of right, are just, but as in regard of evills which they prevent, and the safetie of the comõon weale which they provide for.

. . . . *Eudox.* Nowe truelie, Irenius, yee have meseemes, very well handled this pointe touchinge inconvenyences in

the Cõmon Lawe there, by you observed; and yt seemeth that you
have had a myndefull regard unto the thinges that may concerne
the good of that Realme.　　And yf you cann aswell goe through
with the Statute Lawes of that lande, I will thincke yóu have
not lost all your tyme there.　Therefore, I praye you, nowe take
them to you in hande and tell us what you thincke to bee amisse
in them.

Iren. The Statutes of that realme are not manie, and therefore wee shall the sooner rune through them.　And yet of those
fewe there are sondrie impertinent and unnecessarie : the which
perhappes though at the tyme of the makinge of theme were
very nedeeful, yet nowe through chainge of tyme are cleane
antiquated, and altogether idle : As that which forbiddeth any
to weare theire beardes all on theire upper lip, and none under
the chynne, and that which putteth away saffron shirts and
smockes, and that which restrayneth the using of guylte bridles
and pettronells, and that which appointed to the recorders and
Clarkes Dubline and Drodagh [=Drogheda], to take but ijd.
for the Coppie of a playnte, and that which cõmaundeth bowes
and arrowes, and that which maketh that all Irishmene that
shall converse amonge the Englishe shalbe taken for spies, and
soe punished, and that which forbiddeth persons ameanable
to lawe to enter and distrayne in the lands in the which
they have tittle ; and many other the like which I coulde
rehearse.

Eudox. These, trulie, which you have repeated, seeme very
fryvolous and fruitles ; for by the breach of them little dammage
or inconvenience caun come to the Cõmon-Wealthe, neither,
indeede, yt any transgresse them, shall he seeme worthie of
punishment, scare of blame, savinge be that they abide by the
names of lawes.　But lawes ought to be suche, as that the
keepinge of them should be greatlie for the behoofe of the
Cõmon-Wealth, and the violatinge of them should be very
haynous, and sharply punishable.　But tell us of some more
weightie dislikes in the Statutes then these, and that may more
behouefule importe the reformacon of them.

Iren. There is one or twoe statutes which make the wrong-
full destrayninge of any mans goods against the forme of
Cõmon Lawe to be fellony.　The which statutes seeme surelie to
have benn at firste meant for the greate good of that Realme,
and for restrayninge of a fowle abuse, which then raigned
cõmonly amongst that people, and yet is not altogether layed
aside ; that when any one was indebted to another, he would
first demaunde his debt, and, yf he were not paied, he would

streighte goe and take a distres of his goods or Cattell, where he could finde them, to the value: which he would keepe tyll he was satisfied, and this the simple Churle (as they call him) doth comonly use to doe yet, thorough ignorance of his mis-doing, or evill use that hath long settled amongest them. But this, though it be most unlawfull, yet surely me seemes to hard to make it death, since there is no purpose in the partie to steale the others goods, or to conceale the distres, but doth yt openly, for the most parte before witnesses. And againe, the same statutes are soe slackelie pende, besides that latter of them is so vnsensiblye contryved that yt scarce carieth any reason in yt, that they are often and very easily wrested to the fraude of the subjecte; as yf one goinge to distrayne upon his land or Tenemente, where lawfully he may, yet yf in doinge thereof he transgres the leaste point of the Comon Lawe, he streightlie comitteth fellonie. Or if one by any other occasion take any thing from another, as boyes use sometimes to cap one another, the same is straight fellony. This is a very harde lawe.

Eudox. Neverthelcs the evill use of distrayninge another mans goods, you will not deny but is to be abolished and taken awaye.

Iren. Yt is soe, but not by takinge awaye the subjecte with-all; for that is to violent a medycine, speciallie this use beinge permitted, and made lawfull to some, and to other some, death. As to most of the Corporate Townes there, it is granted by theire charter, that they may, every man by himselfe, without an officer (for that were more tollerable) for any debt, to distrayne the goods of any Irishe, beinge founde within theire liberty, or but passing through theire Townes. And the first permissyon of this was for that in those tymes when that graunt was made, the Irishe were not amesnable to lawe, soe as yt was not saiftie for the Townesman to goe to him forth to demaund his debt, nor possible drawe him into lawe, soe that he had leve to be his own bayliffe, to arrest his saide debtors goods within his owne franchise. The which the Irish seinge, thought yt as lawfull for them to distrayne the Townesmans goods in the countrey where they found yt. And soe [by] ensample of that graunt to Townes-men, they thought yt lawfull, and made yt an use to distrayne one anothers goods for smale debtes. And to say truth, me thinkes yt hard for every tryflyng debt of 2 or 3s. to be dryven to lawe, which is soe farre from them sometymes to be sought; for which me thinkes yt were an heavy ordinance to geve death, especyally to a rude man that is ignorant of

Lawe, and thinketh a common use or graunt to other men a lawe for himselfe.

Eudox. Yea, but the Judge, when it commeth before him to tryall, may easilie deside this doubte, and lay open the intent of the lawe by his better discrecon.

Iren. Yea, but yt is daingerous to leave the sense of a lawe unto there ason or will of Judges, whoe are men and may bee miscaryed by affeccons, and many other meanes, but the lawes ought to be like to stony tables, playne, stedfast, and ymoveable.

. . . Nowe we will proceede to the other like defectes, amonge which there is one generall inconvenience which rayneth allmost throughout all Ireland : and that of the Lords of land, and fre-holders, whoe doe not there use to sett out theire lands to farme, or for terme of yeres, to their teñants, but only from yere to yere, and some during pleasure ; nether indeede will the Irish teñant or husband otherwise take his lande then so longe as he list himself. The reason hereof in the teñant is, for that the landlords there use most shamfully to racke theire tenants, layinge upon him coygnie and livery at pleasure, and exactinge of him besides his covenante, what he please. So that the poore husbandman either dare not binde himselfe to him for longer tyme, or that he thinketh by his contynuall libertie of chainge to keepe his landlorde the rather in awe from wroninge of him. And the reason whic the landlorde will not longer covenante with him is, for that he daylie looketh for chainge and alteracon, and hovereth in expectacon of newe worldes.

Eudox. But what evill comȩth hereby to the comȩonweath ? or what reason is yt that any landlord should not sett, nor any teñante take his land as himselfe list.

Iren. Marry, the evilles that comȩth hereby are greate for by this meanes both the landlord thinketh that he hath his teñante more at commaund, to followe him into what accon soever he will enter, and allso the teñant, beinge left at his liberty, is fitt for every variable occasion of chainge that shalbe offered by tyme : and so much allso the more willinge and ready is hee to runne into the same, for that he hath no such estate in any his holdinge, no suche buyldinge upon any farme, no such costs ymployed in fencing and husbandinge the same, as might withholde him from any such willfull corse, as his lords cause, and his owne lewde disposicon may carry him unto. All which he hath forborne, and spared soe much expence, for that he had no former estate in his tenement, but was only a teñante at will or little more, and soe at will may leave yt.

And this inconvenience maye be reason enough to ground any ordinance for the good of a Com̃on-wealth, against the private behoofe or will of any landlord that shall refuse to graunte any such terme or estate unto his teñante as may tend to the good of the whole Realme.

Eudox. Indeede me seemes yt is a greate willfullnes in any such landlord to refuse to make any longer farmes to theire teñants, as may, besides the generall good of the Realme, be also greatly for theire owne profit and avayle : For what reasonable man will not thinke that the tenement shalbe made much the better for the lords behoofe, yf the teñante may by such meanes be drawen to buylde himselfe some handsome habitacon thereof, to dytch and enclose his grounde, to manure and husband yt as good farmers use? For when his teñants terme shalbe expired, yt will yeilde him, in the renewinge his lease, both a good fyne, and allso a better rente. And also it wil be for the good of the tenent likewise, whoe by such buyld-inges and inclosures shall receave many benefitts : first, by the handsomenes of his howse, he shall take greate comforte of his lief, more saife dwellinge, and a delight to keepe his saide howse neate and cleanely, which nowe beinge as they com̃only are, rather swyne-steades then howses, is the chiefest cause of his soe beastlie manner of life, saluaige condicon, lyinge and lyvinge together with his beaste in one howse, in one rowme, and in one bed, that is the cleane strawe, or rather the fowle dounghill. And to all these other com̃odities he shall in shorte tyme finde a greater added, that is his owne wealth and riches encreased, and wonderfully enlarged, but keeping his cattle in enclosures, where they shall allwayes have fresh pasture, that nowe is all trampled and over runne ; warme cover, that now lyeth open to all weather ; saife beinge, that now are con-tynually filched and stollen. . . . .

Iren. Thus I have, Eudox : as breifly as I could, and as my remembrance would serve, rund through the state of that whole countyre, both to let you see what it nowe is, and also, what yt may be by good care and amendment : not that I take upon me to change the pollicye of so greate a kingdome, or prescribe rules to such wise men as have the handlinge therof, but onely to shewe you the evills, which in my small experience I have observed to be the chiefe hindrance of the reformacon therof ; and by the way of conference to declare my simple opinyon for redresse therof, and establishinge a good course for that government ; which I do not deliver for a perfecte plotte of myne owne invensyon to be onely followed, but as I have learned and understood the same by the consultacons and actyons of very wise Governors and Counsellors whome I have sometymes heard treate thereof. So have I thought good to sett downe a remembraunce of them for myne owne good, and your satisfactyon, that who list to overloke them, although perhaps much wiser them they which have thus advised of that state, yet at leaste, by comparison. hereof, may perhaps better his owne judgement, and by the light of others foregoinge, he may followe after with more ease, and hapely finde a fayrer waye thereunto then they which have gone before.

SIR WALTER RALEIGH.

1552–1618.

THE HISTORIE OF THE WORLD.

By this which wee haue alreadie set downe, is seene the beginning and end of the three first Monarchies of the world ; whereof the Founders and Erectours thought, that they could neuer haue ended. That of *Rome* which made the fourth, was also at this time almost at the highest. Wee haue left it flourishing in the middle of the field ; hauing rooted vp, or cut downe, all that kept it from the eyes and admiration of the world. But after some continuance, it shall begin to lose the beauty it had ; the stormes of ambition shall beat her great boughes and branches one against another ; her leaues shall fall off, her limbes wither, and a rabble of barbarous Nations enter the field, and cut her downe.

Now these great Kings, and conquering Nations, haue bin the subiect of those ancient Histories, which haue bin preserued, and yet remaine among vs ; and withall of so many tragicall Poets, as in the persons of powerfull Princes, and other mighty men haue complained against Infidelitie, Time, Destinie, and most of all against the variable successe of worldly things, and Instabtlitie of Fortune. To these vndertakings, these great Lords of the world haue beene stirred vp, rather by the desire of Fame, which ploweth vp the Aire, and soweth in the Winde ; than by the affection of bearing rule, which draweth after it so much vexation and so many cares. And that this is true, the good aduice of *Cineas* to *Pyrrhus* proues. And certainely, as Fame hath often beene dangerous to the liuing, so is it to the dead of no vse at all ; because separate from knowledge. Which were it otherwise, and the extreame ill bargaine of buying this lasting discourse, vnderstood by them which are dissolued ; they themselues would then rather haue wished, to haue stolne

out of the world without noyse ; than to be put in minde, that they
haue purchased the report of their actions in the world, by
rapine, oppression, and crueltie ; by giuing in spoyle the
innocent and labouring soule to the idle and insolent, and by
hauing emptied the Cities of the world of their ancient
Inhabitants, and fitted them againe with so many and so
variable sorts of sorrowes.

Since the fall of the *Roman* Empire (omitting that of the
Germanes, which had neither greatnesse nor continuance) there
hath beene no State fearfull in the East, but that of the *Turk;*
nor in the West any Prince that hath spred his wings farre
ouer his nest, but the *Spaniard;* who since the time that
Ferdinand expel'd the *Moores* out of *Grenado,* haue made
many attempts to make themselues Masters of al *Europe.*
And it is true, that by the treasures of both *Indies,* and
by the many kingdoms which they possesse in *Europe,*
they are at this day the most powerfull. But as the *Turke* is
now counterpoysed by the *Persian,* so in stead of so many
Millions as haue beene spent by the *English, French,* and
Netherlands in a defensiue Warre, and in diuersions against
them, it is easie to demonstrate, that with the charge of two
hundred thousand pound continued but for two yeeres, or three
at the most, they may not onely be perswaded to liue in peace,
but all their swelling and ouer-flowing streames may bee brought
backe into their naturall channels and old bankes. These two
Nations, I say, are at this day the most eminent, and to be
regarded ; the one seeking to roote out the Christian Religion
altogether, the other the truth and sincere profession therof,
the one to ioyne all *Europe* to *Asia,* the other the rest of all
Europe to *Spaine.*

For the rest, if we seeke a reason of the succession and continuance of this boundlesse ambition in mortall men, we may
adde to that which hath beene already said ; That the Kings
and Princes of the world haue alwaies laid before them,
the actions, but not the ends of those great Ones which
preceded them. They are alwayes transported with the
glorie of the one, but they neuer minde the miserie of the
other, till they finde the experience in themselues. They
neglect the aduice of *God,* while they enioy life, or hope it ; but
they follow the counsell of Death, vpon his first approach. It
is hee that puts into man all wisedome of the world, without
speaking a word ; which *God* with all the words of his Law,
promises, or threats, doth infuse. *Death,* which hateth and
destroyeth man, is beleeued ; God, which hath him and loues

him, is alwaies deferred. *I haue considered* (saith *Salomon*) *all the workes that are vnder the Sunne, and behold, all is vanitie, and vexation of spirit :* but who beleeues it, till Death tells it vs ? It was Death, which opening the conscience of *Charles* the fift, made him enioyne his sonne *Philip* to restore *Nauarre* ; and King *Francis* the first of *France*, to command that iustice should be done vpon the Murderers of the Protestants in *Merindol* and *Cabrieres*, which til then he neglected. It is therefore Death alone that can suddenly make man to know himselfe. He tells the proud and insolent, that they are but Abiects, and humbles them at the instant ; makes them crie, complaine, and repent, yea, euen to hate their forepassed happinesse. He takes the account of the rich, and proues him a beggar ; a naked beggar, which hath interest in nothing, but in the grauell that fills his mouth. He holds a glasse before the eyes of the most beautifull, and makes them see therein, their deformitie and rottennesse ; and they acknowledge it.

O eloquent, iust, and mighty Death ! whom none could aduise, thou hast perswaded ; what none hath dared thou hast done ; and whom all the world hath flattered, thou only has cast out of the world and despised : thou hast drawne together all the farre stretched greatnesse, all the pride, crueltie, and ambition of man, and couered it all ouer with these two narrow words, *Hic iacet.*

RICHARD HOOKER.

1553–1600.

LAW AND ORDER.

HE that goeth about to perswade a multitude, that they are not so well governed as they ought to be, shall never want attentive and favourable hearers; because they know the manifold defects, whereunto every kinde of regiment is subject, but the secret lets and difficulties, which in publick proceedings are innumerable and inevitable; they have not ordinarily the judgement to consider. And because such as openly reproove supposed disorders of State are taken for principall friends to the common benefit of all, and for men that carry singular freedom of mind; under this fair and plausible colour whatsoever they utter, passeth for good and currant. That which wanteth in the weight of their speech, is supplied by the aptnesse of mens minds to accept and beleeve it. Whereas on the other side, if we maintain things that are established, we have not only to strive with a number of heavie prejudices deeply rooted in the hearts of men, who think that herein we serve the time, and speak in favour of the present State, because thereby we either hold or seek preferment; but also to bear such exceptions as mindes so averted before-hand usually take against that which they are loth should be powred into them. . . .

Without order there is no living in publike Society, because the want thereof is the mother of confusion, whereupon division of necessity followeth, and out of division, destruction. The Apostle therefore giving instruction to publike Societies, requireth that all things be orderly done: Order can have no place in things, except it be settled amongst the persons that shall by office be conversant about them. And if things and persons be ordered, this doth imply that they are distinguished by degrees. For order is a graduall disposition : The whole world consisting of parts so many, so different, is by this only thing upheld ; hee which framed them hath set them in order: The very Deity it self both keepeth and requireth for ever this to be kept as a Law, that wheresoever there is a coaugmentation of many, the lowest be knit unto the highest, by that which being interjacent, may cause each to cleave to the other, and so all to continue one. This order of things and persons in publike Societies, is the work of Policie, and the proper instrument thereof in every degree in power, power being that hability which we have of our selves, or receive from others for performance of any action. If the action which we are to perform be conversant about matters of meer Religion, the power of performing it is then spirituall ; And if that power be such as hath not any other to over-rule it, we terme it Dominion, or Power supream ; so farre as the bounds thereof extend. When therefore Christian Kings are said to have Spirituall Dominion or supream Power in Ecclesiasticall affaires and causes, the meaning is, that within their own Precincts and Territories, they have Authority and Power to command even in matters of Christian Religion, and that there is no higher nor greater that can in those cases over-command them, where they are placed to raign as Kings. But withall we must likewise note that their power is termed supremacy, as being the highest, not simply without exception of any thing. For what man is so brain-sick, as not to except in such speeches God himselfe the King of all Dominion ? who doubteth, but that the King who receiveth it, must hold it of, and order the Law according to that old axiome, *Attribuat Rex legi, quod lex attribuit ei potestatem :* And againe, *Rex non debet esse sub homine, sed sub deo & lege.*

. . . . Wherefore that here we may briefly end : of Law there can be no less acknowledged, than that her seat is the bosom of God, her voice the harmony of the world : all things in heaven and earth do her homage, the very least as feeling her care, and the greatest as not exempted from her power : both Angels and men and creatures of what condition soever, though each in different sort and manner, yet all with uniform consent, admiring her as the mother of their peace and joy.

Ecclesiastical Polity.

LANCELOT ANDREWES.

1555–1626.

From a Sermon Preached before Qveene Elizabeth, at Greenwich, on Wednesday the xi. of March, A.D. MDLXXXIX. Psalme. lxxv. Ver. iii. Liquefacta est terra, & omnes qui habitant in ea : Ego confirmavi Columnas ejus. The earth, and all the Jnhabitants thereof are dissolved : but J will establish the Pillars of it.

IT was MOSES the Man of GOD, that, by speciall direction from GOD, first began, and brought up this order, to make *Musique* the conveigher of mens duties into their mindes (*Deut.* 31, 19.) And DAVID sithence hath continued it, and brought it to perfection, in this Booke, as having a speciall grace and felicitie in this kinde : He, for *Songs;* and his Sonne SALOMON for *Proverbs.* By which two (that is) by the *vnhappy Adage,* and by a *wanton song, Sathan* hath ever breathed most of his infection and poison into the minde of man.

In which holy and heavenly vse of his harpe, he doth, by his tunes of *Musique,* teach men how to sett themselves in *tune* (*Psal.* 15.) How not onely to tune themselves, but how to tune their households (*Psal.* 101.) And not onely there, but (heer) in this *Psalme,* how to preserve harmonie, or (as he termeth it) how to sing *Ne perdas,* to a Common-wealth. So saith the *Inscription,* which *Saint Augustine* very fittly calleth the *key* of every *Psalme.*

For, the time of setting this song (by generall consent of all Expositors) being the later end of the long dissention, between the Houses of *David* and *Saul;* evident it is, the estate of the Land was very neer to a *Perdas,* and needed *Ne perdas* to be soong unto it.

For, besides the great overthrow in the Mountaines of *Gilboa,* given by the enemie, wherin the king and three of his sonnes were slaine, and a great part of the Countrey surprised by the *Philistin;* the *Desolation of a divided kingdome, was come upon them too.* For, within themselves, they were at *Cujus est terra?* (2. *Sam.* 3. 12.) even at Civill warrs : At the beginning, but a *play;* (So *Abner* termeth it, 2. Sam. 2. 14.) but *bitternesse* at the end, as the same *Abner* confesseth, *ver.* 26. Surely, it was a weake State and low brought : So much doth *David* imply (in the fore-part of the *verse*) that he found the Land a weake land, by meanes, the strength and *Pillers* of it, were all out of course, by the mis-government of *Saul.* But then withall (in the later part of the *verse*) he professeth, he will leave it a Land of strength, by *re-establishing the Pillars* . and re-edifying the State new againe. *The earth &c.*

The stile whereof runneth in the termes of *Architecture:* very aptly resembling the government, to a frame of building ; the same sett upon and borne up by certaine *Bases* and *Pillars* (the strength whereof assureth, or the weakenesse endangereth the whole :) and *David* himselfe to a skillfull Builder, surveying the *pillers*, and searching into the decayes ; repairing their ruines and setting them into course againe. . . . .

FROM A SERMON PREACHED BEFORE QVEENE ELIZABETH,

At Hampton Court, on Wednesday, being the vi. of March, A.D. MDXCIIII. Memores estote Vxoris Lot. Remember Lot's Wife. A Part of the Chapter read this Morning, by order of the Church, for ii. Lesson.

THE words are few, and the sentence short ; no one in Scripture so short. But it fareth with *Sentences* as with *coynes* : In coines, they that in smallest compasse conteine greatest value, are best esteemed : and, in sentences, those that in fewest words comprise most matter, are most praised. Which, as of all sentences it is true ; so specially of those that are marked with *Memento.* In them, the shorter, the better ; the better, and the better carried away, and the better kept ; and the better called for when we need it. And such is this heere ; of rich contents, and with all exceeding compendious : So that, we must needs be without all excuse, it being but three words, and but five syllables, if we do not remember it.

The Sentence is our SAVIOUR'S. uttered by Him upon this

occasion. Before, (in *Verse* 18.) He had said : that the dayes of the *Sonne* of *man should be as the dayes of* LOT, in two respects. In respect of the sodeinesse of the destruction that should come : and in respect of the securitie of the people, on whom it should come. For, the *Sodomites* laughed at it ; and *Lot's* Wife (it should seeme) but slightly regarded it. Being then in *Lot's* storie, verie fitly, and by good consequence, out of that storie, He leaveth as a *Memento*, before He leaveth it.

There are in *Lot's* storie, two very notable monuments of GOD'S judgement. The *Lake of Sodome*, and LOT'S *Wive's Piller.* The one, the punishment of *resolute sinne* ; the other of *faint virtue.* For, the *Sodomites* are an example of impenitent wilfull sinners : and *Lot's* wife of imperseverant and relapsing righteous persons.

. . . . *Looking back* might proceed of divers causes ; So might this of hers, but that CHRIST'S application directs us. The verse before saith, *Somewhat in the house*, something left behind affected her : Of which He giveth us warning. She grew weary of trouble, and of shifting so oft : From *Vr* to *Haran ;* thence, to *Canaan ;* thence, to *Egypt ;* thence to *Canaan* againe ; then to *Sodom ;* and now to *Zoar ;* and that, in her old daies, when she would fainest have been at rest. Therefore, in this wearisome conceit of new trouble now to beginn ; and withall remembring the convenient seat, she had in *Sodome*, she even desired to *die by her flesh-potts*, and to be buried in *the grave of lust :* wished them at *Zoar*, that would, and her selfe at *Sodom* againe : desiring rather to end her life with ease in that *Stately city*, then to remove, and be safe perhapps, and perhapps not, in the *desolate mountaines.* And this was the sinne of restinesse of soul, which affected her eyes and knees, and was the cause of all the former. When men wery of a good course, which long they have holden, for a little ease or wealth, or (I wote not what) other secular respect, fall away in the end : so losing the praise and fruict of their former perseverance, and relapsing into the danger and destruction, from which they had so neer escaped.

Behold, these were the sinnes of *Lot's wife ;* A wavering of mind : Slow stepps : the convulsion of her neck : all these caused her wearinesse and feare of new trouble, shee preferring SODOM'S *ease* before ZOAR'S *safety. Remember Lot's wife.*

SIR FRANCIS BACON,

VISCOUNT ST. ALBANS—1561–1626.

OF THE TRUE GREATNESSE OF KINGDOMES AND ESTATES.

THE Speech of *Themistocles* the *Athenian*, which was Haughtie and Arrogant, in taking so much to Himselfe, had been a Graue and Wise Obseruation and Censure, applied at large to others. Desired at a Feast to touch a Lute, he said ; *He could not fiddle, but yet he could make a small Towne, a great Citty.* These Words (holpen a little with a Metaphore) may expresse two differing Abilities, in those that deale in Businesse of Estate. For if a true Suruey be taken, of Counsellours and Statesmen, there may be found (though rarely) those, which can make an *Small State Great*, and yet cannot *Fiddle* : As on the other side, there will be found a great many, that can *fiddle* very cunningly, but yet are so farre from being able to make a *Small State Great*, as their Gift lieth the other way ; To bring a Great and Flourishing Estate to Ruine and Decay. And certainly, those Degenerate Arts and Shifts, whereby many Counsellours and Gouernours, gaine both *Fauour* with their Masters, and Estimation with the Vulgar, deserue no better name then *Fidling* ; Being Things, rather pleasing for the time, and gracefull to themselues onely, then tending to the Weale and Aduancement of the State, which they serue. There are also (no doubt) Counsellours and Gouernours, which may be held sufficient, (*Negotijs peres,*) Able to mannage Affaires, and to keepe them from *Precipices*, and manifest in Inconueniences ; which neuerthelesse, are farre from the Abilitie, to raise and Amplifie an Estate, in Power, Meanes, and Fortune. But be the workemen what they may be, let vs speake of the Work ; That is, The true *Greatnesse of Kingdomes and Estates ;* and the *Meanes* thereof. An Argument, fit for Great and Mightie Princes, to haue in their hand ; To the end, that neither by Ouer-measuring their Forces, they leese themselues in vaine Enterprises ; Nor on the other side, by vnderualuing them, they descend to Fearefull and Pusillanimous Counsells.

The *Greatnesse* of an Estate in Bulke and Territorie, doth fall vnder Measure ; And the *Greatnesse* of Finances and Reuenuew doth fall vnder Computation. The Population may appeare by Musters : And the Number and Greatnesse of Cities and Townes, by Cards and Maps. But yet there is not any Thing amongst Ciuill Affaires, more subiect to Errour, then the right valuation, and true Iudgement, concerning the Power and Forces of an Estate. The *Kingdome* of *Heauen* is compared, not to any great Kernell or Nut, but to a *Graine* of *Mustard-seed;* which is one of the least Graines, but hath in it a Propertie and Spirit, hastily to get vp and spread. So are there States, great in Territorie, and yet not apt to Enlarge, or Command ; And some, that haue but a small Dimension of Stemme, and yet apt to be the Foundations of Great Monarchies.

Walled Townes, Stored Arcenalls and Armouries, Goodly Races of Horse, Chariots of Warre, Elephants, Ordnances, Artillery, and the like : All this is but a Sheep in a Lion's Skin, except the Breed and disposition of the People, be stout and warlike. Nay Number (it selfe) in Armies, importeth not much, where the People is of weake Courage : For (as *Virgil* saith) *It neuer troubles a Wolfe, how many the sheepe be.* The Armie of the *Persians*, in the Plaines of *Arbela*, was such a vast Sea of People, as it did somewhat astonish the Commanders in *Alexanders* Armies ; Who came to him therefore, and wisht him, to set vpon them by Night ; But hee answered, *He would not pilfer the Victory.* And the Defeat was Easie. When *Tigranes* the *Armenian*, being incamped vpon a Hill, with 400000. Men, discouered the Armies of the *Romans*, being not aboue 140000. Marching towards him, he made himselfe Merry with it, and said ; *Yonder Men, are too Many for an Ambassage, and too Few for a Fight.* But before the Sunne sett, he found them enough, to giue him the Chace, with infinite Slaughter. Many are the Examples, of the great oddes between Number and Courage : So that a Man may truly make a Iudgement ; That the Principle Point of *Greatness* in any *State*, is to haue a Race of Military Men. Neither is Money the Sinewes of Warre, (as it is triuially said) where the Sinewes of Mens Armes, in Base and Effeminate People, are failing. For *Solon* said well to *Cræsus* (when in Ostentation he shewed him his Gold) *Sir, if any Other come, that hath better Iron then you, he will be Master of all his Gold.* Therefore let any Prince or State, thinke soberly of his Forces, except his *Militia* of Natiues, be of good and Valiant Soldiers. And let Princes, on the other side, that haue Subiects of Martiall disposition, know their owne strength; vnlesse they be otherwise wanting vnto Themselues. As for *Mercenary Forces,* (which is the Help in' this Case) all Examples shew; That whatsoeuer Estate or Prince doth rest vpon them; *Hee may spread his Feathers for a time, but he will mew them soone after.*

The *Blessing* of *Iudah* and *Issachar* will neuer meet; *That the same People or Nation, should be both The Lions whelpe, and the Asse betweene Burthens:* Neither will it be, that a People ouer-laid with *Taxes,* should euer become Valiant, and Martiall. It is true, that *Taxes* leuied by Consent of the Estate, doe abate Mens Courage lesse; as it hath beene seene notably, in the *Excises* of the *Low Countries;* And in some degree, in the *Subsidies* of *England.* For you must note, that we speake now, of the Heart, and not of the Purse. So that, although the same *Tribute* and *Tax,* laid by Consent, or by Imposing, be all one to the Purse, yet it workes diuersly vpon the Courage. So that you may conclude; *That no People, ouer-charged with Tribute, is fit for Empire.*

Let States that aime at *Greatnesse,* take heed how their *Nobility* and *Gentlemen,* doe multiply too fast. For that maketh the Common Subiect, grow to be a Peasant, and Base Swaine, driuen out of Heart, and in effect but the *Gentlemans* Labourer. Euen as you may see in Coppice Woods; *If you leaue your staddles too thick, you shall neuer haue cleane Vnderwood, but Shrubs and Bushes.* So in the Countries, if the *Gentlemen* be too many, the *Commons* will be base; And you will bring it to that, that not the hundred poll, will be fit for an Hermet: Especially as to the *Infantery,* which is the Nerue of an Army: And so there will be Great Population, and Little Strength. This, which I speake of, hath been no where better seen, then by comparing of *England* and *France;* whereof *England,* though farre lesse in Territory and Population, hath been (neuerthelesse) an Ouermatch; In regard, the *Middle People* of *England,* make good Souldiers, which the *Peasants* of *France* doe not. And herein, the deuice of King *Henry* the Seuenth, (whereof I haue spoken largely in the *History of his Life*) was Profound, and Admirable; In making Farmes, and houses of Husbandry, of a Standard; That is, maintained with such a Proportion of Land vnto them, as may breed a Subiect, to liue in Conuenient Plenty, and no **Seruile** Condition ; And to keepe the Plough in the Hands of the Owners, and not meere Hirelings. And thus indeed, you shall attaine to *Virgils* Character, which he giues to Ancient *Italy.*

———*Terra potens Armis atque vbere Glebœ.*

Neither is that State (which for any thing I know, is almost peculiar to *England,* and hardly to be found any where else, except it be perhaps in *Poland*) to be passed ouer ; I meane the State of *Free Seruants* and *Attendants* vpon *Noblemen* and *Gentlemen ;* which are no waies inferiour, vnto the *Yeomanry,* for Armes. And therefore, out of all Question, the Splendour, and Magnificence, and great Retinues, and Hospitality of *Noblemen,* and *Gentlemen,* receiue into Custome, doth much conduce, vnto *Martiall Greatnesse.* Whereas, contrariwise, the Close and Reserued living, of *Noblemen,* and *Gentlemen,* causeth a Penury ot *Military Forces.*

By all meanes, it is to be procured, that the *Trunck* of *Nebuchadnezzars* Tree of *Monarchy,* be great enough, to beare the Branches, and the Boughes ; That is, That the *Naturall Subiects,* of the Crowne or State, beare a sufficient Proportion to the *Stranger Subiects,* that they gouerne. Therefore all States, that are liberall of Naturalization towards Strangers, are fit for *Empire.* For to thinke, that an Handfull of People, can, with the greatest Courage, and Policy in the World, embrace too large Extent of Dominion, it may hold for a time, but it will faile suddainly. The Spartans were a nice People, in Point of Naturalization ; whereby, while they kept their Compasse, they stood firme ; But when they did spread, and their Boughs were becommen too great, for their Stem, they became a Windfall vpon the suddaine. Neuer any State was, in this Point, so open to receiue *Strangers,* into their Body, as were the *Romans.* Therfore it sorted with them accordingly ; For they grew to the greatest *Monarchy.* Their manner was, to grant Naturalization, (which they called *Ius Ciuitates*) and to grant it in the highest Degree ; That is, Not onely *Ius Commercij, Ius Connubij, Ius Hæriditatis ;* But also, *Ius Suffragij,* and *Ius Honorum.* And this, not to Singular Persons alone, but likewise to whole Families ; yea to Cities, and sometimes to Nations. Adde to this, their Custome of *Plantation* of *Colonies ;* whereby the Roman Plant, was remoued into the Soile, of other Nations. And putting both Constitutions together, you will say, that it was not the *Romans* that spread vpon the *World ;* But it was the *World* that spred vpon the *Romans :*

And that was the sure way of *Greatnesse*. I haue marueiled
sometimes at *Spaine*, how they claspe and containe so large
Dominions, with so few Naturall *Spaniards:* But sure, the
whole Compasse of *Spaine*, is a very Great Body of a Tree;
Farre aboue *Rome*, *Sparta*, at the first. And besides, though
they haue not had that vsage, to Naturalize liberally; yet they
haue that, which is next to it; That is *To employ, almost
indifferently, all Nations, in their Militia of ordinary Soldiers:*
yea, and sometimes in their *Highest Commands*. Nay, it
seemeth at this instant, they are sensible of this want of
Natiues; as by the *Pragmaticall Sanction*, now published and
appeareth.

If is certaine, that *Sedentary*, and *Within-doore Arts*, and
delicate Manufactures (that require rather the Finger, then the
Arme) haue, in their Nature, a Contrariety, to a Military
disposition. And generally, all Warlike People, are a little
idle; And loue Danger better then Trauaile; Neither must
they be too much broken of it, if they shall be preserued in
vigour. Therefore, it was great aduantage, in the Ancient
States of *Sparta*, *Athens*, *Rome*, and others, that they had the
vse of *Slaues*, which commonly did rid those Manufactures.
But that is abolished, in greatest part, by the *Christian Law*.
That which commeth nearest to it, is, to leaue those Arts chiefly
to Strangers, (which for that purpose are the more easily to be
receiued) and to containe, the principall Bulke of the vulgar
Natiues, within those three kinds, *Tillers* of the Ground; *Free
Seruants*; and *Handy-Crafts-Men*, of Strong, and Manly Arts,
as Smiths, Masons, Carpenters, &c.; Not reckoning Professed
Souldiers.

But aboue all, for *Empire* and *Greatnesse*, it importeth most;
That a Nation doe professe Armes, as their principall Honour,
Study, and Occupation. For the Things, which we formerly
haue spoken of, are but *Habilitations* towards Armes : And
what is *Habilitation* without *Intention* and *Act?* *Romulus*,
after his death (as they report, or faigne) sent a Present to the
Romans; That, aboue all, they should intend Armes; And
then, they should proue the greatest *Empire* of the World. The
Fabrick of the State of *Sparta*, was wholly (though not wisely)
framed, and composed, to that Scope and End. The *Persians*
and *Macedonians*, had it for a flash. The *Galls*, *Germans*,
Goths, *Saxons*, *Normans*, and others, had it for a Time. The
Turks haue it, at this day, though in great Declination. Of
Christian *Europe*, they that haue it, are, in effect, onely the
Spaniards. But it is so plaine, *That euery Man profiteth in*

that hee most intendeth, that it needeth not to be stood vpon. It is enough to point at it ; That no Nation, which doth not directly professe Armes, may looke to haue *Greatnesse* fall into their Mouths. And, on the other side, it is a most Certaine Oracle of Time ; That those States, that continue long in that Profession (as the *Romans* and *Turks* principally haue done) do wonders. And those, that haue professed Armes but for an Age, haue notwithstanding, commonly, attained that *Greatnesse* in that Age, which maintained them long after, when their ·Profession and Exercise of Armes hath growen to decay.

Incident to this Point is ; For a State, to haue those Lawes or Customes, which may reach forth vnto them, iust Occasions (as may be pretended) of Warre. For there is that Iustice imprinted, in the Nature of Men, that they enter not vpon Wars (whereof so many Calamities doe ensue) but vpon some, at the least Specious, Grounds and Quarrels. The *Turke*, hath at hand, for Cause of Warre, the Propagation of his Law or Sect ; A Quarell that he may alwaies Command. The *Romans*, though they esteemed, the Extending the Limits of their Empire, to be Great Honour to their Generalls, when it was done, yet they neuer rested vpon that alone, to begin a Warre. First therefore, let Nations, that pretend to *Greatnesse*, haue this ; That they be sensible of Wrongs, either vpon Borderers, Merchants, or Politique Ministers ; And that they sit not too long vpon a Prouocation. Secondly, let them be prest, and ready, to giue Aids and Succours, to their Confederates : As it euer was with the *Romans* : In so much, as if the Confederate, had Leagues Defensiue with diuers other States, and vpon Inuasion offered, did implore their Aides seuerally, yet the *Romans* would euer bee the formost, and leaue it to none Other to haue the Honour. As for the Warres, which were anciently made, on the behalfe, of a kinde of Parlie, or tacite Conformitie of Estate, I doe not see how they may be well iustified : As when the *Romans* made a Warre for the Libertie of *Grecia* : Or when the *Lacedemonians*, and *Athenians*, made Warres, to set vp or pull downe *Democracies* and *Oligarchies* : Or when Warres were made by Forrainers, vnder the pretence of Iustice, or Protection, to deliuer the Subiects of others, from Tyrannie, and Opression ; And the like. Let it suffice, That no Estate expect to be *Great*, that is not awake, vpon any iust Occasion of Arming.

No Body can be healthfull without *Exercise*, neither Naturall Body, nor Politique : And certainly, to a Kingdome or Estate, a Iust and Honourable Warre, is the true *Exercise*. A Ciuill

Warre, indeed, is like the Heat of a Feauer ; But a Forraine
Warre, is like the Heat of *Exercise*, and serueth to keepe the
Body in Health : For in a Slothfull Peace, both Courages will
effeminate, and Manners Corrupt. But howsoever it be a
Happinesse, without all Question, for *Greatnesse*, it maketh, to
bee still, for the most Part, in Armes : And the Strength of a
Veteran Armie, (though it be a chargeable Businesse) alwaies
on Foot, is that, which commonly giueth the Law ; Or at least
the Reputation amongst all Neighbour States ; As may well
bee seene in *Spaine ;* which hath had, in one Part or other, a
Veteran Armie, almost continually, now by the space of
Six-score yeeres.

To be Master of the *Sea*, is an Abridgement of a Monarchy.
Cicero writing to *Atticus*, of *Pompey* his *Preparation* against
Cæsar, saith ; *Confilium Pompeij planè Themistocleum est ;
Putat enim, qui Mari potitur, cum Rerum potiri.* And, without doubt, *Pompey* had tired out *Cæsar*, if upon vaine Confidence, he had not left that Way. We see the great Effects of
Battailes by *Sea*. The Battaile of *Actium* decided the Empire of
the World. The Battaile of *Lepanto* arrested the greatnesse of
the *Turke*. There be many Examples, where *Sea-Fights* haue
beene Finall to the warre ; But this is, when Princes or States,
haue set up their Rest, vpon the Battailes. But thus much is
certain ; That hee that Commands the *Sea*, is at great liberty,
and may take as much, and as little of Warre, as he will.
Whereas those, that be strongest by land, are many times
neuerthelesse in great Straights. Surely, at this Day, with vs of
Europe, the Vantage of Strength at *Sea* (which is one of the
Principall Dowries of this Kingdome of *Great Brittaine*) is
great : Both because, most of the Kingdomes of *Europe*, are
not meerely Inland, but girt with the *Sea*, most part of their
Compasse ; And because, the Wealth of both *Indies*, seemes in
great Part, but an Accessary, to the Command of the *Seas*.

The *Warres* of *Latter Ages*, seeme to be made in the
Darke, in Respect of the Glory and Honour, which reflected
vpon men, from the *Warres* in *Ancient Time*. There be now,
for Martiall Encouragement, some Degrees and Orders of
Chiualry ; which neuerthelesse, are conferred promiscuously,
vpon Soldiers, and no Soldiers ; And some Remembrance per-
haps vpon the Scutchion ; And some Hospitals for Maimed
Soldiers ; And such like Things. But in Ancient Times ; The
Trophies erected vpon the Place of the Victory ; The Funerall
Laudatiues and Monuments for those that died in the Wars ; The
Crowns and Garlands Personal ; The Stile of Emperour, which

the Great Kings of the World after borrowed ; The Triumphes of
the Generalls vpon their Returne ; The great Donatiues and
Largesses vpon the Disbanding of the Armies ; were Things
able to enflame all Mens Courages. But aboue all, That of the
Triumph, amongst the *Romans*, was not Pageants or Gauderie,
but one of the Wisest and Noblest Institutions, that euer was.
For it contained three Things ; Honour to the Generall ; Riches
to the Treasury out of the Spoiles ; And Donations to the Army.
But that Honour, perhaps, were not fit for *Monarchies;* Except
it be in the Person of the *Monarch* himselfe, or his Sonnes ; As
it came to passe, in the Times of the *Roman Emperours*, who
did impropriate the Actuall Triumphs to Themselues, and their
Sonnes, for such Wars, as they did atchieue in Person : And
left onely, for Wars atchieued by subiects, some Triumphall
Garments, and Ensignes to the Generall.

 To conclude ; No Man can, by *Care taking* (as the *Scripture*
saith) *adde a Cubite to his Stature;* in this little Modell of a
Mans Body: But in the Great Frame of *Kingdomes*, and
Common Wealths, it is in the Power of Princes, or Estates, to
adde Amplitude and *Greatnesse* to their *Kingdomes*. For by
introducing such Ordinances, Constitutions, and Customes, as
we haue now touched, they may sow *Greatnesse*, to their
Posteritie, and Succession. But these Things are commonly
not Obserued, but left to take their Chance.

Essays.

CHARACTER OF HENRY VII.

This King *(to speake of him in Tearmes equall to his deseruing)*
was one of the best sort of Wonders ; *a* Wonder *for* Wisemen.
He had Parts (both in his Vertues, *and his* Fortune) *not so fit for*
a Common-place, *as for* Obseruation. *Certainely hee was* Religious, *both in his* Affection, *and* Obseruance. *But as hee could*
see cleare (for those times) through Superstition, *so he would*
be blinded (now and then) by Humane Policie. *He aduanced*
Church-men ; *hee was tender in the Priuiledge of* Sanctuaries,
though they wrought him much mischiefe. Hee built and
endowed many Religious Foundations, *besides his* Memorable
Hospital *of the* Sauoy. *And yet was hee a great* Almes-giuer *in*
secret ; which shewed, that his Workes in publique *were dedi-*
cated rather to GODS Glorie, *then his* Owne. *Hee professed*
alwayes to loue and seeke Peace ; *and it was his vsuall* Preface

in his Treaties ; That when CHRIST came into the *World, Peace* was sung ; and when HEE went out of the *World, Peace* was bequeathed. *And this* Vertue *could not proceede out of* Feare, *or* Softnesse ; *for hee was* Valiant *and* Actiue, and *therefore (no doubt) it was truely* Christian *and* Morall. *Yet hee knew the way to* Peace, *was not to seeme to bee desious to auoide* Warres. *Therefore would he make* Offers, *and* Fames *of* Warres, *till hee had mended the* Conditions *of* Peace. *It was also much, that one that was so great a* Louer *of* Peace, *should be so happy in* Warre. *For his* Armes (*either in* Forraine *or* Ciuill Warres) *were neuer* Infortunate ; *neither did he know what a* Disaster *meant. The* Warre *of his* Coming in, *and the* Rebellions *of the* Earle *of* Lincolne, *and the* Lord AWDLEY *were ended by* Victorie. *The* Warres *of* France *and* Scotland, *by* Peaces *sought at his hands. That of* Brittaine, *by accident of the* Dukes *death. The* Insurrection *of the* Lord LOVEL, *and that of* PERKIN *at* Excester, *and in* Kent, *by flight of the* Rebells, *before they came to* Blowes. *So that his* Fortune *of* Armes *was still* Inviolate. *The rather sure, for that in the quenching of the* Commotions *of his* Subiects, *hee euer went in* Person. *Sometimes reseruing himselfe to backe and second his* Lieutenants, *but euer in* Action ; *and yet that was not meerly* Forwardnesse, *but partly* Distrust of others.

Hee did much maintaine and countenance his Lawes. *Which (neuerthelesse) was no* Impediment *to him to worke his* Will. *For it was so handled, that neither* Prerogatiue, *nor* Profit *went to* Diminution. *And yet as hee would sometimes straine vp his* Lawes *to his* Prerogatiue, *so would hee also let downe his* Prerogatiue *to his* Parliament. *For* Minte, *and* Warres, *and* Marshall Discipline, (*things of Absolute Power*) *he would neuerthelesse bring to* Parliament. Justice *was well administred in his time, saue where the* King *was* Partie : *Saue also, that the* Counsell-Table *intermeddled too much with* Meum *and* Tuum. *For it was a very* Court *of* Iustice *during his time, especially in the Beginning. But in that part both of* Iustice *and* Policie *which is the* Durable Part, *and cut (as it were) in in* Brasse *or* Marble (*which is* The making of good Lawes) *hee did excell. And with his* Iustice, *hee was also a* Mercifull Prince. *As in whose time, there were but three of the* Nobilitie *that suffered; the* Earle *of* Warwicke, *the* Lord Chamberlaine, *and the* Lord AWDLEY. *Though the first two were in stead of* Numbers, *in the* Dislike *and* Obloquie *of the* People. *But there were neuer so great* Rebellions, *expiated with so little* Bloud, *drawne by the hand of Justice, as the two* Rebellions *of* Black-heath *and*

Excester. *As for the* Serueritie *vsed vpon those which were taken in* Kent, *it was but vpon a* Scumme *of People. His* Pardons *went euer both before, and after his* Sword. *But then he had withall a strange kind of* Interchanging *of large and unexpected* Pardons, *with seuere* Executions. *Which (his Wisedome considered) could not bee imputed to any* Inconstancie, *or* Inequalitie; *but either to some* Reason *which we do not know, or to a* Principle *he had set vnto himselfe,* That hee would vary, and trie both wayes in turne. *But the lesse* Bloud *hee drew, the more hee tooke of* Treasure. *And (as some construed it) hee was the more sparing in the* One, *that hee might bee the more pressing in the* Other; *for both would haue beene intollerable. Of* Nature *assuredly hee coueted to accumulate* Treasure, *and was a little* Poore *in admiring* Riches. *The* People (*into whome there is infused, for the preseruation of* Monarchies, *a naturall Desire to discharge their* Princes, *though it bee with the vniust charge of their* Counsellors *and* Ministers) *did impute this vnto* Cardinal MORTON, *and Sir* REGINALD BRAY. *Who (as it after appeared) as* Counsellors *of ancient Authoritie with him, did so second his* Humours, *as neuerthelesse they did temper them. Whereas* EMPSON *and* DVDLEY *that followed, beeing Persons that had no* Reputation *with him (otherwise then by the seruile following of his Bent) did not giue way onely (as the first did) but shape him way to those* Extremities, *for which himselfe was touched with remorse at his Death, and which his* Successor *renounced, and sought to purge. This* Excesse *of his, had at that time many* Glosses *and* Interpretations. *Some thought the continuall* Rebellions *wherewith he had beene vexed, had made him grow to hate his* People. *Some thought it was done to pull downe their* Stomacks, *and to keepe them low. Some, for that hee would leaue his* Sonne *a* Golden-fleece. *Some suspected he had some high* Designe *vpon* Forraine *Parts. But those perhaps shall come nearest the truth, that fetch not their reasons so farre of; but rather impute it to* Nature, Age, Peace, *and a* Mind *fixed vpon no other* Ambition *or* Pursuit. *Wherevnto I shall adde, that hauing euery day Occasion to take notice of the* Necessities *and* Shifts *for Monie of other great* Princes *abroad, it did the better (by Comparison) set of to him the* Felicitie *of full* Cofers. *As to his expending of* Treasure, *hee neuer spared Charge which his* Affaires *required; and in his* Buildings *was* Magnificent, *but his* Rewards *wery very limitted. So that his* Liberalitie *was rather vpon his owne* State *and* Memorie, *then vpon the* Deserts *of others.*

Hee was of an High Mind, *and loued his owne* Will, *and his owne* Way ; *as one that reuered himselfe, and would* Raigne *indeed.* Had he been a Priuate-man ; *he would haue been termed* Proud. *But in a Wise* Prince, *it was but keeping of* Distance, *which indeed hee did towards all ; not admitting any neare or full* Approach, *neither to his* Power *or to his* Secrets. *For he was gouerned by none.* His Queene *(notwithstanding shee had presented him with diuers* Children, *and with a* Crowne *also, though hee would not acknowledge it) could doe nothing with him.* His Mother *hee reuerenced much, heard little.* For *any* Person *agreeable to him for* Societie *(such as was* HASTINGS *to King* EDWARD *the Fourth, or* CHARLES BRANDON *after to King* HENRY *the Eigth) hee had none :* Except wee should account for such Persons, FOXE, *and* BRAY, *and* EMPSON, *because they were so much with him.* But it was but as the Instrument *is much with the* Workman. *Hee had nothing in him of* Vaine-glorie, *but yet kept* State *and* Maiestie *to the height ; Beeing sensible, That* Maiestie *maketh the People bow, but* Vaine-glorie *boweth them.*

To his Confederates *abroad he was* Constant *and* Iust, *but not* Open. *But rather such was his* Inquirie, *and such his* Closenesse, *as they stood in the* Light *towards him, and hee stood in the* Darke *to them.* Yet without Strangenesse, *but with a semblance of mutuall* Communication *of Affaires.* As for little Enuies, *or* Emulations *vpon* Forraine Princes *(which are frequent with many Kings) hee had neuer any ; but went substantially to his owne* Businesse. *Certaine it is, that though his* Reputation *was great at home, yet it was greater abroad.* For Forrainers *that could not see the Passages of* Affaires, *but made their Judgements vpon the* Issues *of them, noted that he was euer in* Strife, *and euer a* Loft. *Jt grew also from the* Aires, *which the* Princes *and* States *abroad receiued from their* Ambassadors *and* Agents *here ; which were attending the* Court *in great number.* Whom hee did not onely content with Courtesie, Reward, *and* Priuatenesse ; *but (vpon such* Conferences *as passed with them) put them in* Admiration, *to finde his* Vniuersall Insight *into the Affaires of the World.* Which though hee did sucke chiefely ; from themselues : yet that which hee had gathered from them all, seemed Admirable *to euery one.* So that they did write euer to their Superiours *in high termes, concerning his* Wisedome *and* Art *of* Rule. Nay, when they were returned, they did commonly maintaine Intelligence *with him. Such a* Dexteritie *hee had to impropriate to himselfe all* Forraine Instruments.

Hee was carefull and liberall to obtaine good Intelligence *from all parts abroad.   Wherein hee did not onely vse his* Interest *in* the Leigers *here, and his* Pensioners *which hee had both in the Court of* Rome, *and other the Courts of* Christen-dome ; *but the* Industrie *and* Vigilancie *of his owne* Ambassa-dors *in Forraine parts.   For which purpose, his* Instructions *were euer* Extreame, Curious, *and* Articulate ; *and in them more* Articles *touching* Inquisition, *then touching* Negotiation. *Requiring likewise from his* Ambassadors *an* Answere, *in par-ticular distinct* Articles, *respectiuely to his* Questions.

As for his secret Spialls, *which hee did imploy both at home and abroad, by them to discouer what* Practises *and* Conspiracies *were against him, surely his* case *required it : Hee had such* Moles *perpetually working and casting to vndermind him.   Neither can it be reprehended.   For if* Spialls *bee lawfull against lawfull* Enemies, *much more against* Conspirators, *and* Traitors.   *But indeed to giue them* Credence *by* Othes *or* Curses, *that cannot bee well maintained ; For those are too holy* Vestments *for a* Dis-guise.   *Yet surely there was this further* Good *in his employing of these* Flies *and* Familiars ; *That as the vse of them was cause that many* Conspiracies *were reuealed, so the* Fame *and* Suspition *of them kept (no doubt) many* Conspiracies *from beeing attempted.*

Towards his Queene *hee was nothing* Vxorious, *nor scarce* Indulgent ; *but* Companiable, *and* Respectiue, *and without* Iealousie.   *Towards his* Children *he was full of* Paternall Affection, *Carefull of their* Education, *aspiring to their* High Aduancement, *regular to see that they should not want of any due* Honour *and* Respect, *but not greatly willing to cast any* Popular Lustre *vpon them.*

To his Councell *hee did referre much, and sate oft in Person ; knowing it to bee the Way to assist his* Power, *and informe his* Iudgement.   *In which respect also hee was fairely patient of* Libertie, *both of* Aduise, *and of* Vote, *till himselfe were declared. Hee kept a straight hand on his* Nobilitie, *and chose rather to aduance* Clergie-men *and* Lawyers, *which were more* Obsequious *to him, but had lesse* Interest *in the* People ; *which made for his* Absolutenesse, *but not for his* Safetie.   *Jn so much as (I am perswaded) it was none of the* Causes *of his troublesome* Raigne ; *for that his* Nobles, *though they were* Loyall *and* Obedient, *yet did not* Co-operate *with him, but let euery man goe his owne Way.   Hee was not afraid of an* Able Man, *as* Lewis *the Eleuenth was.   But contrariwise, he was serued by the* Ablest Men *that were to bee found ; without which his* Affaires *could not haue prospered as they did.   For* Warre, Bedford, Oxford,

Svrrey, Dawbeney, Brooke, Poynings. *For other* Affaires, Morton, Foxe, Bray, *the Prior of* Lanthony, Warham, Vrswicke, Hyssey, Frowicke, *and others. Neither did hee care how* Cunning *they were, that hee did imploy; For hee thought himselfe to haue the* Master-Reach. *And as hee chose well, so hee held them vp well. For it is a strange thing, that though he were a* Darke Prince, *and infinitely* Suspitious, *and his Times full of* Secret Conspiracies *and* Troubles ; *yet in Twentie fowre yeares* Raigne, *hee neuer put downe, or discomposed* Counsellor, *or neare* Seruant, *saue onely* Stanley, *the Lord* Chamberlaine. *As for the* Disposition *of his* Subiects *in Generall towards him, it stood thus with him ; That of the* Three Affections, *which naturally tie the hearts of the* Subiects *to their* Soueraignes, Love, Feare, *and* Reuerance ; *hee had the* last *in height, the* second *in good measure, and so little of the* first, *as hee was beholding to the other* Two.

Hee was a Prince, Sad, Serous, *and full of* Thoughts *and secret* Obseruations, *and full of* Notes *and* Memorialls *of his owne hand, especially touching* Persons. *As, whom to Employ, whom to Reward, whom to Enquire of, whom to Beware of, what were the* Dependencies, *what were the* Factions, *and the like ; keeping (as it were) a* Iournall *of his* Thoughts. *There is to this day a merrie* Tale ; *That his* Monkie *(set on as it was thought by one of his Chamber) tore his Principall* Note-Booke *all to pieces, when by chance it lay forth. Whereat the* Court *(which liked not those* Pensiue *Accompts) was almost tickled with sport.*

Hee was indeed full of Apprehensions *and* Suspitions. *But as hee did easily take them, so hee did easily checke them, and master them : whereby they were not dangerous, but troubled himselfe more then others. It is true, his* Thoughts *were so many, as they could not well alwayes stand together ; but that which did good one way, did hurt another. Neither did he at some times waigh them aright in their proportions. Certainely, that* Rumour *which did him so much mischiefe (That the* Duke of Yorke *should bee saued, and aliue) was (at the first) of his owne nourishing ; because hee would haue more* Reason *not to raigne in the* Right *of his* Wife. *Hee was* Affable, *and both* Well *and* Faire-Spoken ; *and would vse strange* Sweetnesse *and* Blandishments *of* Words, *where hee desired to effect or perswade anything that hee tooke to heart. Hee was rather* Studious, *then* Learned ; *reading most* Bookes *that were of any worth, in the* French-tongue. *Yet hee vnderstood the* Latine, *as appeareth in that* Cardinal Hadrian, *and others, who could very well haue written* French, *did vse to write to him in* Latine.

For his Pleasures, *there is no Newes of them. And yet by his* Instructions *to* MARSIN, *and* STILE, *touching the* Queene *of* Naples, *it seemeth hee could Jnterrogate well touching* Beautie. *Hee did by* Pleasures, *as great* Princes *doe by* Banquets, *come and looke a little vpon them, and turn away. For neuer* Prince *was more wholly giuen to* his Affaires, *nor in them more of himselfe; In so much, as in* Triumphs *of* Iusts, *and* Tourneys, *and* Balles, *and* Masques (*which they then called* Disguises) *hee was rather a* Princely *and* Gentle Spectator, *then seemed much to bee delighted.*

No doubt, in him as in all men (*and most of all in* Kings) *his* Fortune *wrought vpon his* Nature, *and his* Nature *vpon his* Fortune. *Hee attayned to the* Crowne, *not onely from a priuate* Fortune, *which might indow him with Moderation; but also from the* Fortune *of an* Exiled Man, *which had quickened in him all* Seedes *of* Obseruation *and* Industrie. *And his* Times *being rather* Prosperous, *then* Calme, *had raised his* Confidence *by* Successe, *but almost marred his* Nature *by* Troubles. *His* Wisdome, *by often* euading *from* Perils, *was turned rather into a* Dexteritie *to deliuer himselfe from* Dangers, *when they pressed him, then into a* Prouidence *to preuent and remove them a farre of. And euen in* Nature, *the* Sight *of his* Minde *was like some* Sights *of* Eyes; *rather strong at hand, then to carrie a farre of. For his* Witt *increased vpon the* Occasion; *and so much the more, if the* Occasion *were sharpened by* Danger. *Againe, whether it were the shortnesse of his* Fore-sight, *or the strength of his* Will, *or the dazeling of his* Suspition, *or what it was; Certaine it is, that the perpetuall* Troubles *of his* Fortunes (*there being no more matter out of which they grew*) *could not have beene without some great* Defects, *and mayne* Errours *in his* Nature, Customes, *and* Proceedings, *which he had enough to doe to saue and helpe, with a thousand little* Industries *and* Watches. *But those doe best appeare in the* Storie *it selfe. Yet take him with all his* Defects, *if a* Man *should compare him with the* Kings *his* Concurrents, *in* France *and* Spaine, *he shall find him more* Politique *then* LEWIS *the twelfth of* France, *and more* Entire *and* Sincere *then* FERDINANDO *of* Spaine. *But if you shall change* LEWIS *the twelfth, for* LEWIS *the eleuenth, who lived a little before; then the* Consort *is more perfect. For that* LEWIS *the* Eleuenth, FERDINANDO, *and* HENRY, *may bee esteemed for the* Tres Magi *of* Kings *of those* Ages. *To conclude, If this* King *did no greater* Matters, *it was long of himselfe; for what he minded, he compassed.*

Hee was a Comely Personage, *a little aboue* lust Stature, *well and straight limmed, but slender.* His Countenance *was* Reuerend, *and a little like a* Churchman : *And as it was not* strange *or* darke, *so neyther was it* Winning *or* Pleasing, *but as the Face of one well disposed. But it was to the Disaduantage of the* Painter ; *for it was best when hee spake.*

His Worth *may beare a* Tale *or two, that may put vpon him somewha. that may seeme* Diuine. *When the* Ladie MARGARET *his* Mother *had diuers great* Sutors *for* Marriage, *she dreamed one Night,* That one in the likenesse of a Bishop in Pontificall habit did tender her EDMVND Earle of Richmond (the Kings Father) for her Husband. *Neither had she euer any* Child *but the* King, *though she had three* Husbands. *One day when* King HENRY *the Sixth (whose* Innocencie *gaue him* Holines) *was washing his hands at a great* Feast, *and cast his* Eye *vpon* King HENRY, *then a young* Youth, *he said;* This is the Lad, that shall possesse quietly that, that we now striue for. *But that that was truely* Diuine *in him, was that he had the* Fortune *of a* True Christian, *as well as of a* Great King, *in liuing* Exercised, *and dying* Repentant. *So as hee had an happie* Warrefare *in both* Conflicts, *both of* Sinne, *and the* Crosse.

Hee was borne at Pembrooke Castle, *and lyeth buried at* Westminster, *in one of the Statelyest and Daintiest Monuments of* Europe, *both for the* Chappell, *and for the* Sepulcher. *So that he dwelleth more richly* Dead, *in the* Monument *of his* Tombe, *then hee did* Aliue *in* Richmond, *or any of his* Palaces. *J could wish he did the like, in this* Monument *of his* Fame.

The Historie of the Raigne of King
HENRY *the Seventh.*

ROBERT SOUTHWELL, S.J.

1562 ?–1595.

[Robert Southwell was born at Horsham St Faith's, a suppressed Benedictine House in the County of Norfolk. As an infant, he was stolen by a gipsy. He studied theology at Paris and Douay; in 1578 he entered the Society of Jesus. He was ordained Priest in 1584; two years later he came to England, and he was executed in 1595.]

THE GIFTS OF YOUTH.

To the worshipful his very good father Mr. R. S. his dutiful son R. S. wisheth all happiness.

IN children of former ages it hath been thought so behoveful a point of duty to their parents, in presence by serviceable offices, in absence by other effectual significations, to yield proof of their thankful minds, that neither any child could omit it without touch of ungratefulness, nor the parents forbear it without nice displeasure. But now we are fallen into sore calamity of times, and the violence of heresy hath crossed this course both of virtue and nature, that these ingrafted laws, never infringed by the most savage and brute creatures, cannot of God's people without peril be observed. I am not of so unnatural a kind, of so wild an education, or so unchristian a spririt, as not to remember the root out of which I branched, or to forget my secondary maker and author of my being. It is not the carelessness of a cold affection, nor the want of a due and reverent respect that has made me such a stranger to my native home, and so backward in defraying the debt of a thankful mind, but only the iniquity of these days, that maketh my presence perilous, and the discharge of my duties an occasion of danger. I was loth to enforce an unwilling courtesy upon any, or, by seeming officious, to become offensive; deeming it better to let time digest the fear that my return into the realm had bred in my kindred, than abruptly intrude myself, and to purchase their dangers, whose good will I so highly esteem. I never doubted but that the belief, which to all my friends by descent and pedigree is, in a manner, hereditary, framed in them a right persuasion of my present calling, not suffering them to measure their censures of me by the ugly terms and odious epithets wherewith heresy hath sought to discredit my functions, but rather by the reverence of so worthy a sacrament, and the sacred usages of all former ages. Yet, because I might easily perceive by apparent conjectures, that many were more willing to hear of me than from me, and readier to praise than to use my endeavours, I have hitherto bridled my desire to see them by the care and jealousy of their safety ; and banishing myself from the scene of my cradle in my own country, I have lived like a foreigner, finding among strangers that which, in my nearest blood, I presumed not to seek. But now, considering that delay may have qualified fear, and knowing my person only to import danger to others, and my persuasion to none but myself, I thought it high time to utter my sincere and dutiful mind, and to open a vent to my zealous affection, which I have so long smothered and suppressed in silence. For not only the original law of nature written in all children's hearts, and derived from the breast of their mother, is a continual solicitude urging me in your behalf, but the sovereign decree enacted by the Father of heaven, ratified by his Son, and daily repeated by the instinct of the Holy Ghost, bindeth every child in the due of Christianity to tender the state and welfare of his parents, and is a motive that alloweth no excuse, but of necessity presseth to performance of duty. Nature by grace is not abolished, nor destroyed, but perfected ; neither are the impressions razed or annulled, but suited to the ends of grace and nature. And if its affections be so forcible, that even in hell, where rancour and despite, and all feelings of goodness are overwhelmed by malice, they moved the rich glutton, by experience of his own misery, to have compassion of his kindred, how much more in the Church of God, where grace quickeneth, charity inflameth, and nature's good inclinations are abetted by supernatural gifts, ought the like piety to prevail. And, who but those more merciless than damned creatures, would see their dearest friends plunged in the like perils, and not be wounded by deep remorse at their lamentable and imminent hazard? If in beholding a mortal enemy wrought and tortured with deadly pains, the strongest heart softeneth with some sorrows ; if the most frozen and fierce mind cannot but thaw and melt with pity even when it knows such person to suffer his deserved torments ; how much less can the heart of a child consider those that bred him into this world, to be in the fall to far more bitter extremities, and not bleed with grief at their uncomfortable case. Surely, for mine own part, though I challenge not the prerogative of the best disposition, yet am I not of so harsh and churlish a humour, but that it is a continual corrective and cross unto me, that, whereas my endeavours have reclaimed many from the brink of perdition, I have been less able to employ them, where they were most due ; and was barred from affording to my dearest friends that which hath been eagerly sought and beneficially obtained by mere strangers. Who hath more interest in the grape than he who planted the vine ? who more right to the crop than he who sowed the corn ? or where can the child owe so great service as to him to whom he is indebted for his very life and being? With young Tobias I have travelled far, and brought home a freight of spiritual substance to enrich you, and medicinable receipts against your ghostly maladies. I have, with Esau, after long toil in pursuing a long and painful chace, returned with the full prey, you were wont to love ; desiring thereby to insure your blessing. I have in this general famine of all true and Christian food, with Joseph, prepared abundance of the bread of angels for the repast of your soul. And now my desire is that my drugs may cure you, my prey delight you, and my provision feed you, by whom I have been cured, enlightened, and fed myself ; that your courtesies may, in part, be countervailed, and my duty, in some sort performed. Despise not, good Sire, the youth of your son, neither deem your God measureth his endowments by number of years. Hoary senses are often couched under youthful locks, and some are riper in the spring, than others in the autumn of their age. God chose not Esau himself, nor his eldest son, but young David to conquer Goliath and to rule his people ; not the most aged person, but Daniel, the most innocent youth, delivered Susannah from the iniquity of the judges. Christ, at twelve years of age, was found in the temple questioning with the greatest doctors. A true Elias can conceive, that a litttle cloud may cast a large and abundant shower ; and the scripture teacheth us, that God unveileth to little ones that which He concealeth from the wisest sages. His truth is not abashed by the minority of the speaker : for out of the mouths of infants and sucklings He can perfect His praises. Timothy was young, and yet a principal pastor : St. John, a youth, and yet an apostle ; yea, and the angels appearing in youthful semblance, gave us a proof that many glorious gifts may be shrouded under tender shapes.

Works.

ROBERT BURTON.

1576–1640.

REMEDIES AGAINST DISCONTENT.

MANY grievances there are, which happen to mortals in this life, from friends, wives, children, servants, masters, companions, neighbours, our own defaults, ignorance, errours, intemperance, indiscretion, infirmities, &c. a many good remedies to mitigate and oppose them, many divine precepts to counterpoise our hearts, special antidotes both in scriptures and humane authors, which who so will observe, shall purchase much ease and quietness unto himself, I will point at a few. Those prophetical, apostolical admitions are well known to all; what Solomon, Siracides, our Saviour Christ himself hath said tending to this purpose, as *Fear God: obey the prince: be sober and watch: pray continually: be angry, but sin not: remember thy last: fashion not yourselves to this world,* &c. *apply your selves to the times: strive not with a mighty man: recompence good for evil: let nothing be done through contention or vain-glory, but with meekness of mind, every man esteeming of others better then himself: love one another;* or that epitome of the law and the prophets, which our Saviour inculcates, *love God above all, thy neighbour as thyself;* and, *whatsoever you would that men should do unto you you, so do unto them,* which Alexander Severus writ in letters of gold, and used as a motto, and Heirom commends to Celantia as an excellent way, amongst so many inticements and worldly provocations, to rectify her life. Out of humane authors take these few cautions—*Know thy self. Be contented with thy lot. Trust not wealth, beauty, nor parasites: they will bring thee to destruction. Have peace with all men, war with vice. Be not idle. Look before you leap. Beware of "Had I wist." Honour thy parents: speak well of friends. Be temperate in foure things,* lingua, loculis, oculis, poculis. *Watch*

thine eye. Moderate thine expences. Hear much: speak little.
Sustine et abstine. *If thou seest ought amiss in another, mend it in thyself. Keep thine own counsell; reveal not thy secrets; be silent in thine intentions. Give not ear to tale-tellers, bablers: be not scurrilous in conversation: jest without bitterness: give no cause of offence. Set thine house in order. Take heed of suretiship.* Fide et diffide: *as a fox on the ice, take heed whom you trust. Live not beyond thy means. Give chearfully. Pay thy dues willingly. Be not a slave to thy mony. Omit not occasion; embrace opportunity; loose no time. Be humble to thy superiors, respective to thine equals, affable to all, but not familiar. Flatter no man. Lie not: dissemble not. Keep thy word and promise, be constant in a good resolution. Speak truth. Be not opiniative: maintain no factions. Lay no wagers: make no comparisons. Find no faults, meddle not with other mens matters. Admire not thyself. Be not proud or popular. Insult not.* Fortunam reverenter habe. *Fear not that which cannot be avoided. Grieve not for that which cannot be recalled. Undervalue not thy self. Accuse no man, commend no man, rashly. Go not to law without great cause. Strive not with a greater man. Cast not off an old friend. Take heed of a reconciled enemy. If thou come as a guest, stay not too long. Be not unthankful. Be meek, merciful, and patient. Do good to all. Be not fond of fair words. Be not a newter in a faction. Moderate thy passions. Think no place without a witness. Admonish thy friend in secret: commend him in publike. Keep good company. Love others, to be loved thy self.* Ama, tanquam osurus. Amicus tardo fias. *Provide for a tempest.* Noli irritare crabrones. *Do not prostitute thy soul for gain. Make not a fool of thy self, to make others merry. Marry not an old crony, or a fool, for mony. Be not over sollicitous or curious. Seek that which may be found. Seem not greater then thou art. Take thy pleasure soberly.* Ocymum ne terito. *Live merrily as thou canst. Take heed by other mens examples. Go as thou wouldst be met: sit as thou wouldst be found. Yield to the time; follow the stream. Wilt thou live free from fears and cares? Live innocently, keep thy self upright; thou needest no other keeper, &c.* Look for more in Isocrates, Seneca, Plutarch, Epictetus, &c. a, for defect, consult with cheese-trenchers and painted cloths.

AGAINST MELANCHOLY IT SELF.

Every man, saith Seneca, *thinks his own burthen the heaviest;* and a melancholy man, above all others, complains most. Weariness of life, abhorring all company and light ; fear, sorrow, suspition, anguish of mind, bashfulness, and those other dread symtomes of body and mind, must needs aggravate this misery ; yet, conferred to other maladies, they are not so hainous as they be taken. For, first, this disease is either in habit or disposition, curable or incurable. If new and in disposition, 'tis commonly pleasant, and may be helped. If inveterate, or an habit, yet they have *lucida intervalla,* sometimes well, and sometimes ill ; or if more continuate, as the Vejentes were to the Romans, 'tis *hostis magis assiduus quam gravis,* a more durable enemy then dangerous ; and, amongst many inconveniences, some comforts are annexed to it. First, it is not catching ; and, as Erasmus comforted himself, when he was greivously sick of the stone, though it was most troublesome, and an intolerable pain to him, yet it was no whit offensive to others, not lothsome to the spectators, gastly, fulsom, terrible, as plagues, apoplexies, leprosies, wounds, sores, tetters, pox, pestilent agues are, which either admit of no company, terrify or offend those that are present. In this malady, that which is, is wholly to themselves ; and those symptomes not so dreadful, if they be compared to the opposite extreams. They are most part bashful, suspicious, solitary, &c. therefore no such ambitious, impudent intruders, as some are, no sharkers, no cunnicatchers, no prolers, no smel-feasts, praters, panders, parasites, bawds, drunkards, whoremasters : necessity and defect compels them to be honest ; as Micio told Demea in the comedy,

> Haec si neque ego neque tu fecimus,
> Non sivit egestas facere nos :

if we be honest, 'twas poverty made us so : if we melancholy men be not as bad as he that is worst, 'tis our dame Melancholy kept us so :

> Non deerat voluntas sed facultas.

Besides they are freed in this from many other infirmities ; solitariness makes them more apt to contemplate, suspition wary, which is a necessary humour in these times ; *nam, pol, qui maxime cavet, sæpe is cautor captus est :* he that takes most heed, is often circumvented and overtaken. Fear and sorrow keep them temperate and sober, and free them from many disolute acts, which jollity and boldness thrust men upon ; they are therefore no *sicarii*, roaring boyes, theeves, or assassinates. As they are soon dejected, so they are as soon, by soft words and good perswasions, reared. Wearisomeness of life makes them they are not so besotted on the transitory vain pleasures of the world. If they dote in one thing, they are wise and well understanding in most other. If it be inveterate, they are *insensati*, most part doting, or quite mad, insensible of any wrongs, ridiculous to others, but most happy and secure to themselves. Dotage is a state which many much magnifie and commend : so is simplicity, and folly, as he said,

> Hic furor, O Superi, sit mihi pepetuus.

Some think fools and disards live the merriest lives, as Ajax in Sophocles ; *nihil scire vita jucundissima ;* 'tis the pleasantest life to know nothing ; *iners malorum remedium ignorantia ;* ignorance is a down-right remedy of evils. These curious arts and laborius sciences, Galens, Tullies, Aristotles, Justinians, do but trouble the world, some think ; we might live better with that illiterate Virginian simplicity, and gross ignorance ; entire ideots do best ; they are not macerated with cares, tormented with fears and anxiety, as other wise men are : for, as he said, if folly were a pain, you should hear them houl, roar, and cry out in every house, as you go by in the street ; but they are most free, jocund, and merry, and, in come countries, as amongst the Turks, honoured for saints, and abundantly maintained out of the common stock. They are no dissemblers, lyers, hypocrites ; for fools and mad men tell commonly truth. In a word, as they are distressed, so are they pittied ; which some hold better then to be envied, better to be said then merry, better to be foolish and quiet, *quam sapere et ringi*, to be wise and still vexed ; better to be miserable then happy : of two extremes it is the best.

EXERCISE RECTIFIED OF BODY AND MINDE.

To that great inconvenience, which comes on the one side by immoderate and unseasonable exercise, too much solitariness and idleness on the other, must be opposed, as an antidote, a moderate and seasonable use of it, and that both of body and minde, as a most materiall circumstance, much conducing to this cure, and to the generall preservation of our health. The heavens themselves run continually round ; the sun riseth and sets ; the moon increaseth and decreaseth ; stars and planets keep their constant motions ; the aire is still tossed by the winds ; the waters eb and flow, to their conservation no doubt, to teach us that we should ever be in action. For which cause Hierom prescribes Rusticus the monk, that he be alwayes occupied about some business or other, *that the devill do not finde him idle.* Seneca would have a man do something, though it be to no purpose. Xenophon wisheth one rather to play at tables, dice, or make a jester of himself (though he might be far better imployed) than do nothing. The Ægyptians of old, and many flourishing commonwealths since, have enjoyned labour and exercise to all sorts of men, to be of some vocation and calling, and to give an account of their time, to prevent those greivous mischiefs that come by idleness ; *for, as fodder, whip, and burthen, belong to the asse, so meat, correction, and worke, unto the servant,* Ecclus. 33. 23. The Turks injoyn all men whatsoever, of what degree, to be of some trade or other : the grand Signior himself is not excused. *In our memory* (saith Sabellicus) *Mahomet the Turke, he that conquered Greece, at that very time when he heard ambassadours of other princes, did either carve or cut wooden spoones, or frame something upon a table.* This present sultan makes notches for bows. The Jews are most severe in this examination of time. All wel-governed places, towns, families, and every discreet person will be a law unto himself. But, amongst us, the badge of gentry is idleness : to be of no calling, not to labour (for that's derogatory to their birth), to be a meer spectator, a drone, *fruges consumere natus,* to have no necessary employment to busie himself about in church and commonwealth (some few governers exempted), *but to rise to eat, &c.* to spend his dayes in hawking, hunting, &c. and such like disports and recreations (which our casuists tax), are the sole exercise almost and ordinary actions of our nobility, and in which they are too immoderate. And thence it comes to pass, that in city and country so many grievances of body and mind, and this ferall disease of melancholy so frequently rageth, and now domineers almost all over Europe amongst our great ones. They know not how to spend their times (disports excepted, which are all their business), what to do, or otherwise how to bestow themselves ; like our modern Frenchmen, that had rather lose a pound of blood in a single combate, than a drop of sweat in any honest labour. Every man almost hath something or other to employ himself about, some vocation, some trade : but they do all by ministers and servants ; *ad otia duntaxat se natos existimant, imo ad sui ipsius plerum et que aliorum perniciem,* as one freely taxeth such kinde of men : they are all for pastimes ; 'tis all their study ; all their invention tends to this alone, to drive away time, as if they were born, some of them, to no other ends. Therefore to correct and avoid these errors and inconveniences, our divines, physicians, and politicians, so much labour, and so seriously exhort : and for this disease in particular, *there can be no better cure than continuall business,* as Rhasis holds, *to have some employment or other, which may set their minde aworke, and distract their cogitations.* Riches may not easily be had without labour and industry, nor learning without study ; neither can our health be preserved without bodily exercise. If it be of the body, Guianerius allowes that exercise which is gentle, *and still after those ordinary frications,* which must be used every morning. Montaltus (*cap.* 26) and Jason Pratensis use almost the same words, highly commending exercise, if it be moderate : *a wonderful help, so used,* Crato calls it, *and a great means to preserve our health, as adding strength to the whole body, increasing naturall heat, by means of which, the nutriment is well concocted in the stomacke, liver, and veines, few or no crudities left, is happily distributed over all the body.* Besides, it expells excrements by sweat, and other insensible vapours ; in so much that Galen prefers exercise before all physick, rectification of diet, or any regimen in what kinde soever ; 'tis Natures physician. Fulgentius (out of Gordonius, *de conserv. vit. hom. lib.* 1 *cap.* 7) tearms exercise *a spur of a dull sleepy nature, the comforter of the members, cure of infirmity, death of diseases, destruction of all mischiefes and vices.* The fittest time for exercise is a little before dinner, a little before supper, or at any time when the body is empty. Montanus (*consil.* 31) prescribes it every morning to his patient, and that, as Calenus addes, *after he hath done his ordinary needs, rubbed his body, washed his hands and face, combed his head, and gargarized.* What kinde of exercise he should use, Galen tells us, *lib.* 2 *et* 3. *de sanit. tuend.* and in what measure, *till the body be ready to sweat,* and roused up, *ad ruborem,* some say, *non ad sudorem,* lest it should dry the body too much ; others injoyn those wholesome businesses, as to dig so long in his garden, to hold the plough, and the like. Some prescribe frequent and violent labour and exercises, as sawing every day, so long together, (*epid.* 6. Hippocrates confounds them) but that is in some cases, to some peculiar men ; the most forbid, and will by no means have it go farther than a beginning sweat, as being perilous if it exceed.

Of these labours, exercises, and recreations, which are likewise included, some properly belong to the body, some to the mind, some more easie, some hard, some with delight, some without, some within doors, some naturall, some are artificiall. Amongst bodily exercises, Galen commends *ludum parvæ pilæ*, to play at ball : be it with the hand or racket, in tenniscourts, or otherwise, it exerciseth each part of the body, and doth much good, so that they sweat not too much. It was in great request of old amongst the Greeks, Romanes, Barbarians, mentioned by Homer, Herodotus, and Plinius. Some write, that Aganella, a fair maide of Corcyra, was the inventer of it ; for she presented the first ball that ever was made, to Nausica, the daughter of king Alcinoüs, and taught her how to use it.

The ordinary sports which are used abroad, are hawking, hunting : *hilares venandi labores,* one calls them, because they recreate body and minde ; another, *the best exercise that is, by which alone many have been freed from all ferall diseases.* Hegesippus (*lib.* 1. *cap.* 37) relates of Herod, that he was eased of a greivous melancholy by that means. Plato (7 *de leg.*) highly magnifies it, dividing it into three parts, by land, water, ayre. Xenophon (in *Cyropæd.*) graces it with a great name, *Deorum munus,* the gift of the Gods, a princely sport, which they have ever used, saith Langius, (*epist.* 59. *lib.* 2) as well for health as pleasure, and do at this day, it being the sole almost and ordinary sport of our noblemen in Europe, and elsewhere all over the world. Bohemus (*de mor. gent. lib.* 3. *cap.* 12) stiles it therefore *studium nobilium ; communiter venantur, quod sibi solis licere contendunt ;* 'tis all their study, their exercise, ordinary business, all their talk : and indeed some dote too much after it ; they can do nothing else, discourse of naught else. Paulus Jovius (*descr. Brit.*) doth in some sort tax our *English nobility for it, for living in the country so much, and too frequent use of it, as if they had no other means but hawking and hunting to approve themselves gentlemen with.*

Hawking comes neer to hunting, the one in the aire, as the other on the earth, a sport as much affected as the other, by some preferred. It was never heard of amongst the Romans, invented some 1200 years since, and first mentioned by Firmicus *lib* 5, *cap.* 8. The Greek emperours began it, and now nothing so frequent : he is nobody, that in the season hath not a hawke on his fist : a great art, and many books written of it. It is a wonder to hear what is related of the Turkes officers in this behalf, how many thousand men are employed about it, how many hawks of all sorts, how much revenewes consumed on that only disport, how much time is spent at Adrianople alone every year to that purpose. The Persian kings hawk after butterflies with sparrows, made to that use, and stares ; lesser hawks for lesser games they have, and bigger for the rest, that they may produce their sport to all seasons. The Muscovian emperours reclaime eagles to fly at hindes, foxes, &c. and such a one was sent for a present to Queen Elizabeth : some reclaime ravens, castrils, pies, &c. and man them for their pleasures.

Fowling is more troublesome, but all out as delightsome to some sorts of men, be it with guns, lime, nets, glades, ginnes, strings, baits, pitfalls, pipes, calls, stawking-horses, setting-dogs, coy-ducks, &c. or otherwise. Some much delight to take larks with day-nets, small birds with chaffe-nets, plovers, partridge, herons, snite, &c. Henry the third, king of Castile, (as Mariana the Jesuite reports of him, *lib.* 3. *cap.* 7.) was much affected *with catching of quailes:* and many gentlemen take a singular pleasure at morning and evening to go abroad with their quaile-pipes, and will take any paines to satisfie their delight in that kinde. The Italians have gardens fitted to such use, with nets, bushes, glades, sparing no cost or industry, and are very much affected with the sport. Tycho Brahe, that great astronomer, in the Chorography of his Isle of Huena, and castle of Uraniburge, puts down his nets, and manner of catching small birds as an ornament, and a recreation, wherein he himself was sometimes employed.

Fishing is a kinde of hunting by water, be it with nets, weeles, baits, angling or otherwise, and yeelds all out as much pleasure to some men, as dogs, or hawk, *when they draw their fish upon the bank*, saith Nic. Henselius, *Silesiographiæ cap.* 3, speaking of that extraordinary delight his countrymen took in fishing, and in making of pooles. James Dubravius, that Moravian, in his book *de pisc* telleth, how travelling by the highway side in Silesia, he found a nobleman *booted up to the groines*, wading himself, pulling the nets, and labouring as much as any fisherman of them all : and when some belike objected to him the baseness of his office, he excused himself, *that if other men might hunt hares, why should not he hunt carpes?* Many gentlemen in like sort, with us, will wade up to the arm-holes, upon such occasions, and voluntarily undertake that to satisfie their pleasure, which a poor man for a good stipend would scarce be hired to undergo. Plutarch, in his book *de soler. animal.* speaks against all fishing, *as a filthy, base, illiberall imployment, having neither wit nor perspicacity in it, nor worth the labour.* But he that shall consider the variety of baits, for all seasons, and pretty devices which our anglers have invented, peculiar lines, false flies, severall sleights, &c. will say, that it deserves like commendation, requires as much study and perspicacity as the rest, and is to be preferred before many of them ; because hawking and hunting are very laborious, much riding, and many dangers accompany them ; but this is still and quiet : and if so be the angler catch no fish, yet he hath a wholesome walk to the brook side, pleasant shade, by the sweet silver streams ; he hath good aire, and sweet smels of fine fresh meadow flowers ; he hears the melodious harmony of birds ; he sees the swans, herons, ducks, water-hens, cootes, &c. and many other fowle, with their brood, which he thinketh better than the noise of hounds, or blast of hornes, and all the sport that they can make.

Many other sports and recreations there be, much in use, as ringing, bowling, shooting, which Askam commends in a just volume, and hath in former times been injoyned by statute, as a defensive exercise, and an honour to our land, as well may witness our victories in France ; keelpins, tronks, coits, pitching bars, hurling, wrestling, leaping, running, fencing, mustring, swimming, wasters, foiles, foot-ball, balown, quintans, &c. and many such, which are the common recreations of the country folks ; riding of great horses, running at rings, tilts and turnaments, horse-races, wilde-goose chases, which are the disports of greater men, and good in themselves, though many gentlemen by that means, gallop quite out of their fortunes.

But the most pleasant of all outward pastimes is that of Aretæus, *deambulatio per amœna loca,* to make a petty progress, a merry journey now and then with some good companions, to visit friend, see cities, castles, towns,

> Visere sæpe amnes nitidos, peramœnaque Tempe,
> Et placidas summis sectari in montibus auras :

> To see the pleasant fields, the crystall fountains,
> And take the gentle aire amongst the mountains :

to walk amongst orchards, gardens, bowers, mounts, and arbours, artificiall wildernesses, green thickets, arches, groves, lawns, rivulets, fountains and such like pleasant places, like that Antiochian Daphne, brooks, pooles, fishponds, betwixt wood and water, in a fair meadow, by a river side, *ubi variæ avium cantationes, florum colores, pratorum frutices, &c.* to disport in some pleasant plain, park, run up a steep hill sometimes, or sit in a shady seat, must needs be a delectable recreation. *Hortus principis et domus ad delectationem facta, cum sylvâ, monte, et piscinâ, vulgo La Montagna :* the princes garden at Ferrara, Schottus highly magnifies, with the groves, mountaines, ponds, for a delectable prospect : he was much affected with it : a Persian paradise, or pleasant parke, could not be more delectable in his sight. S. Bernard, in the description of his monastery, is almost ravished with the pleasures of it. *A sick man* (saith he) *sits upon a green bank ; and, when the dog-star parcheth the plaines, and dries up rivers, he lies in a shadie bowre,*

Fronde sub arboreâ ferventia temperat astra,

and feeds his eyes with variety of objects, hearbs, trees : and to comfort his misery, he receives many delightsome smels, and fils his ears with that sweet and various harmony of birdes. Good God! (saith he) *what a company of pleasures hast thou made for man!* He that should be admitted on a sudden to the sight of such a palace as that of Escuriall in Spain, or to that which the Moores built at Granado, Fountenblewe in France, the Turkes gardens in his seraglio, wherein all manner of birds and beasts are kept for pleasure, wolves, bears, lynces, tygers, lyons, elephants, &c. or upon the banks of that Thracian Bosphorus : the popes Belvedere in Rome as pleasing as those *horti pensiles* in Babylon, or that Indian kings delightsome garden in Ælian ; or those famous gardens of the Lord Cantelow in France, could not choose, though he were never so ill apaid, but be much recreated for the time ; or many of our noblemens gardens at home. To take a boat in a pleasant evening, and with musick to row upon the waters, which Plutarch so much applaudes, Ælian admires, upon the river Peneus, in those Thessalian fields beset with green bayes, where birds so sweetly sing, that passengers, enchanted as it were with their heavenly musick, *omnium laborum et curarum obliviscantur,* forget forthwith all labours, care and grief ; or in a gundilo through the grand canale in Venice, to see those goodly palaces, must needs refresh and give content to a melancholy dull spirit. Or to see the inner roomes of a fairbuilt and sumptuous ædifice, as that of the Persian kings so much renowned by Diodorus and Curtius, in which all was almost beaten gold, chaires, stooles, thrones, tabernacles, and pillars of gold, plane trees, and vines of gold, grapes of precious stones, all the other ornaments of pure gold,

> (Fulget gemma toris, et iaspide fulva supellex ;
> Strata micant Tyrio——)

with sweet odours and perfumes, generous wines, opiparous fare, &c. besides the gallantest young men, the fairest virgins, *puellæ scitulæ ministrantes*, the rarest beauties the world could afford, and those set out with costly and curious attires, *ad stuporem usque spectantium*, with exquisite musick, as in Trimalchions house, in every chamber, sweet voices ever sounding day and night, *incomparabilis luxus*, all delights and pleasures in each kinde which to please the senses could possibly be devised or had, *convivæ coronati, deliciis ebrii, &c.* Telemachus in Homer is brought in as one ravished almost, at the sight of that magnificent palace, and rich furniture of Menelaus, when he beheld

> Æris fulgorem, et resonantia tecta corusco
> Auro, atque electro nitido, sectoque elephanto,
> Argentoque simul.   Talis Jovis ardua sedes,
> Aulaque Cœlicolûm stellans splendescit Olympo.
>
> Such glittering of gold and brightest brass to shine,
> Cleer amber, silver pure, and ivory so fine :
> Jupiters lofty palace, where the gods do dwell,
> Was even such a one, and did it not excell.

It will *laxare animos*, refresh the soule of man, to see fair-built cities, streets, theaters, temples, obelisks, &c. The temple of Jerusalem was so fairly built of white marble, with so many pyramids covered with gold ; *tectumque templi, fulvo coruscans auro, nimio suo fulgore obcæcabat oculos itinerantium*, was so glorious and so glistered afar off, that the spectators might not well abide the sight of it. But the inner parts were all so curiously set out with cedar, gold, jewels, &c. (as he said of Cleopatras palace in Egypt,

> ——————Crassumque trabes absconderat aurum)

that the beholders were amazed. What so pleasant as to see some pageant or sight go by, as at coronations, weddings, and such like solemnities ;—to see an embassadour or a prince met, received, entertained with masks, shewes, fireworks, &c.—to see two kings fight in single combat, as Porus and Alexander, Canutus and Edmond Ironside, Scanderbeg and Ferat Bassa the Turke, when not honour alone but life it self is at stake, (as the poet of Hector,

> ———————— nec enim pro tergore tauri,
> Pro bove nec certamen erat, quæ præmia cursûs
> Esse solent, sed pro magni vitâque animâque
> Hectoris);——

to behold a battle fought, like that of Crescy, or Agencourt, or Poictiers, *quâ nescio* (saith Froissard) *an vetustas ullam pro-ferre possit clariorem;*—to see one of Cæsars triumphs in old Rome revived, or the like ;—to bee present at an interview, as that famous of Henry the 8th, and Francis the first, so much renowned all over Europe ; *ubi tanto apparatu* (saith Hubertus Vellius) *tamque triumphali pompâ ambo reges cum eorum conjugibus coiêre, ut nulla unquam ætas tam celebria festa viderit aut audierit,* no age ever saw the like. So infinitely pleasant are such shews, to the sight of which often times they will come hundreths of miles, give any mony for a place, and remember many years after with singular delight. Bodine, when he was embassador in England, said he saw the noblemen go in their robes to the parliament house, *summâ cum jucunditate vidimus;* he was much affected with the sight of it. Pomponius Columna, saith Jovius in his life, saw 13 Frenchmen, and so many Italians, once fight for a whole army : *quod jucundissimum spectaculum in vitâ dicit suâ,* the pleasantest sight that ever he saw in his life. Who would not have been affected with such a spectacle ? Or that single combat of Breaute the Frenchman, and Anthony Schets a Dutchman, before the walls of Sylvaducis in Brabant, anno 1600. They were 22 horse on the one side, as many on the other, which, like Livies Horatii, Torquati, and Corvini, fought for their own glory and countries honour, in the sight and view of their whole city and army. When Julius Cæsar warred about the bankes of Rhene, there came a barbarian prince to see him and the Roman army ; and when he had beheld Cæsar a good while, *I see the gods now,* (saith he) *which before I heard of, nec feliciorem ullam vitæ meæ aut optavi aut sensi diem :* it was the happiest day that ever he had in his life. Such a sight alone were able of it self to drive away melancholy ; if not for ever, yet it must needs expell it for a time. Radzivilius was much taken with the bassas palace in Cairo ; and, amongst many other objects which that place afforded, with that solemnity of cutting the bankes of Nilus, by Imbram Bassa, when it overflowed, besides two or three hundred guilded gallies on the water, he saw two millions of men gathered together on the land, with turbants as white as snow; and twas a goodly sight. The very reading of feasts, triumphs, interviews, nuptials, tilts, turnaments, combats, and monomachies, is most acceptable and pleasant. Franciscus Modius hath made a large collection of such solemnities in two great tomes, which who so will may peruse. The inspection alone of those curious iconographies of temples and palaces, as that of the Lateran church in Albertus Durer, that of the temple of Jerusalem in Josephus, Adricomius, and Villalpandus: that of the Escuriall in Guadas, of Diana at Ephesus in Pliny, Neros goldon palace in Rome, Justinians in Constantinople, that Peruvian Ingos in Cusco, *ut non ab hominibus, sed a dæmoniis, constructum videatur;* S. Marks in Venice by Ignatius, with many such: *priscorum artificum opera* (saith that interpreter of Pausanias) the rare workmanship of those ancient Greeks, in theaters, obelisks, temples, statues, gold, silver, ivory, marble images, *non minore ferme, quum leguntur, quam quum cernuntur, animum delectatione complent,* affect one as much by reading almost, as by sight.

The country hath his recreations, the city his severall gymnicks and exercises, may-games, feasts, wakes, and merry meetings, to solace themselves. The very being in the country, that life it self, is a sufficient recreation to some men, to enjoy such pleasures, as those old patriarks did. Dioclesian the emperour was so much affected with it, that he gave over his scepter, and turned gardiner. Constantine wrote 20 books of husbandry. Lysander, when embassadours came to see him, bragged of nothing more, than of his orchard: *hi sunt ordines mei.* What shall I say of Cincinnatus, Cato, Tully, and many such? how have they been pleased with it, to prune, plant, inoculate, and graft, to shew so many severall kindes of pears, apples, plums, peaches, &c.

> Nunc captare feras laqueo, nunc fallere visco,
> Atque etiam magnos canibus circumdare saltus,
> Insidias avibus moliri, incendere vepres.

> Sometimes with traps deceive, with line and string
> To catch wild birds and beasts, encompassing
> The grove with dogs, and out of bushes firing.

> ——————— et nidos avium scrutari, &c.

Jucundus, in his preface to Cato, Varro, Columella, &c. put out by him, confesseth of himself, that he was mightily delighted with these husbandry studies, and took extraordinary pleasure in them. If the theorick or speculation can so much affect, what shall the place and exercise it self, the practick part, do? The same confession I find in Herbastein, Porta, Camerarius, and many others, which have written of that subject. If my testimony were ought worth, I could say as much of myself; I am *vere Saturninus;* no man ever took more delight in springs, woods, groves, gardens, walks, fishponds, rivers, &c. But

> Tantalus a labris sitiens fugientia captat
> Flumina ;

and so do I : *velle licet; potiri non licet.*

Anatomy of Melancholy.

EDWARD HERBERT,

LORD HERBERT OF CHERBURY.

1581–1648.

CHARACTER OF HENRY VIII.

OUR King having long laboured under the burden of an extreme fat and unwieldly body, and together being afflicted with a sore leg, took (at the Palace of *Westminster*, in *January*, this yeer) his deathbed ; being for the rest not without sense of his present condition. For he both caused a Church of the Franciscans in *London* (lately supprest) to be opened again, and made a Parish Church, endowing it with 500 Marks *per annum;* and (March, 1546.) bestowed both the ground and buildings of the said *Covent*, as also the adjoyning hospital of *St. Bartholomew*, on the City, for the relief of the poor : where now is the fair Hospital called Christ-Church : suppress'd the Stews on the Bank-side, and made his last Will and Testament, the Originall whereof yet having not seen, I shall mention no otherwise.

As for *Sanders* affirmation, that he was not desirous to be reconciled to the Roman Church ; and that his Courtiers (especially those who had profited themselves of Abbeys) did divert him ; and that the Bishops rested doubtfull what to answer, lest they should be entrapped ; and how *Winchester* did cunningly evade the danger, I leave to his credit. Others affirming, that he desired to speak with *Cranmer*, who yet not coming sooner then that the King was speechlesse (though in good memory) the King extended his hand to him ; and that thereupon *Cranmer* besought him to give some signe of his trust in God by Christ, and that the King should strain his hand. Howsoever, it may be collected, that he died (January 28. 1547.) religiously and penitently, when he had reigned seven and thirty yeers, nine months, and six days ; and after he had lived five and fifty years and seven months ; and was carryed to *Windsor*, where he had begun a fair Monument, and founded a Colledge for thirteen poor Knights, and two Priests to pray for his soul.

And now if the Reader (according to my manner in other great Personages) do expect some Character of this Prince, I must affirm, (as in the beginning) that the course of his life being commonly held various and diverse from it self, he will hardly suffer any, and that his History will be his best Character and description. Howbeit, since others have so much defamed him, as will appear by the following Objections, I shall strive to rectifie their understandings who are impartiall lovers of truth ; without either presuming audaciously to condemn a Prince, heretofore Soveraign of our Kingdom, or omitting the just freedom of an Historian.

And because his most bitter censures agree, that he had all manner of perfection either of nature or education ; and that he was (besides) of a most deep judgement in all Affairs to which he applyed himself ; a Prince not onely liberall and indulgent to his Family, and Court, and even to strangers, whom he willingly saw ; and one that made choice both of able and good men for the Clergy, and of wise and grave Counsellors for his State-Affairs ; and above all, a Prince of a Royall courage : I shall not controvert these points, but come to my particular observations. According to which, I finde him to have been ever most zealous of his Honour and Dignity ; insomuch, that his most questioned passages were countenanced either with home or forraign Authority : so many Universities of *Italy* and *France* maintaining his repudiating of Queen *Katherin* of *Spain;* and his Parliament (for the rest) authorizing the Divorces and decapitations of his following Wives, the dissolutions of the Monasteries, and divers others of his most branded Actions : So that by his Parliaments in publick, and Juries in private Affairs, he at least wanted not colour and pretext to make them specious to the World ; which also he had reason to affect : Outward esteem and reputation being the same to great Persons which the skin is to the fruit, which though it be but a slight and delicate cover, yet without it the fruit will presently discolour and rot.

As for matter of State, I dare say, never Prince went upon a truer Maxime for this Kingdom ; which was, to make himself Arbiter of Christendom : and had it not cost him so much, none had ever proceeded more wisely. But as he would be an Actor (for the most part) where he needed onely be a Spectator, he both engaged himself beyond what was requisite, and by calling in the money he lent his Confederates and Allyes, did often disoblige them when he had most need of their friendship. Yet thus he was the most active Prince of his time. The examples whereof are so frequent in his History, that there was no Treaty, or almost Conventicle in Christendom, wherein he had not his particular Agent and interest ; which, together with his intelligence in all Countries, and concerning all affairs, and the pensions given for that purpose, was one of his vast ways for spending of money.

Again, I observe, that there never was Prince more delighted in Interviews, or (generally) came off better from them. To which also, as his goodly personage and excellent qualities did much dispose him, so they gave him a particular advantage and lustre. Howbeit, as these Voyages were extreme costly, so when he made use thereof to conclude a Treaty, it did not alwayes succeed ; especially where credit was yeelded to any single and private word. Insomuch, that at his last being with *Francis* (where he intended, upon his bare promise, *lier la partie* for the most important Affairs of Christendom) he found himself so much frustrated and deceived.

At home it was his manner to treat much with his Parliaments ; where, if gentle means served not, he came to some degrees of the rough : though more sparingly, that he knew his people did but too much fear him. Besides, he understood well, that fowl wayes are not always passable, nor to be used (especially in suspected and dangerous times) but where others fail. However, it may be noted, That none of his Predecessours understood the temper of Parliaments better then himself, or that prevailed himself more dexteriously of them. Therefore, without being much troubled at the tumultuous beginnings of the rasher sort, he would give them that leave, which all new things must have, to settle. Which being done, his next care was to discover and prevent those privie combinations that were not for his service. After which, coming to the point of Contribution, he generally took strict order, (by his Commissioners) that Gentlemen in the Country should not spare each other ; but that the true or (at least) neer approaching value of every mans Goods and Lands should be certified. And this hee did the rather, because hee knew the custome of his people was to reckon with him about their Subsidies, and indeed, rather to number, then to weigh their Gifts.

As for his faults, I finde that of opiniate and wilfull much objected : Insomuch, that the impressions privately given him

by any Court-whisperer, were hardly or never to be effaced.
And herein the persons neer him had a singular ability ; while
beginning with the· commendations of those they would
disgrace, their manner was to insinuate such exceptions, as
they would discommend a man more in few words, then
commend him in many : Doing therein like cunning wrestlers,
who to throw one down, first take him up. Besides, this wilful-
nesse had a most dangerous quality annexed to it (especially
towards his later end) being an intense jealousie almost of all
persons and affairs, which disposed him easily to think the
worst. Whereas it is a greater part of wisdom to prevent,
then to suspect. These conditions again being armed with
power, produced such terrible effects, as stiled him both at
home and abroad by the name of *Cruell;* which also hardly
can be avoyded ; especially, if that Attribute be due, not onely
to those Princes who inflict capitall punishments frequently,
and for small crimes, but to those who pardon not all that are
capable of mercy. And for testimonies in this kinde, some
urge two Queens, one Cardinal (*in procinctu,* at least) or two,
(for *Poole* was condemned, though absent) ; Dukes, Marquesses,
Earls, and Earls Sons, twelve ; Barons and Knights, eighteen ;
Abbots, Priors, Monks and Priests, seventy seven ; of the more
common sort, between one Religion and another, huge multitudes. Hee gave some proofs yet that he could forgive ;
though, as they were few and late, they served not to recover
him the name of a Clement Prince. As for Covetousnesse, or
Rapine, another main fault observed by *Sanders,* as extending
not onely to a promiscuous overthrow of Religious Houses, but
a notable derogation of Title of Supreme Head of the Church
in his Dominions : (and the rather, that he still retained the
substance of the Roman Catholick Religion) nothing, that I
know, can on those terms palliate it, unlesse it might be
collected, that the Religious Orders in his Kingdom would have
assisted those who threatened Invasion from abroad, and that
hee had no other extraordinary means than their Revenues
then left to defend himself. For certainly, the publick pretext,
taken from their excessive numbers in proportion to a well-
composed State, or the inordinate and vitious life of the
general sort, cannot sufficiently excuse him ; since, together
with the supernumerary and debauched Abbeys, Priories and
Nunneries, he subverted and extinguished the good and
opportune ; without leaving any Receptacle for such as through
age or infirmity being unapt for secular businesse, would end
their dayes in a devout and a retired life. Nevertheless, as he

erected divers new Bishopricks, increased the number of Colledges, and the stipend of Readers in the Universities, and did many other pious works, it is probable he intended some reparation. Though (as the Roman Catholick party conceives it) they were neither satisfactory for, nor equivalent to the desolations and ruines hee procured, when yet he should pretend that the Revenues and number of the Gentry and Soldatesque of the Kingdome were augmented thereby. Howbeit, as in this act of overthrowing Monasteries, his parliaments were deeply engaged, it will be dangerous to question the authority thereof, since things done by publick Vote, where they finde not reason, make it; neither have many Laws other ground then the constitution of the times; which yet afterwards changing, leave their interpretation doubtfull: Insomuch, that posterity might justly abrogate them when the causes thereof ceased, had they the power to do it. For which regard also I shall not interpose my opinion otherwise, then that this King had met with no occasion to do that which hath caused so much scandal to him and his Parliaments.

But whereas *Sanders* hath remarked Covetousnesse as a great vice in this King, I could wish it had been with more limitation, and so as he noted the other extreme (being Prodigality) for the greater fault: The examples of both being so pregnant in the King's Father and himself. The first, by an exact inquiry into the corruptions and abuses of his Officers and Subjects, and the prevailing himself thereof to bring all into good order; and the getting of money together, whether by ordinary or extraordinary means (onely when they were not manifestly unjust): and lastly, by frugality, acquiring to himself the name of *prudent* at home, and *puissant* abroad; as being known to have in his coffers always as much as would pay an Army Royall. Whereas this King, so often exhausting his Treasury, that he was constrained at last to have recourse to unusual and grievous ways for relieving his wants, did not onely disaffect his Subjects in great part (as appeared in the Rebellion of the Northern men and others, though to their confusion) but exposed his Kingdom to the Invasion of his Neighbours: who knowing (as all Princes do) to about how much their Revenues amount, and that there remained no longer any ready way to improve them, did collect thence what forces he could furnish; and consequently, would have assayled him at home, but that mutuall divisions did hinder them. Whereby it appears, that what in *Henry* VII is call'd by some Covetousnesse, was a royall Vertue: whereas the excessive and needlesse expences of *Henry* VIII drew after them those miserable consequences which the World hath so much reproached. Howbeit, there may be occasion to doubt, whether the immense Treasure which *Henry* the VII left behinde him, were not (accidentally) the cause of those ils that followed : while the young Prince his Son, finding such a mass of money, did first carelesly spend, and after strive to supply as he could.

As for the third vice, wherewith he was justly charged, being Lust and Wantonness ; there is little to answer, more then that it was rather a personall fault, than damageable to the Publick : Howbeit, they who reprove it, ought not onely to examine circumstances (which much aggravate or extenuate the fact) but even the complexions of men. That concupiscence which in some is a vice, being in others a disease of Repletion, in others a necessity of nature. It doth not yet appear that this fault did hasten the death of his Queens ; he being noted more for practising of private pleasures, then secret mischiefs ; so that if any undue motive did cooperate herein, it may be thought an inordinate desire to have Posterity (especially masculine) which might be the undoubted Heirs of him and the Kingdom, rather than any thing else.

With all his crimes yet, he was one of the most glorious Princes of his time : Insomuch, that not onely the chief Potentates of Christendome did court him, but his Subjects in generall did highly reverence him, as the many tryals he put them to, sufficiently testifie : which yet expired so quickly, that it may be truly said, All his Pomp died with him ; his Memory being now exposed to obloquy, as his Accusers will neither admit Reason of State to cover any where, or Necessity to excuse his Actions. For, as they were either discontented Clergy-men (for his relinquishing the Papall Authority, and overthrowing the Monasteries); or offended Women (for divers severe examples against their sex) that first oppos'd and cry'd him down, the clamour hath been the greater : So that although one *William Thomas* a Clerk to the Councel to *Edward* the Sixth, and living about the latter times of *Henry* the Eighth's Reign, did in great part defend him in an Italian Book, printed *Anno* 1552, it hath not availed.

But what this Prince was, and whether, and how far forth excusable in point of State, Conscience or Honour, a diligent observation of his Actions, together with a conjuncture of the times, will (I conceive) better declare to the judicious Reader, then any factious relation on what side whatsoever. To conclude ; I wish I could leave him in his grave.

The Life and Reign Of King Henry the Eighth.

THOMAS HOBBES.

1588-1679.

Of the Liberty *of Subjects.*

Liberty, or Fredome, signifieth (properly) the absence of Opposition ; (by Opposition, I mean externall Impediments of motion ;) and may be applyed no lesse to Irrationall, and Inanimate creatures, than to Rationall. For whatsoever is so tyed, or environed, as it cannot move, but within a certain space, which space is determined by the opposition of some externall body, we say it hath not Liberty to go further. And so of all living creatures, whilest they are imprisoned, or restrained, with walls, or chayns ; and of the water whilest it is kept in by banks, or vessels, that otherwise should spread it selfe into a larger space, we use to say, they are not at Liberty, to move in such manner, as without those externall impediments they would. But when the impediment of motion, is in the constitution of the thing it selfe, we use not to say, it wants the Liberty ; but the Power to move ; as when a stone lyeth still, or a man is fastned to his bed by sicknesse.

And according to this proper, and generally received meaning of the word, *A* Free-Man, *is he, that in those things, which by his strength and wit is able to do, is not hindred to doe what he has a will to.* But when the words *Free,* and *Liberty,* are applyed to any thing but *Bodies,* they are abused ; for that which is not subject to Motion, is not subject to Impediment : And therefore, when 'tis said (for example) The Way is Free, no Liberty of the way is signified, but those that walk in it without stop. And when we say a Guift is Free, there is not meant any Liberty of the Guift, but of the Giver, that was not bound by any law, or Covenant to give it. So when we *speak Freely,* it is not the Liberty of voice, or pronunciation, but of the man, whom no law hath obliged to speak otherwise then he did. Lastly, from the use of the word *Free-will*, no Liberty can be inferred of the will, desire, or inclination, but the Liberty of the man ; which consisteth in this, that he finds no stop, in doing what he has the will, desire, or inclination to doe.

Feare and Liberty are consistent ; as when a man throweth his goods into the Sea for *feare* the ship should sink, he doth it neverthelesse very willingly, and may refuse to doe it if he will : It is therefore the action, of one that was *free* ; so a man some-times pays his debt, only for *feare* of Imprisonment, which because no body hindred him from detaining, was the action of a man at *liberty*. And generally all actions which men doe in Common-wealths, for *feare* of the law, are actions, which the doers had *liberty* to omit.

Liberty, and *Necessity* are Consistent : As in the water, that hath not only *liberty*, but a *necessity* of descending by the Channel ; so likewise in the Actions which men voluntarily doe : which, because they proceed from their will, proceed from *liberty* ; and yet, because every act of mans will, and every desire, and inclination proceedeth from some cause, and that from another cause, in a continuall chaine, (whose first link is in the hand of God the first of all causes,) proceed from *necessity*. So that to him that could see the connexion of those causes, the *necessity* of all mens voluntary actions, would appeare manifest. And therefore God, that seeth and disposeth all things, seeth also that the *liberty* of man in doing what he will, is accompanied with the *necessity* of doing that which God will, & no more, nor lesse. For though men may do many things, which God does not command, nor is therefore Author of them ; yet they can have no passion, nor appetite to any thing, of which appetite Gods will is not the cause. And did not his will assure the *necessity* of mans will, and consequently of all that on mans will dependeth, the *liberty* of men would be a contradiction, and impediment to the omnipotence and *liberty* of God. And this shall suffice, (as to the matter in hand) of that naturall *liberty*, which only is properly called *liberty*.

But as men, for the atteyning of peace, and conservation of themselves thereby, have made an Artificiall Man, which we call a Common-wealth ; so also have they made Artificiall Chains, called *Civill Lawes*, which they themselves, by mutuall covenants, have fastned at one end to the lips of that Man, or Assembly, to whom they have given the Soveraigne Power ; and at the other end to their own Ears. These Bonds in their own nature but weak, may neverthelesse be made to hold, by the danger, though not by the difficulty of breaking them.

In relation to these Bonds only it is, that I am to speak now, of the *Liberty* of *Subjects*. For seeing there is no Common-wealth in the world, wherein there be Rules enough set down, for the regulating of all the actions, and words of men, (as being a thing impossible :) it followeth necessarily, that in all kinds of actions, by the laws prætermitted, men have the Liberty, of doing what their own reasons shall suggest, for the most profit-able to themselves. For if wee take Liberty in the proper sense, for corporall Liberty; that is to say, freedome from chains, and prison, it were very absurd for men to clamor as they doe, for the Liberty they so manifestly enjoy. Againe, if we take Liberty, for an exemption from Lawes, it is no lesse absurd, for men to demand as they doe, that Liberty, by which all other men may be masters of their lives. And yet as absurd as it is, this is it they demand ; not knowing that the Lawes are of no power to protect them, without a Sword in the hands of man, or men, to cause those laws to be put in execution. The Liberty of a Subject, lyeth therefore only in those things, which in regulating their actions, the Soveraign hath prætermitted : such as is the Liberty to buy, and sell, and otherwise contract with one another ; to choose their own aboad, their own diet, their own trade of life, and institute their children as they themselves think fit ; & the like.

Neverthelesse we are not to understand, that by such Liberty, the Soveraign Power of life, and death, is either abolished, or limited. For it has been already shewn, that nothing the Soveraign Representative can doe to a Subject, on what pre-tence soever, can properly be called Injustice, or Injury ; because every Subject is Author of every act the Soveraign doth ; so that he never wanteth Right to anything, otherwise, than as he himself is the Subject of God, and bound thereby to observe the laws of Nature. And therefore it may, and doth often happen in Common-wealths, that a Subject may be put to death, by the command of the Soveraign Power ; and yet neither do the other wrong : As when *Jeptha* caused his daughter to be sacri-ficed ; In which, and the like cases, he that so dieth, had Liberty to doe the action, for which he is neverthelesse, without Injury put to death. And the same holdeth also in a Soveraign Prince, that putteth to death an Innocent Subject. For though the action be against the law of Nature, as being contrary to Equitie, (as was the killing of *Uriah*, by *David ;*) yet it was not an Injury to *Uriah ;* but to *God*. Not to *Uriah*, because the right to doe what he pleased, was given to him by *Uriah* himself : And yet to *God* because *David* was *Gods* Subject ; and prohibited all Iniquitie by the law of Nature. Which distinction, *David* himself, when he repented the fact, evidently confirmed, saying, *To thee only have I sinned.* In the same manner, the people of *Athens*, when they banished the most potent of their Common-wealth for ten years, thought they committed no Injustice ; and yet they never questioned what crime he had done ; but what hurt he would doe : Nay they commanded the banishment of they knew not whom ; and every Citizen bringing his Oystershell into the market place, written with the name of him he desired should be banished, without actuall accusing him, sometimes banished an *Aristides*, for his reputation of Justice ; And sometimes a scurrilous Jester, as *Hyperbolus*, to make a Jest of it. And yet a man cannot say, the Soveraign people of *Athens* wanted right to banish them ; or an *Athenian* the Libertie to Jest, or to be Just.

The Libertie, whereof there is so frequent, and honorable mention, in the Histories, and Philosophy of the Antient Greeks, and Romans, and in the writings, and discourse of those that from them have received all their learning in the Politiques, is not the Libertie of Particular men ; but the Libertie of the Common-wealth : which is the same with that, which every man then should have, if there were no Civil Laws, nor Common-wealth at all. And the effects of it also be the same. For as amongst masterlesse men, there is perpetuall war, of every man against his neighbour ; no inheritance, to transmit to the Son, nor to expect from the Father ; no propriety of goods, or Lands ; no security, but a full and absolute Libertie in every Particular man : So in States, and Common-wealths not dependent on one another, and Common-wealth, (not every man) has an absolute Libertie, to doe what it shall judge (that is to say, what that Man, or Assemblie that representeth it, shall judge) most conducing to their benefit. But withall, they live in the condition of a perpetuall war, and upon the confines of battel, with their frontiers armed, and canons planted against their neighbours round about. The *Athenians*, and *Romanes* were free ; that is, free Common-wealths : not that any particular men had the Libertie to resist their own Representative ; but that their Representative had the Libertie to resist, or invade other people. There is written on the Turrets of the city of *Luca* in great characters at this day, the word *LIBERTAS ;* yet no man can thence inferre, that a particular man has more Libertie, or Immunitie from the service of the Commonwealth there, than in *Constantinople.* Whether a Commonwealth be Monarchicall, or Popular, the Freedome is still the same.

But it is an easy thing, for men to be deceived, by the specious name of Libertie ; and for want of Judgement to distinguish, mistake that for their Private Inheritance, and Birthright, which is the right of the Publique only. And when the same errour is confirmed by the authority of men in reputation for their writings in this subject, it is no wonder if it produce sedition, and change of Government. In these westerne parts of the world, we are made to receive our opinions concerning the Institution, and Rights of Common-weaths, from *Aristotle*, *Cicero*, and other men, Greeks and Romanes, that living under Popular States, derived those Rights, not from the Principles of Nature, but transcribed them into their books, out of the Practise of their own Common-weaths, which were Popular ; as the Grammarians describe the Rules of Language, out of the Practise of the time ; or the Rules of Poetry, out of the Poems of *Homer* and *Virgil*. And because the Athenians were taught, (to keep them from desire of changing their Government,) that they were Free-men, and all that lived under Monarchy were slaves ; therefore *Aristotle* puts it down in his *Politiques* (*lib.* 6. *cap.* 2.) *In democracy*, Liberty *is to be supposed : for 'tis commonly held, that no man is* Free *in any other Government*. And as *Aristotle;* so *Cicero*, and other Writers have grounded their Civill doctrine, on the opinions of the Romans, who were taught to hate Monarchy, at first, by them that having deposed their Soveraign, shared amongst them the Soveraignty of *Rome;* and afterwards by their Successors. And by reading of these Greek, and Latine Authors, men from their childhood had gotten a habit (under a false shew of Liberty,) of favouring tumults, and of licentious controlling the actions of their Soveraigns ; and again of controlling those controllers, with the effusion of so much blood ; as I think I may truly say, there was never any thing so deerly bought, as these Western parts have bought the learning of the Greek and Latine tongues. . . . . .

Of those things that Weaken, or tend to the
DISSOLUTION *of a Common-wealth.*

THOUGH nothing can be immortall, which mortals make ; yet, if men had the use of reason they pretend to, their Common-wealths might be secured, at least, from perishing by internall diseases. For by the nature of their Institution, they are designed to live, as long as Man-kind, or as the Lawes of Nature, or as Justice it selfe, which gives them life. Therefore when they come to be dissolved, not by externall violence, but intestine disorder, the fault is not in men, as they are the *Matter;* but as they are the *Makers,* and orders of them. For men, as they become at last weary of irregular justling, and hewing one another, and desire with all their hearts, to conforme themselves into one firme and lasting edifice; so for want, both of the art of making fit Lawes, to square their actions by, and also of humility, and patience, to suffer the rude and combersome points of their present greatnesse to be taken off, they cannot without the help of a very able Architect, be compiled, into any other than a crasie building, such as hardly lasting out their own time, must assuredly fall upon the heads of their posterity.

Amongst the *Infirmities* therefore of a Common-wealth, I will reckon in the first place, those that arise from an Imperfect Institution, and resemble the diseases of a naturall body, which procced from a Defectuous Procreation.

Of which, this is one, *That a man to obtain a Kingdome, is sometimes content with lesse Power, than to the Peace, and defence of the Common-wealth is necessarily required.* From whence it commeth to passe, that when the exercise of the Power layd by, is for the publique safety to be resumed, it hath the resemblance of an unjust act; which disposeth great numbers of men (when occasion is presented) to rebel; In the same manner as the bodies of children, gotten by diseased parents, are subject either to untimely death, or to purge the ill quality, derived from their vicious conception, by breaking out into biles and scabbs. And when Kings deny themselves some such necessary Power, it is not alwayes (though sometimes) out of ignorance of what is necessary to the office they undertake; but many times out of a hope to recover the same again at their pleasure: Wherein they reason not well; because such as will hold them to their promises, shall be maintained against them by forraign Common-wealths; who in order to the good of their own Subjects let slip few occasions to *weaken* the estate of their Neighbours. So was *Thomas Becket* Archbishop of *Canterbury,* supported against *Henry* the Second, by the Pope; the subjection of Ecclesiastiques to the Common-wealth, having been dispensed with by *William the Conquerour* at his reception, when he took an Oath, not to infringe the liberty of the Church.

And so were the *Barons,* whose power was by *William Rufus* (to have their help in transferring the Succession from his Elder brother, to himselfe,) encreased to a degree, inconsistent with the Soveraign Power, maintained in their Rebellion against King *John* by the French.

Nor does this happen in Monarchy onely. For whereas the stile of the antient Roman Common-wealth, was, *The Senate, and People of Rome ;* neither Senate, nor People pretended to the whole Power ; which first caused the seditions of *Tiberius Gracchus, Caius Gracchus, Lucius Saturninus,* and others ; and afterwards the warres between the Senate and the People, under *Marius* and *Sylla ;* and again under *Pompey* and *Cæsar,* to the extinction of their Democraty, and the setting up of Monarchy.

The people of *Athens* bound themselves but from one onely Action ; which was, that no man on pain of death should propound the renewing of the warre for the Island of *Salamis ;* And yet thereby, if *Solon* had not caused to be given out he was mad, and afterwards in gesture and habit of a mad-man, and in verse, propounded it to the People that flocked about him, they had had an enemy perpetually in readinesse, even at the gates of their Citie ; such dammage, or shifts, are all Common-wealths forced to, that have their Power never so little limited.

In the second place, I observe the *Diseases* of a Common-wealth, that proceed from the poyson of seditious doctrines ; whereof one is, *That every private man is Judge of Good and Evill actions.* This is true in the condition of meer Nature, where there are no Civill Lawes ; and also under Civill Government, in such cases as are not determined by the Law. But otherwise, it is manifest, that the measure of Good and Evill actions, is the Civill Law ; and the Judge the Legislator, who is alwayes representative of the Common-wealth. From this false doctrine, men are disposed to debate with themselves, and dispute the commands of the Common-wealth ; and afterwards to obey, or disobey them, as in their private judgements they shall think fit. Whereby the Common-wealth is distracted and *Weakened.*

Another doctrine repugnant to Civill Society, is, that *whatsoever a man does against his Conscience, is Sinne ;* and it dependeth on the presumption of making himself judge of Good and Evill. For a mans Conscience, and his Judgement is the same thing ; and as the Judgement, so also the Conscience may be erroneous. Therefore, though he that is subject to no Civill Law, sinneth in all he does against his Conscience, because he has no other rule to follow but his own reason ; yet it is not so with him that lives in a Common-wealth ; because the Law is the publique Conscience, by which he hath already undertaken to be guided. Otherwise in such diversity, as there is of private consciences, which are but private opinions, the Common-wealth must needs be distracted, and no man dare to obey the Soveraign Power, further than it shall seem good in his own eyes.

It hath been also commonly taught, *That Faith and Sanctity, are not to be attained by Study and Reason, but by supernaturall Inspiration, or Infusion.* Which granted, I see not why any man should render a reason of his Faith ; or why every Christian should not be also a Prophet ; or why any man should take the Law of his Country, rather than his own Inspiration, for the rule of his action. And thus wee fall again into the fault of taking upon us to Judge of Good and Evill ; or to make Judges of it, such private men as pretend to be supernaturally Inspired, to the Dissolution of all Civill Government. Faith comes by hearing, and hearing by those accidents, which guide us into the presence of them that speak to us ; which accidents are all contrived by God Almighty ; and yet are not supernaturall, but onely, for the great number of them that concurre to every effect, unobservable. Faith, and Sanctity, are indeed not very frequent ; but yet they are not Miracles, but brought to pass by education, discipline, correction, and other naturall wayes, by which God worketh them in his elect, at such times as he thinketh fit. And these three opinions, pernicious to Peace and Government, have in this part of the world, proceeded chiefly from the tongues, and pens of unlearned Divines ; who joyning the words of Holy Scripture together, otherwise than is agreeable to reason, do what they can, to make men think that Sanctity and Naturall Reason, cannot stand together.

A fourth opinion, repugnant to the nature of a Common-wealth, is this, *That he that hath the Soveraign Power, is subject to the Civill Lawes.* It is true, that Soveraigns are all subject to the Lawes of Nature ; because such lawes be Divine, and cannot by any man, or Common-wealth be abrogated. But to those Lawes which the Soveraign himselfe, that is, which the Common-wealth maketh, he is not subject. For to be subject to Lawes is to be subject to the Common-wealth, that is to the Soveraign Representative, that is to himselfe ; which is not subjection, but freedome from the Lawes. Which errour, because it setteth the Lawes above the Soveraign, setteth also a

Judge above him, and a Power to punish him ; which is to make a new Soveraign ; and again for the same reason a third, to punish the second ; and so continually without end, to the Confusion, and Dissolution of the Common-wealth.

A Fifth doctrine, that tendeth to the Dissolution of a Common-wealth, is, *That every private man has an absolute Propriety in his Goods ; such, as excludeth the Right of the Soveraign.* Every man has indeed a Propriety that excludes the Right of every other Subject : And he has it onely from the Soveraign Power ; without the protection whereof every other man should have equall Right to the same. But if the Right of the Soveraign also be excluded, he cannot performe the office they have put him into ; which is, to defend them both from forraign enemies, and from the injuries of one another ; and consequently there.is no longer a Common-wealth.

And if the Propriety of Subjects, exclude not the Right of the Soveraign Representative to their Goods ; much lesse to their offices of Judicature, or Execution, in which they Represent the Soveraign himselfe.

There is a Sixth doctrine, plainly, and directly against the essence of a Common-wealth ; and 'tis this, *That the Soveraign Power may be divided.* For what is it to divide the Power of a Common-wealth, but to dissolve it ; for Powers divided mutually destroy each other. And for these doctrines, men are chiefly beholding to some of those, that making profession of the Lawes, endeavour to make them depend upon their own learning, and not upon the Legislative Power.

And as False Doctrine, so also often-times the example of different Government in a neighbouring Nation, disposeth men to alteration of the forme already setled. So the people of the Jewes were stirred up to reject God, and to call upon the prophet *Samuel,* for a King after the manner of the Nations : So also the lesser Cities of *Greece,* were continually disturbed with seditions of the Aristocraticall, and Democraticall factions ; one part of almost every Common-wealth, desiring to imitate the Lacedæmonians ; the other, the Athenians. And I doubt not, but many men, have been contented to see the late troubles in *England,* out of an imitation of the Low Countries ; supposing there needed no more to grow rich, than to change, as they had done, the forme of their Government. For the constitution of mans nature, is of it selfe subject to desire novelty : When therefore they are provoked to the same, by the neighbourhood also of those that have been enriched by it, it is almost impossible for them, not to be content with those that solicite them to change ; and love the first beginnings, though they be grieved with the continuance of disorder ; like hot blouds, that having gotten the itch, tear themselves with their own nayles, till they can endure the smart no longer.

And as to Rebellion in particular against Monarchy ; one of the most frequent causes of it, is the Reading of the books of Policy, and Histories of the antient Greeks, and Romans ; from which, young men, and all others that are unprovided of the Antidotes of solid Reason, receiving a strong, and delightfull impression, of the great exploits of warre, atchieved by the Conductors of their Armies, receive withall a pleasing Idea of all they have done besides ; and imagine their great prosperity, not to have proceeded from the æmulation of particular men, but from the vertue of their popular forme of government : Not considering the frequent Seditions, and Civill Warres, produced by the imperfection of their Policy. From the reading, I say, of such books, men have undertaken to kill their Kings, because the Greek and Latine writers, in their books, and discourses of Policy, make it lawfull, and laudable, for any man so to do ; provided, before he do it, he call him Tyrant. For they say not *Regicide*, that is, killing of a King, but *Tyrannicide*, that is, killing of a Tyrant is lawfull. From the same books, they that live under a Monarch conceive an opinion, that the Subjects in a Popular Common-wealth enjoy Liberty ; but that in a Monarchy they are all Slaves. I say, they that live under a Monarchy conceive such an opinion ; not they that live under a Popular Government : for they find no such matter. In summe, I cannot imagine, how any thing can be more prejudiciall to a Monarchy, than the allowing such books to be publiquely read, without present applying such correctives of discreet Masters, as are fit to take away their Venime : Which Venime I will not doubt to compare to the biting of a mad Dogge, which is a disease the Physicians call *Hydrophobia*, or *fear of Water*. For as he that is so bitten, has a continuall torment of thirst, and yet abhorreth water ; and is in such an estate, as if the poysons endeavoured to convert him into a Dogge : So when a Monarchy is once bitten to the quick, by those Democraticall writers, that continually snarl at the estate ; it wanteth nothing more than a strong Monarch, which neverthelesse out of a certain *Tyrannophobia*, or fear of being strongly governed, when they have him, they abhorre.

As there have been Doctors, that hold there be three Soules in a man ; so there be also that think there may be more Soules, (that is, more Soveraigns,) than one, in a Common-wealth ; and set up a *Supremacy* against the *Soveraignty; Canons* against *Lawes;* and a *Ghostly Authority* against the *Civill;* working on mens minds, with words and distinctions, that of themselves signifie nothing, but bewray (by their obscurity) that there walked (as some think invisibly) another Kingdome, as it were a Kingdome of Fayries, in the dark. Now seeing it is manifest, that the Civill Power, and the Power of the Common-wealth is the same thing ; and that Supremacy, and the Power of making Canons, and granting Faculties, im-plyeth a Common-wealth ; it followeth, that where one is Soveraign, another Supreme ; where one can make Lawes, and another make Canons ; there must needs be two Common-wealths, of one & the same Subjects ; which is a Kingdome divided in it selfe, and cannot stand. For notwithstanding the insignificant distinction of *Temporal* and *Ghostly*, they are still two Kingdomes, and every Subject is subject to two Masters. For seeing the *Ghostly* Power challengeth the Right to declare what is Sinne, it challengeth by consequence to declare what is Law (Sinne being nothing but the transgression of the Law ;) and again, the Civill Power challenging to declare what is Law, every Subject must obey two Masters, who both will have their Commands be observed as Law ; which is impossible. Or, if it be but one Kingdome, either the *Civill*, which is the Power of the Common-wealth, must be subordinate to the *Ghostly*, and then there is no Soveraignty by the *Ghostly;* or the *Ghostly* must be subordinate to the *Temporall*, and then there is no *Supremacy* but the *Temporall.* When therefore these two Powers oppose one another, the Common-wealth cannot but be in great danger of Civill warre, and Dissolution. For the *Civill* Authority being more visible, and standing in the cleerer light of naturall reason, cannot choose but draw to it in all times a very considerable part of the people : And the *Spirituall,* though it stand in the darknesse of Schoole distinctions, and hard words ; yet because the fear of the Darknesse, and Ghosts, and greater than other fears, cannot want a party sufficient to Trouble, and sometimes to Destroy a Common-wealth. And this is a Disease which not infitly may be compared to the Epilepsie, or Falling-sicknesse (which the Jews tooks to be one kind of possession by Spirits) in the Body Naturall. For as in this Disease. There is an unnatural spirit, or wind in the head that obstructeth the roots of the Nerves, and moving them violently, taketh away the motion which naturally they should have from the power of the Soule in the Brain, and thereby causeth violent, and irregular motions (which men call Convul⁴sions) in the parts ; insomuch as he that is seized therewith, falleth down sometimes into the water, and sometimes into the fire, as a man deprived of his senses ; as also in the Body Politique, when the Spirituall Power, moveth the Members of a Common-wealth, by the terrour of punishments, and hope of rewards, (which are the Nerves of it,) otherwise than by the Civill Power (which is the Soule of the Common-wealth) they ought to be moved ; and by strange, and hard words suffocates, their understanding, it must needs thereby Distract the people, and either Overwhelm the Common-wealth with Oppression, or cast it into the Fire of a Civill Warre.

Sometimes also in the meer Civill government, there be more than one Soule : As when the Power of levying mony, (which is the Nutritive faculty,) has depended on a Assembly ; the Power of conduct and command, (which is the Motive faculty,) on one man ; and the Power of making Lawes, (which is the Rationall faculty,) on the accidentall consent, not onely of those two, but also of a third ; This endangereth the Common-wealth, sometimes for want of consent to good Lawes ; but most often for want of such Nourishment as is necessary to Life, and Motion. For although few perceive, that such government, is not government, but division of the Common-wealth into three Factions, and call it mixt Monarchy ; yet the truth is, that it is not one independent Common-wealth, but three independent Factions ; nor one Representative Person, but three.   In the Kingdome of God, there may be three Persons independent, without breach of unity in God that Reigneth, but where men Reign, that be subject to diversity of opinions, it cannot be so.   And therefore if the King bear the person of the People, and the generall Assembly bear also the person of the People, and another Assembly bear the person of a Part of the people, they are not one Person, nor one Soveraign, but three Persons, and three Soveraigns.

To what Disease in the Naturall Body of man, I may exactly compare this irregularity of a Common-wealth, I know not. But I have seen a man, that had another man growing out of his side, with an head, armes, breast, and stomach, of his own : If he had had another man growing out of his other side, the comparison might then have been exact.

Hitherto I have named such Diseases of a Common-wealth, as are of the greatest and most present danger.   There be other, not so great ; which neverthelesse are not unfit to be observed.   At first, the difficulty of raising Mony for the

necessary uses of the Common-wealth ; especially in the
approach of warre. This difficulty ariseth from the opinion,
that every Subject hath of a Propriety in his lands and goods,
exclusive of the Soveraigns Right to the use of the same. From
whence it commeth to passe, that the Soveraign Power, which
foreseeth the necessities and dangers of the Common-wealth,
(finding the passage of mony to the publique Treasure
obstructed, by the tenacity of the people,) whereas it ought to
extend it selfe, to encounter, and prevent such dangers in their
beginnings, contracteth it selfe as long as it can, and when it
cannot longer, struggles with the people by stratagems of Law,
to obtain little summes, which not sufficing, he is fain at last
violently to open the way for present supply, or Perish ; and
being put often to these extremities, at last reduceth the people
to their due temper ; or else the Common-wealth must perish.
Insomuch as we may compare this Distemper very aptly to an
Ague ; wherein, the fleshy parts being congealed, or by venom-
ous matter obstructed ; the Veins which by their naturall course
empty themselves into the Heart, are not, (as they ought to be)
supplyed from the Arteries, whereby there succeedeth at first a
cold contraction, and trembling of the limbes ; and afterwards a
hot, and strong endeavour of the Heart, to force a passage for
the Bloud ; and before it can do that, contenteth it selfe with
the small refreshments of such things as coole for a time, till
(if Nature be strong enough) it break at last the contumacy of
the parts obstructed, and dissipateth the venome into sweat ;
or (if Nature be too weak) the Patient dyeth.

Again, there is sometimes in a Common-wealth, a Disease,
which resembleth the Pleurisie ; and that is, when the Treasure
of the Common-wealth, flowing out of its due course, is gathered
together in too much abundance, in one, or a few private men,
by Monopolies, or by Farmers of the Publique Revenues ; in
the same manner as the Blood in a Pleurisie, getting into
the Membrane of a breast, breedeth there an Inflammation,
accompanied with a Fever, and painfull stitches.

Also, the Popularity of a potent Subject, (unless the Common-
wealth have very good caution of his fidelity,) is a dangerous
Disease ; because the people (which should receive their motion
from the Authority of the Soveraign,) by the flattery, and by the
reputation of an ambitious man, are drawn away from their
obedience to the Lawes, to follow a man, of whose vertues and
designes they have no knowledge. And this is commonly of
more danger in a Popular Government, than in a Monarchy ;
· because an Army is of so great force, and multitude, as it may

easily be made believe, they are the people. By this means it was, that *Julius Cæsar*, who was set up by the People against the Senate, having won to himselfe the affections of his Army, made himselfe Master, both of Senate and People. And this proceeding of popular, and ambitious men, is plain Rebellion ; and may be resembled to the effects of Witchcraft.

Another infirmity of a Common-wealth, is the immoderate greatnesse of a Town, when it is able to furnish out of its own Circuit, the number, and expence of a great Army : As also the great number of Corporations ; which are as it were many lesser Common-wealths in the bowels of a greater, like wormes in the entrayls of a naturall man. To which may be added, the Liberty of Disputing against absolute Power, by pretenders to Politicall Prudence ; which though bred for the most part in the Lees of the people ; yet animated by False Doctrines, are perpetually medling with the Fundamentall Lawes, to the molestation of the Common-wealth ; like the little Wormes, which Physicians call *Ascarcides.*

We may further adde, the insatiable appetite, or *Bulimia*, of enlarging Dominion ; with the incurable *Wounds* thereby many times received from the enemy ; and the *Wens*, of ununited conquests, which are manny times a burthen, and with lesse danger lost, than kept ; As also the *Lethargy* of Ease and *Consumption* of Riot and Vain Expence.

Lastly, when in a warre (forraign, or intestine,) the enemies get a finall Victory ; so as (the forces of the Common-wealth keeping the field no longer) there is no further protection of Subjects in their loyalty ; then is the Common-wealth DISSOLVED, and every man at liberty to protect himselfe by such courses as his own discretion shall suggest unto him. For the Soveraign, is the publique Soule, giving Life and Motion to the Common-wealth ; which expiring, the Members are governed by it no more, than the Carcasse of a man, by his departed (though Immortall) Soule. For though the Right of a Soveraign Monarch cannot be extinguished by the act of another ; yet the Obligation of the members may. For he that wants protection, may seek it anywhere ; and when he hath it, is obliged (without fraudulent pretence or having submitted himselfe out of fear,) to protect his Protection as long as he is able. But when the Power of an Assembly is once suppressed, the Right of the same perisheth utterly ; because the Assembly it selfe is extinct ; and consequently, there is no possibility for the Soveraignty to re-enter.

Leviathan.

GEORGE HERBERT.

1593–1632.

THE PARSON'S LIFE.

THE countrey parson is exceeding exact in his life, being holy, just, prudent, temperate, bold, grave, in all his wayes. And because the two highest points of life wherein a Christian is most seen are patience and mortification—patience in regard of afflictions ; mortification in regard of lusts and affections, and the stupifying and deading of all the clamarous powers of the soul—therefore he hath thoroughly studied these, that he may be an absolute master and commander of himself for all the purposes which God hath ordained him. Yet in these points he labours most in those things which are most apt to scandalize his parish. And first, because countrey people live hardly, and therefore as feeling their own sweat, and consequently knowing the price of money, are offended much with any who by hard usage increase their travell, the countrey parson is very circumspect in avoiding all covetousnesse, neither being greedy to get, nor niggardly to keep, nor troubled to lose any worldly wealth ; but in all his words and actions slighting and disesteeming it, even to a wondring that the world should so much value wealth, which in the day of wrath hath not one dramme of comfort for us. Secondly, because luxury is a very visible sin, the parson is very careful to avoid all the kinds thereof; but especially that of drinking, because it is the most popular vice ; into which, if he come, he prostitutes himself both to shame and sin, and by having ' fellowship with the unfruitfull works of darknesse,' he disableth himself of authority to reprove them ; for sins make all equall whom they finde together, and then they are worst who ought to be best. Neither is it for the servant of Christ to haunt innes or tavernes or alehouses, to the dishonour of his person and office. The parson doth not so, but orders his life in such a fashion, that when death takes him, as the Jewes and Judas did Christ, he may say as He did, ' I sate daily with you teaching in the temple.'   Thirdly, because countrey people (as indeed all honest men) do much esteem their word, it being the life of buying and selling, and dealing in the world ; therefore the parson is very strict in keeping his word, though it be to his own hinderance, as knowing that if he be not so he wil quickly be discovered and disregarded: neither will they beleeve him in the pulpit whom they cannot trust in his conversation. As for oaths and apparell, the disorders thereof are also very manifest.   The parson's yea is *yea*, and nay *nay;* and his apparell plaine, but reverend and clean, without spots or dust or smell ; the purity of his mind breaking out and dilating itselfe even to his body, cloaths, and habitation.

A Priest to the Temple.

IZAAK WALTON.

1593–1683.

OLD SONGS.

Pisc. Look, under that broad *Beechtree* I sate down when I was last this way a fishing, and the birds in the adjoining Grove seemed to have a friendly contention with an Echo, whose dead voise seemed to live in a hollow cave, near to the brow of that Primrosehil ; there I sate viewing the Silver streams glide silently towards their center, the tempestuous Sea, yet sometimes opposed by rugged roots, and pibble stones, which broke their waves, and turned them into fome : and sometimes viewing the harmless Lambs, some leaping securely in the cool shade, whilst others sported themselves in the cheerful Sun ; and others were craving comfort from the swolne Udders of their bleating Dams. As I thus sate, these and other sights had so fully possest my soul, that I thought as the Poet has happily exprest it :

> *I was for that time lifted above earth ;*
> *And possest Joyes not promis'd in my birth.*

As I left this place, and entered into the next field, a second pleasure entertained me, 'twas a handsome Milk-maid, that had cast away all care, and sang like a *Nightingale;* her voice was good, and the Ditty fitted for it ; 'twas that smooth Song which was made by *Kit Marlow,* now at least fifty years ago ; and the Milk-maid's mother sung an answer to it, which was made by Sir *Walter Raleigh* in his younger dayes.

They were old fashioned Poetry, but choicely good, I think much better then that now in fashion in this critical age. Look yonder, on my word, yonder they be both a milking again : I will give her the *Chub,* and perswade them to sing those two songs to us.

The Angler's Life.

And now, Scholer, my direction for fly-fishing is ended with this showre, for it has done raining, and now look about you, and see how pleasantly that Meadow looks, nay and the earth smels as sweetly too. Come let me tell you what holy Mr. *Herbert* saies of such dayes and Flowers as these, and then we will thank God that we enjoy them, and walk to the River and sit down quietly and try to catch the other brace of *Trouts.*

> *Sweet day, so cool, so calm, so bright,*
> *The bridal of the earth and skie,*
> *Sweet dews shall weep thy fall to night,*
> > *for thou must die.*

> *Sweet Rose, whose hew angry and brave*
> *Bids the rash gazer wipe his eye,*
> *Thy root is ever in its grave,*
> > *and thou must die.*

> *Sweet Spring, ful of sweet days and roses,*
> *A box where sweets compacted lie ;*
> *My Musick shewes you have your closes,*
> > *and all must die.*

> *Only a sweet and virtuous soul,*
> *Like seasoned timber never gives,*
> *But when the whole world turns to cole,*
> > *then chiefly lives.*

Viat. I thank you, good Master, for your good direction for fly-fishing, and for the sweet enjoyment of the pleasant day, which is so far spent without offence to God or man : and I thank you for the sweet close of your discourse with Mr. Herberts Verses, which I have heard, loved Angling ; and I do the rather believe it, because he had a spirit suitable to Anglers, and to those Primitive Christians that you love, and have so much commended.

Pisc. Well, my loving Scholer, and I am pleased to know that you are so well pleased with my direction and discourse ; and I hope you will be pleased too, if you find a *Trout* at one of our Angles, which we left in the water to fish for it self ; you shall chuse which shall be yours, and it is an even lay, one catches ; And let me tell you, this kind of fishing, and laying Night-hooks, are like putting money to use, for they both work

for the Owners, when they do nothing but sleep, or eat, or
rejoice, as you know we have done this last hour, and sate as
quietly and free from cares under this *Sycamore*, as Virgils
Tityrus and his *Melibœus* did under their broad *Beech* tree :
No life, my honest Scholer, no life so happy, and so pleasant as
the Anglers, unless it be the Beggers life in Summer ; for then
only they take no care but are as happy as we Anglers.

The Compleat Angler.

SIR THOMAS BROWNE.

1605-1682.

RELIGIO MEDICI.

NOR truely doe I thinke the lives of any were ever correspond-
ent, or in all points conformable unto their doctrines ; it is evident that *Aristotle* transgressed the rule of his owne Ethicks ; the
Stoicks that condemne passion, and command a man to laugh
in *Phalaris* his Bull, could not endure without a groane a fit of
the stone or collick. The *Scepticks* that affirmed they knew
nothing, even in that opinion confute themselves, and thought
they knew more than all the world beside. *Diogenes* I hold to
bee the most vaine glorious man of his time, and more ambitious in refusing all honours, than *Alexander* in rejecting none.
Vice and the Devill put a fallacie upon our reasons, and,
provoking us too hastily to run from it, entangle and profound
us deeper in it. The duke of *Venice*, that weds himselfe unto
the sea, by a ring of Gold, I will not argue of prodigality,
because it is a solemnity of good use and consequence in the
State. But the Philosopher that threw his money into the Sea
to avoyd avarice, was a notorious prodigal. There is no road
or ready way to verture, it is not an easie point of art to
disentangle our selves from this riddle, or web of sin : To
perfect vertue, as to Religion, there is required a Panoplia, or
compleat armour, that whilst we lye at close ward against one
vice we lie not open to the vennie of another : And indeed wiser
discretions that have the thred of reason to conduct them, offend
without a pardon ; whereas under heads may stumble without
dishonour. There goe so many circumstances to piece up one
good action, that it is a lesson to be good, and wee are forced to
be virtuous by the booke. Againe, the practice of men holds not
an equall pace, yea, and often runnes counter to their Theory ; we
naturally know what is good, but naturally pursue what is evill :

the Rhetoricke wherewith I perswade another cannot perswade my selfe : there is a depraved appetite in us, that will with patience heare the learned instructions of Reason ; but yet perform no farther than agrees to its owne irregular Humour. In briefe, we all are monsters, that is, a composition of man and beast, wherein we must endeavour to be as the Poets fancy that wise man *Chiron*, that is, to have the Region of Man above that of Beast, and sense to sit but at the feete of reason. Lastly, I doe desire with God, that all, but yet affirme with men, that few shall know salvation, that the bridge is narrow, the passage straite unto life ; yet those who doe confine the Church of God, either to particular Nations, Churches, or Families, have made it farre narrower than our Saviour ever meant it.

The vulgarity of those judgments that wrap the church of God in *Strabo's* cloak and restraine it unto Europe, seeme to mee as bad Geographers as *Alexander*, who thought hee had conquer'd all the world when hee [had] not subdued the halfe of any part thereof : For wee cannot deny the Church of God both in Asia and Africa, if we doe not forget the peregrinations of the Apostles, the deaths of their Martyrs, the sessions of many and even in our reformed judgment lawfull councells, held in those parts in the minoritie and nonage of ours : nor must a few differences more remarkable in the eyes of man than perhaps in the judgement of God, excommunicate from heaven one another, much lesse those Christians who are in a manner all Martyrs, maintaining their faith in the noble way of persecution, and serving God in the fire, whereas we honour him but in the sunshine. 'Tis true we all hold there is a number of Elect and many be saved, yet take our opinions together, and from the confusion thereof, there will be no such thing as salvation, nor shall any one be saved ; for first the church of *Rome* condemneth us, wee likewise them ; the Sub-reformists and Sectaries sentence the Doctrine of our Church as damnable, the Atomist, or Familist reprobates all these, and all these them againe. Thus whilst the mercies of God doth promise us heaven, our conceits and opinions exclude us from that place. There must be therefore more than one Saint *Peter*, particular Churches and Sects usurpe the gates of heaven, and turne the key against each other, and thus we goe to heaven against each others will, conceits and opinions, and with as much uncharity as ignorance, doe erre, I feare in points, not onely of our own, but on[e] anothers salvation.

I beleeve many are saved who to man seeme reprobated, and many are reprobated, who in the opinion and sentence of man, stand elected ; there will appeare at the last day, strange, and unexpected examples, both of his justice and his mercy, and therefore to define either is folly in man, and insolency, even in the devils ; those acute and subtill spirits, in all their sagacity, can hardly divine who shall be saved, which if they could prognostick, their labour were at an end ; nor need they compasse the earth, seeking whom they may devoure. Those who upon a rigid application of the Law, sentence *Solomon* unto damnation, condemne not onely him, but themselves, and the whole world ; for by the letter and written Word of God, we are without exception in the state of death, but there is a prerogative of God, and an arbitrary pleasure above the letter of his owne Law, by which alone wee can pretend unto salvation, and through which *Solomon* might be as easily saved as those who condemne him.

The number of those who pretend unto salvation, and those infinite swarmes who thinke to passe through the eye of this needle, have much amazed me. That name and compellation of *little Flocke*, doth not comfort, but deject, my devotion, especially when I reflect upon mine owne unworthinesse, wherein, according to my humble apprehensions, I am below them all. I beleeve there shall never be an Anarchy in Heaven, but as there are Hierarchies amongst the Angels, so shall there be degrees of priority amongst the Saints. Yet is it (I protest) beyond my ambition to aspire unto the first rankes, my desires onely are, and I shall be happy therein, to be but the last man, and bring up the Rere in Heaven.

CHRISTIAN MORALS.

VALUE the Judicious, and let not mere acquests in minor parts of Learning gain thy preexistimation. 'Tis an unjust way of compute to magnify a weak Head for some Latin abilities, and to undervalue a solid Judgment, because he knows not the genealogy of *Hector*. When that notable King of *France* would have his son to know but one sentence in Latin, had it been a good one, perhaps it had been enough. Natural parts and good Judgments rule the World. States are not governed by Ergotisms. Many have Ruled well, who could not perhaps define a Commonwealth, and they who understand not the Globe of the Earth command a great part of it. Where natural Logick prevails not, Artificial too often faileth. When Nature fills the Sails, the Vessel goes smoothly on, and when Judgment is the Pilot, the Ensurance need not be high. When Industry builds upon Nature, we may expect Pyramids : where that foundation is wanting, the structure must be low. They do most by Books, who could do much without them, and he that chiefly ows himself unto himself is the substantial Man.

Let thy Studies be free as thy Thoughts and Contemplations : but fly not only upon the wings of Imagination ; Joyn Sense unto Reason, and Experiment unto Speculation, and so give life unto Embryon Truths, and Verities yet in their Chaos. There is nothing more acceptable unto the Ingenious World, than this noble Eluctation of Truth ; wherein, against the tenacity of Prejudice and Presciption, this Century now prevaileth. What Libraries of new Volumes aftertimes will behold, and in what a new World of Knowledge the eyes of our Posterity may be happy, a few Ages may joyfully declare ; and is but a cold thought unto those, who cannot hope to behold this Exantlation of Truth, or that obscured Virgin half out of the Pit. Which might make some content with a commutation of the time of their lives, and to commend the fancy of the *Pythagorean* metempsychosis ; whereby they might hope to enjoy this happiness in their third or fourth selves, and behold that in *Pythagoras*, which they now but foresee in *Euphorbus*. The World, which took but six days to make, is like to take six thousand to make out : mean while old Truths voted down begin to resume their places, and new ones arise upon us ; wherein there is no comfort in the happiness of *Tully's* Elizium, or any satisfaction from the Ghosts of the Ancients, who knew so little of what is now well known. Men disparage not Antiquity, who prudently exalt new Enquiries, and make not them the Judges of Truth, who were but fellow Enquirers of it. Who can but magnify the Endeavours of *Aristotle*, and the noble start which Learning had under him ; or less than pitty the slender progression made upon such advantages ? While many Centuries were lost in repetitions and transcriptions sealing up the Book of Knowledge. And therefore rather than to swell the leaves of Learning by fruitless Repetitions, to sing the same Song in all Ages, nor adventure at Essays beyond the attempt of others, many would be content that some would write like *Helmont* or *Paracelsus;* and be willing to endure the monstrosity of some opinions, for divers singular notions requiting such aberrations.

Confound not the distinctions of thy Life which Nature hath divided : that is, Youth, Adolescence, Manhood, and old Age, nor in these divided Periods, wherein thou art in a manner Four, conceive thyself but One. Let every division be happy in its proper Virtues, nor one Vice run through all. Let each distinction have its salutary transition, and critically deliver thee from the imperfections of the former, so ordering the whole, that Prudence and Virtue may have the largest Section. Do as a Child but when thou art a Child, and ride not on a Reed at twenty. He who hath not taken leave of the follies of his Youth, and in his maturer state scarce got out of that division, disproportionately divideth his Days, crowds up the latter part of his life, and leaves too narrow a corner for the Age of Wisdom ; and so hath room to be a man scarce longer than he hath been a Youth. Rather than to make this confusion, anticipate the Virtues of Age, and live long without the infirmities of it. So may'st thou count up thy Days as some do *Adams*, that is, by anticipation ; so may'st thou be coetaneous unto thy Elders, and a Father unto thy contemporaries.

Live unto the Dignity of thy Nature, and leave it not disputable at last, whether thou hast been a Man, or since thou art a composition of Man and Beast, how thou hast predominantly passed thy days, to state the denomination. Un-man not therefore thy self by a Beastial transformation, nor realize old Fables. Expose not thy self by four-footed manners unto monstrous draughts, and *Caricatura* representations. Think not after the old *Pythagorean* conceit, what Beast thou may'st be after death. Be not under any Brutal *metempsychosis*, while thou livest, and walkest about erectly under the scheme of Man. In thine own circumference, as in that of the Earth, let the Rational Horizon be larger than the sensible, and the Circle of Reason than of Sense. Let the Divine part be upward, and the Region of Beast below. Otherwise, 'tis but to live invertedly, and with thy Head unto the Heels of thy *Antipodes*. Desert not thy title to a Divine particle and union with invisibles. Let true Knowledge and Virtue tell the lower World thou art a part of the higher. Let thy thoughts be of things which have not entred into the Hearts of Beasts : Think of things long past, and long to come : Acquaint thyself with the *Choragium* of the Stars, and consider the vast expansion beyond them. Let Intellectual Tubes give thee a glance of things, which visive Organs reach not. Have a glimpse of incomprehensibles, and Thoughts of things, which Thoughts but tenderly touch. Lodge immaterials in thy Head : ascend unto invisibles : fill thy Spirit with Spirituals, with the mysteries of Faith, the magnalities of Religion, and thy Life with the Honour of God ; without which, though Giants in Wealth and Dignity, we are but Dwarfs and Pygmies in Humanity, and may hold a pitiful rank in that triple division of mankind into Heroes, Men, and Beasts. For though human Souls are said to be equal, yet is there no small inequality in their operations ; some maintain the allowable Station of Men ; many are far below it ; and some have been so divine, as to approach the *Apogeum* of their Natures, and to be in the *Confinium* of Spirits.

URNE BURIALL.

NOW since these dead bones have already out-lasted the living ones of *Methuselah*, and in a yard under ground, and thin walls of clay, out-worn all the strong and specious buildings above it ; and quietly rested under the drums and tramplings of three conquests ; What Prince can promise such diuturnity unto his Reliques, or might not gladly say,

Sic ego componi versus in ossa velim.

Time which antiquates Antiquities, and hath an art to make dust of all things, hath yet spared these *minor* Monuments. In vain we hope to be known by open and visible conservatories, when to be unknown was the means of their continuation and obscurity their protection : If they dyed by violent hands, and were thrust into their Urnes, these bones become considerable, and some old philosophers would honour them, whose souls they conceived most pure, which were thus snatched from their bodies ; and to retain a stranger propension unto them : whereas they weariedly left a languishing corps, and with faint desires of re-union. If they fell by long and aged decay, yet wrapt up in the bundle of time, they fell into indistinction, and made but one blot with Infants. If we begin to die when we live, and long life be but a prolongation of death : our life is a sad composition ; We live with death, and die not in a moment. How many pulses made up the life of *Methuselah*, were work for *Archimedes:* Common Counters summe up the life of *Moses* his man. Our dayes become considerable like petty sums by minute accumulations ; where numerous fractions make up but small round numbers ; and our days of a span long make not one little finger.

If the nearnesse of our last necessity, brought a nearer conformity unto it, there were a happinesse in hoary hairs, and no calamity in half senses.   But the long habit of living indisposeth us for dying ; When Avarice makes us the sport of death ; When even *David* grew politickly cruell ; and *Solomon* could hardly be said to be the wisest of men.   But many are too early old, and before the the date of age.   Adversity stretcheth our days, misery make *Alcmenas* nights,[*] and time hath no wings unto it.   But the most tedious being is that which can unwish it self, content to be nothing, or never to have been, which was beyond the *male*-content of *Job*, who cursed not the day of his life, but his Nativity : Content to have so farre been, as to have a Title to future being ; Although he had lived here but in a hidden state of life, and as it were an abortion.

What Song the *Syrens* sang, or what name *Achilles* assumed when he hid himself among women, though puzling Questions, are not beyond all conjecture.   What time the persons of these Ossuaries entred the famous Nations of the dead, and slept with Princes and Counsellours, might admit a wide solution.   But who were the proprietaries of these bones, or what bodies these ashes made up, were a question above Antiquarism.   Not to be resolved by man, nor easily perhaps by spirits, except we consult the Provinciall Guardians, or tutellary Observators.   Had they made as good provision for their names, as they have done for their Reliques, they had not so grossly erred in the art of perpetuation.   But to subsist in bones, and be but Pyramidally extant is a fallacy in duration.   Vain ashes, which in the oblivion of names, persons, times, and sexes, have found unto themselves, a fruitlesse continuation, and only arise unto late posterity, as Emblemes of mortall vanities ; Antidotes against pride, vainglory, and madding vices.   Pagan vain-glories which thought the world might last for ever, had encouragement for ambition, and finding no *Atropos* unto the immortality of their Names, were never dampt with the necessity of oblivion.   Even old ambitions had the advantage of ours, in the attempts of their vain-glories, who acting early, and before the probable Meridian of time, have by this time found great accomplishment of their designes, whereby the ancient *Heroes* have already out-lasted their Monuments and Mechanicall preservations.   But in this latter Scene of time we cannot expect such Mummies unto our

---

[*] One night as long as three.

memories, when ambition may fear the Prophecy of *Elias*, and *Charles* the fifth can never hope to live within two *Methuselah's* of *Hector*.

And therefore restlesse inquietude for the diuturnity of our memories unto present considerations, seems a vanity almost out of date, and superannuated peece of folly. We cannot hope to live so long in our names, as some have done in their persons, one face of *Janus* holds no proportion unto the other. 'Tis too late to be ambitious. The great mutations of the world are acted, or time may be too short for our designes. To extend our memories by Monuments, whose death we dayly pray for, and whose duration we cannot hope, without injury to our expectations, in the advent of the last day, were a contradiction to our beliefs. We whose generations are ordained in this setting part of time, are providentially taken off from such imaginations. And being necessitated to eye the remaining particle of futurity, are naturally constituted unto thoughts of the next world, and cannot excusably decline the consideration of that duration, which maketh Pyramids pillars of snow, and all that's past a moment.

Circles and right lines limit and close all bodies, and the mortall right-lined circle, must conclude and shut up all. There is no antidote against the *Opium* of time, which temporally considereth all things ; Our Fathers finde their graves in our short memories, and sadly tell us how we may be buried in our Survivors. Grave-stones tell truth scarce forty years : Generations passe while some trees stand, and old Families last not three Oaks. To be read by bare Inscriptions like many in *Gruter*, to hope for Eternity by Ænigmaticall Epithetes, or first letters of our names, to be studied by Antiquaries, who we were, and have new Names given us like many of the Mummies, are cold consolations unto the Students of perpetuity, even by everlasting Languages.

To be content that times to come should only know there was such a man, not caring whether they knew more of him, was a frigid ambition in *Cardan:* disparaging his horoscopal inclination and judgement of himself, who cares to subsist like *Hippocrates* Patients, or *Achilles* horses in *Homer*, under naked nominations, without deserts and noble acts, which are the balsame of our memories, the *Entelechia* and soul of our subsistences. To be namelesse in worthy deeds exceeds an infamous history. The *Canaanitish* woman lives more happily without a name, then *Herodias* with one. And who would not rather have been the good theef, then *Pilate?*

But the iniquity of oblivion blindely scattereth her poppy

and deals with the memory of men without distinction to merit of perpetuity.   Who can but pity the founder of the Pyramids? *Herostratus* lives that burnt the Temple of *Diana*, he is almost lost that built it ; Time hath spared the Epitaph of *Adrians* horse, confounded that of himself.   In vain we compute our felicities by the advantage of our good names, since bad have equall durations ; and *Thersites* is like to live as long as *Agamemnon*, without the favour of the everlasting Register : Who knows whether the best of men be known? or whether there be not more remarkable persons forgot, then any that stand remembred in the known account of time?   The first man had been as unknown as the last, and *Methuselahs* long life had been his only Chronicle.

Oblivion is not to be hired : The greater part must be content to be as though they had not been, to be found in the register of God, not in the record of man.   Twenty seven names make up the first story, and the recorded names ever since contain not one living Century.   The number of the dead long exceedeth all that shall live.   The night of time far surpasseth the day, and who knows when was the Æquinox.   Euery houre addes unto that current Arithmetique, which scarce stands one moment.   And since death must be the *Lucina* of life, and even Pagans could doubt whether thus to live, were to dye.   Since our longest Sunne sets at right descensions, and makes but winter arches, and therefore it cannot be long before we lie down in darknesse, and have our light in ashes.   Since the brother of death daily haunts us with dying *memento's*, and time that grows old it self, bids us hope no long duration : Diuturnity is a dream and folly of expectation.

Darknesse and light divide the course of time, and oblivion shares with memory, a great part even of our living beings ; we slightly remember our felicities, and the smartest stroaks of affliction leave but short smart upon us.   Sense endureth no extremities, and sorrows destroy us or themselves.   To weep into stones are fables.   Afflictions induce callosities, miseries are slippery, or fall like snow upon us, which notwithstanding is no unhappy stupidity.   To be ignorant of evils to come, and forgetful of evils past, is a mercifull provision in nature, whereby we digest the mixture of our few and evil dayes, and our delivered senses not relapsing into cutting remembrances, our sorrows are not kept raw by the edge of repetitions.   A great part of Antiquity contented their hopes of subsistency with a transmigration of their souls.   A good way to continue their memories, while having the advantage of plurall successions, they could not but act something remarkable in such variety of beings, and enjoying the fame of their passed selves, make accumulation of glory unto their last durations. Others rather then be lost in the uncomfortable night of nothing, were content to recede into the common being, and make one particle of the publick soul of all things, which was no more then to return into their unknown and divine Originall again. Ægyptian ingenuity was more unsatisfied, contriving their bodies in sweet consistencies, to attend the return of their souls. But all was vanity, feeding the winde, and folly. The Ægyptian Mummies, which *Cambyses* or time hath spared, avarice now consumeth. Mummie is become Merchandise, *Misraim* cures wounds, and *Pharaoh* is sold for balsoms.

In vain do individuals hope for Immortality, or any patent from oblivion, in preservations below the Moon : Men have been deceived even in their flatteries above the Sun, and studied conceits to perpetuate their names in heaven. The various Cosmography of that part hath already varied the names of contrived constellations ; *Nimrod* is lost in *Orion*, and *Osyris* in the Dogge-starre. While we look for incorruption in the heavens, we finde they are but like the Earth ; Durable in their main bodies, alterable in their parts : whereof beside Comets and new Stars, perspectives begin to tell tales. And the spots that wander about the Sun, with *Phaetons* favour, would make clear conviction.

There is nothing strictly immortall, but immortality ; whatever hath no beginning may be confident of no end. All others have a dependent being, and within the reach of destruction, which is the peculiar of that necessary essence that cannot destroy it self ; And the highest strain of omnipotency to be so powerfully constituted, as not to suffer even from the power of it self. But the sufficiency of Christian Immortality frustrates all earthly glory, and the quality of either state after death, makes a folly of posthumous memory. God who can only destroy our souls, and hath assured our resurrection, either of our bodies or names hath directly promised no duration. Wherein there is so much of chance that the boldest Expectants have found unhappy frustration ; and to hold long subsistence, seems but a scape in oblivion. But man is a Noble Animal, splendid in ashes, and pompous in the grave, solemnizing Nativities and Deaths with equall lustre, nor omitting Ceremonies of bravery, in the infamy of his nature.

Life is a pure flame, and we live by an invisible Sun within us. A small fire sufficeth for life, great flames seemed too little after death, while men vainly affected precious pyres, and to burn like *Sardanapalus*, but the wisedom of funeral Laws found the folly of prodigall blazes, and reduced undoing fires, unto the rule of sober obsequies, wherein few could be so mean as not to provide wood, pitch, a mourner, and an Urne.

Five Languages secured not the Epitaph of *Gordianus;* The man of God lives longer without a Tomb then any by one, invisibly interred by Angels, and adjudged to obscurity, though not without some marks directing humane discovery. *Enoch* and *Elias* without either tomb or buriall, in an anomalous state of being, are the great Examples of perpetuity, in their long and living memory, in strict account being still on this side death, and having a late part yet to act upon this staye of earth.   If in the decretory term of the world we shall not all dye but be changed, according to received translation ; the last day will make but few graves ; at least quick Resurrections will anticipate lasting Sepultures ; Some Graves will be opened before they be quite closed, and *Lazarus* be no wonder.   When many that feared to dye shall groane that they can dye but once, the dismal state is the second and living death, when life puts despair on the damned ; when men shall wish the coverings of Mountaines, not of Monuments, and annihilation shall be courted.

While some have studied Monuments, others have studiously declined them : and some have been so vainly boisterous, that they durst not acknowledge their Graves ; wherein *Alaricus* seems most subtle, who had a River turned to hide his bones at the bottome.   Even *Sylla* that thought himself safe in his Urne, could not prevent revenging tongues, and stones thrown at his Monument.   Happy are they whom privacy makes innocent, who deal so with men in this world, that they are not afraid to meet them in the next, who when they dye, make no commotion among the dead, and are not toucht with that poeticall taunt of *Isaiah.*

Pyramids, Arches, Obelisks, were but irregularities of vain-glory, and wilde enormities of ancient magnanimity.   But the most magnanimous resolution rests in the Christian Religion, which trampleth upon pride, and sets on the neck of ambition, humbly pursuing that infallible perpetuity, unto which all others must diminish their diameters, and be poorly seen in Angles of contingency.

Pious spirits who passed their dayes in raptures of futurity, made little more of this world, then the world that was before it, while they lay obscure in the Chaos of pre-ordination, and night of their fore-beings. And if any have been so happy as truly to understand Christian annihilation, extasis, exolution, liquefaction, transformation, the kisse of the Spouse, gustation of God, and ingression into the divine shadow, they have already had an handsome anticipation of heaven ; the glory of the world is surely over, and the earth in ashes unto them.

To subsist in lasting Monuments, to live in their productions, to exist in their names, and prædicament of *Chymera's*, was large satisfaction unto old expectations, and made one part of their *Elyziums.* But all this is nothing in the Metaphysicks of true belief. To live indeed is to be again ourselves, which being not only an hope but an evidence in noble believers ; 'Tis all one to lye in St. *Innocents* Churchyard, as in the Sands of *Ægypt :* Ready to be anything, in the exstasie of being ever, and as content with six foot as the Moles of *Adrianus.*

Lucan

——— *Tabesne cadavera solvat,*
An rogus haud refert. ———

THOMAS FULLER.

1608–1661.

OXFORD.—*BUILDINGS.*

THE Colleges in *Oxford*, advantaged by the vicinity of fair *Free-stone*, do for the generality of their structure carry away the credit from all in Christendom, and equal any for the largeness of their endowments.

It is not the least part of *Oxfords* happiness, that a moity of her Founders were Prelates, (whereas *Cambridge* hath but three Episcopal Foundations, *Peter-house*, *Trinity-hall*, and *Jesus*) who had an experimental knowledge, what belonged to the necessities and conveniences of Scholars, and therefore have accomodated them accordingly ; principally in providing them the patronages of many good Benefices, whereby the Fellows of those Colleges are plentifully maintained, after their leaving of the University.

Of the Colleges *University* is the oldest, *Pembroke* the youngest, *Christ-church* the greatest, *Lincoln* (by many reputed) the least, *Magdalen* the neatest, *Wadham* the most uniform, *New-college* the strongest, and *Jesus college* (no fault but its unhappiness) the poorest ; and if I knew which was the richest, I would not tell, seeing concealment in this kind is the safest. *New-college* is most proper for Southern, *Exeter* for Western, *Queens* for Northern, *Brazen-nose* for North-western men, *St. Johns* for *Londoners*, *Jesus* for Welshmen ; and at other Colleges almost indifferently for men of all Countries. *Merton* hath been most famous for School-men. *Corpus Chresti* (formerly called *Trilingue Collegium*) for Linguists, *Christ-church* for Poets, *All-souls* for Orators, *New-college* for Civilians, *Brazen-nose* for Disputants, *Queens college* for Metaphysicians, *Exeter* for a late series of *Regius Professors ;* *Magdalen* for ancient, *St. Johns* for modern Prelates : and all eminent in some one kind or other. And if any of these Colleges were transported into forreign parts, it would alter its *kind,* (or degree at least) and presently of a College *proceed* an University, as equal to most, and superiour to many, *Academics* beyond the Seas.

Before I conclude with these Colleges, I must confess how much I was posed with a passage which I met with in the *Epistles* of *Erasmus,* writing to his familiar friend *Ludovicus Vives,* then residing in *Oxford, in collegis Apum,* in the College of Bees, according to his direction of his Letter : I knew all Colleges may metaphorically be termed the *Colleges of Bees,* wherein the industrious Scholers live under the rule of one Master : In which respect *St. Hierom* advised *Rusticus* the Monk to busie himself in making *Bee-hives,* that from thence he might learn, *Monasteriorum ordinem & Regiam disciplinam,* the order of Monasteries and discipline of Kingly government. But why any one College should be so signally called, and which it was, I was at a loss ; till at last seasonably satisfied that it was *Corpus Christi :* whereon no unpleasant story doth depend ;

In the year 1630. the *Leads* over *Vives* his Study being decayed, were taken up and new cast, by which occasion the Stall was taken, and with it an incredible mass of Honey. But the *Bees,* as presaging their intended and imminent destruction (whereas they were never known to have swarmed before) did that Spring (to preserve their famous kind) send down a fair swarm into the Presidents Garden : The which in the year 1633. yielded two Swarms, one whereof pitched in the Garden for the President, the other they sent up as a new Colony into their old Habitation, there to continue the memory of this *mellifluous Doctor,* as the University styled him in a Letter to the Cardinal.

It seems these *Bees* were *Aborigines,* from the first building of the Colledge, being called *Collegium Apum* in the Founders Statutes, and so is *John Claymand,* the first President thereof, saluted by *Erasmus.*

THE LIBRARY.

IF the *Schools* may be resembled to the Ring, the *Library* may the better be compared to the Diamond therein : not so much for the *bunching forth* beyond the rest, as the *preciousness* thereof, in some respects equalling any in *Europe*, and in most kinds exceeding all in *England*, yet our Land hath ever been φιλοβίβλος, much given to the love of Books, and let us *Fleet the Cream* of a few of the primest Libraries in all ages.

In the infancy of *Christianity*, that at *York* bare away the Bell, founded by Archbishop *Egbert* (and so highly praised by *Alevinus* in his Epistle to *Charles* the Great) but long since abolished.

Before the dissolution of *Abbies*, when all Cathedrals and Convents had their Libraries, that at *Ramsey* was the greatest *Rabbin*, spake the most and best *Hebrew*, abounding in *Iewish*, and not defective in other Books.

In that age of *Lay-Libraries* (as I may term them, as belonging to the City) I behold that pertaining to *Guild-Hall* as a *Principal*, founded by *Richard Whittington*, whence three Cart loads of choice *Manuscripts* were carried in the reign of King *Edward* the sixth on the promise of [never performed] Restitution.

Since the *Reformation*, that of *Benet* in *Cambridge* hath for *Manuscripts* exceeded any (thank the cost and care of *Mathew Parker*) *Collegiate Library* in *England.*

Of late *Cambridge* Library, augmented with the Arch-Episcopal Library of *Lambeth*, is grown the second in the Land.

As for private *Libraries* of Subjects, that of Treasurer *Burlies* was the best for the use of a *States-man*, the Lord *Lumlies* for an *Historian*, the late Earl of *Arundels* for an *Herald*, Sir *Robert Cottons* for an *Antiquary*, and Arch-Bishop *Ushers* for a *Divine.* Many other excellent *Libraries* there were of particular persons, Lord *Brudnels*, Lord *Hattons*, &c. routed by our Civil Wars, and many Books which scaped the execution are fled, [transported] into *France, Flanders*, and other forraign parts.

To return to *Oxford* Library (which stands like *Diana* amongst her *Nymphs*, and) surpasseth all the rest for rarity and multitude of Books ; so that if any be wanting on any subject, it is because the world doth not afford them. This Library was founded by *Humphrey* the Good Duke of *Gloucester;* confounded in the raign of *Edward* the sixth, by* those who I list not to name ; re-founded by worthy Sir *Thomas Bodley*, and the bounty of daily Benefactors.

Worthies.

* By the Protestants.

JOHN MILTON.

1608–1674

FROM *AREOPAGITICA*.

TRUTH indeed came once into the world with her divine Master, and was a perfect shape most glorious to look on : but when he ascended, and his Apostles after him were laid asleep, then straight arose a wicked race of deceivers, who as that story goes of the *Ægyptian Typhon* with his conspirators, how they dealt with the good *Osiris*, took the virgin Truth, hewed her lovely form into a thousand peeces, and scatter'd them to the four winds. From that time ever since, the sad friends of Truth, such as durst appear, imitating the carefull search that *Isis* made for the mangl'd body of *Osiris*, went up and down gathering up limb by limb still as they could find them. We have not yet found them all, Lords and Commons, nor ever shall doe, till her Masters second comming ; he shall bring together every joynt and member, and shall mould them into an immortall feature of loveliness and perfection. Suffer not these licencing prohibitions to stand at every place of opportunity forbidding and disturbing them that continue seeking, that continue to do our obsequies to the torn body of our martyr'd Saint. We boast our light ; but if we look not wisely on the Sun it self, it smites us into darknes. Who can discern those planets that are oft *Combust*, and those stars of brightest magnitude that rise and set with the Sun, untill the opposite motion of their orbs bring them to such a place in the firmament, where they may be seen evning or morning. The light which we have gain'd, was giv'n us, not to be ever staring on, but by it to discover onward things more remote from our knowledge. It is not the unfrocking of a Priest, the unmitring of a Bishop, and the removing him from off the *Presbyterian* shoulders that will make us a happy Nation, no, if other things

as great in the Church, and in the rule of life both economicall
and politicall be not lookt into and reform'd, we have lookt so
long upon the blaze that *Zuinglius* and *Calvin* hath beacon'd
up to us, that we are stark blind. There be who perpetually
complain of schisms and sects, and make it such a calamity
that any man dissents from their maxims. 'Tis their own pride
and ignorance which causes the disturbing, who neither will
hear with meekness, nor can convince, yet all must be
supprest which is not found in their *Syntagma.* They are
the troublers, they are the dividers of unity, who neglect and
permit not others to unite those dissever'd peeces which are yet
wanting to the body of Truth. To be still searching what we
know not, by what we knew, still closing up truth to truth as we
find it (for all her body is *homogeneal,* and proportionall) this is
the golden rule in *Theology* as well as in Arithmetick, and makes
up the best harmony in a Church ; not the forc't and outward
union of cold, and neutrall, and inwardly divided minds.

Lords and Commons of England, consider what Nation it is
wherof ye are, and wherof ye are the governours : a Nation
not slow and dull, but of a quick, ingenious, and piercing spirit,
acute to invent, suttle and sinewy to discours, not beneath the
reach of any point the highest that human capacity can soar to.
Therefore the studies of learning in her deepest Sciences have
bin so ancient, and so eminent among us, that Writers of good
antiquity, and ablest judgment have bin perswaded that ev'n
the school of *Pythagoras,* and the *Persian* wisdom took begin-
ing from the old Philosophy of this Island. And that wise and
civill Roman, *Julius Agricola,* who govern'd once here for
Cæsar, preferr'd the naturall wits of Britain, before the labour'd
studies of the French. Nor is it for nothing that the grave
and frugal *Transylvanian* sends out yearly from as farre
as the mountanous borders of *Russia,* and beyond the
Hercynian wildernes, not their youth, but their stay'd men,
to learn our language and our *theologic* arts. Yet that
which is above all this, the favour and the love of heav'n
we have great argument to think in a peculiar manner
propitious and propending towards us. Why else was this
Nation chos'n before any other, that out of her as out of
Sion, should be proclaim'd and sounded forth the first tidings
and trumpet of Reformation to all *Europ.* And had it not bin
the obstinat perverseness of our Prelats against the divine
and admirable spirit of *Wicklef,* to suppresse him as a schis-
matic and *innovator,* perhaps neither the *Bohemian Husse*
and *Jerom,* no nor the name of *Luther,* or of *Calvin* had

bin ever known : the glory of reforming all our neighbours had bin compleatly ours. But now, as our obdurate Clergy have with violence demean'd the matter, we are become hitherto the latest and the backwardest Schollers, of whom God offer'd to have made us the teachers. Now once again by all concurrence of signs, and by the generall instinct of holy and devout men, as they daily and solemnly expresse their thoughts, God is decreeing to begin some new and great period in his Church, ev'n to the reforming of Reformation it self : what does he then but reveal Himself to his servants, and as his manner is, first to his English-men ; I say as his manner is, first to us, though we mark not the method of his counsels, and are unworthy. Behold now this vast City ; a City of refuge, the mansion house of liberty, encompast and surrounded with his protection ; the shop of warre hath not there more anvils and hammers waking, to fashion out the plates and instruments of armed Justice in defence of beleagur'd Truth, then there be pens and heads there, sitting by their studious lamps, musing, searching, revolving new notions and idea's wherewith to present, as with their homage and their fealty the approaching Reformation : others as fast reading, trying all things, assenting to the force of reason and convincement. What could a man require more from a Nation so pliant and so prone to seek after knowledge. What wants there to such a towardly and pregnant soile, but wise and faithfull labourers, to make a knowing people, a Nation of Prophets, of Sages, and of Worthies. We reck'n more then five months yet to harvest ; there need not be five weeks, had we but eyes to lift up, the fields are white already. Where there is much desire to learn, there of necessity will be much arguing, much writing, many opinions ; for opinion in good men is but knowledge in the making. Under these fantastic terrors of sect and schism, we wrong the earnest and zealous thirst after knowledge and understanding which God hath stirr'd up in this City. What some lament of, we rather should rejoice at, should rather praise this pious forwardnes among men, to reassume the ill deputed care of their Religion into their own hands again. A little generous prudence, a little forbearance of one another, and som grain of charity might win all these diligencies to joyn, and unite into one generall and brotherly search after Truth ; could we but foregoe this Prelaticall tradition of crowding free consciences and Christian liberties into canons and precepts of men. I doubt not, if some great and worthy stranger should come amongst us, wise to discern the mould and temper of a people, and how to govern it, observing the high hopes and aims, the diligent alacrity of our extended thoughts and reasonings in the pursuance of truth and freedom, but that he would cry out as *Pirrhus* did, admiring the Roman docility and courage, if such were my *Epirots*, I would not despair the greatest design that could be attempted to make a Church or Kingdom happy. Yet these are the men cry'ed out against for schismaticks and sectaries ; as if, while the Temple of the Lord was building, some cutting, some squaring the marble, others hewing the cedars, there should be a sort of irrationall men who could not consider there must be many schisms and many dissections made in the quarry and in the timber, ere the house of God can be built. And when every stone is laid artfully together, it cannot be united into a continuity, it can but be contiguous in this world ; neither can every peece of the building be of one form ; nay rather the perfection consists in this, that out of many moderat varieties and brotherly dissimilitudes that are not vastly disproportionall arises the goodly and the gracefull symmetry that commends the whole pile and structure. Let us therefore be more considerat builders, more wise in spirituall architecture, when great reformation is expected. For now the time seems come, wherein *Moses* the great Prophet may sit in heav'n rejoycing to see that memorable and glorious wish of his fulfill'd, when not only our sev'nty Elders, but all the Lords people are become Prophets. No marvell then though some men, and some good men too perhaps, but young in goodnesse, as *Joshua* then was, envy them. They fret, and out of their own weaknes are in agony, lest these divisions and subdivisions will undoe us. The adversary again applauds, and waits the hour, when they have brancht themselves out, saith he, small anough into parties and partitions, then will be our time. Fool ! he sees not the firm root, out of which we all grow, though into branches : nor will beware, untill hee see our small divided maniples cutting through at every angle of his ill united and unweildy brigade. And that we are to hope better of all these supposed sects and schisms, and that we shall not need that solicitude honest perhaps though over timorous of them that vex in his behalf, but shall laugh in the end, at those malicious applauders of our differences, I have these reasons to perswade me.

First, when a City shall be as it were besieg'd and blockt about, her navigable river infested, inrodes and incursions round, defiance and battell oft rumor'd to be marching up ev'n to her walls, and suburb trenches, that then the people, or the greater part, more then at other times, wholly tak'n up with the study of highest and most important matters to be reform'd, should be disputing, reasoning, reading, inventing, discoursing, even to a rarity, and admiration, things not before discourst or writt'n of, argues first a singular good will, contentednesse, and confidence in your prudent foresight, and safe government, Lords and Commons ; and from thence derives it self to a gallant bravery and well grounded contempt of their enemies, as if there were no small number of as great spirits among us, as his was, who when Rome was nigh besieg'd by *Hanibal*, being in the City, bought that peece of ground at no cheap rate, whereon *Hanibal* himself encampt his own regiment. Next it is a lively and cherfull presage of our happy successe and victory. For as in a body, when the blood is fresh, the spirits pure and vigorous, not only to vital, but to rationall faculties, and those in the acutest, and the pertest operations of wit and suttlety, it argues in what good plight and constitution the body is, so when the cheerfulnesse of the people is so sprightly up, as that it has, not only wherewith to guard well its own freedom and safety, but to spare, and to bestow upon the solidest and sublimest points of controversie, and new invention, it betok'n us not degenerated, nor drooping to a fatall decay, by casting off the old and wrincl'd skin of corruption to outlive these pangs and wax young again, entring the glorious waies of Truth and prosperous vertue destin'd to become great and honourable in these latter ages. Methinks I see in my mind a noble and puissant Nation rousing herself like a strong man after sleep, and shaking her invincible locks : Methinks I see her as an Eagle muing her mighty youth, and kindling her undazl'd eyes at the full midday beam ; purging and unscaling her long abused sight at the fountain it self of heav'nly radiance, while the whole noise of timorous and flocking birds, with those also that love the twilight, flutter about, amaz'd at what she means, and in their envious gabble would prognosticat a year of sects and schisms.

EDWARD HYDE,

EARL OF CLARENDON.

1609–1674.

FALKLAND.

IF the celebrating the memory of eminent and extraordinary persons, and transmitting their great virtues, for the imitation of posterity, be one of the principal ends and duties of history, it will not be thought impertinent, in this place, to remember a loss which no time will suffer to be forgotten, and no success or good fortune could repair. In this unhappy battle (first battle of Newbury, Septr. 20, 1643) was slain the lord viscount Falkland ; a person of such prodigious parts of learning and knowledge, of that inimitable sweetness and delight in conversation, of so flowing and obliging a humanity and goodness to mankind, and of that primitive simplicity and integrity of life, that if there were no other brand upon this odious and accursed civil war, than that single loss, it must be most infamous, and execrable to all posterity.

Turpe mori, post te, solo non posse dolore.

Before this parliament, his condition of life was so happy that it was hardly capable of improvement. Before he came to be twenty years of age, he was master of a noble fortune, which descended to him by the gift of a grandfather, without passing through his father or mother, who were then both alive, and not well enough contented to find themselves passed by in the descent. His education for some years had been in Ireland, when his father was lord deputy ; so that, when he returned in England, to the possession of his fortune, he was unentangled with any acquaintance or friends, which usually grow up by the custom of conversation ; and therefore was to make a pure

election of his company ; which he chose by other rules than
were prescribed to the young nobility of that time. And it
cannot be denied, though he admitted some few to his friendship for the agreeableness of their natures, and their undoubted
affection to him, that his familiarity and friendship, for the most
part was with men of the most eminent and sublime parts, and
of untouched reputation in point of integrity ; and such men
had a title to his bosom.

He was a great cherisher of wit, and fancy, and good parts in
any man ; and, if he found them clouded with poverty or want,
a most liberal and bountiful patron towards them, even above
his fortune ; of which, in those administrations, he was such a
dispenser, as, if he had been trusted with it to such uses, and if
there had been the least of vice in his expense, he might have
been thought too prodigal. He was constant and pertinacious
in whatsoever he resolved to do, and not to be wearied by any
pains that was necessary to that end. And therefore having
once resolved not to see London, which he loved above all
places, till he had perfectly learned the Greek tongue, he went
to his own house in the country, and pursued it with that inde-
fatigable industry, that it will not be believed in how short a
time he was master of it, and accurately read all the Greek
historians.

In this time, his house being within little more than ten
miles of Oxford, he contracted familiarity and friendship with
the most polite and accurate men of that university; who found
such an immenseness of wit, and such a solidity of judgment in
him, so infinite a fancy, bound in by a most logical ratiocina-
tion, such a vast knowledge, that he was not ignorant in
anything, yet such an excessive humility, as if he had known
nothing, that they frequently resorted, and dwelt with him, as
in a college situated in a purer air ; so that his house was a
university in a less volume ; whither they came not so much for
repose as study ; and to examine and refine those grosser
propositions, which laziness and consent made current in vulgar
conversation.

Many attempts were made upon him by the instigation of his
mother (who was a lady of another persuasion in religion, and
of a most masculine understanding, allayed with the passion
and infirmities of her own sex) to prevent him in his piety to
the church of England, and to reconcile him to that of Rome ;
which they prosecuted with the more confidence, because he
declined no opportunity or occasion of conference with those of
that religion, whether priests or laies ; having diligently studied

the controversies, and exactly read all, or the choicest of the
Greek and Latin fathers, and having a memory so stupendous,
that he remembered, on all occasions, whatsoever he read.
And he was so great an enemy to that passion and un-
charitableness, which he saw produced, by difference of
opinion, in matters of religion, that in all those disputations
with priests, and others of the Roman church, he affected to
manifest all possible charity to their persons, and estimation of
their parts ; which made them retain still some hope of his
reduction, even when they had given over offering farther
reasons to him for that purpose. But this charity towards
them was much lessened, and any correspondence with them
quite declined, when, by sinister arts, they had corrupted his
two younger brothers, being both children, and stolen them
from his house, and transported them beyond seas, and perverted his sisters : upon which occasion he writ two large
discourses against the principal positions of that religion, with
that sharpness of style, and full weight of reason, that the
church is deprived of great jewels in the concealment of them,
and that they are not published to the world.

He was superior to all those passions and affections which
attend vulgar minds, and was guilty of no other ambition than
of knowledge, and to be reputed a lover of all good men ; and
that made him too much a contemner of those arts, which must
be indulged in the transactions of human affairs. In the last
short parliament he was a burgess in the house of commons ;
and, from the debates which were then managed with all
imaginable gravity and sobriety, he contracted such a reverence
to parliaments, that he thought it really impossible they could
ever produce mischief or inconvenience to the kingdom ; or
that the kingdom could be tolerably happy in the intermission
of them. And from the unhappy and unseasonable dissolution
of that convention, he harboured, it may be, some jealousy and
prejudice to the court, to which he was not before immoderately
inclined ; his father having wasted a full fortune there, in those
offices and employments by which other men use to obtain a
greater. He was chosen again this parliament to serve in the
same place, and, in the beginning of it, declared himself very
sharply and severely against those exorbitances, which had been
most grievous to the state ; for he was so rigid an observer of
established laws and rules, that he could not endure the least
breach or deviation from them ; and thought no mischief so
intolerable as the presumption of ministers of state to break
positive rules, for reasons of state ; or judges to transgress

known laws, upon the title of conveniency, or necessity ; which made him so severe against the earl of Strafford and the lord Finch, contrary to his natural gentleness and temper : insomuch as they who did not know his composition to be as free from revenge, as it was from pride, thought that the sharpness to the former might proceed from the memory of some unkindnesses, not without a mixture of injustice, from him towards his father. But without doubt he was free from those temptations, and in both cases was only misled by the authority of those, who, he believed, understood the laws perfectly ; of which himself was utterly ignorant ; and if the assumption, which was then scarce controverted, had been true, "that an endeavour to overthrow "the fundamental laws of the kingdom was treason," a strict understanding might make reasonable conclusions to satisfy his own judgment, from the exorbitant parts of their several charges.

. . . . He had a courage of the most clear and keen temper, and so far from fear, that he seemed not without some appetite of danger ; and therefore, upon any occasion of action, he always engaged his person in those troops, which he thought, by the forwardness of the commanders, to be the most like to be farthest engaged ; and in all such encounters he had about him an extraordinary cheerfulness, without at all affecting the execution that usually attended them, in which he took no delight, but took pains to prevent it, when it was not, by resistance, made necessary ; insomuch that at Edge-hill, when the enemy was routed, he was like to have incurred great peril, by interposing to save those who had thrown away their arms, and against whom, it may be, others were more fierce for their having thrown them away : so that a man might think, he came into the field chiefly out of curiosity to see the face of danger, and charity to prevent the shedding of blood. Yet in his natural inclination be acknowledged he was addicted to the profession of a soldier ; and shortly after he came to his fortune, before he was of age, he went into the Low Countries, with a resolution of procuring command, and to give himself up to it, from which he was diverted by the complete inactivity of that summer : so he returned into England, and shortly after entered upon that vehement course of study we mentioned before, till the first alarm from the north ; then again he made ready for the field, and though he received some repulse in the command of a troop of horse, of which he had a promise, he went a volunteer with the earl of Essex.

From the entrance into this unnatural war, his natural

cheerfulness and vivacity grew clouded, and a kind of sadness and dejection of spirit stole upon him, which he had never been used to ; yet being one of those who believed that one battle would end all differences, and that there would be so great a victory on one side, that the other would be compelled to submit to any conditions from the victor, (which supposition and conclusion generally sunk into the minds of most men, and prevented the looking after many advantages, that might then have been laid hold of,) he resisted those indispositions, *et in luctu, bellum inter remedia erat.* But after the king's return from Brentford, and the furious resolution of the two houses not to admit any treaty for peace, those indispositions, which had before touched him, grew into a perfect habit of uncheerfulness ; and he, who had been so exactly easy and affable to all men, that his face and countenance was always present, and vacant to his company, and held any cloudiness, and less pleasantness of the visage, a kind of rudeness or incivility, became, on a sudden, less communicable ; and thence very sad, pale, and exceedingly affected with the spleen. In his clothes and habit, which he had minded before always with more neatness, and industry, and expense, than is usual to so great a soul, he was now not only incurious, but too negligent : and in his reception of suitors, and the necessary or casual addresses to his place, so quick, and sharp, and severe that there wanted not some men, (strangers to his nature and disposition,) who believed him proud and imperious, from which no mortal man was ever more free.

It is true, that as he was of a most incomparable gentleness, and even submission to good, and worthy, and entire men, so he was naturally (which could not but be more evident in his place, which objected him to another conversation and inter-mixture, than his own election would have done) *adversus malos injucundus;* and was so ill a dissembler of his dislike and disinclination to ill men, that it was not possible for such not to discern it. There was once, in the house of commons, such a declared acceptation of the good service an eminent member had done to them, and, as they said to the whole kingdom, that it was moved, he being present, "that the speaker might, in the name of the whole house, give him thanks ; and then, that every member might, as a testimony of his particular acknowledgment, stir or move his hat towards him ;" the which, (though not ordered) when very many did, the lord Falkland, (who believed the service itself not to be of that moment, and that an honourable and generous person could not have stooped to it for any recompense,) instead of moving his hat, stretched both his arms out, and clasped his hands together upon the crown of his hat, and held it close down to his head ; that all men might see, how odious that flattery was to him, and the very approbation of the person, though at that time most popular.

When there was any overture or hope of peace, he would be more erect and vigorous, and exceedingly solicitous to press anything which he thought might promote it ; and sitting among his friends, often, after a deep silence and frequent sighs, would, with a shrill and sad accent, ingeminate the word Peace, Peace ; and would passionately profess " that the very " agony of the war, and the view of the agony and desolation the " kingdom did and must endure, took his sleep from him, and " would shortly break his heart." This made some think, or pretend to think, " that he was so much enamoured on peace, " that he would have been glad the king should have bought it any price ;" which was a most unreasonable calumny. As if a man, that was himself the most punctual and precise in every circumstance that might reflect upon conscience or honour, could have wished the king to have committed a trespass against either. And yet this senseless scandal made some impression upon him, or at least he used it for an excuse of the daringness of his spirit ; for at the leaguer before Gloucester, when his friend passionately reprehended him for exposing his person unnecessarily to danger, (for he delighted to visit the trenches, and nearest approaches, and to discover what the enemy did,) as being so much beside the duty of his place, that it might be understood rather to be against it, he would say merrily, " that his office could not take away the privilege of his " age ; and that a secretary in war might be present at the " greatest secret of danger ;" but withal alleged seriously, " that " it concerned him to be more active in enterprises of hazard, " than other men ; that all might see, that his impatiency for " peace proceeded not from pusillanimity, or fear to adventure " his own person."

In the morning before the battle, as always upon action, he was very cheerful, and put himself into the first rank of the lord Byron's regiment, then advancing upon the enemy, who had lined the hedge on both sides with musketeers ; from whence he was shot with a musket in the lower part of the belly, and in the instant falling from his horse, his body was not found till the next morning ; till when, there was some hope he might have been a prisoner ; though his nearest friends, who knew his

temper, received small comfort from that imagination. Thus
fell that incomparable young man, in the four and thirtieth year
of his age, having so much despatched the true business of life,
that the eldest rarely attained to that immense knowledge, and
the youngest enter not into the world with more innocency:
whosoever leads such a life needs not be the less anxious upon
how short a warning it is taken from him.

History of the rebellion.

JEREMY TAYLOR.

1613–1667.

INTRODUCTION TO A SERMON

Preached in Saint Maries Church in Oxford. Vpon the Anniversary of the Gunpowder-Treason. To the Most Reverend Father in God, William, by Divine providence Lord Archbishop of Canterbury His Grace, Primate of all England, and Metropolitan, Chancellor of the University of Oxford, and one of his Maiesties Most Honourable Privy Councell.

My Most Humble Good Lord !
May it please your Grace,

IT was obedience to my *Superiour* that ingaged me upon this last Anniversary commemoration of the great Goodnesse of God Almighty to our King and Country in the discouery of the most damnable *Powder-Treason.* It was a blessing which no tongue could express, much lesse mine, which had scarce learned to speake, at least, was most unfit to speake in the Schooles of the Prophets. *Delicata autem est illa obedientia quæ causas quærit.* It had beene no good argument of my obedience to have disputed the inconvenience of my person, and the unaptnesse of my parts for such an imployment. I knew God, out of the mouth of Infants, could acquire his praise, and if my heart were actually as *Votive* as my tongue should have beene, it might bee one of Gods *Magnalia* to perfect his owne praise out of the weaknesse and imperfection of the Organ. · So as I was able, I endeavour'd to performe it, having my obedience ever ready for my excuse to men, and my willingnesse to perform my duty, for the assoylment of my selfe before God ; part of which I hope was accepted, and I have no reason to think, that the other was not pardoned.

When I first thought of the Barbarisme of this Treason, I wondred not so much at the thing itselfe as by what meanes it was possible for the Divell to gaine so strong a party in mens resolutions, as to move them to undertake a businesse so abhorring from Christianity, so evidently full of extreame danger to their lives, and so certainly to incurre the highest wrath of God Almighty.   My thoughts were thus rude at first; but after a strict inquisition I found it was apprehended as a businesse (perhaps full of danger to their bodies, but) advantagious to their soules, consonant to the obligation of all Christians, and meritorious of an exceeding weight of Glory, for now it was come to passe, which our dear Master foretold, *Men should kill us, and thinke they did God good service in it.* I could not thinke this to be a part of any mans religion, nor doe I yet believe it.   For it is so apparently destructive of our deare Master his Royal lawes of *Charity & obedience,* that I must not be so uncharitable as to thinke they speak their owne minde truly, when they professe their beliefe of the lawfulnesse and necessity in some cases of rebelling against their lawfull Prince, and using all means to throw him from his kingdome, though it be by taking of his life.   But it is but iust that they who breake the bonds of duty to their Prince, should likewise forfeit the lawes of charity to themselves, and if they say not true, yet to bee more uncharitable to their owne persons, then I durst be, though I had their own warrant.   Briefly (Most R. Father) I found amongst them of the Roman party such prevailing opinions, as could not consist with loyalty to their Prince, in case hee were not the Popes subiect, and these so generally believed, and somewhere obtruded under perill of their soules, that I could not but point at these dangerous rocks, at which I doubt not, but the loyalty of many hath suffered shipwrack, and of thousands more might, if a higher *starre* had not guided them better, then their own Pilots.

I could not therefore but thinke it very likely that this Treason might spring from the same Fountaine; and I had concluded so in my first meditations, but that I was willing to consider, whether or no it might not bee that these men were rather exasperated than perswaded, and whether it were not that the severity of our lawes against them might rather provoke their intemperate zeal, then religion thus move their setled conscience.   It was a materiall consideration, because they ever did and still doe fill the world with outcries against our lawes for making a rape upon their consciences, have printed Catalogues of their English Martyrs, drawn Schemes of most strange tortures imposed on their Priests, such as were unimaginable, by *Nero*, or *Dioclesian*, or any of the worst and cruellest enemies of Christianity, endeavouring thus to make us partly guilty of our own ruine, and so washing their hands in token of their own innocence, even then when they were dipping them in the blood Royall, and would have emptyed the best veynes in the whole kingdome to fill their *Lavatory*. But I found all these to be but Calumnies, strong accusations upon weak presumptions, and that the cause did rest where I had begun, I meane, upon the pretence of the *Catholique cause*, and that the imagin'd iniquity of the Lawes of *England* could not be made a vaile to cover the deformity of their intentions, for our Laws were Just, Honourable, and Religious.

Concerning these and some other appendices to the business of the day ; I expressed some part of my thoughts, which because happily they were but a just truth, and this truth not unseasonable for these last times, in which (as S. Paul prophesyed) *men would be fierce, Traytors, heady, and high-minded, creeping into houses, leading silly women captive*, it pleased some who had power to command me, to wish me to a publicatiõ of these my short and sudden meditations, that (if it were possible) even this way I might express my duty to *God* and the *King*.

ANDREW MARVELL.

1620–1678.

ON ENGLISH SOVEREIGNTY.

THERE has now for divers years a design been carried on to change the lawful Government of England into an absolute Tyranny, and to convert the established Protestant Religion into downright Popery : than both which, nothing can be more destructive or contrary to the interest and happiness, to the constitution and being of the king and kingdom.

For if we first consider the State, the kings of England rule not upon the same terms with those of our neighbour nations, who, having by force or by address usurped that due share which their people had in the government, are now for some ages in the possession of an arbitrary power (which yet no prescription can make legal) and exercise it over their persons and estates in a most tyrannical manner. But here the subjects retain their proportion in the Legislature ; the very meanest commoner of England is represented in Parliament, and is a party to those laws by which the Prince is sworn to govern himself and his people. No money is to be levied but by the common consent. No man is for life, limb, goods, or liberty, at the Soveraign's discretion : but we have the same right (modestly understood) in our propriety that the prince hath in his regality ; and in all cases where the King is concerned, we have our just remedy as against any private person of the neighbourhood, in the Courts of Westminster Hall or in the High Court of Parliament. His very Prerogative is no more than what the Law has determined. His Broad Seal, which is the legitimate stamp of his pleasure, yet is no longer currant, than upon the trial it is found to be legal. He cannot commit any person by his particular warrant. He cannot himself be witness in any cause : the ballance of publick justice being so delicate, that not the hand only but even the

breath of the Prince would turn the scale. Nothing is left to
the King's will, but all is subjected to his authority : by which
means it follows that he can do no wrong, nor can he receive
wrong ; and a King of England keeping to these measures, may
without arrogance, be said to remain the onely intelligent Ruler
over a rational People. In recompense therefore and acknowledgment of so good a Government under his influence, his
person is most sacred and inviolable ; and whatsoever excesses
are committed against so high a trust, nothing of them is
imputed to him, as being free from the necessity or temptation ;
but his ministers only are accountable for all, and must answer
it at their perils. He hath a vast revenue constantly arising
from the hearth of the Householder, the sweat of the Labourer,
the rent of the Farmer, the industry of the Merchant, and consequently out of the estate of the Gentleman : a large competence
to defray the ordinary expense of the Crown, and maintain its
lustre. And if any extraordinary occasion happen, or be but
with any probable decency pretended, the whole Land at whatsoever season of the year does yield him a plentiful harvest. So
forward are his people's affections to give even to superfluity,
that a forainer (or English-man that hath been long abroad)
would think they could neither will nor chuse, but that the
asking of a supply were a meer formality, it is so readily granted.
He is the fountain of all honours, and has moreover the distribution of so many profitable offices of the Household, of the
Revenue, of State, of Law, of Religion, of the Navy, and (since
his present Majestie's time) of the Army, that it seems as if the
Nation could scarce furnish honest men enow to supply all those
imployments. So that the Kings of England are in nothing
inferiour to other Princes, save in being more abridged from
injuring their own subjects : but have as large a field as any of
external felicity, wherein to exercise their own virtue, and so
reward and incourage it in others. In short, there is nothing
that comes near in Government to the Divine Perfection, than
where the Monarch, as with us, enjoys a capacity of doing all
the good imaginable to mankind, under a disability to all that
is evil.

An account of the growth of popery, and
arbitrary government in England, &c.

JOHN BUNYAN.

1628–1688.

VANITY-FAIR.

THEN I saw in my Dream, that when they were got out of the Wilderness, they presently saw a Town before them, and the name of that Town is *Vanity;* and at the Town there is a *Fair* kept, called *Vanity-Fair;* It is kept all the Year long, it beareth the name of *Vanity-Fair,* because the Town where 'tis kept *is lighter then Vanity;* and also, because all that is there sold, or that cometh thither, is Vanity. As is the saying of the wise, *All that cometh is vanity.*

This Fair is no new erected business, but a thing of Ancient standing ; I will shew you the original of it.

Almost five thousand years agone, there were Pilgrims walking to the Cœlestial City, as these two honest persons are ; and *Beelzebub, Apollyon,* and *Legion,* with their Companions, perceiving by the path that the Pilgrims made, that their way to the City lay through *this Town* of *Vanity,* they contrived here to set up a Fair ; a Fair wherein should be sold of *all sorts of Vanity,* and that it should last all the year long. Therefore at *this Fair* are all such Merchandize sold, As Houses, Lands, Trades, Places, Honours, Preferments, Titles, Countreys, Kingdoms, Lusts, Pleasures and Delights of all sorts, as Whores, Bauds, Wives, Husbands, Children, Masters, Servants, Lives, Blood, Bodies, Souls, Silver, Gold, Pearls, precious Stones, and what not.

And moreover, at this Fair there is at all times to be seen Juglings, Cheats, Games, Plays, Fools, Apes, Knaves, and Rogues, and that of all sorts.

Here are to be seen, and that for nothing, Thefts, Murders, Adultries, False-swearers, and that of a blood-red colour.

And as in others fairs of less moment, there are the several

Rows and Streets, under their proper names, where such and such Wares are vended : So here likewise, you have the proper Places, Rows, Streets, (*viz.* Countreys, and Kingdoms,) where the Wares of this Fair are soonest to be found : Here is the *Britain* Row, the *French* Row, the *Italian* Row, the *Spanish* Row, the *German* Row, where several sorts of Vanities are to be sold. But as in other *fairs* some one Commodity is as the chief of all the *fair*, so the Ware of *Rome* and her Merchandize is greatly promoted in *this fair:* Only our *English* Nation, with some others, have taken a dislike thereat.

Now, as I said, the way to the Cælestial City lyes just thorow *this Town*, where this lusty Fair is kept ; and he that will go to the City, and yet not go thorow this Town, *must* needs *go out of the World.* The Prince of Princes himself, when here, went through *this Town* to his own Countrey, and that upon a *Fair-day too:* Yea, and as I think, it was *Beelzebub*, the chief Lord of this *Fair*, that invited him to buy of his *Vanities;* yea, would have made him Lord of the *Fair*, would he but have done him Reverence as he went thorow the *Town*. Yea, because he was such a person of Honour, *Beelzebub* had him from *Street* to *Street*, and shewed him all the Kingdoms of the World in a little time, that he might, if possible, a'ure that Blessed One, to *cheapen* and *buy* some of his *Vanities*. But he had no mind to the Merchandize, and therefore left the *Town*, without laying out so much as one Farthing upon these *Vanities*. This *Fair* therefore is an Ancient thing, of long standing, and a very great *Fair.*

Now these Pilgrims, as I said, must needs go thorow this *fair:* Well, so they did ; but behold, even as they entred into the *fair*, all the people in the *fair* were moved, and the Town it self as it were in a Hubbub about them ; and that for several reasons : For,

First, The Pilgrims were cloathed with such kind of Raiment, as was diverse from the Raiment of any that Traded in that *fair*. The people therefore of the *fair* made a great gazing upon them : Some said they were Fools, some they were Bedlams, and some they are Outlandish-men.

Secondly, And as they wondred at their Apparel, so they did likewise at their Speech, for few could understand what they said ; they naturally spoke the Language of *Canaan*, but they that kept the *fair*, were they men of this World : So that from one end of the *fair* to the other, they seemed *Barbarians* each to the other.

Thirdly, But that which did not a little amuse the Merchandizers, was, that these Pilgrims set very light by all their Wares, they cared not, so much as to look upon them : and if they called upon them to buy, they would put their fingers into their ears, and cry, *Turn away mine eyes from beholding vanity;* and look upwards, signifying their Trade and Traffick was in Heaven.

One chanced mockingly, beholding the carriages of the men, to say unto them, What will ye buy? but they, looking gravely upon them, said, *We buy the Truth.* At that, there was an occasion taken to despise the men the more ; some mocking, some taunting, some speaking reproachfully, and some calling upon others to smite them. At last things came to an hubbub and great stir in the *fair*, in so much that all order was confounded. Now was word presently brought to the *great one* of the *fair*, who quickly came down, and deputed some of his most trusty friends to take these men into examination, about whom the *fair* was almost overturned. So the men were brought to examination ; and they that sat upon them, asked them whence they came, whether they went, and what they did there in such an unusual Garb? The men told them, that they were Pilgrims and Strangers in the World, and that they were going to their own Countrey, which was the Heavenly *Jerusalem;* and they had given none occasion to the men of the Town, nor yet to the Merchandizers, thus to abuse them, and to let them in their Journey. Except it was, for that, when one asked them what they would buy, they said they would *buy the Truth.* But they that were appointed to examine them, did not believe them to be any other than Bedlams and Mad, or else such as came to put all things into a confusion in the *fair*. Therefore they took them and beat them, and besmeared them with dirt, and then put them into the Cage, that they might be made a Spectacle to all the men of the *fair*. There therefore they lay for some time, and were made the objects of any mans sport, or malice, or revenge. The great one of the *fair* laughing still at all that befell them. But the men being patient, and not rendering railing for railing, but contrarywise blessing, and giving good words from bad, and kindness for injuries done : Some men in the *fair* that were more observing, and less prejudiced than the rest, began to check and blame the baser sort for their continual abuses done by them to the men : They therefore in angry manner let fly at them again, counting them as bad as the men in the Cage, and telling them that they seemed confederates, and should be made partakers of their misfortune. The other replied, that for aught they could see, the men were quiet, and

sober, and intended no body any harm ; and that there were
many that Traded in their *fair*, that were more worthy to be
put into the Cage, yea, and Pillory too, then were the men that
they had abused. Thus, after divers words had passed on both
sides, (the men themselves behaving themselves all the while
very wisely and soberly before them) they fell to some blows,
and did harm one to another. Then were these two poor men
brought before their Examiners again, and there charged as
being guilty of the late Hubbub that had been in the *fair*. So
they beat them pitifully, and hanged Irons upon them, and led
them in Chaines, up and down the *fair*, for an example and a
terror to others, lest any should further speak in their behalf, or
joyn themselves unto them. But *Christian* and *Faithful*
behaved themselves yet more wisely, and received the ignominy
and shame that was cast upon them, with so much meekness
and patience, that it won to their side (though but few in comparison of the rest) several of the men in the *fair*. This put
the other party yet into a greater rage, insomuch that they
concluded the death of these two men. Wherefore they
threatened that the Cage nor Irons should serve their turn, but
that they should die, for the abuse they had done, and for
eluding the men of the *fair*.

Then they were remanded to the Cage again until further
order should be taken with them. So they put them in, and
made their feet fast in the Stocks.

The Pilgrim's Progress.

JOHN TILLOTSON.

1630-1694.

SERMON XXX.—THE DUTY AND REASON OF PRAYING FOR GOVERNOURS.

Preach'd on the 29th of May, 1693. 1 Tim. ii., 1, 2.—I exhort therefore, that first of all, supplications, prayers, intercessions, and giving of thanks be made for all men: for Kings, and for all that are in authority; that we may lead a quiet and peaceable life, in all godliness and honesty.

I NEED not tell any here, that *this day* is appointed by authority for an *anniversary solemnity*, in a grateful commemoration of the great mercy of God to these nations, in putting an end to the intestine wars and confusions of many years, in restoring to us our ancient government and laws, in bringing home, as upon *this day*, the rightful heir of these kingdoms, to the crown and throne of his fathers : And tho' the glory of *this day* hath not been a little sullied and obscured by many things which have happen'd since that time, fitter now to be buried in silence and oblivion, than to be mentioned and raked up ; yet it hath pleased God, in scattering those black clouds which not long since hung over us, to restore *this day* to its first lustre and brightness ; so that we may now with great joy look back upon it, as designed by the wise providence of God to make way for the happiness which we now enjoy under *their present majesties*, by whom, under God, we have been deliver'd from that terrible and imminent danger which threatened our *religion* and *laws*, and the very *constitution* itself of our *antient government*. And to this occasion, no kind of argument can be more proper and suitable, than that which the *text* affords to our consideration, in this injunction of *St. Paul* to *Timothy*, to take care that in the public worship of God, *supplications* and *thanksgivings* be put up to God, *for Kings, and all that are in authority.*

. . . . Government is necessary to the welfare of mankind, because it is the great band of human society, the guard of its peace, and the security of every man's person and property; and therefore we are concerned as much as is possible, both to pray for our governours, and to bless God for them; because without them we should be in a most wretched condition. Mankind would be unavoidably miserable without government; humane society would presently disband, and all things would run into confusion. It is a remarkable saying of one of the Jewish masters, *pray for the happiness of the kingdom or government; for if it were not for the fear of that, men would devour one another alive.* And *Josephus* tells us, that *when the Jews were made subject to the Romans* (tho' it was by conquest) *twice a day they offered up sacrifices for the life and safety of the emperor.* And this was very agreeable to what God had commanded that people by his prophet, in a much like case, when the *jews* were conquered by the King of *Babylon*, and carried away captives, *Jer.* 29. 7. *Seek the peace of the city whither I have caused you to be carried away captives, and pray unto the Lord for it; for in the peace thereof shall ye have peace.* And surely the reason is much stronger, why we should pray for our *natural* princes and governours.

. . . . Without government there could be no such thing as property in any thing beyond our own persons; for nothing but laws can make property, and laws are the effect of government and authority: Nay, without government, we have no security of our persons and lives, much less of any thing that belongs to us, and is at present in our possession. Were we not protected by laws (which are the effect of government) we could have no safety, no quiet enjoyment of any thing; but every man must be perpetually upon his guard against all the world, and exposed to continual violence and injuries from those, who are too many, and too strong for him; so that all our quiet and security from fear and danger, from the fraud and oppression of those who are more crafty and powerful than ourselves, from endless confusions and distractions, and from a state of perpetual feud and war with all mankind, is entirely due and owing to civil government.

And this alone is so unspeakable a benefit, that without it, *men*, of all creatures, would be the most miserable; because all that wit and sagacity, all that cunning and contrivance, which mankind hath above the brute creatures, would but enable them to do so much the more mischief to one another, and to devise and find out more powerful and effectual means and instruments to harm and destroy one another.

In short, that we live, and that we live well, in any tolerable condition either of safety or plenty, and that we are able to call any thing our own for one day, or for one hour; that we are not in perpetual terror and apprehension of mortal dangers, and that we are at any time free from the invasion of what we at present possess, by the fraud and force of others, is solely the effect of this great blessing and divine appointment of government, to preserve the peace of humane society, and by wise and wholsome laws, to tie up mens hands from mutual injuries and violence. Upon this all the comfort and all the security of humane laws does depend. From hence it comes to pass (that as the scripture expresseth it) *we may sit down every man under his own vine, and under his own fig-tree, and that there shall be none to make us afraid.* So that if security is necessary to the comfort and happiness of mankind; then goverment is so too: For without this, the societies of men would presently dissolve and fall in pieces, and all things would run into confusion and disorder.

. . . . And now to *apply* this to ourselves, and to the occasion of *this day.* By all that hath been said, we cannot but be convinced what cause we have to bless God for *that happy government* which we live under, *that excellent constitution,* under the gentle influences whereof *we* enjoy more liberty, more plenty, and more security from all manner of injury and oppression, than *any nation* this day on the face of the earth. Therefore with what thankfulness should we *this day* commemorate the happy restoration of this government to us, after the miserable distinctions and confusions of twenty years, by the restoration and return of our banished *sovereign,* in so peaceable, and yet so wonderful a manner, that a remembrance of it, even at this distance, is almost still matter of amazement to us !

Blessed be the Lord God of Israel, who above doth wondrous things.

And with our joyful praises, let us join our most devout and fervent prayers to almighty God, *for the king's and queen's majesties, and for all that are in authority.* And I may truly say, that there was hardly ever greater reason and occasion for it, from both our distractions at home, and our dangers from abroad ; never was there greater need of our earnest supplications and prayers, than at *this* time, when our armies and fleets are in motion, and when God seems already to have given us some earnest of good success ; blessed be his great and glorious name.

We have indeed a great army, and a more powerful fleet, than ever this nation sent forth ; but unless God be on our side, and favour our cause, in vain are all our preparations ; for whenever his providence is pleased to interpose, by strength shall no man prevail. Have we not reason then to cry mightily unto God, when the only strength of the nation is at stake, when our sins and provocations are so many and great, and there lies so heavy a load of guilt upon us ? When the person of his sacred majesty is exposed to so much hazard, not only *in the high places of the field,* but from the *restless attempts* of the malicious and implacable enemies of our peace and religion, *that he would be graciously pleased to go forth with our armies and fleets,* and *not remember our iniquities against us, but save us for his mercies sake ?*

We are too apt to murmur and complain of miscarriages, and the ill management of affairs ; but surely the best thing we can do, and that which best becomes us, is to look forward, and to turn our censures of our governours and their actions, into humble supplications to God in their behalf, and in behalf of the whole nation ; *that he would be pleased to turn us every one from the evil of our ways, that he may return to us, and have mercy on us, that so iniquity may not be our ruin; but that he may rejoice over us to do us good, and may at last think thoughts of peace towards us, thoughts of good and not of evil, to give us an expected end of our troubles.*

Let us then betake ourselves to the proper work of *this day,* hearty *prayers* and *thanksgivings to almighty God, for the king and queen, and for all that are in authority; that as he hath been pleased by a wonderful providence, to rescue us from the imminent dangers we were in, and from all our fears, by the happy advancement of their majesties to the throne of these kingdoms; so he would of his infinite goodness still preserve and continue to us* this light of our eyes, and breath of our nostrils, *princes of that great clemency and goodness, which render them the true representatives of God upon earth, and the most gracious governours of men.*

And let us earnestly beseech him, *that he would confirm and strengthen them in all goodness, and make them wise as angels of God, to discern betwixt good and evil, that they may know how to go in and out before this great people; that he would give them the united affections of their people, and a heart to study and seek their good all the days of their lives.*

And finally, *That he would be pleased to continue so great a blessing to us, and to grant them a long and prosperous reign over us, and that their posterity in this royal family may endure for ever,* and their throne as the days of heaven ; *that under them the people of these nations, we and the generations to come,* may lead quiet and peaceable lives in all goodness and honesty.

Works.

GEORGE SAVILE,

MARQUESS OF HALIFAX.

1630–1695.

THE CHARACTER OF A TRIMMER.

OUR Trimmer is so fully satisfied of the truth of these principles by which he is directed, in reference to the public, that he will neither be hectored and threatened, laughed nor drunk out of them ; and instead of being converted by the arguments of his adversaries to their opinions, he is very much confirmed in his own by them. He professes solemnly, that were it in his power to choose, he would rather have his ambition bounded by the commands of a great and wise master, than let it range with a popular license, though crowned with success ; yet he cannot commit such a sin against the glorious thing called Liberty, nor let his soul stoop so much below itself, as to be content without repining to have his reason wholly subdued, or the privilege of acting like a sensible creature torn from him by the imperious dictates of unlimited authority, in what hand soever it happens to be placed. What is there in this that is so criminal, as to deserve the penalty of that most singular apophthegm, "A Trimmer is worse than a rebel !" What do angry men ail, to rail so against moderation ? Does it not look as if they were going to some very scurvy extreme, that is too strong to be digested by the more considering part of mankind ? These arbitrary methods, besides the injustice of them, are, God be thanked, very unskilful too ; for they fright the birds, by talking so loud, from coming into the nets that are laid for them ; and when men agree to rifle a house, they seldom give warning, or blow a trumpet ; but there are some small statesmen, who are so full charged with their own expectations, that they cannot contain.

And kind Heaven, by sending such a seasonable curse upon their undertakings, has made their ignorance an antidote against their malice. Some of these cannot treat peaceably; yielding will not satisfy them, they will have men by storm. There are others that must have plots to make their service more necessary, and have interest to keep them alive, since they are to live upon them ; and persuade the king to retrench his own greatness, so as to shrink into the head of a party, which is the betraying him into such an unprincely mistake, and to such a wilful diminution of himself, that they are the last enemies he ought to allow himself to forgive. Such men, if they could, would prevail with the sun to shine only upon them and their friends, and to leave all the rest of the world in the dark. This is a very unusual monopoly, and may come within the equity of the law, which makes it treason to imprison the king : When such unfitting bounds are put to his favour, and he confined to the narrow limits of a particular set of men, that would inclose him ; these honest and loyal gentlemen, if they may be allowed to bear witness for themselves, make a king their engine, and degrade him into a property, at the very time that their flattery would make him believe they paid divine worship to him. Besides these, there is a flying squadron on both sides, they are afraid the world should agree ; small dabblers in conjuring, that raise angry apparitions to keep men from being reconciled, like wasps that fly up and down, buz and sting men to keep them unquiet ; but these insects are commonly short-lived creatures, and no doubt in a little time mankind will be rid of them. They were giants at least who fought once against heaven, but for such pigmies as these to contend against it, is such a provoking folly, that the insolent bunglers ought to be laughed and hissed out of the world for it. They should consider, there is a soul in that great body the people, which may for a time be drowsy and unactive, but when the leviathan is roused, it moves like an angry creature, and will neither be convinced nor resisted. The people can never agree to show their united powers, till they are extremely tempted and provoked to it ; so that to apply cupping-glasses to a great beast naturally disposed to sleep, and to force the tame thing, whether it will or no, to be valiant, must be learned out of some other book than Machiavil, who would never have prescribed such a preposterous method. It is to be remembered, that if princes have law and authority on their sides, the people on theirs may have Nature, which is a formidable adversary. Duty, Justice, Religion, nay, even human prudence too, bids the people suffer anything rather than resist ; but uncorrected Nature, where'er it feels the smart, will run to the nearest remedy. Men's passions, in this case, are to be considered as well as their duty, let it be never so strongly enforced ; for if their passions are provoked, they being as much a part of us as our limbs, they lead men into a short way of arguing, that admits no distinction ; and from the foundation of self-defence, they will draw inferences that will have miserable effects upon the quiet of a government.

Our Trimmer therefore dreads a general discontent, because he thinks it differs from a rebellion, only as a spotted fever does from the plague, the same species under a lower degree of malignity ; it works several ways, sometimes like a slow poison that has its effects at a great distance from the time it was given ; sometimes like dry flag prepared to catch at the first fire, or like seed in the ground ready to sprout up on the first shower : In every shape 'tis fatal, and our Trimmer thinks no pains or precaution can be so great as to prevent it.

In short, he thinks himself in the right, grounding his opinion upon that truth, which equally hates to be under the oppressions of wrangling sophistry on the one hand, or the short dictates of mistaken authority on the other.

Our Trimmer adores the goddess Truth, though in all ages she has been scurvily used, as well as those that worshipped her : 'Tis of late become such a ruining virtue, that Mankind seems to be agreed to commend and avoid it ; yet the want of practice, which repeals the other laws, has no influence upon the law of truth, because it has root in Heaven, and an intrinsic value in itself, that can never be impaired : She shows her greatness in this, that her enemies, even when they are successful, are ashamed to own it. Nothing but power full of truth has the prerogative of triumphing, not only after victories, but in spite of them, and to put conquest herself out of countenance. She may be kept under and suppressed, but her dignity still remains with her, even when she is in chains. Falsehood with all her impudence, has not enough to speak ill of her before her face : such majesty she carries about her, that her most prosperous enemies are fain to whisper their treason ; all the power upon the earth can never extinguish her : she has lived in all ages ; and let the mistaken zeal of prevailing authority christen any opposition to it with what name they please, she makes it not only an ugly and unmannerly, but a dangerous thing to persist : She has lived very retired indeed, nay, sometimes so buried, that only some few of the discerning part of Mankind could have a glimpse of her ; with all that, she has eternity in her, she knows not how to die, and from the darkest clouds that shade and cover her, she breaks from time to time with triumph for her friends, and terror to her enemies.

Our Trimmer therefore, inspired by this divine virtue, thinks fit to conclude with these assertions, that our climate is a Trimmer, between that part of the world where men are roasted, and the other where they are frozen : That our church is a Trimmer, between the frenzy of platonic visions, and the lethargic ignorance of popish dreams : That our laws are Trimmers, between the excess of unbounded power, and the extravagance of liberty not enough restrained : That true virtue hath ever been thought a Trimmer, and to have its dwelling in the middle between the two extremes : That even God Almighty himself is divided between his two great attributes, his Mercy and his Justice.

In such company, our Trimmer is not ashamed of his name, and willingly leaves to the bold champions of either extreme, the honour of contending with no less adversaries than Nature, Religion, Liberty, Prudence, Humanity, and Common Sense.

Works.

JOHN DRYDEN.

1631–1700.

POSTSCRIPT TO "REMARKS ON SETTLE'S *'EMPRESS OF MOROCCO.'*"

SOME who are pleased with the bare sound of verse, or the rumbling of robustious nonsense, will be apt to think Mr. Settle too severely handled in this pamphlet; but I do assure the reader, that there are a vast number of errours passed by, perhaps as many or more than are taken notice of, both to avoid the tediousness of the work and the greatness. It might have occasioned a volume upon such a trifle. I dare affirm that no objections in this book are fruitless cavils : but if through too much haste Mr. Settle may be accused of any seeming fault, which may reasonably be defended, let the passing by many gross errours without reprehension compound for it. I am not ignorant that his admirers, who most commonly are women, will resent this very ill ; and some little friends of his, who are smatterers in poetry, will be ready for most of his gross errours to use that much mistaken plea of *poetica licentia*, which words fools are apt to use for the palliating the most absurd nonsense in any poem. I cannot find when poets had liberty from any authority to write nonsense, more than any other men. Nor is that plea of *poetica licentia* used as a subterfuge by any but weak professors of that art, who are commonly given over to a mist of fancy, a buzzing of invention, and a sound of something like sense, and have no use of judgment. They never think thoroughly, but the best of their thoughts are like those we have in dreams, imperfect ; which, though perhaps we are often pleased with, sleeping, we blush at, waking. The licentious wildness and extravagance of such men's conceits have made poetry contemned by some, though it be very unjust for any to condemn the science for the weakness of some of the professors.

Men that are given over to fancy only, are little better than madmen. What people say of fire, viz. that it is a good servant, but an ill master, may not unaptly be applied to fancy ; which, when it is too active, rages, but when cooled and allayed by the judgment, produces admirable effects.　But this rage of fancy is never Mr. Settle's crime ; he has too much phlegm, and too little choler, to be accused of this.　He has all the pangs and throes of a fanciful poet, but is never delivered of any more perfect issue of his phlegmatick brain, than a dull Dutch-woman's sooterkin is of her body.

His style is very muddy, and yet much laboured ; for his meaning (for sense there is not much,) is most commonly obscure, but never by reason of too much height, but lowness. His fancy never flies out of sight, but often sinks out of sight : —but now I hope the reader will excuse some digression upon the extravagant use of fancy and poetical licence.

Fanciful poetry and musick, used with moderation, are good ; but men who are wholly given over to either of them, are commonly as full of whimsies as diseased and splenetick men can be.　Their heads are continually hot, and they have the same elevation of fancy sober, which men of sense have when they drink.　So wine used moderately does not take away the judgment, but used continually, debauches men's under-standings, and turns them into sots, making their heads continually hot by accident, as the others are by nature ; so mere poets and mere musicians are as sottish as mere drunkards are, who live in a continual mist, without seeing or judging any thing clearly.

A man should be learned in several sciences, and should have a reasonable, philosophical, and in some measure a mathe-matical head, to be a complete and excellent poet ; and besides this, should have experience in all sorts of humours and manners of men ; should be thoroughly skilled in conversation, and should have a great knowledge of mankind in general. Mr. Settle having never studied any sort of learning but poetry, and that but slenderly, as you may find by his writings, and having besides no other advantages, must make very lame work on't ; he himself declares he neither reads, nor cares for conver-sation, so that he would persuade us he is a kind of fanatick in poetry, and has a light within him, and writes by an inspiration ; which (like that of the heathen prophets) a man must have no sense of his own when he receives ; and no doubt he would be thought inspired, and would be reverenced extremely in the country where Santons are worshipped.　But some will I doubt not object, that poetry should not be reduced to the strictness of mathematicks ; to which I answer, it ought to be so far mathematical as to have likeness and proportion, since they will all confess that it is a kind of painting.　But they will perhaps say, that a poem is a picture to be seen at a distance, and therefore ought to be bigger than the life. I confess there must be a due distance allowed for the seeing of any thing in the world; for an object can no more be seen at all too near, than too far off the eye : but granting that a poem is a picture to be viewed at a great distance, the distance and the bigness ought to be so suited, as though the picture be much bigger than the life, yet it must not seem so ; and what miserable mistakes some poets make for want of knowing this truly, I leave to men of sense to judge ; and by the way, let us consider that dramatick poetry, especially the English, brings the picture nearer the eye, than any other sort of poetry.

But some will say after this, what licence is left for poets? Certainly the same that good poets ever took, without being faulty, (for surely the best were so sometimes, because they were but men,) and that licence is fiction ; which kind of poetry is like that of landscape-painting ; and poems of this nature, though they be not *vera*, ought to be *verisimilia*.

The great art of poets is either the adorning and beautifying of truth, or the inventing pleasing and probable fictions. If they invent impossible fables, like some of Æsop's, they ought to have such morals couched under them, as may tend to the instruction of mankind or the regulation of manners, or they can be of no use ; nor can they really delight any but such as would be pleased with Tom Thumb, without these circumstances. But there are some pedants, who will quote authority from the ancients for the faults and extravagancies of some of the moderns ; who being able to imitate nothing but the faults of the classick authors, mistake them for their excellencies. I speak with all due reverence to the ancients, for no man esteems their perfections more than myself, though I confess I have not that blind implicit faith in them which some ignorant schoolmasters would impose upon us, to believe in all their errours, and own all their crimes : to some pedants every thing in them is of that authority, that they will create a new figure of rhetorick out of the fault of an old poet. I am apt to believe the same faults were found in them, when they wrote, which men of sense find now ; but not the excellencies which schoolmasters would persuade us : yet I must say now,

Nobis non licet esse tam disertis,
*Musas qui colimus severiores.**

* Martial. Epigr. ix. 12.

Prose Works.

ROBERT SOUTH.

1633–1716

OF THE FATAL IMPOSTURE AND FORCE OF WORDS.

THE generality of Mankind is wholly and absolutely governed by *Words* and Names : *Without;* nay, for the most part, even *against* the knowledge Men have of things.   The Multitude, or Common Rout, like a Drove of Sheep, or an Herd of Oxen, may be managed by any Noise, or Cry, which their Drivers shall accustom them to.

And, he who will set up for a skillfull manager of the Rabble, so long *as they have but Ears to hear*, needs never enquire, whether they have any *understanding* whereby to judge ; but with two or three popular, empty Words, such as *Popery and Superstition, Right of the Subject, Liberty of Conscience, Lord Jesus Christ* well tuned and humour'd ; may whistle them backwards and forwards, upwards and downwards, till he is weary ; and get up upon their Backs when he is so.

As for the *meaning* of the Word it self, that may shift for it self; And, as for *the Sense and Reason of it*, that has little or nothing to doe here ; only let it sound full and round, and chime right to the Humour, which is at present a Gog, (just as a big, long, rattling Name is said to command even Adoration from a *Spaniard,*) and, no doubt, with this powerfull, senseless Engine the *Rabble-driver*, shall be able to carry all before him, or to draw all after him, as he pleases.   For, a plausible, insignificant Word, in the mouth of an expert Demagogue, is a dangerous and a dreadfull Weapon.

You know, when *Cæsar's* Army mutinied, and grew troublesome, no Argument from Interest, or Reason, could satisfie or appease them : But, as soon as he gave them the Appellation of *Quirites*, the Tumult was immediately hush'd ; and all were quiet and content, and took that *one Word* in good payment for all.   Such is the trivial slightness and levity of most minds. And indeed, take any Passion of the Soul of Man, while it is predominant, and a float, and, just in the critical height of it, nick it with some *lucky*, or *unlucky* Word, and you may as certainly over-rule into your own purpose, as a spark of Fire, falling upon Gun-powder, will infallibly blow it up.

The Truth is, he who shall duly consider these matters, will find that there is a certain *bewitchery*, or fascination in Words, which makes them operate with a force beyond what we can naturally give an account of.   For, would not a man think, ill Deeds, and shrewd Turns, should reach further, and strike deeper than ill Words?   And yet many Instances might be given, in which Men have much more easily pardoned ill things *done*, than ill Things *said* against them :   Such a peculiar rancour and venom doe they leave behind them in men's Minds, and so much more poysonously and incurably does the Serpent bite with his *Tongue*, than with his *Teeth*.

Nor are Men prevailed upon at this odd, unaccountable rate, by bare Words, only through a *defect* of Knowledge ; but sometimes also doe they suffer themselves to be carried away with these *Puffs of Wind*, even *contrary* to Knowledge and Experience itself.   For otherwise, how could Men be brought to surrender up their reason, their Interest, and their Credit to Flattery?   Gross, fulsome, abusive Flattery ; indeed more abusive and reproachfull upon a true estimate of Things and Persons, than the rudest Scoffs, and the sharpest Invectives. Yet so it is, that though Men know themselves utterly void of those Qualities and Perfections, which the impudent Sycophant, at the same time, both ascribes to them, and in his Sleeve laughs at them for believing ; nay, though *they know* that the Flatterer himself knows the falsehood of his own Flatteries, yet they swallow the fallacious Morsel, love the Impostor, and with both arms Hug the Abuse ; And that to such a degree, that no Offices of Friendship, no real Services shall be able to lie in the Balance against those luscious Falsehoods, which Flattery shall feed the Mind of a *Fool in Power* with ; The *sweetness* of the one infinitely over-comes the *substance* of the other.

And therefore, you shall seldom see, that such an one cares to have Men of Worth, Honesty, and Veracity about him ; For, such persons cannot fall down and worship Stocks and Stones, though they are placed never so high above them.   But their *Yea* is *Yea*, and their *Nay, Nay;* and, they cannot admire a *Fox* for his sincerity, a *Wolf* for his Generosity, nor an *Ass* for his Wit and Ingenuity ; And therefore can never be acceptable to those whose whole Credit, Interest, and Advantage lies in their not appearing to the World, what they are really in themselves.   None are, or can be welcome to such, but those who Speak *Paint* and *Wash;* for that is the thing they *love;* and, no wonder, since it is the Thing they *need.*

There is hardly any Rank, Order or Degree of Men, but more or less have been captivated, and enslaved by Words.   It is a Weakness, or rather a Fate, which attends both high and low.   The Statesman, who holds the Helm, as well as the Peasant who holds the Plough.   So that if ever you find an *Ignoramus* in Place or Power, and can have so little Conscience, and so much Confidence, as to tell him to his face, that he has a Wit and understanding above all the World beside ; and *That what his own Reason cannot suggest to him, neither can the United Reasons of all Mankind put together;* I dare undertake, that, as fulsome a Dose as you give him, he shall readily take it down, and admit the Commendation, though he cannot believe the Thing : *Blanditiæ etiam cùm excluduntur placent;* says *Seneca.*   Tell him, that no History or Antiquity can match his Policies and his Conduct ; and presently the Sot (because he knows neither History, nor Antiquity) shall begin to *measure himself by himself,* (which is the only sure way for him not to fall short ;) and so immediately amongst his *outward Admirers, and his inward Despisers,* Vouched also by a *Teste Me-ipso,* he steps forth an exact Politician ; and, by a wonderfull, and new way of Arguing, proves himself *no fool,* because, forsooth, the Sycophant, who tells him so, is an Egregious *Knave.*

But to give you a yet grosser Instance of the force of Words, and of the extreme Variety of man's Nature in being influenced by them, hardly shall you meet with any person, Man or Woman, so aged, or ill-favoured, but if you will venture to commend them for their Comeliness ; nay, and for their Youth too ; though *Time out of mind* is wrote upon every line of their face ; yet they shall take it very well at your hands, and begin to think with themselves, that certainly they have some Perfections, which the generality of the World are not so happy as to be aware of.

But now, are not these (think we) strange Self-delusions, and yet attested by common Experience, almost every day?   But whence, in the mean time, can all this proceed, but from that besotting Intoxication, which this *Verbal* Magick (as I may so call it) brings upon the Mind of Man?   For, can any thing in Nature have a more certain, deep, and undeniable Effect, than

Folly has upon man's Mind, and Age upon his Body? And yet we see, that in both these, Words are able to perswade men out of what they *find* and *feel*, to reverse the very Impressions of Sense, and to amuse men with Fancies and Paradoxes even in spight of Nature, and Experience. But, since it would be endless to pursue all the Particulars in which this Humour shews it self; whosoever would have one full, lively and complete view of an empty, shallow, self-opinion'd Grandee, surrounded by his Flatterers, (like a choice Dish of Meat by a company of fellows *commending*, and *devouring* it at the same time,) let him cast his Eye upon *Ahab* in the midst of his false Prophets, 1. *Kings* 22. Where we have them all with one Voice for giving him a cast of their Court-Prophecy, and sending him, in a Compliment, to be Knockt on the Head at *Ramoth Gilead.* But, says *Jehosaphat*, (who smelt the *Parasite* through the *Prophet*) in the 7th. *verse. Is there not a Prophet of the Lord besides, that we may enquire of him? Why yes, says Ahab, there is yet one man by whom we may enquire of the Lord; but I hate him, for he doth not prophesy Good concerning me, but Evil.* Ah! that was his crime; the poor man was so *good* a *Subject*, and so *bad* a *Courtier*, as to venture to serve, and save his Prince, whether he would or no; for, it seems, to give *Ahab* such warning, as might infallibly have prevented his Destruction, was esteemed by him *Evil*, and to push him on head-long into it, because he was fond of it, was accounted *Good*. These were his new measures of *Good* and *Evil*. And therefore, those who knew how to *make their Court* better, (as the Word is) tell him a bold Lye in God's Name, and therewith sent him packing to his certain doom; thus calling *Evil good* at the cost of their Prince's Crown, and his Life too. But what cared they? they knew that it would please, and that was enough for them; there being always a sort of Men in the World, (whom others have an Interest to serve by,) who had rather a great deal be *pleased*, than be *safe*. *Strike* them under the *fifth Rib;* provided at the same time you *kiss* them too, as *Joab* served *Abner*, and you may both destroy and oblige them with the same blow.

Accordingly in the 30th. of *Isaiah*, we find some arrived to that pitch of Sottishness, and so much in love with their own Ruin, as to own plainly and roundly what they would be at; in the 10th verse; *Prophesie not unto us, say they, right things, but prophesie to us smooth things.* As if they had said, Doe but oil the Razor for us, and let us alone to cut our own Throats. Such an Enchantment is there in Words; and so fine a thing does it seem to some, to be ruined plausibly, and to be ushered to their destruction with Panegyrick and Acclamation ; A shamefull, though irrefragable Argument of the absurd Empire and Usurpation of Words over Things ; and, that the greatest Affairs, and most important Interests of the World, are carried on by Things, not as they *are*, but as they are *called.*

A Sermon preached on May the 9th, 1686.

ON PLAINNESS OF SPEECH.

A SECOND property of the ability of speech, conferred by Christ upon his apostles, was its unaffected plainness and simplicity : it was to be easy, obvious and familiar ; with nothing in it strained or far-fetched : no affected scheme, or airy fancies, above the reach or relish of an ordinary apprehension ; no, nothing of all this ; but their grand subject was truth, and consequently above all these petit arts, and poor additions ; as not being capable of any greater lustre or advantage, than to appear just as it is. For there is a certain majesty in plainness ; as the proclamation of a prince never frisks it in tropes or fine conceits, in numerous and well turned periods, but commands in sober, natural expressions. A substantial beauty, as it comes out of the hands of nature, needs neither paint nor patch ; things never made to adorn, but to cover something that would be hid. It is with expression, and the clothing of a man's conceptions, as with the clothing of a man's body. All dress and ornament supposes imperfection, as designed only to supply the body with something from without, which it wanted, but had not of its own. Gaudery is a pitiful and mean thing, not extending farther than the surface of the body ; nor is the highest gallantry considerable to any, but to those, who would hardly be considered without it : for in that case indeed there may be great need of an outside, when there is little or nothing within.

And thus also it is with the most necessary and important truths ; to adorn and clothe them is to cover them, and that to obscure them. The eternal salvation and damnation of souls are not things to be treated of with jests and witticisms. And he who thinks to furnish himself out of plays and romances with language for the pulpit, shews himself much fitter to act a part in the revels, than for a cure of souls.

"I speak the words of soberness," said Saint Paul, (Acts, xxvi.

25 ;) and I preach the gospel not with the "enticing words of man's wisdom," (1 Cor. ii. 4.) This was the way of the apostles' discoursing of things sacred. Nothing here "of the fringes of the north star;" nothing of "nature's becoming unnatural;" nothing of the "down of angels' wings," or "the beautiful locks of cherubims:" no starched similitudes introduced with a "Thus have I seen a cloud rolling in its airy mansion," and the like. No, these were sublimities above the rise of the apostolic spirit. For the apostles, poor mortals, were content to take lower steps, and to tell the world in plain terms, "that he who believed should be saved, and that he who believed not should be damned." And this was the dialect which pierced the conscience, and made the hearers cry out, "Men and brethren, what shall we do?" It tickled not the ear, but sunk into the heart : and when men came from such sermons, they never commended the preacher for his taking voice or gesture ; for the fineness of such a simile, or the quaintness of such a sentence ; but they spoke like men conquered with the overpowering force and evidence of the most concerning truths ; much in the words of the two disciples going to Emmaus ; "Did not our hearts burn within us, while he opened to us the Scriptures ?"

In a word, the apostles' preaching was therefore mighty, and successful, because plain, natural, and familiar, and by no means above the capacity of their hearers ; nothing being more preposterous, than for those who were professedly aiming at men's hearts to miss the mark, by shooting over their heads.

A Sermon preached on the 30th of April, 1668.

DANIEL DEFOE.

1661–1731.

A SEASONABLE *WARNING* AND *CAUTION*

Against *The Insinuations* of Papists and *Jacobites* in Favour of the *Pretender.*

Why how now *England!* what ail'st thee now ? What Evil Spirit now possesseth thee ! O thou Nation famous for espousing Religion, and defending Liberty ; Eminent in all Ages for pulling down Tyrants, and adhering steddily to the Fundamentals of thy own Constitution. That has not only secur'd thy own Rights, and Handed them down Unimpair'd to every succeeding Age, but has been the Sanctuary of other Oppress'd Nations ; the strong Protector of Injur'd Subjects against the Lawless Invasion of Oppressing Tyrants.

To Thee the Oppressed Protestants of *France* ow'd, for some Ages ago, the Comfort of being powerfully Supported, while their own King, wheedl'd by the Lustre of a Crown, became Apostate, and laid the Foundation of their Ruin among themselves ; In Thee their Posterity find a Refuge, and flourish in thy Wealth and Trade, when Religion and Liberty find no more Place in their own Country.

To Thee the distressed *Belgii* owe the powerful Assistance by which they took up Arms, in Defence of Liberty and Religion, against *Spanish* Cruelty, the Perfidious Tyranny of their Kings, and the Rage of the Bloody Duke *D'Alva.*

From Thee the Confederate *Hollanders* receiv'd Encouragement to join in that Indissoluble Union which has since reduc'd the Invincible Power of the *Spaniards*, and from whence has been rais'd the most Flourishing Commonwealth in the World.

By thy assistance they are become the Bulwark of the

Protestant Religion, and of the Liberties of *Europe* ; and have many Times since gratefully employ'd that Force in thy Behalf ; and by their Help, Thou, who first gav'st them Liberty, hast more than Once rescu'd and preserv'd thy Own.

To Thee the present Protestant Nations of *Europe* owe, their being at this Day freed from the just Apprehensions of the growing Greatness of *France* ; and to thy Power, when acted by the Glorious Protector of thy Liberty, King *William*, is the whole Christian World indebted, for depriving the *French* Tyrant of the Hopes and Prospects of Universal Monarchy.

To thy Blood, thy Treasure, the Conduct of thy Generals, and the Vigour of thy Councils ; are due, the Glory, the Fame, the Praises, and the Advantages of Twenty Years War, for the establishing and restoring the Liberty and Religion of *Europe*.

When Posterity shall enquire into the Particulars of this Long and Bloody War ; the Battles, Sieges and stupendous Marches of Armies, which, as well with Loss as with Victory, have been the Subject of thy History ; it will for Ever be frequent in their Mouths ; *HERE* the *British* Troops fighting with dreadful Fury and their usual Constancy, shed their Blood in Defence of the Protestant Cause, and left a Bloody Victory to God's Enemies and their own ; as at *Steenkirk*, *Landen*, *Camaret*, *Almanza*, *Brihenga*, and the like ; Or, *HERE* the *British* Troops, with their usual Valour, carried all before them, and Conquer'd in Behalf of the Protestant Interest, and *Europe's* Liberties ; as at *Blenheim*, *Ramilies*, *Barcelona*, *Oudenard*, *Sarragossa*, *Blaregnies*, &c. Here the *British* Navies Triumph'd over *French* Greatness ; as at *Cherburgh*, *La Hogue*, *Gibraltar*, &c. There their Land-Forces reduc'd the most Impregnable Fortresses ; as at *Namure*, *Lisle*, *Menin*, *Tournay*, &c.

And wherefore has all this *English* and *British* blood been spilt ? Wherefore thy Nation *Exhausted;* Thy Trade *Sunk* and *Interrupted;* Thy Veins *Open'd ?* Why hast Thou struggled thus long, and with so much Vigour, as well with *French* Tyranny Abroad, as Popish Factions at Home, but to preserve Entire the Religion and Liberties of *Europe*, and particularly of this Nation, and to preserve our Posterity from Slavery and Idolatry ? Principles truly Noble, worthy a Nation's Blood to protect, and worthy a Nation's treasure to save.

But what has all this been for ? And to what Intent and Purpose was all this Zeal, if you will Sink under the Ruin of the very Fabrick ye have pull'd down ? If ye will give up the Cause after ye have gain'd the Advantage, and yield your selves up after you have been Delivered ; to what Purpose then has all this been done ? Why all the Money expended ? Why all this Blood spilt ? To what End is *France* said to be reduc'd, and Peace now concluded, if *the same* Popery, *the same* Tyranny, *the same* Arbitrary Methods of Government shall be received among you again ? Sure your Posterity will stand amazed to consider how Lavish this Age has been of their Money, and their Blood, and to how little Purpose ; since no Age since the Creation of the World can show us a Time when ever any Nation spent so much Blood and Treasure *to End* just where *they Begun :* As, if the Arts of our Enemies prevail, we are like to do.

Let us reason a little together on these Things, and let us inquire a little, *Why*, and *for what Reason* Britain, so lately the Glory of *Europe ;* so lately the Terror of *France*, the Bullwark of Religion, and the Destroyer of Popery, should be brought to be the Gazing-stock of the World ? And why is it that her Neighbours expect every Hour to hear that She is going back to *Egypt*, and having given up her Liberty, has made it her own Choice to submit to the Stripes of her *Taskmasters*, and make Bricks without Straw.

We that are *Englishmen*, and live from Home among the Protestants of other Nations, cannot but be sensible of this Alteration, and we bear the Reproaches of those who speak freely of the Unhappy Change which appears in the Temper of our Countrymen at Home. It is astonishing to all the World to hear that the Common People of *England* should be turn'd from the most Riveted Aversions, to a Coldness and Indifferency in Matters of Popery and the Pretender : That they, who with so unanimous a Resolution deposed the late King *James*, as well for his Invasions of their Liberty as of their Religion ; and who with such Marks of Contempt drove him and his pretended Progeny out of the Nation, should, without any visible Alteration of Circumstances, be Drawn-in to favour the Return of that Race with all the certain Additions of *Popish Principles* in *Religion ; French Principles* in Government ; *Revenge* for Family Injuries : *Restoration* of Abdicated and Impoverish'd Votaries ; aud the certain *Support* of a Party at Home, whose Fortunes and Losses must be Restor'd and Repair'd out of the Ruins of their Country's Liberties.

To what Purpose was the Revolution ? Why did you mock your selves at so vast an Expence ? Why did you cry in your Oppressions to God and the Prince of *Orange* to deliver you ? Why did you rise as one Man against King *James* and his Popish Adherents ? Why was your Fury so great, and your

Opposition so Universal, that altho' he had a good Army of Veteran, Disciplin'd Troops, and a powerful Assistance from *France* ready to fall in and joyn him, yet durst not, when got all together, venture to look you in the Face, but fled *like* Darkness before the Sun, *like* Guilt before the Sword of Justice; or *as* a Murtherer from the Avenger of Blood? *Was it all* that you might the better weaken your selves by Ages of War, and *They might Return again*, and bind you like *Samson*, when your Strength was departed.

JONATHAN SWIFT.

1667–1745.

LORD PETER.

I HAVE now, with much pains and study, conducted the reader to a period where he must expect to hear of great revolutions. For no sooner had our learned brother, so often mentioned, got a warm house of his own over his head than he began to look big and to take mightily upon him ; insomuch that, unless the gentle reader, out of his great candour, will please a little to exalt his idea, I am afraid he will henceforth hardly know the hero of the play when he happens to meet him ; his part, his dress, and his mien being so much altered.

He told his brothers he would have them to know that he was their elder, and consequently his father's sole heir ; nay, a while after, he would not allow them to call him brother, but *Mr.* PETER, and then he must be styled *Father* PETER ; and sometimes, *My Lord* PETER. To support this grandeur, which he soon began to consider could not be maintained without a better *fonde* than what he was born to, after much thought, he cast about at last to turn projector and virtuoso, wherein he so well succeeded, that many famous discoveries, projects, and machines, which bear great vogue and practice at present in the world, are owing entirely to lord PETER'S invention. I will deduce the best account I have been able to collect of the chief among them, without considering much the order they came out in ; because I think authors are not well agreed as to that point.

I hope, when this treatise of mine shall be translated into foreign languages (as I may without vanity affirm that the labour of collecting, the faithfulness in recounting, and the great usefulness of the matter to the public, will amply deserve that justice), that the worthy members of the several academies abroad, especially those of France and Italy, will favourably accept these humble offers for the advancement of universal knowledge. I do also advertise the most reverend fathers, the Eastern missionaries, that I have, purely for their sakes, made use of such words and phrases as will best admit an easy turn into any of the oriental languages, especially the Chinese. And so I proceed with great content of mind, upon reflecting how much emolument this whole globe of the earth is likely to reap by my labours.

The first undertaking of lord Peter was, to purchase a large continent, lately said to have been discovered in *terra australis incognita.* This tract of land he bought at a very great penny-worth from the discoverers themselves (though some pretended to doubt whether they had ever been there), and then retailed it into several cantons to certain dealers, who carried over colonies, but were all shipwrecked in the voyage. Upon which lord Peter sold the said continent to other customers again, and again, and again, and again, with the same success.

The second project I shall mention was his sovereign remedy for the worms, especially those in the spleen. The patient was to eat nothing after supper for three nights : as soon as he went to bed he was carefully to lie on one side, and when he grew weary to turn upon the other ; he must also duly confine his two eyes to the same object ; and by no means break wind at both ends together without manifest occasion. These prescriptions diligently observed, the worms would void insensibly by perspiration, ascending through the brain.

A third invention was the erecting of a whispering-office for the public good and ease of all such as are hypochondriacal or troubled with the colic ; as likewise of all eavesdroppers, physicians, midwives, small politicians, friends fallen out, repeating poets, lovers happy or in despair, bawds, privy-counsellors, pages, parasites, and buffoons ; in short, of all such as are in danger of bursting with too much wind. An ass's head was placed so conveniently that the party affected might conveniently with his mouth accost either of the animal's ears ; to which he was to apply close for a certain space, and by a fugitive faculty, peculiar to the ears of that animal, receive immediate benefit, either by eructation, or expiration, or evomitation.

Another very beneficial project of lord Peter's was, an office of insurance for tobacco-pipes, martyrs of the modern zeal, volumes of poetry, shadows, ———, and rivers ; that these, nor any of these, shall receive damage by fire. Whence our friendly

societies may plainly find themselves to be only transcribers
from this original; though the one and the other have been of
great benefit to the undertakers, as well as of equal to the
public.

Lord PETER was also held the original author of puppets
and raree-shows; the great usefulness whereof being so
generally known, I shall not enlarge farther upon this
particular.

But another discovery, for which he was much renowned, was
his famous universal pickle. For, having remarked how your
common pickle in use among housewives was of no farther
benefit than to preserve dead flesh and certain kinds of
vegetables, Peter, with great cost as well as art, had contrived a
pickle proper for houses, gardens, towns, men, women, children,
and cattle; wherein he could preserve them as sound as insects
in amber. Now, this pickle, to the taste, the smell, and the
sight, appeared exactly the same with what is in common
service for beef, and butter, and herrings, and has been often
that way applied with great success; but, for its many sovereign
virtues, was a quite different thing. For Peter would put in a
certain quantity of his powder pimperlimpimp, after which it
never failed of success. The operation was performed by
spargefaction, in a proper time of the moon. The patient who
was to be pickled, if it were a house, would infallibly be
preserved from all spiders, rats, and weasels; if the party
affected were a dog, he should be exempt from mange, and
madness, and hunger. It also infallibly took away all scabs,
and lice, and scalled heads from children, never hindering the
patient from any duty, either at bed or board.

But of all Peter's rarities he most valued a certain set of bulls,
whose race was by great fortune preserved in a lineal descent
from those that guarded the golden fleece. Though some, who
pretended to observe them curiously, doubted the breed had
not been kept entirely chaste, because they had degenerated
from their ancestors in some qualities, and had acquired others
very extraordinary, by a foreign mixture. The bulls of Colchis
are recorded to have brazen feet; but whether it happened by
ill pasture and running, by an allay from intervention of other
parents, from stolen intrigues; whether a weakness in their
progenitors had impaired the seminal virtue, or by a decline
necessary through a long course of time, the originals of nature
being depraved in these latter sinful ages of the world;
whatever was the cause, it is certain that lord Peter's bulls were
extremely vitiated by the rust of time in the metal of their feet,

which was now sunk into common lead. However, the terrible roaring peculiar to their lineage was preserved ; as likewise that faculty of breathing out fire from their nostrils, which, notwithstanding, many of their detractors took to be a feat of art, to be nothing so terrible as it appeared, proceeding only from their usual course of diet, which was of squibs and crackers. However, they had two peculiar marks, which extremely distinguished them from the bulls of Jason, and which I have not met together in the description of any other monster beside that in Horace :

"Varias inducere plumas ;"

and

"Atrum desinat in piscem."

For these had fishes' tails, yet upon occasion could outfly any bird in the air. Peter put these bulls upon several employs. Sometimes he would set them a-roaring to fright naughty boys, and make them quiet. Sometimes he would send them out upon errands of great importance ; where, it is wonderful to recount (and perhaps the cautious reader may think much to believe it), an *appetitus sensibilis* deriving itself through the whole family from their noble ancestors, guardians of the golden fleece, they continued so extremely fond of gold, that if Peter sent them abroad, though it were only upon a compliment, they would roar, and spit, and belch, and piss, and fart, and snivel out fire, and keep a perpetual coil, till you flung them a bit of gold ; but then, *pulveris exigui jactu*, they would grow calm and quiet as lambs. In short, whether by secret connivance or encouragement from their master, or out of their own liquorish affection to gold, or both, it is certain they were no better than a sort of sturdy, swaggering beggars ; and where they could not prevail to get an alms, would make women miscarry, and children fall into fits, who to this very day usually call sprights and hobgoblins by the name of bull-beggars. They grew at last so very troublesome to the neighbourhood, that some gentlemen of the north-west got a parcel of right English bull-dogs, and baited them so terribly that they felt it ever after.

I must needs mention one more of lord Peter's projects, which was very extraordinary, and discovered him to be master of a high reach and profound invention. Whenever it happened that any rogue of Newgate was condemned to be hanged, Peter would offer him a pardon for a certain sum of money; which, when the poor caitiff had made all shifts to scrape up and send, his lordship would return a piece of paper in this form :—

"To all mayors, sheriffs, jailors, constables, bailiffs, hang-men, etc. Whereas we are informed that A. B. remains in the hands of you, or some of you, under the sentence of death. We will and command you, upon sight hereof, to let the said prisoner depart to his own habitation, whether he stands condemned for murder, sodomy, rape, sacrilege, incest, treason, blasphemy, etc., for which this shall be your sufficient warrant ; and if you fail hereof, G— d—mn you and yours to all eternity. And so we bid you heartily farewell.

Your most humble
Man's man,
Emperor PETER."

The wretches, trusting to this, lost their lives and money too.

I desire of those whom the learned among posterity will appoint for commentators upon this elaborate treatise, that they will proceed with great caution upon certain dark points, wherein all who are not *verè adepti* may be in danger to form rash and hasty conclusions, especially in some mysterious paragraphs, where certain *arcana* are joined for brevity sake, which in the operation must be divided. And I am certain that future sons of art will return large thanks to my memory for so grateful, so useful an *innuendo.*

It will be no difficult part to persuade the reader that so many worthy discoveries met with great success in the world ; though I may justly assure him that I have related much the smallest number ; my design having been only to single out such as will be of most benefit for public imitation, or which best served to give some idea of the reach and wit of the inventor. And therefore it need not be wondered at if by this time lord Peter was become exceeding rich : but, alas ! he had kept his brain so long and so violently upon the rack, that at last it shook itself, and began to turn round for a little ease. In short, what with pride, projects, and knavery, poor Peter was grown distracted, and conceived the strangest imaginations in the world. In the height of his fits, as it is usual with those who run mad out of pride, he would call himself God Almighty, and sometimes monarch of the universe. I have seen him (says my author) take three old high-crowned hats, and clap them all on his head three storey high, with a huge bunch of keys at his girdle, and an angling-rod in his hand. In which guise, whoever went to take him by the hand in the way of salutation, Peter with much grace, like a well-educated spaniel, would present them with his foot, and if they refused his civility, then he would raise it as high as their chaps, and give them a damned kick on the mouth, which has ever since been called a salute. Whoever walked by without paying him their compliments, having a wonderful strong breath, he would blow their hats off into the dirt. Meantime his affairs at home went upside down, and his two brothers had a wretched time ; where his first *boutade* was to kick both their wives one morning out of doors, and his own too ; and in their stead gave orders to pick up the first three strollers that could be met with in the streets. A while after he nailed up the cellar-door, and would not allow his brothers a drop of drink to their victuals. Dining one day at an alderman's in the city, Peter observed him expatiating, after the manner of his brethern, in the praises of his sirloin of beef. "Beef," said the sage magistrate, "is the king of meat ; beef comprehends in it the quintessence of partridge, and quail, and venison, and pheasant, and plum-pudding, and custard." When Peter came home he would needs take the fancy of cooking up this doctrine into use, and apply the precept, in default of a sirloin, to his brown loaf. "Bread," says he, "dear brothers, is the staff of life ; in which bread is contained, inclusive, the quintessence of beef, mutton, veal, venison, partridge, plum-pudding, and custard ; and, to render all complete, there is intermingled a due quantity of water, whose crudities are also corrected by yeast or barm, through which means it becomes a wholesome fermented liquor, diffused through the mass of the bread." Upon the strength of these conclusions, next day at dinner was the brown loaf served up in all the formality of a city feast. "Come, brothers," said Peter, "fall to, and spare not ; here is excellent good mutton ; or hold, now my hand is in, I will help you." At which word, in much ceremony, with fork and knife, he carves out two good slices of a loaf, and presents each on a plate to his brothers. The elder of the two, not suddenly entering into lord Peter's conceit, began with very civil language to examine the mystery. " My lord," said he, " I doubt, with great submission, there may be some mistake."—"What," says Peter, "you are pleasant ; come then, let us hear this jest your head is so big with."— " None in the world, my lord ; but, unless I am very much deceived, your lordship was pleased a while ago to let fall a word about mutton, and I would be glad to see it with all my heart."—"How," said Peter, appearing in great surprise, " I do not comprehend this at all." Upon which the younger interposing to set the business aright, "My lord," said he, "my brother, I suppose, is hungry, and longs for the mutton your lordship has promised us to dinner."—"Pray," said Peter, "take me along with you; either you are both mad, or disposed to be merrier than I approve of; if you there do not like your piece I will carve you another; though I should take that to be the choice bit of the whole shoulder."—"What then, my lord," replied the first, "it seems this is a shoulder of mutton all this while?"—"Pray, sir," says Peter, "eat your victuals, and leave off your impertinence, if you please, for I am not disposed to relish it at present:" but the other could not forbear, being over-provoked at the affected seriousness of Peter's countenance: "By G—, my lord," said he, "I can only say, that to my eyes, and fingers, and teeth, and nose, it seems to be nothing but a crust of bread." Upon which the second put in his word: " I never saw a piece of mutton in my life so nearly resembling a slice from a twelvepenny loaf."—"Look ye, gentlemen," cries Peter, in a rage; "to convince you what a couple of blind, positive, ignorant, wilful puppies you are, I will use but this plain argument: by G—, it is true, good, natural mutton as any in Leadenhall-market; and G— confound you both eternally if you offer to believe otherwise." Such a thundering proof as this left no farther room for objection; the two unbelievers began to gather and pocket up their mistake as hastily as they could. "Why, truly," said the first, "upon more mature consideration——"—"Ay," says the other, interrupting him, "now I have thought better on the thing, your lordship seems to have a great deal of reason."—"Very well," said Peter; "here, boy, fill me a beer-glass of claret; here's to you both with all my heart." The two brethren, much delighted to see him so readily appeased, returned their most humble thanks, and said they would be glad to pledge his lordship. "That you shall," said Peter; "I am not a person to refuse you anything that is reasonable: wine, moderately taken, is a cordial; here is a glass a-piece for you; it is true natural juice from the grape, none of your damned vintner's brewings." Having spoke thus, he presented to each of them another large dry crust, bidding them drink it off, and not be bashful, for it would do them no hurt. The two brothers, after having performed the usual office in such delicate conjunctures, of staring a sufficient period at lord Peter and each other, and finding how matters were likely to go, resolved not to enter on a new dispute, but let him carry the point as he pleased; for he was now got into one of his mad fits, and to argue or expostulate farther would only serve to render him a hundred times more untractable.

I have chosen to relate this worthy matter in all its circumstances, because it gave a principal occasion to that great and famous rupture which happened about the same time among these brethren, and was never afterwards made up. But of that I shall treat at large in another section.

However, it is certain that lord Peter, even in his lucid intervals, was very lewdly given in his common conversation, extremely wilful and positive, and would at any time rather argue to the death than allow himself once to be in an error. Besides, he had an abominable faculty of telling huge palpable lies upon all occasions ; and not only swearing to the truth, but cursing the whole company to hell if they pretended to make the least scruple of believing him. One time he swore he had a cow at home which gave as much milk at a meal as would fill three thousand churches ; and, what was yet more extraordinary, would never turn sour. Another time he was telling of an old sign-post, that belonged to his father, with nails and timber enough in it to build sixteen large men of war. Talking one day of Chinese waggons, which were made so light as to sail over mountains, " Z— ds," said Peter, " where's the wonder of that ? By G—, I saw a large house of lime and stone travel over sea and land (granting that it stopped sometimes to bait) above two thousand German leagues." * And that which was the good of it, he would swear desperately all the while that he never told a lie in his life ; and at every word, " By G—, gentlemen, I tell you nothing but the truth ; and the d—l broil them eternally that will not believe me."

In short, Peter grew so scandalous, that all the neighbourhood began in plain words to say he was no better than a knave. And his two brothers, long weary of his ill-usage, resolved at last to leave him ; but first they humbly desired a copy of their father's will, which had now lain by neglected time out of mind. Instead of granting this request he called them damned sons of whores, rogues, traitors, and the rest of the vile names he could muster up. However, while he was abroad one day upon his projects, the youngsters watched their opportunity, made a shift to come at the will, and took a *copia vera*, by which they presently saw how grossly they had been abused ; their father having left them equal heirs, and strictly commanded that whatever they got should lie in common among them all. Pursuant to which their next enterprise was to break open the cellar-door, and get a little good drink, to

* The Chapel of Loretto, which travelled from the Holy Land to Italy. — *Hawkesworth.*

spirit and comfort their hearts. In copying the will they had met another precept against whoring, divorce, and separate maintenance ; upon which their next work was to discard their concubines, and send for their wives. While all this was in agitation there enters a solicitor from Newgate, desiring lord Peter would please procure a pardon for a thief that was to be hanged to-morrow. But the two brothers told him he was a coxcomb to seek pardons from a fellow who deserved to be hanged much better than his client ; and discovered all the method of that imposture in the same form I delivered it a while ago, advising the solicitor to put his friend upon obtaining a pardon from the king. In the midst of all this clutter and revolution, in comes Peter with a file of dragoons at his heels, and gathering from all hands what was in the wind, he and his gang, after several millions of scurrilities and curses, not very important here to repeat, by main force very fairly kicked them both out of doors, and would never let them come under his roof from that day to this.

A Tale of a Tub.

THE BATTLE OF THE BOOKS.

THE guardian of the regal library,* a person of great valour, but chiefly renowned for his humanity, had been a fierce champion for the moderns ; and, in an engagement upon Parnassus, had vowed, with his own hands, to knock down two of the ancient chiefs, who guarded a small pass on the superior rock ; but, endeavouring to climb up, was cruelly obstructed by his own unhappy weight and tendency towards his centre ; a quality to which those of the modern party are extremely subject ; for, being light-headed, they have, in speculation, a wonderful agility, and conceive nothing too high for them to mount ; but, in reducing to practice, discover a mighty pressure about their posteriors and their heels. Having thus failed in his design, the disappointed champion bore a cruel rancour to the ancients ; which he resolved to gratify by showing all marks of his favour to the books of their adversaries, and lodging them in the fairest apartments ; when, at the same time, whatever book had the boldness to own itself for an advocate of the ancients was buried alive in some obscure corner, and

* The Honourable Mr. Boyle, in the preface to his edition of Phalaris, says he was refused a MS. by the royal librarian, Dr. Bentley.

threatened, upon the least displeasure, to be turned out of doors. Besides, it so happened that about this time there was a strange confusion of place among all the books in the library ; for which several reasons were assigned. Some imputed it to a great heap of learned dust, which a perverse wind blew off from a shelf of moderns into the keeper's eyes. Others affirmed he had a humour to pick the worms out of the schoolmen, and swallow them fresh and fasting : whereof some fell upon his spleen, and some climbed up into his head, to the great perturbation of both. And lastly, others maintained that, by walking much in the dark about the library, he had quite lost the situation of it out of his head ; and therefore, in replacing his books, he was apt to mistake, and clap Des Cartes next to Aristotle ; poor Plato had got between 'Hobbes and the Seven Wise Masters, and Virgil was hemmed in with Dryden on one side and Withers on the other.

Meanwhile those books that were advocates for the moderns chose out one from among them to make a progress through the whole library, examine the number and strength of their party, and concert their affairs. This messenger performed all things very industriously, and brought back with him a list of their forces, in all, fifty thousand, consisting chiefly of light-horse, heavy-armed foot, and mercenaries ; whereof the foot were in general but sorrily armed and worse clad ; their horses large, but extremely out of case and heart ; however, some few, by trading among the ancients, had furnished themselves tolerably enough.

While things were in this ferment, discord grew extremely high ; but words passed on both sides, and ill blood was plentifully bred. Here a solitary ancient, squeezed up among a whole shelf of moderns, offered fairly to dispute the case, and to prove by manifest reason that the priority was due to them from long possession, and in regard of their prudence, antiquity, and, above all, their great merits toward the moderns. But these denied the premises, and seemed very much to wonder how the ancients could pretend to insist upon their antiquity, when it was so plain (if they went to that) that the moderns were much the more ancient of the two. As for any obligations they owed to the ancients, they renounced them all. It is true, said they, we are informed some few of our party have been so mean to borrow their subsistence from you ; but the rest, infinitely the greater number (and especially we French and English), were so far from stooping to so base an example, that there never passed, till this very hour, six words between us.

For our horses were of our own breeding, our arms of our own forging, and our clothes of our own cutting out and sewing. Plato was by chance up on the next shelf, and observing those that spoke to be in the ragged plight mentioned a while ago ; their jades lean and foundered, their weapons of rotten wood, their armour rusty, and nothing but rags underneath ; he laughed loud, and in his pleasant way swore, by ——, he believed them.

Now, the moderns had not proceeded in their late negotiation with secrecy enough to escape the notice of the enemy. For those advocates who had begun the quarrel, by setting first on foot the dispute of precedency, talked so loud of coming to a battle, that Sir William Temple happened to overhear them, and gave immediate intelligence to the ancients : who thereupon drew up their scattered troops together, resolving to act upon the defensive ; upon which, several of the moderns fled over to their party, and among the rest Temple himself. This Temple, having been educated and long conversed among the ancients, was, of all the moderns, their greatest favourite, and became their greatest champion.

Things were at this crisis when a material accident fell out. For upon the highest corner of a large window there dwelt a certain spider, swollen up to the first magnitude by the destruction of infinite numbers of flies, whose spoils lay scattered before the gates of his palace, like human bones before the cave of some giant. The avenues to his castle were guarded with turnpikes and palisadoes, all after the modern way of fortification. After you had passed several courts you came to the centre, wherein you might behold the constable himself in his own lodgings, which had windows fronting to each avenue, and ports to sally out upon all occasions of prey or defence. In this mansion he had for some time dwelt in peace and plenty, without danger to his person by swallows from above, or to his palace by brooms from below ; when it was the pleasure of fortune to conduct thither a wandering bee, to whose curiosity a broken pane in the glass had discovered itself, and in he went ; where, expatiating a while, he at last happened to alight upon one of the outward walls of the spider's citadel ; which, yielding to the unequal weight, sunk down to the very foundation. Thrice he endeavoured to force his passage, and thrice the centre shook. The spider within, feeling the terrible convulsion, supposed at first that nature was approaching to her final dissolution ; or else, that Beelzebub, with all his legions, was come to revenge the death of many thousands of his subjects whom his enemy had slain and devoured. However, he at length valiantly resolved to issue forth and meet his fate. Meanwhile the bee had acquitted himself of his toils, and, posted securely at some distance, was employed in cleansing his wings, and disengaging them from the ragged remnants of the cobweb. By this time the spider was adventured out, when, beholding the chasms, the ruins, and dilapidations of his fortress, he was very near at his wits' end; he stormed and swore like a madman, and swelled till he was ready to burst. At length, casting his eye upon the bee, and wisely gathering causes from events (for they knew each other by sight): A plague split you, said he, for a giddy son of a whore; is it you, with a vengeance, that have made this litter here? could not you look before you, and be d——d? do you think I have nothing else to do (in the devil's name) but to mend and repair after your arse?—Good words, friend, said the bee (having now pruned himself, and being disposed to droll): I'll give you my hand and word to come near your kennel no more; I was never in such a confounded pickle since I was born.—Sirrah, replied the spider, if it were not for breaking an old custom in our family, never to stir abroad against an enemy, I should come and teach you better manners.—I pray have patience, said the bee, or you'll spend your substance, and, for aught I see, you may stand in need of it all, toward the repair of your house.—Rogue, rogue, replied the spider, yet methinks you should have more respect to a person whom all the world allows to be so much your betters.—By my troth, said the bee, the comparison will amount to a very good jest; and you will do me a favour to let me know the reasons that all the world is pleased to use in so hopeful a dispute. At this the spider, having swelled himself into the size and posture of a disputant, began his argument in the true spirit of controversy, with resolution to be heartily scurrilous and angry to urge on his own reasons, without the least regard to the answers or objections of his opposite; and fully predetermined in his mind against all conviction.

Not to disparage myself, said he, by the comparison with such a rascal, what art thou but a vagabond without house or home, without stock or inheritance? born to no possession of your own, but a pair of wings and a drone-pipe. Your livelihood is a universal plunder upon nature; a freebooter over fields and gardens; and, for the sake of stealing, will rob a nettle as easily as a violet. Whereas I am a domestic animal, furnished with a native stock within myself. This large castle (to show my improvements in the mathematics) is all built with my own hands, and the materials extracted altogether out of my own person.

I am glad, answered the bee, to hear you grant at least that I am come honestly by my wings and my voice ; for then, it seems, I am obliged to Heaven alone for my flights and my music ; and Providence would never have bestowed on me two such gifts, without designing them for the noblest ends. I visit indeed all the flowers and blossoms of the field and garden ; but whatever I collect thence enriches myself, without the least injury to their beauty, their smell, or their taste. Now, for you and your skill in architecture and other mathematics, I have little to say : in that building of yours there might, for aught I know, have been labour and method enough ; but, by woeful experience for us both, it is too plain the materials are naught ; and I hope you will henceforth take warning, and consider duration and matter, as well as method and art. You boast indeed of being obliged to no other creature, but of drawing and spinning out all from yourself ; that is to say, if we may judge of the liquor in the vessel by what issues out, you possess a good plentiful store of dirt and poison in your breast ; and, though I would by no means lessen or disparage your genuine stock of either, yet I doubt you are somewhat obliged, for an increase of both, to a little foreign assistance. Your inherent portion of dirt does not fail of acquisitions, by sweepings exhaled from below ; and one insect furnishes you with a share of poison to destroy another. So that, in short, the question comes all to this ; whether is the nobler being of the two, that which, by a lazy contemplation of four inches round, by an over-weening pride, feeding and engendering on itself, turns all into excrement and venom, producing nothing at all but flybane and a cobweb ; or that which, by a universal range, with long search, much study, true judgment, and distinction of things, brings home honey and wax.

This dispute was managed with such eagerness, clamour, and warmth, that the two parties of books, in arms below, stood silent a while, waiting in suspense what would be the issue ; which was not long undetermined ; for the bee, grown impatient at so much loss of time, fled straight away to a bed of roses, without looking for a reply, and left the spider, like an orator, collected in himself, and just prepared to burst out.

It happened upon this emergency that Æsop broke silence first. He had been of late most barbarously treated by a strange effect of the regent's humanity, who had torn off his title-page, sorely defaced one half of his leaves, and chained him fast among a shelf of moderns. Where, soon discovering how high the quarrel was likely to proceed, he tried all his arts, and turned himself to a thousand forms. At length, in the borrowed shape of an ass, the regent mistook him for a modern ; by which means he had time and opportunity to escape to the ancients, just when the spider and the bee were entering into their contest ; to which he gave his attention with a world of pleasure, and when it was ended, swore in the loudest key that in all his life he had never known two cases so parallel and adapt to each other as that in the window and this upon the shelves. The disputants, said he, have admirably managed the dispute between them, have taken in the full strength of all that is to be said on both sides, and exhausted the substance of every argument *pro* and *con*. It is but to adjust the reasonings of both to the present quarrel, then to compare and apply the labours and fruits of each, as the bee has learnedly deduced them, and we shall find the conclusion fall plain and close upon the moderns and us. For pray, gentlemen, was ever anything so modern as the spider in his air, his turns, and his paradoxes? he argues in the behalf of you, his brethren, and himself with many boastings of his native stock and great genius ; that he spins and spits wholly from himself, and scorns to own any obligation or assistance from without. Then he displays to you his great skill in architecture and improvement in the mathematics. To all this the bee, as an advocate retained by us the ancients, thinks fit to answer, that, if one may judge of the great genius or inventions of the moderns by what they have produced, you will hardly have countenance to bear you out in boasting of either. Erect your schemes with as much method and skill as you please ; yet, if the materials be nothing but dirt, spun out of your own entrails (the guts of modern brains), the edifice will conclude at last in a cobweb ; the duration of which, like that of other spiders' webs, may be imputed to their being forgotten, or neglected, or hid in a corner. For anything else of genuine that the moderns may pretend to, I cannot recollect ; unless it be a large vein of wrangling and satire, much of a nature and substance with the spider's poison ; which, however, they pretend to spit wholly out of themselves, is improved by the same arts, by feeding upon the insects and vermin of the age. As for us the ancients, we are content, with the bee, to pretend to nothing of our own beyond our wings and our voice : that is to say, our flights and our language. For the rest, whatever we have got has been by infinite labour and search, and ranging through every corner of nature; the difference is, that, instead of dirt and poison, we have rather chosen to fill our hives with honey and wax; thus furnishing mankind with the two noblest of things, which are sweetness and light.

It is wonderful to conceive the tumult arisen among the books upon the close of this long descant of Æsop : both parties took the hint, and heightened their animosities so on a sudden, that they resolved it should come to a battle. Immediately the two main bodies withdrew, under their several ensigns, to the farther parts of the library, and there entered into cabals and consults upon the present emergency. The moderns were in very warm debates upon the choice of their leaders : and nothing less than the fear impending from their enemies could have kept them from mutinies upon this occasion. The difference was greatest among the horse, where every private trooper pretended to the chief command, from Tasso and Milton to Dryden and Withers. The light-horse were commanded by Cowley and Despreaux. There came the bowmen under their valiant leaders, Des Cartes, Gassendi, and Hobbes ; whose strength was such that they could shoot their arrows beyond the atmosphere, never to fall down again, but turn like that of Evander, into meteors ; or, like the cannon-ball, into stars. Paracelsus brought a squadron of stinkpot-flingers from the snowy mountains of Rhætia. There came a vast body of dragoons, of different nations, under the leading of Harvey[*] their great aga : part armed with scythes, the weapons of death ; part with lances and long knives, all steeped in poison ; part shot bullets of a most malignant nature, and used white powder, which infallibly killed without report. There came several bodies of heavy-armed foot, all mercenaries, under the ensigns of Guicciardini, Davila, Polydore, Virgil, Buchanan, Mariana, Camden, and others. The engineers were commanded by Regiomontanus and Wilkins. The rest was a confused multitude, led by Scotus, Aquinas, and Bellarmine ; of mighty bulk and stature, but without either arms, courage, or discipline. In the last place came infinite swarms of calones, a disorderly rout led by L'Estrange ; rogues and ragamuffins, that follow the camp for nothing but the plunder, all without coats to cover them.

The army of the ancients was much fewer in number ; Homer led the horse, and Pinder the light-horse ; Euclid was chief engineer ; Plato and Aristotle commanded the bowmen ; Herodotus and Livy the foot ; Hippocrates the dragoons ; the allies, led by Vossius and Temple, brought up the rear.

[*] Discoverer of the circulation of the blood.

All things violently tending to a decisive battle, Fame, who much frequented, and had a large apartment formerly assigned her in the regal library, fled up straight to Jupiter, to whom she delivered a faithful account of all that passed betweeen the two parties below ; for among the gods she always tells truth. Jove, in great concern, convokes a council in the milky way. The senate assembled, he declares the occasion of convening them ; a bloody battle just impendent between two mighty armies of ancient and modern creatures, called books, wherein the celestial interest was but too deeply concerned. Momus, the patron of the moderns, made an excellent speech in their favour, which was answered by Pallas, the protectress of the ancients. The assembly was divided in their affections ; when Jupiter commanded the book of fate to be laid before him. Immediately were brought by Mercury three large volumes in folio, containing memoirs of all things past, present, and to come. The clasps were of silver double gilt, the covers of celestial turkey leather, and the paper such as here on earth might pass almost for vellum. Jupiter, having silently read the decree, would communicate the import to none, but presently shut up the book.

Without the doors of this assembly there attended a vast number of light, nimble gods, menial servants to Jupiter : these are his ministering instruments in all affairs below. They travel in a caravan, more or less together, and are fastened to each other, like a link of galley-slaves, by a light chain, which passes from them to Jupiter's great toe : and yet, in receiving or delivering a message, they may never approach above the lowest step of his throne, where he and they whisper to each other through a large hollow trunk. These deities are called by mortal men accidents or events ; but the gods call them second causes. Jupiter having delivered his message to a certain number of these divinities, they flew immediately down to the pinnacle of the regal library, and consulting a few minutes, entered unseen, and disposed the parties according to their orders.

Meanwhile Momus, fearing the worst, and calling to mind an ancient prophecy which bore no very good face to his children the moderns, bent his flight to the region of a malignant deity called Criticism. She dwelt on the top of a snowy mountain in Nova Zembla ; there Momus found her extended in her den, upon the spoils of numberless volumes, half devoured. At her right hand sat Ignorance, her father and husband, blind with age ; at her left, Pride, her mother, dressing her up in the scraps of paper herself had torn. There was Opinion, her

sister, light of foot, hoodwinked, and headstrong, yet giddy and
perpetually turning. About her played her children, Noise and
Impudence, Dulness and Vanity, Positiveness, Pedantry, and
Ill-manners. The goddess herself had claws like a cat ; her
head, and ears, and voice, resembled those of an ass ; her
teeth fallen out before, her eyes turned inward, as if she looked
only upon herself ; her diet was the overflowing of her own
gall ; her spleen was so large as to stand prominent, like a dug
of the first rate ; nor wanted excrescencies in form of teats, at
which a crew of ugly monsters were greedily sucking ; and
what is wonderful to conceive, the bulk of spleen increased
faster than the sucking could diminish it. Goddess, said
Momus, can you sit idly here while our devout worshippers, the
moderns, are this minute entering into a cruel battle, and
perhaps now lying under the swords of their enemies? who
then hereafter will ever sacrifice or build altars to our divinities?
Haste, therefore, to the British isle, and, if possible, prevent
their destruction ; while I make factions among the gods, and
gain them over to our party.

Momus, having thus delivered himself, staid not for an
answer, but left the goddess to her own resentment. Up she
rose in a rage, and, as it is the form upon such occasions, began
a soliloquy : It is I (said she) who gave wisdom to infants and
idiots ; by me children grew wiser than their parents, by me
beaux become politicians, and school-boys judges of philosophy :
by me sophisters debate and conclude upon the depths of
knowledge ; and coffee-house wits, instinct by me, can correct
an author's style, and display his minutest errors without
understanding a syllable of his matter or his language ; by me
striplings spend their judgment, as they do their estate, before
it comes into their hands. It is I who have deposed wit and
knowledge from their empire over poetry, and advanced
myself in their stead. And shall a few upstart ancients dare to
oppose me ?—But come, my aged parent, and you my children
dear, and thou, my beauteous sister ; let us ascend my chariot,
and haste to assist our devout moderns, who are now sacrificing
to us a hecatomb, as I perceive by that grateful smell which
from thence reaches my nostrils.

The goddess and her train, having mounted the chariot,
which was drawn by tame geese, flew over infinite regions,
shedding her influence in due places, till at length she arrived
at her beloved island of Britain ; but in hovering over its
metropolis, what blessings did she not let fall upon her
seminaries of Gresham and Covent-garden ! And now she

reached the fatal plain of St. James's library, at what time the two armies were upon the point to engage ; where, entering with all her caravan unseen, and landing upon a case of shelves, now desert, but once inhabited by a colony of virtuosoes, she staid a while to observe the posture of both armies.

But here the tender cares of a mother began to fill her thoughts and move in her breast : for at the head of a troop of modern bowmen she cast her eyes upon her son Wotton, to whom the fates had assigned a very short thread. Wotton, a young hero, whom an unknown father of mortal race begot by stolen embraces with this goddess. He was the darling of his mother above all her children, and she resolved to go and comfort him. But first, according to the good old custom of deities, she cast about to change her shape, for fear the divinity of her countenance might dazzle his mortal sight and over-charge the rest of his senses. She therefore gathered up her person into an octavo compass : her body grew white and arid, and split in pieces with dryness ; the thick turned into paste-board, and the thin into paper ; upon which her parents and children artfully strewed a black juice, or decoction of gall and soot, in form of letters ; her head, and voice, and spleen, kept their primitive form ; and that which before was a cover of skin did still continue so. In this guise she marched on towards the moderns, undistinguishable in shape and dress from the divine Bentley, Wotton's dearest friend. Brave Wotton, said the goddess, why do our troops stand idle here, to spend their present vigour and opportunity of the day ? away, let us haste to the generals, and advise to give the onset immediately. Having spoken thus, she took the ugliest of her monsters, full glutted from her spleen, and flung it invisibly into his mouth, which, flying straight up into his head, squeezed out his eye-balls, gave him a distorted look, and half over-turned his brain. Then she privately ordered two of her beloved children, Dullness and Ill-manners, closely to attend his person in all encounters. Having thus accoutred him, she vanished in a mist, and the hero perceived it was the goddess his mother.

THE YAHOOS.

THE reader may please to observe, that the following extract of many conversations I had with my master, contains a summary of the most material points, which were discoursed at several times for above two years ; his honour often desiring fuller satisfaction, as I further improved in the Houghnhnm tongue. I laid before him, as well as I could, the whole state of Europe ; I discoursed of trade and manufactures, of arts and sciences ; and the answers I gave to all the questions he made, as they arose upon several subjects, were a fund of conversation not to be exhausted. But I shall here only set down the substance of what passed between us, concerning my own country, reducing it in order as well as I can, without any regard to time or other circumstances, while I strictly adhere to truth. My only concern is, that I shall hardly be able to do justice to my master's arguments and expressions, which must needs suffer by my want of capacity, as well as by a translation into our barbarous English.

In obedience therefore to his honour's commands, I related to him the revolutions under the prince of Orange ; the long war with France, entered into by the said prince, and renewed by his successor, the present queen ; wherein the greatest powers of Christendom were engaged, and which still continued : I computed at his request, that about a million of Yahoos might have been killed, in the whole progress of it ; and perhaps a hundred or more cities taken, and five times as many ships burnt or sunk.

He asked me what were the usual causes or motives that made one county go to war with another. I answered they were innumerable ; but I should only mention a few of the chief. Sometimes, the ambition of princes, who never think they have land or people enough to govern. Sometimes, the corruption of ministers, who engage their master in a war, in order to stifle or divert the clamour of the subjects against their evil administration. Difference in opinions have cost many millions of lives : for instance, whether flesh be bread or bread be flesh ; whether the juice of a certain berry be blood or wine ; whether whistling* be a vice or a virtue ; whether it be better to kiss a post† or to throw it into the fire ; what is the best colour for a coat,‡ whether black, white, red, or gray ; and whether it should be long or short, narrow or wide, dirty or clean, with many more. Neither are any wars so furious and bloody, or of so long continuance, as those occasioned by difference in opinion, especially if it be in things indifferent.

Gulliver's Travels.

* Church music.   † The Cross.
‡ *i.e.*, the clothing of Ecclesiastical ministers.

ALEXANDER POPE.

1688–1744.

A RECEIPT TO MAKE AN EPIC POEM.

For the Fable.

"Take out of any old poem, history books, romance, or legend, for instance Geoffrey of Monmouth, or Don Belianis of Greece, those parts of story which afford most scope for long descriptions. Put these pieces together, and throw all the adventures you fancy into one tale. Then take a hero whom you may choose for the sound of his name, and put him into the midst of these adventures. There let him work, for twelve books ; at the end of which you may take him out ready prepared to conquer, or to marry ; it being necessary that the conclusion of an epic poem be fortunate."

To make an episode.—"Take any remaining adventure of your former collection, in which you could no way involve your hero ; or any unfortunate accident that was too good to be thrown away ; and it will be of use, applied to any other person, who may be lost and evaporate in the course of the work, without the least damage to the composition."

For the moral and allegory.—"These you may extract out of the fable afterwards at your leisure. Be sure you strain them sufficiently."

For the Manners.

"For those of the hero, take all the best qualities you can find in all the celebrated heroes of antiquity ; if they will not be reduced to a constituency, lay them all on a heap upon him. But be sure they are qualities which your patron would be thought to have ; and to prevent any mistake which the world may be subject to, select from the alphabet those capital letters that compose his name, and set them at the head of a dedication before your poem. However, do not absolutely observe the exact quantity of these virtues, if not being determined, whether or no it be necessary for the hero of a poem, to be an honest man.—For the under-characters, gather them from Homer and Virgil, and change the names as occasion serves."

For the Machines.

"Take of deities, male and females, a many as you can use. Separate them into two equal parts, and keep Jupiter in the middle. Let Juno put him in a ferment, and Venus mollify him. Remember on all occasions to make use of volatile Mercury. If you have need of devils, draw them out of Milton's Paradise, and extract your spirits from Tasso. The use of these machines is evident ; for since no epic poem can possibly subsist without them, the wisest way is to reserve them for your greatest necessities. When you cannot extricate your hero by any human means, or yourself by your own wit, seek relief from heaven, and the gods will do your business very readily. This is according to the direct prescription of Horace in his Art of Poetry :

> Nec Deus intersit, nisi dignus vindice nodus
> Inciderit.—
>
> Never presume to make a God appear
> But for a business worthy of a God.
>
> *Roscommon.*

That is to say, a poet should never call upon the gods for their assistance, but when he is in great perplexity."

For the Descriptions.

For a tempest.—"Take Eurus, Zephyr, Auster and Boreas, and cast them together in one verse. Add to these of rain, lightning, and of thunder, the loudest you can, *quantum sufficit.* Mix your clouds and billows well together, till they foam, and thicken your description here and there with a quicksand. Brew your tempest well in your head, before you set it a blowing."

For a battle.—" Pick a large quantity of images and descriptions from Homer's Iliad, with a spice or two of Virgil, and if there remain any overplus you may lay them by for a skirmish. Season it well with smiles, and it will make an excellent battle."

For a burning town.—"If such a description be necessary, because it is certain there is one in Virgil, Old Troy is ready burnt to your hands. But if you fear that would be thought borrowed, a chapter or two of the Theory of the Conflagration, well circumstanced, and done into verse, will be a good succedaneum."

"As for similes and metaphors, they may be found all over the creation ; the most ignorant may gather them, but the danger is in applying them. For this, advise with your bookseller."

FOR THE LANGUAGE.

I mean the diction. "Here it will do well to be an imitator of Milton, for you will find it easier to imitate him in this than anything else. Hebraisms and Grecisms are to be found in him, without the trouble of learning the languages. I knew a painter who, like our poet, had no genius, made his daubings be thought originals by setting them in the smoke. You may in the same manner give the venerable air of antiquity to your piece, by darkening it up and down with old English. With this you may be easily furnished upon any occasion, by the dictionary commonly printed at the end of Chaucer."

I must not conclude without cautioning all writers without genius in one material point, which is never to be afraid of having too much fire in their works. I should advise rather to take their warmest thoughts, and spread them abroad upon paper ; for they are observed to cool before they are read.

Essays.

SIR RICHARD STEELE.

1671–1729.

ELOQUENCE.

*On Eloquence; Talents for Conversation; Urbanus and
Umbratilis; Pedantry.*

Quid voveat dulci nutricula majus alumno,
Quam sapere, et fari possit quæ sentiat?

HOR. Ep. i. 4. S.

IT is no easy matter, when people are advancing in any thing,
to prevent their going too fast for want of patience. This
happens in nothing more frequently than in the prosecution of
studies. Hence it is, that we meet crowds who attempt to be
eloquent before they can speak. They affect the flowers of
rhetoric before they understand the parts of speech. In the
ordinary conversation of this town, there are so many who can,
as they call it, talk well, that there is not one in twenty that
talks to be understood. This proceeds from an ambition to
excel, or, as the term is, to shine in company. The matter is
not to make themselves understood, but admired. They come
together with a certain emulation, rather than benevolence.
When you fall among such companions, the safe way is to give
yourself up, and let the orators declaim for your esteem, and
trouble yourself no further. It is said, that a poet must be
born so; but I think it may be much better said of an orator,
especially when we talk of our town poets and orators : but the
town poets are full of rules and laws; the town orators go
through thick and thin, and are, forsooth, persons of such
eminent natural parts, and knowledge of the world, that they
despise all men as unexperienced scholastics, who wait for an
occasion before they speak, or who speak no more than is

necessary. They had half persuaded me to go to the tavern the other night, but that a gentleman whispered me, ' Pr'ythee, Isaac, go with us ; there is Tom Varnish will be there, and he is a fellow that talks as well as any man in England.'

I must confess, when a man expresses himself well upon any occasion, and his falling into an account of any subject arises from a desire to oblige the company, or from fulness of the circumstance itself, so that his speaking of it at large is occasioned only by the openness of a companion ; I say, in such a case as this, it is not only pardonable, but agreeable, when a man takes the discourse to himself ; but when you see a fellow watch for opportunities for being copious, it is excessively troublesome. A man that stammers, if he has understanding, is to be attended to with patience and good-nature ; but he that speaks more than he needs, has no right to such an indulgence. The man who has a defect in his speech takes pains to come to you, while a man of weak capacity, with fluency of speech, triumphs in outrunning you. The stammerer strives to be fit for your company ; the loquacious man endeavours to show you, you are not fit for his.

With thoughts of this kind do I always enter into that man's company who is recommended as a person that talks well ; but if I were to choose the people with whom I would spend my hours of conversation, they should be certainly such as laboured no farther than to make themselves readily and clearly apprehended, and would have patience and curiosity to understand me. To have good sense, and ability to express it, are the most essential and necessary qualities in companions. When thoughts rise in us fit to utter, among familiar friends there needs but very little care in clothing them.

Urbanus is, I take it, a man one might live with whole years, and enjoy all the freedom and improvement imaginable, and yet be insensible of a contradiction to you in all the mistakes you can be guilty of. His great goodwill to his friends, has produced in him such a general deference in his discourse, that if he differs from you in his sense of any thing, he introduces his own thoughts by some agreeable circumlocution ; or, ' he has often observed such and such a circumstance that made him of another opinion.' Again, where another would be apt to say, 'this I am confident of, I may pretend to judge of this matter as well as any body ;' Urbanus says, 'I am verily persuaded ; I believe one may conclude.' In a word, there is no man more clear in his thoughts and expressions than he is, or speaks with greater diffidence. You shall hardly find one man of any consideration, but you shall observe one of less consequence form himself after him. This happens to Urbanus ; but the man who steals from him almost every sentiment he utters in a whole week, disguises the theft by carrying it with a quite different air. Umbratilis knows Urbanus's doubtful way of speaking proceeds from good-nature and good-breeding, and not from uncertainty in his opinions. Umbratilis, therefore, has no more to do but repeat the thoughts of Urbanus in a positive manner, and appear to the undiscerning a wiser man than the person from whom he borrows : but those who know him, can see the servant in his master's habit ; and the more he struts, the less do his clothes appear his own.

In conversation, the medium is neither to affect silence or eloquence ; not to value our approbation, and to endeavour to excel us who are of your company, are equal injuries. The great enemies therefore to good company, and those who transgress most against the laws of equality, which is the life of it, are, the clown, the wit, and the pedant. A clown, when he has sense, is conscious of his want of education, and with an awkward bluntness, hopes to keep himself in countenance by overthrowing the use of all polite behaviour. He takes advantage of the restraint good-breeding lays upon others not to offend him, to trespass against them, and is under the man's own shelter while he intrudes upon him. The fellows of this class are very frequent in the repetition of the words *rough* and *manly*. When these people happen to be by their fortunes of the rank of gentlemen, they defend their other absurdities by an impertinent courage ; and, to help out the defect of their behaviour, add their being dangerous to their being disagreeable. This gentleman (though he displeases, professes to do so ; and knowing that, dares still go on to do so) is not so painful a companion, as he who will please you against your will, and resolves to be a wit.

This man, upon all occasions, and whoever he falls in company with, talks in the same circle, and in the same round of chat which he has learned at one of the tables of this coffeehouse. As poetry is in itself an elevation above ordinary and common sentiments ; so there is no fop so very near a madman in indifferent company as a political one. He is not apprehensive that the generality of the world are intent upon the business of their own fortune and profession, and have as little capacity as curiosity to enter into matters of ornament or speculation. I remember at a full table in the city, one of these ubiquitary wits was entertaining the company with a soliloquy, for so I call it when a man talks to those who do not understand him, concerning wit and humour. An honest gentleman who sat next to me, and was worth half a plumb, stared at him, and observing there was some sense, as he thought, mixed with his impertinence, whispered me, 'Take my word for it, this fellow is more knave than fool.' This was all my good friend's applause of the wittiest man of talk that I was ever present at, which wanted nothing to make it excellent, but that there was no occasion for it.

The pedant is so obvious to ridicule, that it would be to be one to offer to explain him. He is a gentleman so well known, that there is none but those of his own class who do not laugh at and avoid him. Pedantry proceeds from much reading and little understanding. A pedant among men of learning and sense, is like an ignorant servant giving an account of a polite conversation. You may find he has brought with him more than could have entered into his head without being there, but still that he is not a bit wiser than if he had not been there at all.

Tatler.

ON PROLIXITY.

Favete linguis.—Hor. Od. iii. 2. 2.

Boccalini, in his 'Parnassus,' indicts a laconic writer for speaking that in three words which he might have said in two, and sentences him for his punishment to read over all the works of Guicciardini. This Guicciardini is so very prolix and circumstantial in his writings, that I remember our countryman, doctor Donne, speaking of that majestic and concise manner in which Moses has described the creation of the world, adds, 'that if such an author as Guicciardini were to have written on such a subject, the world itself would not have been able to have contained the books that gave the history of its creation.'

I look upon a tedious talker, or what is generally known by the name of a story-teller, to be much more insufferable than even a prolix writer. An author may be tossed out of your hand, and thrown aside when he grows dull and tiresome; but such liberties are so far from being allowed towards your orators in common conversation, that I have known a challenge sent a person for going out of the room abruptly, and leaving a man of honour in the midst of a dissertation. This evil is at present so very common and epidemical, that there is scarce a coffee-house in town that has not some speakers belonging to it, who utter their political essays, and draw parallels out of Baker's 'Chronicle' to almost every part of her majesty's reign. It was said of two ancient authors, who had very different beauties in their style, 'that if you took a word from one of them, you only spoiled his eloquence ; but if you took a word from the other, you spoiled his sense.' I have often applied the first part of this criticism to several of these coffee-house speakers whom I have at present in my thoughts, though the character that is given to the last of those authors, is what I would recommend to the imitation of my loving countrymen. But it is not only public places of resort, but private clubs and conversations over a bottle, that are infested with this loquacious kind of animal, especially with that species which I comprehend under the name of a story-teller. I would earnestly desire these gentlemen to consider, that no point of wit or mirth at the end of a story can atone for the half hour that has been lost before they come at it. I would likewise lay it home to their serious consideration, whether they think that every man in the company has not a right to speak as well as themselves ? and whether they do not think they are invading another man's property, when they engross the time which should be divided equally among the company to their own private use ?

What makes this evil the much greater in conversation is, that these humdrum companions seldom endeavour to wind up their narrations into a point of mirth or instruction, which might make some amends for the tediousness of them ; but think they have a right to tell any thing that has happened within their memory. They look upon matter of fact to be a sufficient foundation for a story, and give us a long account of things, not because they are entertaining or surprising, but because they are true.

My ingenious kinsman, Mr. Humphry Wagstaff, used to say, ' the life of man is too short for a story-teller.'

Methusalem might be half an hour in telling what o'clock it was : but as for us postdiluvians, we ought to do every thing in haste ; and in our speeches, as well as actions, remember that our time is short. A man that talks for a quarter of an hour together in company, if I meet him frequently, takes up a great part of my span. A quarter of an hour may be reckoned the eight-and-fortieth part of a day, a day the three hundred and sixtieth part of a year, and a year the threescore and tenth part of life. By this moral arithmetic, supposing a man to be in the talking world one third part of the day, whoever gives another a quarter of an hour's hearing, makes him a sacrifice of more than the four hundred thousandth part of his conversable life.

I would establish but one great general rule to be observed in all conversation, which is this, 'that men should not talk to please themselves, but those that hear them.' This would make them consider, whether what they speak be worth hearing ; whether there be either wit or sense in what they are about to say ; and, whether it be adapted to the time when, the place where, and the person to whom, it is spoken.

For the utter extirpation of these orators and story-tellers, which I look upon as very great pests of society, I have invented a watch which divides the minute into twelve parts, after the same manner that the ordinary watches are divided into hours : and will endeavour to get a patent, which shall oblige every club or company to provide themselves with one of these watches, that shall lie upon the table as an hour-glass is often placed near the pulpit, to measure out the length of a discourse.

I shall be willing to allow a man one round of my watch, that is, a whole minute, to speak in ; but if he exceeds that time, it shall be lawful for any of the company to look upon the watch, or to call him down to order.

Provided, however, that if any one can make it appear he is turned of threescore, he may take two, or, if he pleases, three rounds of the watch without giving offence. Provided, also, that this rule be not construed to extend to the fair sex, who shall still be at liberty to talk by the ordinary watch that is now in use. I would likewise earnestly recommend this little automaton, which may be easily carried in the pocket without any incumbrance, to all such as are troubled with this infirmity of speech, that upon pulling out their watches, they may have frequent occasion to consider what they are doing, and by that means cut the thread of the story short, and hurry to a conclusion. I shall only add, that this watch, with a paper of directions how to use it, is sold at Charles Lillie's.

I am afraid a Tatler will be thought a very improper paper to censure this humour of being talkative ; but I would have my readers know that there is a great difference between *tattle* and *loquacity*, as I shall show at large in a following lucubration ; it being my design to throw away a candle upon that subject, in order to explain the whole art of tattling in all its branches and subdivisions.

Tatler.

JOSEPH ADDISON.

1672–1719.

ON ENGLISH TACITURNITY;

The genius of our language, ever tending to abbreviation, favours it.

Est breviate opus, ut currat sententia.
HOR. Sat. i. 10. 9.

I HAVE somewhere read of an eminent person, who used in his private offices of devotion to give thanks to heaven that he was born a Frenchman : for my own part, I look upon it as a peculiar blessing that I was born an Englishman. Among many other reasons, I think myself very happy in my country, as the language of it is wonderfully adapted to a man who is sparing of his words, and an enemy to loquacity.

As I have frequently reflected on my good fortune in this particular, I shall communicate to the public my speculations upon the English tongue, not doubting but they will be acceptable to all my curious readers.

The English delight in silence more than any other European nation, if the remarks which are made on us by foreigners are true. Our discourse is not kept up in conversation, but falls into more pauses and intervals than in our neighbouring countries ; as it is observed, that the matter of our writings is thrown much closer together, and lies in a narrower compass than is usual in the works of foreign authors : for, to favour our natural taciturnity, when we are obliged to utter our thoughts, we do it in the shortest way we are able, and give as quick a birth to our conceptions as possible.

This humour shews itself in several remarks that we may make upon the English language. As first of all, by its abounding in monosyllables, which gives us an opportunity of delivering our thoughts in few sounds. This indeed takes off from the elegance of our tongue, but at the same time expresses our ideas in the readiest manner, and consequently answers the first design of speech better than the multitude of syllables, which make the words of other languages more tuneable and sonorous. The sounds of our English words are commonly like those of string music, short and transient, which rise and perish upon a single touch ; those of other languages are like the notes of wind instruments, sweet and swelling, and lengthened out into variety of modulation.

In the next place we may observe, that where the words are not monosyllables, we often make them so, as much as lies in our power, by our rapidity of pronunciation ; as it generally happens in most of our long words which are derived from the Latin, where we contract the length of the syllables that gives them a grave and solemn air in their own language, to make them more proper for dispatch, and more comformable to the genius of our tongue. This we may find in a multitude of words, as *liberty, conspiracy, theatre, orator, &c.*

The same natural aversion to loquacity has of late years made a very considerable alteration in our language, by closing in one syllable the termination of our preterperfect tense, as in the words *drown'd, walk'd, arriv'd,* for *drowned, walked, arrived,* which has very much disfigured the tongue, and turned a tenth part of our smoothest words into so many clusters of consonants. This is the more remarkable, because the want of vowels in our language has been the general complaint of our politest authors, who nevertheless are the men that have made these retrenchments, and consequently very much increased our former scarcity.

This reflexion on the words that end in *ed*, I have heard in conversation from one of the greatest geniuses this age has produced. I think we may add to the foregoing observation, the change which has happened in our language by the abbreviation of several words that are terminated in *eth*, by substituting an *s* in the room of the last syllable, as in *drowns, walks, arrives,* and innumerable other words, which in the pronunciation of our forefathers were *drowneth, walketh, arriveth.* This has wonderfully multiplied a letter which was before too frequent in the English tongue, and added to that hissing in our language, which is taken so much notice of by foreigners ; but at the same time humours our taciturnity, and eases us of many superfluous syllables.

I might here observe, that the same single letter on many occasions does the office of a whole word, and represents the *his* and *her* of our forefathers. There is no doubt but the ear of a foreigner, which is the best judge in this case, would very much disapprove of such innovations, which indeed we do ourselves in some measure, by retaining the old termination in writing, and in all the solemn offices of our religion.

As in the instances I have given we have epitomized many of our particular words to the detriment of our tongue, so on other occasions we have drawn two words into one, which has likewise very much untuned our language, and clogged it with consonants, as *mayn't, can't, shan't, won't*, and the like, for *may not, can not, shall not, will not, &c.*

It is perhaps this humour of speaking no more than we needs must, which has so miserably curtailed some of our words, that in familiar writings and conversations they often lose all but their first syllables, as in *mob. rep. pos. incog.* and the like; and as all ridiculous words make their first entry into a language by familiar phrases, I dare not answer for these, that they will not in time be looked upon as a part of our tongue. We see some of our poets have been so indiscreet as to imitate Hudibras's doggrel expressions in their serious compositions, by throwing out the signs of our substantives, which are essential to the English language. Nay, this humour of shortening our language had once run so far, that some of our celebrated authors, among whom we may reckon Sir Roger L'Estrange in particular, began to prune their words of all superfluous letters, as they termed them, in order to adjust the spelling to the pronunciation; which would have confounded all our etymologies, and have quite destroyed our tongue.

We may here likewise observe that our proper names, when familiarized in English, generally dwindle to monosyllables, whereas in other modern languages they receive a softer turn on this occasion, by the addition of a new syllable, *Nick* in Italian is *Nicolini*, *Jack* in French *Janot*; and so of the rest.

There is another particular in our language which is a great instance of our frugality of words, and that is the suppressing of several particles which must be produced in other tongues to make a sentence intelligible; this often perplexes the best writers, when they find the relatives *whom, which*, or *they*, at their mercy, whether they may have admission or not; and will never be decided till we have something like an academy, that by the best authorities and rules, drawn from the analogy of languages, shall settle all controversies between grammar and idiom.

I have only considered our language as it shews the genius and natural temper of the English, which is modest, thoughtful, and sincere, and which perhaps may recommend the people, though it has spoiled the tongue. We might perhaps carry the same thought into other languages, and deduce a great part of what is peculiar to them from the genius of the people who speak them. It is certain the light talkative humour of the French has not a little infected their tongue, which might be shewn by many instances ; as the genius of the Italians, which is so much addicted to music and ceremony, has moulded all their words and phrases to those particular uses. The stateliness and gravity of the Spaniards shews itself to perfection in the solemnity of their language ; and the blunt honest humour of the German sounds better in the roughness of the High-Dutch than it would in a politer tongue.

Spectator.

THE USE OF FRENCH TERMS.

On the Introduction of French military terms into English; letter describing the battle of Blenheim.

Si fortenecesse est,
Fingere cinctutis non exaudita Cethegis
Continget : dabiturque licentia sumpta pudenter.
IIor. Ars Poet. 48.

I HAVE often wished, that as in our constitution there are several persons whose business it is to watch over our laws our liberties and commerce, certain men might be set apart as superintendents of our language, to hinder any words of a foreign coin from passing among us ; and in particular to prohibit any French phrases from being current in this kingdom, when those of our own stamp are altogether as valuable. The present war has so adulterated our tongue with strange words, that it would be impossible for one of our great grandfathers to know what his posterity have been doing, were he to read their exploits in a modern newspaper. Our warriors are very industrious in propagating the French language, at the same time that they are so gloriously successful in beating down their power.   Our soldiers are men of strong heads for action, and perform such feats as they are not able to express.   They want words in their own tongue to tell us what it is they achieve, and therefore send us over accounts of their performances in a jargon of phrases, which they learn among their conquered enemies.   They ought, however, to be provided with secretaries, and assisted by our foreign ministers, to tell their story for them in plain English, and to let us know in our mother-tongue what it is our brave countrymen are about.   The French would indeed be in the right to publish the news of the present war in English phrases, and make their campaigns unintelligible. Their people might flatter themselves that things are not so bad as they really are, were they thus palliated with foreign terms, and thrown into shades and obscurity : but the English cannot be too clear in their narrative of those actions, which have raised their country to a higher pitch of glory than it ever yet arrived at, and which will be still the more admired the better they are explained.

For my part, by that time a siege is carried on two or three days, I am altogether lost and bewildered in it, and meet with so many inexplicable difficulties, that I scarce know what side has the better of it, till I am informed by the Tower guns that the place is surrendered.   I do indeed make some allowance for this part of the war, fortifications having been foreign inventions, and upon that account abounding in foreign terms.   But when we have won battles, which may be described in our own language, why are our papers filled with so many unintelligible exploits, and the French obliged to lend us a part of their tongue before we can know how they are conquered ?   They must be made accessory to their own disgrace, as the Britrons were formerly so artificially wrought in the curtain of the Roman theatre, that they seemed to draw it up, in order to give the spectators an opportunity of seeing their own defeat celebrated upon the stage : for so Mr. Dryden has translated that verse in Virgil :—

> Purpurea intexti tollunt aulæa Britanni.
>
> GEORG. iii. 25.

> Which interwoven Britons seem to raise,
> And shew the triumph that their shame displays.

The histories of all our former wars are transmitted to us in our vernacular idiom, to use the phrase of a great modern critic. I do not find in any of our chronicles that Edward III. ever *reconnoitered* the enemy, though he often discovered the posture of the French, and as often vanquished them in battle. The Black Prince passed many a river without the help of *pontoons,* and filled a ditch with faggots as successfully as the generals of our times do it with *fascines.* Our commanders lose half their praise, and our people half their joy, by means of those hard words and dark expressions in which our newspapers do so much abound. I have seen many a prudent citizen, after having read every article, enquire of his next neighbour what news the mail had brought.

I remember, in that remarkable year, when our country was delivered from her greatest fears and apprehensions, and raised to the greatest height of gladness it had ever felt since it was a nation,—I mean the year of Blenheim,—I had the copy of a letter sent me out of the country, which was written from a young gentleman in the army to his father, a man of a good estate and plain sense : as the letter was very modishly chequered with this modern military eloquence, I shall present my reader with a copy of it.

'Sir,
'Upon the junction of the French and Bavarian armies, they took post behind a great morass, which they thought impracticable. Our general the next day sent a party of horse to reconnoitre them from a little hauteur, at about a quarter of an hour's distance from the army, who returned again to the camp unobserved through several defiles, in one of which they met with a party of French that had been marauding, and made them all prisoners at discretion. The day after, a drum arrived at our camp, with a message which he would communicate to none but the general ; he was followed by a trumpet, who they say behaved himself very saucily, with a message from the Duke of Bavaria. The next morning our army, being divided into two corps, made a movement towards the enemy ; you will hear in the public prints how we treated them, with the other circumstances of that glorious day. I had the good fortune to be in that regiment that pushed the *Gens d'Armes.* Several French battalions, who some say were a corps de réserve, made a show of resistance ; but it only proved a gasconade, for upon our preparing to fill up a little fosse, in order to attack them, they beat the chamade, and sent us *charte blanche.* Their commandant, with a great many other general officers, and troops without number, are made prisoners of war, and will I believe give you a visit in England, the cartel not being yet settled.

Not questioning but those particulars will be very welcome to you, I congratulate you upon them, and am your most dutiful son,' &c.

The father of the young gentleman upon the perusal of the letter found it contained great news, but could not guess what it was.   He immediately communicated it to the curate of the parish, who upon the reading of it, being vexed to see any thing he cou d not understand, fell into a kind of a passion, and told him that his son had sent him a letter that was neither fish, flesh, nor good red-herring.   'I wish,' says he, 'the captain may be *compos mentis;* he talks of a saucy trumpet, and a drum that carries messages ; then who is this *Charte Blanche ?*   He must either banter us, or he is out of his senses.'   The father, who always looked upon the curate as a learned man, began to fret inwardly at his son's usage, and producing a letter which he had written to him about three posts before, 'You see here,' says he, 'when he writes for money he knows how to speak intelligibly enough ; there's no man in England can express himself clearer, when he wants a new furniture for his horse.'   In short, the old man was so puzzled upon the point, that it might have fared ill with his son, had he not seen all the prints about three days after filled with the same terms of art, and that Charles only wrote like other men.

Spectator.

HENRY ST. JOHN,

VISCOUNT BOLINGBROKE.

1678-1751.

THE IDEA OF A PATRIOT KING.

LEWIS THE FOURTEENTH was king in an absolute monarchy, and reigned over a people, whose genius makes it as fit perhaps to impose on them by admiration and awe, as to gain and hold them by affection. Accordingly he kept great state; was haughty, was reserved; and all he said or did appeared to be forethought and planned. His regard to appearances was such, that when his mistress was the wife of another man, and he had children by her every year, he endeavoured to cover her constant residence at court by a place she filled about the queen: and he dined and supped and cohabited with the latter in every apparent respect as if he had had no mistress at all. Thus he raised a great reputation; he was revered by his subjects, and admired by his neighbours: and this was due principally to the art with which he managed appearances, so as to set off his virtues, to disguise his failings and his vices, and by his example and authority to keep a veil drawn over the futility and debauch of his court.

His successor, not to the throne, but to the sovereign power, was a mere rake, with some wit, and no morals; nay, with so little regard to them, that he made them a subject of ridicule in discourse, and appeared in his whole conduct more profligate, if that could be, than he was in principle. The difference between these characters soon appeared in abominable effects; such as, cruelty apart, might recal the memory of Nero, or, in the other sex, that of Messalina, and such as I leave the chroniclers of scandal to relate.

Our Elizabeth was queen in a limited monarchy, and reigned

over a people at all times more easily led than driven ; and at that time capable of being attached to their prince and their country, by a more generous principle than any of those which prevail in our days, by affection. There was a strong prerogative then in being, and the crown was in possession of greater legal power. Popularity was, however, then, as it is now, and as it must be always in mixed government, the sole true foundation of that sufficient authority and influence, which other constitutions give the prince gratis, and independently of the people, but which a king of this nation must acquire. The wise queen saw it, and she saw too, how much popularity depends on those appearances, that depend on the decorum, the decency, the grace, and the propriety of behaviour of which we are speaking. A warm concern for the interest and honour of the nation, a tenderness for her people, and a confidence in their affections were appearances that ran through her whole publick conduct, and gave life and colour to it. She did great things, and she knew how to set them off according to their full value, by her manner of doing them. In her private behaviour she showed great affability, she descended even to familiarity ; but her familiarity was such as could not be imputed to her weakness, and was, therefore, most justly ascribed to her goodness. Though a woman, she hid all that was womanish about her : and if a few equivocal marks of coquetry appeared on some occasions, they passed like flashes of lightning, vanished as soon as they were discerned, and imprinted no blot on her character. She had private friendships, she had favourites : but she never suffered her friends to forget she was their queen ; and when her favourites did, she made them feel that she was so. . . .

What in truth can be so lovely, what so venerable, as to contemplate a king, on whom the eyes of a whole people are fixed, filled with admiration, and glowing with affection ? A king, in the temper of whose government, like that of Nerva, things so seldom allied as empire and liberty are intimately mixed, coexist together inseparably, and constitute one real essence ? What spectacle can be presented to the view of the mind so rare, so nearly divine, as a king possessed of absolute power, neither usurped by fraud, nor maintained by force, but the genuine effect of esteem, of confidence, and affection ; the free gift of liberty, who finds her greatest security in this power, and would desire no other if the prince on the throne could be, what his people wish him to be, immortal ? Of such a prince, and of such a prince alone, it may be said with strict propriety and truth,

> " Volentes
> " Per populos dat jura, viamque affectat Olympo."

Civil fury will have no place in this draught : or if the monster is seen, he must be seen as Virgil describes him,

> " Centum vinctus ahenis
> " Post tergum nodis, fremit horridus ore cruento."

He must be seen subdued, bound, chained, and deprived entirely of power to do hurt. In his place, concord will appear, brooding peace and prosperity on the happy land : joy sitting in every face, content in every heart ; a people unoppressed, undisturbed, unalarmed ; busy to improve their private property and the publick stock ; fleets covering the ocean, bringing home wealth by the returns of industry, carrying assistance or terrour abroad by the direction of wisdom, and asserting triumphantly the right and the honour of Great Britain, as far as waters roll and as winds can waft them.

Those who live to see such happy days, and to act in so glorious a scene, will perhaps call to mind, with some tenderness of sentiment, when he is no more, a man, who contributed his mite to carry on so good a work, and who desired life for nothing so much, as to see a king of Great Britain the most popular man in this country, and a Patriot King at the head of a united people.

Works.

GEORGE BERKELEY.

1684–1753.

ALCIPHRON, OR THE MINUTE PHILOSOPHER.

A DIALOGUE.

DIALOGUE i. i.—I flattered myself, Theages, that before this time I might have been able to have sent you an agreeable account of the success of the affair, which brought me into this remote corner of the country. But instead of this, I should now give you the detail of its miscarriage, if I did not rather choose to entertain you with some amusing incidents, which have helped to make me easy under a circumstance I could neither obviate nor foresee. Events are not in our power ; but it always is, to make a good use even of the very worst. And I must needs own, the course and event of this affair gave opportunity for reflections, that make me some amends for a great loss of time, pains, and expence. A life of action, which takes its issue from the counsels, passions, and views of other men, if it doth not draw a man to imitate, will at last teach him to observe. And a mind at liberty to reflect on its own observations, if it produce nothing useful to the world, seldom fails of entertainment to itself. For several months past I have enjoyed such liberty and leisure in this distant retreat, far beyond the verge of that great whirlpool of business, faction, and pleasure, which is called the *world*. And a retreat in itself agreeable, after a long scene of trouble and disquiet, was made much more so by the conversation and good qualities of my host *Euphranor*, who unites in his own person the philosopher and the farmer, two characters not so inconsistent in nature as by custom they seem to be. *Euphranor*, from the time he left the university, hath lived in this small town, where he is possessed of a convenient house with a hundred acres of land adjoining to it ; which being improved by his own labour, yield him a plentiful subsistence. He hath a good collection, chiefly of old books, left him by a clergyman, his uncle, under whose care he was brought up. And the business of his farm doth not hinder him from making good use of it. He hath read much, and thought more ; his health and strength of body enabling him the better to bear fatigue of mind. He is of opinion that he could not carry on his studies with more advantage in the closet than the field, where his mind is seldom idle while he prunes the trees, follows the plough, or looks after his flocks. In the house of this honest friend I became acquainted with *Crito*, a neighbouring gentleman of distinguished merit and estate, who lives in great friendship with *Euphranor*. Last summer *Crito*, whose parish church is in our town, dining on a Sunday at *Euphranor's*, I happened to inquire after his guests, whom we had seen at church with him the Sunday before. They are both well, said *Crito*, but, having once occasionally conformed, to see what sort of assembly our parish could afford, they had no farther curiosity to gratify at church, and so chose to stay at home. How, said *Euphranor*, are they then dissenters? No, replied *Crito*, they are free-thinkers. . *Euphranor*, who had never met with any of this species or sect of men, and but little of their writings, showed a great desire to know their principles or system. That is more, said *Crito*, than I will undertake to tell you. Their writers are of different opinions. Some go farther, and explain themselves more freely than others. But the current general notions of the sect are best learned from conversation with those who profess themselves of it. Your curiosity may now be satisfied, if you and *Dion* would spend a week at my house with these gentle-men, who seem very ready to declare and propagate their opinions. *Alciphron* is above forty, and no stranger either to men or books. I knew him first at the temple, which, upon an estate's falling to him he quitted, to travel through the polite parts of *Europe*. Since his return he hath lived in the amuse-ments of the town, which being grown stale and tasteless to his palate, have flung him into a sort of splenatic indolence. The young gentleman, *Lysicles*, is a near kinsman of mine, one of lively parts and a general insight into letters, who, after having passed the forms of education, and seen a little of the world, fell into an intimacy with men of pleasure, and free-thinkers, I am afraid much to the damage·of his constitution and his fortune. But what I most regret, is the corruption of his mind by a set of pernicious principles, which, having been observed to survive the passions of youth, forestal even the remote hopes of amendment. They are both men of fashion, and would be agreeable enough, if they did not fancy themselves free-thinkers. But this, to speak the truth, has given them a certain air and manner, which a little too visibly declare they think themselves wiser than the rest of the world. I should therefore be not at all displeased if my guests met with their match, where they least expected it, in a country farmer. I shall not, replied *Euphranor*, pretend to any more than barely to inform myself of their principles and opinions. For this end I propose to-morrow to set a week's task to my labourers, and accept your invitation, if *Dion* thinks good. To which I gave consent. Mean while, said *Crito*, I shall prepare my guests, and let them know that an honest neighbour hath a mind to discourse them on the subject of their free-thinking. And, if I am not much mistaken, they will please themselves with the prospect of leaving a convert behind them, even in a country village. Next morning *Euphranor* rose early, and spent the forenoon in ordering his affairs. After dinner we took our walk to *Crito's*, which lay through half a dozen pleasant fields planted round with plane-trees, that are very common in this part of the country. We walked under the delicious shade of these trees for about an hour before we came to *Crito's* house, which stands in the middle of a small park, beautified with two fine groves of oak and walnut, and a winding stream of sweet and clear water. We met a servant at the door with a small basket of fruit which he was carrying into a grove, where he said his master was with the two strangers. We found them all three sitting under a shade. And after the usual forms at first meeting, *Euphranor* and I sit down by them. Our conversation began upon the beauty of this rural scene, the fine season of the year, and some late improvements which had been made in the adjacent country by new methods of agriculture. When *Alciphron* took occasion to observe, that the most valuable improvements came latest. I should have small temptation, said he, to live where men have neither polished manners, nor improved minds, though the face of the country were ever so well improved. But I have long observed, that there is a gradual progress in human affairs. The first care of mankind is to supply the cravings of nature; in the next place they study the conveniencies and comforts of life. But the subduing prejudices, and acquiring true knowledge, that *Herculean* labour is the last, being what demands the most perfect abilities, and to which all other advantages are preparative. Right, said *Euphranor*, *Alciphron* hath touched our true defect. It was always my opinion, that as soon as we had provided subsistence for the body, our next care should be to improve the mind. But the desire of wealth steps between and engrosseth men's thoughts.

DIALOGUE i. vi.—We will suppose, said *Alciphron*, that I am bred up, for instance in the church of *England*. When I come to maturity of judgment and reflect on the particular worship and opinions of this church, I do not remember when or by what means they first took possession of my mind, but there I find them from time immemorial. Then casting an eye on the education of children, from whence I can make a judgment of my own, I observe they are instructed in religious matters before they can reason about them, and consequently that all such instruction is nothing else but filling the tender mind of a child with prejudices. I do therefore reject all those religious notions, which I consider as the other follies of my childhood. I am confirmed in this way of thinking, when I look abroad into the world, where I observe papists, and several sects of dissenters, which do all agree in a general profession of belief in Christ, but d.ffer vastly one from another in the particulars of faith and worship. I then enlarge my view so as to take in *Jews* and *Mahometans*, between whom and the christians I perceive indeed some small agreement in the belief of one God ; but then they have each their distinct laws and revelations, for which they profess the same regard. But extending my view still further to heathenish and idolatrous nations, I discover an endless variety, not only in particular opinions and modes of worship, but even in the very notion of a deity, wherein they widely differ one from another, and from all the forementioned sects. Upon the whole, instead of truth simple and uniform, I perceive nothing but discord, opposition, and wild pretensions, all springing from the same source, to wit the prejudices of education. From such reasonings and reflections as these, thinking men have concluded that all religions are alike false and fabulous. One is a Christian, another a Jew, a third a Mahometan, a fourth an idolatrous Gentile, but all from one and the same reason, because they happen to be bred up each in his respective sect. In the same manner, therefore, as each of these contending parties condemns the rest, so an unprejudiced stander-by will condemn and reject them altogether, observing that they all draw their origin from the same fallacious principle, and are carried on by the same artifice to answer the same ends of the priest and the magistrate.

DIALOGUE v. xix.—ALC. But there is a sort of war and warriors

peculiar to christendom, which the heathens had no notion of:
I mean disputes in theology and polemical divines, which the
world hath been wonderfully pestered with : these teachers of
peace, meekness, concord, and what not! if you take their
word for it : but, if you cast an eye upon their practice, you
find them to have been in all ages the most contentious,
quarrelsome, disagreeing crew that ever appeared upon earth.
To observe the skill and sophistry, the zeal and eagerness, with
which those barbarians the school divines, split hairs and
contest about chimœras, gives me more indignation as being
more absurd and a greater scandal to human reason, than all
the ambitious intrigues, cabals, and politics of the court of
Rome. CRI. If divines are quarrelsome, that is not so far
forth as divine, but as undivine and unchristian. Justice is a
good thing ; and the art of healing is excellent ; nevertheless,
in the administering of justice or physic men may be wronged
or poisoned. But as wrong cannot be justice, or the effect of
justice, so poison cannot be medicine or the effect of medicine,
so neither can pride nor strife be religion or the effect of
religion. Having premised this, I acknowledge, you may often
see hot-headed bigots engage themselves in religious as well as
civil parties, without being of credit or service to either. And
as for the schoolmen in particular, I do not in the least think
the christian religion concerned in the defence of them, their
tenets or their method of handling them ; but, whatever
futility there may be in their notions, or inelegancy in their
language, in pure justice to truth one must own, they neither
banter nor rail nor declaim in their writings, and are so far
from shewing fury or passion, that perhaps an impartial judge
will think, the minute philosophers are by no means to be compared with them, for keeping close to the point, or for temper
and good manners. But after all, if men are puzzled, wrangle,
talk nonsense, and quarrel about religion, so they do about law,
physic, politics, and everything else of moment. I ask whether
in these professions, or in any other, where men have refined
and abstracted, they. do not run into disputes, chicane,
nonsense, and contradictions, as well as in Divinity? And yet
this doth not hinder but there may be many excellent rules,
and just notions, and useful truths in all those professions. In
all disputes human passions too often mix themselves, in proportion as the subject is conceived to be more or less important.
But we ought not to confound the cause of men with the cause
of God, or make human follies an objection to divine truths. It
is easy to distinguish what looks like wisdom from above, and

what proceeds from the passion and weakness of men. This is so clear a point, that one would be tempted to think, the not doing it was an effect, not of ignorance, but, of something worse.

DIALOGUE v. xxiv. ALC. There is, I must needs say, one sort of learning undoubtedly of Christian original, and peculiar to the universities ; where our youth spend several years in acquiring that mysterious jargon of scholasticism ; than which there could never have been contrived a more effectual method, to perplex and confound human understanding. It is true, gentlemen are untaught by the. world what they have been taught at the college : but then their time is doubly lost. CRI. But what if this scholastic learning was not of Christian but of Mahometan original, being derived from the *Arabs?* And what if this grievance of gentlemen's spending several years in learning and unlearning this jargon, be all grimace and a specimen only of the truth and candour of certain minute philosophers, who raise great invectives from slight occasions, and judge too often without inquiring ? Surely it would be no such deplorable loss of time, if a young gentleman spent a few months upon that so much despised and decried art of logic, *a surfeit of which is by no means the prevailing nuisance of this age.** It is one thing to waste one's time in learning and unlearning the barbarous terms, wire-drawn distinctions, and prolix sophistry of the schoolmen, and another to attain some exactness in defining and arguing : things perhaps not altogether beneath the dignity even of a minute philosopher. There was indeed a time, when logic was considered as its own object ; and that art of reasoning, instead of being transferred to things turned alto-gether upon words and abstractions ; which produced a sort of leprosy in all parts of knowledge, corrupting and converting them into hollow verbal disputations in a most impure dialect. But those times are past ; and that, which had been cultivated as the principal learning for some ages, is now considered in another light, and by no means makes that figure in the universities, or bears that part in the studies of young gentle-men educated there, which is pretended by those admirable reformers of religion and learning, the minute philosophers.

DIALOGUE vii. xxxi.—CRI. In order to cure a distemper, you should consider what produced it. Had men reasoned themselves into a wrong opinion, one might hope to reason them out of it. But this is not the case ; the infidelity of most minute philosophers seeming an effect of very different motives

---

* The italics are mine.—A. G.

from thought and reason, little incidents, vanity, disgust, humour, inclination, without the least assistance from reason, are often known to make infidels. Where the general tendency of a doctrine is disagreeable, the mind is prepared to relish and improve everything that with the least pretence seems to make against it. Hence the coarse manners of a country curate, the polite ones of a chaplain, the wit of a minute philosopher, a jest, a song, a tale can serve instead of a reason for infidelity. *Bupalus** preferred a rake in the church, and then made use of him as an argument against it. Vice, indolence, faction, and fashion produce minute philosophers, and meer petulancy not a few. Who then can expect a thing so irrational and capricious should yield to reason? It may, nevertheless, be worth while to argue against such men, and expose their fallacies, if not for their own sake, yet for the sake of others ; as it may lessen their credit, and prevent the growth of their sect, by removing a prejudice in their favour, which sometimes inclines others as well as themselves to think they have made a monopoly of human reason.

XXXIII.—On all occasions, we ought to distinguish the serious, modest, ingenuous man of sense, who hath scruples about religion, and behaves like a prudent man in doubt, from the minute philosophers, those profane and conceited men, who must needs proselyte others to their own doubts. When one of this stamp presents himself, we should consider what species he is of : Whether a first or a second-hand philosopher, a libertine, or scorner, or sceptic? Each character requiring a peculiar treatment. Some men are too ignorant to be humble, without which there can be no docility : But though a man must in some degree have thought and considered to be capable of being convinced, yet it is possible the most ignorant may be laughed out of his opinions. I knew a woman of sense reduce two minute philosophers, who had long been a nuisance to the neighbourhood, by taking her cue from their predominant affectations. The one set up for being the most incredulous man upon earth, the other for the most unbounded freedom. • She observed to the first, that he who had credulity sufficient to trust the most valuable things, his life and fortune, to his apothecary and lawyer, ridiculously affected the character of incredulous, by refusing to trust his soul, a thing in his own account but a meer trifle, to his parish-priest. The other, being what you call a beau, she made sensible how absolute a slave he was in

---

* *i.e.,* gave a preferment to.

point of dress, to him the most important thing in the world, while he was earnestly contending for a liberty of thinking, with which he never troubled his head ; and how much more it concerned and became him to affect an independency on fashion, and obtain scope for his genius, where it was best qualified to exert itself. The minute philosophers at first hand are very few, and considered in themselves, of small consequence : but their followers, who pin their faith upon him, are numerous, and not less confident than credulous ; there being something in the air and manner of these seccnd-hand philosophers, very apt to disconcert a man of gravity and argument, and much more difficult to be born than the weight of their objections.

XXXIV.—*Crito* having made an end, *Euphranor* declared it to be his opinion, that it would much conduce to the public benefit, if, instead of discouraging free-thinking, there was erected in the midst of this free country a dianœtic academy, or seminary for free-thinkers, provided with retired chambers, and galleries, and shady walks and groves, where, after seven years spent in silence and meditation, a man might commence a genuine free-thinker, and from that time forward, have licence to think what he pleased, and a badge to distinguish him from counterfeits. In good earnest, said *Crito*, I imagine that thinking is the great *desideratum* of the present age ; and that the real cause of whatever is amiss, may justly be reckoned the general neglect of education, in those who need it most, the people of fashion. What can be expected where those who have the most influence, have the least sense, and those who are sure to be followed set the worst example ? Where youth so uneducated are yet so forward ? Where modesty is esteemed pussillanimity, and a deference to years, knowledge, religion, laws, want of sense and spirit ? Such untimely growth of genius would not have been valued or encouraged by the wise men of antiquity ; whose sentiments on this point are so ill suited to the genius of our times, that it is to be feared modern ears·could not bear them. But however ridiculous such maxims might seem to our *British* youth, who are so capable and so forward to try experiments, and mend the constitution of their country, I believe it will be admitted by men of sense, that if the governing part of mankind would in these days, for experiment's sake, consider themselves in the old *Homerical* light as pastors of the people, whose duty it was to improve their flock, they would soon find that this is to be done by an education very different from the modern, and othergess maxims than those of the minute philosophy. If our youth were really inured to thought and reflexion, and an acquaintance with the excellent writers of antiquity, we should soon see that licentious humour, vulgarly called free-thinking, banished from the presence of gentlemen, together with ignorance and ill taste ; which as they are inseparable from vice, so men follow vice for the sake of pleasure, and fly from virtue through an abhorrence of pain. Their minds therefore betimes should be formed and accustomed to receive pleasure and pain from proper objects, or, which is the same thing, to have their inclinations and aversions rightly placed. Καλῶς χαίρειν ἤ μισεῖν. This according to *Plato* and *Aristotle*, was the ὀρθή παιδεία, the right education. And those who, in their own minds, their health, or their fortunes, feel the cursed effects of a wrong one, would do well to consider, they cannot better make amends for what was amiss in themselves, than by preventing the same in their posterity. While *Crito* was saying this, company came in, which put an end to our conversation.

Alciphron.

HENRY FIELDING.

1707–1754.

An interview between parson ADAMS *and parson* TRULLIBER.

PARSON ADAMS came to the house of Parson Trulliber, whom he found stript into his waistcoat, with an apron on, and a pail in his hand, just come from serving his hogs ; for Mr. Trulliber was a parson on Sundays, but all the other six days might more properly be called a farmer. He occupied a small piece of land of his own, besides which he rented a considerable deal more. His wife milked his cows, managed his dairy, and followed the markets with butter and eggs. The hogs fell chiefly to his care ; which he carefully waited on at home, and attended to fairs ; on which occasion he was liable to many jokes, his own size being with much ale rendered little inferior to that of the beasts he sold. He was indeed one of the largest men you should see, and could have acted the part of Sir John Falstaff without stuffing. Add to this, that the rotundity of his belly was considerably increased by the shortness of his stature, his shadow ascending very near as far in height, when he lay on his back, as when he stood on his legs. His voice was loud and hoarse, and his accents extremely broad ; to complete the whole, he had a stateliness in his gait, when he walked, not unlike that of a goose, only he stalked slower.

Mr. Trulliber being informed that somebody wanted to speak to him, immediately slipt off his apron, and clothed himself in an old nightgown ; being the dress in which he always saw his company at home. His wife, who informed him of Mr. Adams's arrival, had made a small mistake ; for she had told her husband, ' She believed there was a man come for some of his ' hogs.' This supposition made Mr. Trulliber hasten with the utmost expedition to attend his guest. He no sooner saw Adams, than not in the least doubting the cause of his errand

to be what his wife had imagined, he told him, 'He was come
'in very good time ; that he expected a dealer that very after-
'noon,' and added, 'they were all pure and fat, and upwards
'of 20 score apiece.'   Adams answered, 'He believed he did
'not know him.'   'Yes, yes,' cried Trulliber, 'I have seen
'you often at fair ; why, we have dealt before now, mun, I
'warrant you, yes, yes,' cries he, 'I remember thy face very well,
'but won't mention a word more till you have seen them,
'though I have never sold thee a flitch of such bacon as is now
'in the stye.'   Upon which he laid violent hands on Adams,
and dragged him into the hogstye, which was indeed but two
steps from his parlour window.   They were no sooner arrived
there, than he cried out, 'Do but handle them ; step in, friend,
'art welcome to handle them, whether thou dost buy or no.'
At which words, opening the gate, he pushed Adams into the
pigstye, insisting on it, that he should handle them, before he
would talk one word with him.   Adams, whose natural com-
placence was beyond any artificial, was obliged to comply before
he was suffered to explain himself ; and laying hold on one of
their tails, the unruly beast gave such a sudden spring, that he
threw poor Adams all along in the mire.   Trulliber, instead of
assisting him to get up, burst into a laughter, and entering the
stye, said to Adams, with some contempt, 'Why, dost not
'know how to handle a hog ?'   and was going to lay hold of
one himself ; but Adams, who thought he had carried his com-
placence far enough, was no sooner on his legs, than he escaped
out of the reach of the animals, and cried out, *Nihil habeo cum
porcis :* 'I am a clergyman, Sir, and am not come to buy hogs.'
Trulliber answered, 'He was sorry for the mistake ; but that
'he must blame his wife ;' adding, 'she was a fool, and
'always committed blunders.'   He then desired him to walk in
and clean himself ; that he would only fasten up the stye and
follow him.   Adams desired leave to dry his great coat, wig
and hat by the fire, which Trulliber granted.   Mrs. Trulliber
would have brought him a bason of water to wash his face ;
but her husband bid her be quiet, like a fool as she was, or she
would commit more blunders, and then directed Adams to the
pump.   While Adams was thus employed, Trulliber conceiving
no great respect for the appearance of his guest, fastened the
parlour door, and now conducted him into the kitchen ; telling
him, he believed a cup of drink would do him no harm, and
whispered his wife to draw a little of the worst ale.   After a
short silence, Adams said, 'I fancy, Sir, you already perceive
'me to be a clergyman.'   'Ay, ay,' cries Trulliber, grinning ;

' I perceive you have some cassock ; I will not venture to caale
'it a whole one.' Adams answered, 'It was indeed none of
'the best ; but he had the misfortune to tear it about ten years
'ago in passing over a stile.' Mrs. Trulliber returning with the
drink, told her husband, 'She fancied the gentleman was a
'traveller, and that he would be glad to eat a bit.' Trulliber
bid her hold her impertinent tongue ; and asked her, 'If parsons
'used to travel without horses?' adding, 'He supposed the
'gentleman had none by his having no boots on.' 'Yes, Sir,
'yes,' says Adams, 'I have a horse, but I have left him behind
me.' 'I am glad to hear you have one,' says Trulliber ; 'for I
'assure you, I don't love to see clergymen on foot ; it is not
'seemly, nor suiting the dignity of the cloth.' Here Trulliber
made a long oration on the dignity of the cloth (or rather
gown) not much worth relating, till his wife had spread the
table, and set a mess of porridge on it for his breakfast. He
then said to Adams, 'I don't know, friend, how you come to
'caale on me ; however, as you are here, if you think proper to
'eat a morsel, you may.' Adams accepted the invitation, and
the two parsons sat down together ; Mrs. Trulliber waiting
behind her husband's chair, as was, it seems, her custom.
Trulliber eat heartily, but scarce put any thing in his mouth
without finding fault with his wife's cookery. All which the
poor woman bore patiently. Indeed, she was so absolute an
admirer of her husband's greatness and importance, of which
she had frequent hints from his own mouth, that she almost
carried her adoration to an opinion of his infallibility. To say
the truth, the parson had exercised her more ways than one ;
and the pious woman had so well edified by her husband's
sermons, that she had resolved to receive the bad things of this
world together with the good. She had indeed been at first a
little contentious ; but he had long since got the better ; partly
by her love for this ; partly by her fear of that ; partly by
her religion ; partly by the respect he paid himself ; and
partly by that which he received from the parish : She
had, in short, absolutely submitted, and now worshipped
her husband as Sarah did Abraham, calling him (not lord,
but) master. Whilst they were at table, her husband gave
her a fresh example of his greatness ; for as she had just
delivered a cup of ale to Adams, he snatched it out of his
hand, and crying out, 'I caal'd vurst,' swallowed down the
ale. Adams denied it ; it was referred to the wife, who, though
her conscience was on the side of Adams, durst not give it
against her husband. Upon which he said, 'No, Sir, no ; I

'should not have been so rude to have taken it from you, if you
'had caal'd vurst; but I'd have you know I'm a better man
'than to suffer the best he in the kingdom to drink before me in
'my own house, when I caale vurst."

As soon as their breakfast was ended, Adams began in the
following manner : 'I think, Sir, it is high time to inform you
'of the business of my embassy. I am a traveller, and am
'passing this way in company with two young people, a lad and
'a damsel, my parishioners, towards my own cure ; we stopt at
'a house of hospitality in the parish, where they directed me to
'you, as having the cure.' '———Though I am but a curate,'
says Trulliber, 'I believe I am as warm as the vicar himself, or
'perhaps the rector of the next parish too; I believe I could
'buy them both.' 'Sir," cries Adams, 'I rejoice thereat.
'Now, Sir, my business is, that we are by various accidents
'stript of our money, and are not able to pay our reckoning,
'being seven shillings. I therefore request you to assist me
'with the loan of those seven shillings, and also seven shillings
'more, which peradventure, I shall return to you ; but if not, I
'am convinced you will joyfully embrace such an opportunity
'of laying up a treasure in a better place than any this world
'affords.'

Suppose a stranger, who entered the chambers of a lawyer,
being imagined a client, when the lawyer was preparing his
palm for the fee, should pull out a writ against him. Suppose
an apothecary, at the door of a chariot, containing some great
doctor of eminent skill, should, instead of directions to a patient,
present him with a potion for himself. Suppose a minister
should, instead of a good round sum, treat my Lord——or Sir
——or Esq ;——with a good broomstick. Suppose a civil
companion, or a led captain, should, instead of virtue, and
honour, and beauty, and parts, and admiration ; thunder vice,
and infamy, and ugliness, and folly, and contempt, in his
patron's ears. Suppose when a tradesman first carries in his
bill, the man of fashion should pay it ; or suppose, if he did so,
the tradesman should abate what he had overcharged, on the
supposition of waiting. In short,—suppose what you will, you
never can, nor will suppose any thing equal to the astonishment
which seized on Trulliber, as soon as Adams had ended his
speech. A while he rolled his eyes in silence ; sometimes surveying Adams, then his wife, then casting them on the ground,
then lifting them up to heaven. At last, he burst forth in the
following accents : 'Sir, I believe I know where to lay up my
'little treasure as well as another ; I thank G—, if I am not so

‘warm as some, I am content ; that is a blessing greater than
‘riches ; and he, to whom that is given, need ask no more.
‘To be content with a little, is greater than to possess the
‘world ; which a man may possess without being so.   Lay up
‘my treasure ! what matters where a man's treasure is, whose
‘heart is in the scriptures ? there is the treasure of the
‘christian.’   At these words the water ran from Adams's eyes ;
and catching Trulliber by the hand in a rapture, ‘ Brother,’ says
he, ‘ heavens bless the accident by which I came to see you ; I
‘ would have walked many a mile to have communed with you ;
‘and, believe me, I will shortly pay you a second visit ; but my
‘friends, I fancy, by this time, wonder at my stay ; so let me
‘have the money immediately.’   Trulliber then put on a stern
look, and cried out, ‘ Thou dost not intend to rob me ? ’   At
which the wife, bursting into tears, fell on her knees, and
roared out, ‘ O dear Sir ! for heaven's sake don't rob my master,
‘we are but poor people.’   ‘ Get up for a fool, as thou
‘art, and go about thy business,’ said Trulliber, ‘ dost
‘think the man will venture his life ? he is a beggar, and no
‘robber.’   ‘ Very true, indeed,’ answered Adams.   ‘ I wish,
‘with all my heart, the tithing-man was here,’ cries Trulliber,
‘ I would have thee punished as a vagabond for thy impudence.
‘Fourteen shillings indeed !   I won't give thee a farthing.   I
‘believe thou art no more a clergyman than the woman there
‘(pointing to his wife) ; but if thou art, dost deserve to have thy
‘gown stript over thy shoulders, for running about the country
‘in such a manner.’   ‘ I forgive your suspicions,’ says Adams ;
‘but suppose I am not a clergyman, I am, nevertheless, thy
‘brother ; and thou, as a christian, much more as a clergyman,
‘art obliged to relieve my distress.’   ‘ Dost preach to me ? ’
replied Trulliber, ‘ dost pretend to instruct me in my duty ? ’
‘Isacks, a good story,’ cries Mrs. Trulliber, ‘ to preach to my
‘master.’   ‘ Silence, woman,’ cries Trulliber.   ‘ I would have
‘thee know, friend,’ (addressing himself to Adams) ‘ I shall not
‘learn my duty from such as thee ; I know what charity is,
‘better than to give to vagabonds.’   ‘ Besides, if we were
‘inclined, the poor's rate obliges us to give so much charity,’
cries the wife.—‘ Pugh ! thou art a fool.   Poor's rate ! hold thy
‘nonsense,’ answered Trulliber ; and then, turning to Adams,
he told him, ‘ He would give him nothing.’   ‘ I am sorry,’
answered Adams, ‘ that you do know what charity is, since you
‘practise it no better ; I must tell you, if you trust to your
‘knowledge for your justification, you will find yourself deceived,
‘though you should add faith to it, without good works.’

'Fellow,' cries Trulliber, 'dost thou speak against faith in my
'house? Get out of my doors, I will no longer remain under
'the same roof with a wretch who speaks wantonly of faith and
'the scriptures.' 'Name not the scriptures,' says Adams.
'How! not name the scriptures! Do you disbelieve the scrip-
'tures?' cries Trulliber. 'No, but you do,' answered Adams,
'If I may reason from your practice ; for their commands
'are so explicit, and their rewards and punishments so im-
'mense, that it is impossible a man should stedfastly believe
'without obeying. Now, there is no command more express,
'no duty more frequently enjoined, than charity. Whoever,
'therefore, is void of charity, I make no scruple of pronouncing
'that he is no christian.' 'I would not advise thee,' says
Trulliber, 'to say that I am no christian ; I won't take it of
'you ; for I believe I am as good a man as thyself:' (and
indeed, though he was now rather too corpulent for athletic exercises, he had, in his youth, been one of the best boxers and
cudgel-players in the county.) His wife, seeing him clench his
fist, interposed, and begged him not to fight, but shew himself a
true christian, and take the law of him. As nothing could
provoke Adams to strike, but an absolute assault on himself or
his friend, he smiled at the angry look and gestures of Trulliber ;
and telling him, he was sorry to see such men in orders, departed
without further ceremony.

Joseph Andrews.

SAMUEL JOHNSON.

1709-1784.

THE PATRIOT.

Addressed to the Electors of Great Britain, 1774.

They bawl for freedom in their senseless mood,
   Yet still revolt when truth would set them free ;
   Licence they mean, when they cry liberty,
For who loves that must first be wise and good.—MILTON.

To improve the golden moment of opportunity, and catch the good that is within our reach, is the great art of life. Many wants are suffered, which might once have been supplied ; and much time is lost in regretting the time which had been lost before.

At the end of every seven years comes the Saturnalian season, when the freemen of Great Britain may please themselves with the choice of their representatives. This happy day has now arrived, somewhat sooner than it could be claimed.

To select and depute those, by whom laws are to be made, and taxes to be granted, is a high dignity and an important trust : and it is the business of every elector to consider, how this dignity may be well sustained, and this trust faithfully discharged.

It ought to be deeply impressed on the minds of all who have voices in this national deliberation, that no man can deserve a seat in parliament who is not a PATRIOT. No other man will protect our rights, no other man can merit our confidence.

A PATRIOT is he whose publick conduct is regulated by one single motive, the love of his country ; who, as an agent in parliament, has for himself neither hope nor fear, neither kindness nor resentment, but refers every thing to the common interest.

That of five hundred men, such as this degenerate age affords, a majority can be found thus virtuously abstracted, who will affirm? Yet there is no good in despondence: vigilance and activity often effect more than was expected. Let us take a patriot where we can meet him; and that we may not flatter ourselves by false appearances, distinguish those marks which are certain from those which may deceive: for a man may have the external appearance of a Patriot, without the constituent qualities; as false coins have often lustre, though they want weight.

Some claim a place in the list of patriots by an acrimonious and unremitting opposition to the court.

This mark is by no means infallible. Patriotism is not necessarily included in rebellion. A man may hate his king, yet not love his country. He that has been refused a reasonable or unreasonable request, who thinks his merit underrated, and sees his influence declining, begins soon to talk of natural equality, the absurdity of *many made for one*, the original compact, the foundation of authority, and the majesty of the people. As his political melancholy increases, he tell us, and perhaps dreams, of the advances of the prerogative, and the dangers of arbitrary power; yet his design in all his declamation is not to benefit his country, but to gratify his malice.

These, however, are the most honest of the opponents of government; their patriotism is a species of disease; and they feel some part of what they express. But the greater, far the greater number of those who rave and rail, and inquire and accuse, neither suspect nor fear, nor care for the publick; but hope to force their way to riches by virulence and invective, and are vehement and clamorous, only that they may be sooner hired to be silent.

A man sometimes starts up a patriot, only by disseminating discontent, and propagating reports of secret influence, of dangerous counsels, of violated rights, and encroaching usurpation.

This practice is no certain note of patriotism. To instigate the populace with rage beyond the provocation, is to suspend publick happiness, if not to destroy it. He is no lover of his country, that unnecessarily disturbs its peace. Few errours, and few faults of government can justify an appeal to the rabble; who ought not to judge of what they cannot understand, and whose opinions are not propagated by reason, but caught by contagion.

The fallaciousness of this note of patriotism is particularly apparent, when the clamour continues after the evil is past. They who are still filling our ears with Mr. Wilkes, and the freeholders of Middlesex, lament a grievance that is now at an end. Mr. Wilkes may be chosen, if any will choose him, and the precedent of his exclusion makes not any honest, or any decent man, think himself in danger.

It may be doubted whether the name of a Patriot can be fairly given as the reward of secret satire, or open outrage To fill the newspapers with sly hints of corruption and intrigue, to circulate the Middlesex Journal and London Packet, may, indeed, be zeal ; but it may likewise be interest and malice. To offer a petition, not expected to be granted : to insult a king with a rude remonstrance, only because there is no punishment for legal insolence, is not courage, for there is no danger ; nor patriotism, for it tends to the subversion of order, and lets wickedness loose upon the land, by destroying the reverence due to sovereign authority.

It is the quality of patriotism to be jealous and watchful, to observe all secret machinations, and to see public dangers at a distance. The true lover of his country is ready to communicate his fears, and to sound the alarm, whenever he perceives the approach of mischief. But he sounds no alarm, when there is no enemy : he never terrifies his countrymen till he is terrified himself. The patriotism therefore may be justly doubted of him, who professes to be disturbed by incredibilities ; who tells, that the last peace was obtained by bribing the princess of Wales ; that the king is grasping at arbitrary power ; and that because the French, in the new conquests, enjoy their own laws, there is a design at court of abolishing in England the trial by juries.

Still less does the true Patriot circulate opinions which he knows to be false. No man, who loves his country, fills the nation with clamourous complaints, that the Protestant religion is in danger, because *Popery is established in the extensive province of Quebec*—a falsehood so open and shameless, that it can need no confutation among those who know that of which it is almost impossible for the most unenlightened zealot to be ignorant.

That Quebec is on the other side of the Atlantic, at too great a distance to do much good or harm to the European world :

That the inhabitants, being French, were always Papists, who are certainly more dangerous as enemies, than as subjects :

That though the province be wide, the people are few,

probably not so many as may be found in one of the larger English counties :

That persecution is not more virtuous in a Protestant than a Papist ; and that while we blame Lewis the Fourteenth for his dragoons and his galleys, we ought, when power comes into our hands, to use it with greater equity :

That when Canada with its inhabitants was yielded, the free enjoyment of their religion was stipulated ; a condition, of which king William, who was no propagator of Popery, gave an example nearer home, at the surrender of Limerick :

That in an age, where every mouth is open for *liberty of conscience*, it is equitable to show some regard to the conscience of a Papist, who may be supposed, like other men, to think himself safest in his own religion ; and that those, at least, who enjoy a toleration, ought not to deny it to our new subjects.

If liberty of conscience be a natural right, we have no power to withhold it ; if it be an indulgence, it may be allowed to Papists, while it is not denied to other sects.

A patriot is necessarily and invariably a lover of the people. But even this mark may sometimes deceive us.

The people is a very heterogeneous and confused mass of the wealthy and the poor, the wise and the foolish, the good and the bad. Before we confer on a man, who caresses the people, the title of patriot, we must examine to what part of the people, he directs his notice. It is proverbially said, that he who dissembles his own character, may be known by that of his companions. If the candidate of patriotism endeavours to infuse right opinions into the higher ranks, and by their influence to regulate the lower; if he consorts chiefly with the wise, the temperate, the regular, and the virtuous, his love of the people may be rational and honest. But if his first or principal application be to the indigent, who are always inflammable ; to the weak, who are naturally suspicious ; to the ignorant, who are easily misled ; and to the profligate, who have no hope but from mischief and confusion ; let his love of the people be no longer boasted. No man can reasonably be thought a lover of his country, for roasting an ox, or burning a boot, or attending the meeting at Mile-End, or registering his name in the Lumber Troop. He may, among the drunkards, be a hearty fellow, and among sober handicraftsmen, a free-spoken gentleman ; but he must have some better distinction before he is a patriot.

Works.

DAVID HUME.

1711–1776.

OF MIRACLES—PART I.

THERE is, in Dr. Tillotson's writings, an argument against the *real presence*, which is as concise, and elegant, and strong, as any argument can possibly be supposed against a doctrine, so little worthy of a serious refutation. It is acknowledged on all hands, says that learned prelate, that the authority, either of the Scripture or of tradition, is founded merely on the testimony of the apostles, who were eye witnesses to those miracles of our Saviour, by which He proved his divine mission. Our evidence, then, for the truth of the *Christian* religion, is less than the evidence for the truth of our senses ; because, even in the first authors of our religion, it was no greater ; and it is evident it must diminish in passing from them to their disciples ; nor can any one rest such confidence in their testimony, as in the immediate object of his senses. But a weaker evidence can never destroy a stronger ; and therefore, were the doctrine of the real presence ever so clearly revealed in Scripture, it were directly contrary to the rules of just reasoning to give our assent to it. It contradicts sense, though both the Scripture and tradition, on which it is supposed to be built, carry not such evidence with them as sense ; when they are considered merely as external evidences, and are now brought home to every one's breast, by the immediate operation of the Holy Spirit.

Nothing is so convenient as a decisive argument of this kind, which must at least *silence* the most arrogant bigotry and superstition, and free us from their impertinent solicitations. I flatter myself, that I have discovered an argument of a like nature, which, if just, will, with the wise and learned, be an everlasting check to all kinds of superstitious delusion, and consequently will be useful as long as the world endures. For so long, I presume, will the accounts of miracles and prodigies be found in all history, sacred and profane.

Though experience be our only guide in reasoning concerning matters of fact ; it must be acknowledged, that this guide is not altogether infallible, but in some cases is apt to lead us into errors. One who, in our climate, should expect better weather in any week of June than in one of December, would reason justly and conformably to experience ; but it is certain, that he may happen, in the event, to find himself mistaken. However, we may observe, that, in such a case, he would have no cause to complain of experience ; because it commonly informs us beforehand of the uncertainty, by that contrariety of events, which we may learn from a diligent observation. All effects follow not with like certainty from their supposed causes. Some events are found, in all countries and all ages, to have been constantly conjoined together : Others are found to have been more variable, and sometimes to disappoint our expectations : so that, in our reasonings concerning matter of fact, there are all imaginable degrees of assurance, from the highest certainty to the lowest species of moral evidence.

A wise man, therefore, proportions his belief to the evidence. In such conclusions as are founded on an infallible experience, he expects the event with the last degree of assurance, and regards his past experience as a full *proof* of the future existence of that event. In other cases, he proceeds with more caution : He weighs the opposite experiments : He considers which side is supported by the greater number of experiments : To that side he inclines, with doubt and hesitation ; and when at last he fixes his judgment, the evidence exceeds not what we properly call *probability*. All probability, then, supposes an opposition of experiments and observations, where the one side is found to overbalance the other, and to produce a degree of evidence proportioned to the superiority. A hundred instances of experiments on one side, and fifty on another, afford a doubtful expectation of any event ; though a hundred uniform experiments, with only one that is contradictory, reasonably beget a pretty strong degree of assurance. In all cases, we must balance the opposite experiments, where they are opposite, and deduct the smaller number from the greater, in order to know the exact force of the superior evidence.

To apply these principles to a particular instance, we may observe, that there is no species of reasoning more common, more useful, and even necessary to human life, than that which is derived from the testimony of men, and the reports of eye witnesses and spectators. This species of reasoning, perhaps, one may deny to be founded on the relation of cause and effect. I shall not dispute about a word. It will be sufficient to observe, that our assurance in any argument of this kind is derived from no other principle than our observation of the veracity of human testimony, and of the usual conformity of facts to the reports of· witnesses. It being a general maxim that no objects have any discoverable connection together, and that all the inferences which we can draw from one to another, are founded merely on our experience of their constant and regular conjunction ; it is evident, that we ought not to make an exception to this maxim in favour of human testimony, whose connection with any event seems, in itself, as little necessary as any other. Were not the memory tenacious to a certain degree ; had not men commonly an inclination to truth and a principle of probity ; were they not sensible to shame, when detected in a falsehood : were not these, I say, discovered by *experience* to be qualities inherent in human nature, we should never repose the least confidence in human testimony. A man delirious, or noted for falsehood and villany, has no manner of authority with us.

And as the evidence, derived from witnesses and human testimony, is founded on past experience, so it varies with the experience, and is regarded either as a *proof* or a *probability*, according as the conjunction between any particular kind of report, and any kind of object, has been found to be constant or variable. There are a number of circumstances to be taken into consideration in all judgments of this kind ; and the ultimate standard, by which we determine all disputes, that may arise concerning them, is always derived from experience and observation. Where this experience is not entirely uniform on any side, it is attended with an unavoidable contrariety in our judgments, and with the same opposition and mutual destruction of argument as in every other kind of evidence. We frequently hesitate concerning the reports of others. We balance the opposite circumstances which cause any doubt or uncertainty ; and when we discover a superiority on any side, we incline to it ; but still with a diminution of assurance, in proportion to the force of its antagonist.

This contrariety of evidence, in the present case, may be derived from several different causes ; from the opposition of contrary testimony ; from the character or number of the witnesses ; from the manner of their delivering their testimony ; or from the union of all these circumstances. We entertain a suspicion concerning any matter of fact, when the witnesses contradict each other ; when they are but few, or of a doubtful character ; when they have an interest in what they affirm ; when they deliver their testimony with hesitation, or, on the contrary, with too violent asseverations. There are many other particulars of the same kind, which may diminish or destroy the force of any argument derived from human testimony.

Suppose, for instance, that the fact, which the testimony endeavours to establish, partakes of the extraordinary and the marvellous ; in that case, the evidence resulting from the testimony admits of a diminution greater or less, in proportion as the fact is more or less unusual. The reason why we place any credit in witnesses and historians, is not derived from any *connection* which we perceive, *à priori*, between testimony and reality, but because we are accustomed to find a conformity between them. But when the fact attested is such a one as has seldom fallen under our observation, here is a contest of two opposite experiences, of which the one destroys the other as far as its force goes ; and the superior can only operate on the mind by the force which remains. The very same principle of experience which gives us a certain degree of assurance in the testimony of witnesses, gives us also, in this case, another degree of assurance against the fact which they endeavour to establish ; from which contradiction there necessarily arises a counterpoise, and mutual destruction of belief and authority.

I should not believe such a story were it told me by Cato, was a proverbial saying in Rome, even during the lifetime of that philosophical patriot. The incredibility of a fact, it was allowed, might invalidate so great an authority.

The Indian prince, who refused to believe the first relations concerning the effects of frost, reasoned justly ; and it naturally required very strong testimony to engage his assent to facts that arose from a state of nature with which he was unacquainted, and which bore so little analogy to those events of which he had had constant and uniform experience. Though they were not contrary to his experience, they were not conformable to it.

But in order to increase the probability against the testimony of witnesses, let us suppose, that the fact which they affirm, instead of being only marvellous, is really miraculous ; and suppose also, that the testimony, considered apart and in itself, amounts to an entire proof ; in that case, there is proof against proof, of which the strongest must prevail, but still with a diminution of its force, in proportion to that of its antagonist.

A miracle is a violation of the laws of nature ; and as a firm and unalterable experience has established these laws, the proof against a miracle, from the very nature of the fact, is as entire as any argument from experience can possibly be imagined. Why is it more than probable, that all men must die ; that lead cannot of itself remain suspended in the air ; that fire consumes wood, and is extinguished by water ; unless it be, that these events are found agreeable to the laws of nature, and there is required a violation of these laws, or in other words, a miracle to prevent them ? Nothing is esteemed a miracle, if it ever happen in the common course of nature. It is no miracle that a man seemingly in good health should die on a sudden ; because such a kind of death, though more unusual than any other, has yet been frequently observed to happen. But it is a miracle, that a dead man should come to life ; because that has never been observed in any age or country. There must, therefore, be a uniform experience against every miraculous event, otherwise the event would not merit that appellation. And as an uniform experience amounts to a proof, there is here a direct and full *proof* from the nature of the fact against the existence of any miracle ; nor can such a proof be destroyed, or the miracle rendered credible, but by an opposite proof, which is superior.

The plain consequence is (and it is a general maxim worthy of our attention), " That no testimony is sufficient to establish a miracle, unless the testimony be of such a kind, that its falsehood would be more miraculous than the fact which it endeavours to establish : And even in that case there is a mutual destruction of arguments, and the superior only gives us an assurance suitable to that degree of force which remains after deducting the inferior." When any one tells me, that he saw a dead man restored to life, I immediately consider with myself, whether it be more probable that this person should either deceive or be deceived, or that the fact which he relates should really have happened. I weigh the one miracle against the other ; and according to the superiority which I discover, I pronounce my decision, and always reject the greater miracle. If the falsehood of his testimony would be more miraculous than the event which he relates ; then, and not till then, can he pretend to command my belief or opinion.

LAURENCE STERNE.

1713–1769.

ON HOBBY HORSES.

De gustibus non est disputandum: that is, there is no disputing against Hobby-horses ; and, for my part, I seldom do ; nor could I with any sort of grace had I been an enemy to them at the bottom, for happening at certain intervals and changes of the moon to be both fiddler and painter, according as the fly stings : be it known to you, that I keep a couple of pads myself, upon which in their turns (nor do I care who knows it), I frequently ride out and take the air ; though sometimes, to my shame be it spoken, I take somewhat longer journeys than what a wise man would think altogether right, but the truth is, I am not a wise man ; and besides am a mortal of so little consequence in the world, it is not much matter what I do ; so I seldom fret or fume at all or about it : nor does it much disturb my rest when I see such great lords and tall personages as hereafter follow, such, for instance, as my Lord A, B, C, D, E, F, G, H, I, K, L, M, N, O, P, Q, and so on, all of a row, mounted upon their several horses ; some with large stirrups, getting on in a more grave and sober pace ; others, on the contrary, tucked up to their very chins, with whips across their mouths, scourging and scampering it away like so many little parti-coloured devils astride a·mortgage, and as if some of them were resolved to break their necks. So much the better, say I to myself ; for in case the worst should happen, the world would make a shift to do excellently well without them ; and for the rest, why, God speed them ; even let them ride on without any opposition from me ; for were their lordships unhorsed this very night, 'tis ten to one but that many of them would be worse mounted by one half before to-morrow morning.

Not many of these instances therefore can be said to break

in upon my rest. But there is an instance, which I own puts me off my guard, and that is when I see one born for great actions, and, what is still more for his honour, whose nature ever inclines him to good ones, when I behold such a one, my lord, like yourself, whose principles and conduct are as generous and noble as his blood, and whom for that reason a corrupt world cannot spare one moment; when I see such a one, my lord, mounted, though it is but for a minute beyond the time which my love to my country has prescribed to him, and my zeal for his glory wishes, then, my lord, I cease to be a philosopher, and in the first transport of an honest impatience, I wish the Hobby-horse with all his fraternity at the devil.

'MY LORD,
"I maintain this to be a dedication, notwithstanding its singularity in the three great essentials, of matter, form, and place: I beg, therefore, you will accept it as such, and that you will permit me to lay it with the most respectful humility at your lordship's feet, when you are upon them, which you can be when you please; and that is, my lord, whenever there is occasion for it, and I will add to the best purposes too. I have the honour to be,
"My lord, your lordship's most obedient,
'And most devoted, and most humble servant,
"TRISTRAM SHANDY."

I solemnly declare to all mankind that the above dedication was made for no one prince, prelate, Pope, or potentate, duke, marquis, earl, viscount, or baron, of this or any other realm in Christendom; nor has it yet been hawked about, or offered publicly or privately, directly or indirectly, to any one person or personage, great or small; but is honestly a true virgin dedication, untried on upon any soul living.

I labour this point so particularly merely to remove any offence or objection which might arise against it from the manner in which I propose to make the most of it; which is the putting it up fairly to public sale, which I now do.

Every author has a way of his own in bringing his points to bear; for my own part, as I hate chaffering and higgling for a few guineas in a dark entry, I resolved within myself, from the very beginning, to deal squarely and openly with your great folks in this affair, and try whether I should not come off the better by it.

If therefore there is any one duke, marquis, earl, viscount, or baron in these His Majesty's dominions who stands in need of a tight, genteel dedication, and whom the above will suit (for, by-the-by, unless it suits in some degree, I will not part with it), it is much at his service for fifty guineas, which I am positive is twenty guineas less than it ought to be afforded for by any man of genius.

My lord, if you examine it over again, it is far from being a gross piece of daubing, as some dedications are. The design, your lordship sees, is good, the colouring transparent, the drawing not amiss, or, to speak more like a man of science, and measure my piece in the painter's scale, divided into 20, I believe, my lord, the outlines will turn out as 12, the composition as 9, the colouring as 6, the expression 13 and a half, and the design—if I may be allowed, my lord, to understand my own design, and supposing absolute perfection in designing—to be as 20, I think it cannot well fall short of 19. Besides all this, there is keeping in it, and the dark strokes in the Hobby-horse (which is a secondary figure, and a kind of background to the whole) give great force to the principal lights in your own figure, and make it come off wonderfully, and besides there is an air of originality in the *tout ensemble.*

Be pleased, my good lord, to order the sum to be paid into the hands of Mr. Dodsley, for the benefit of the author ; and in the next edition care shall be taken that this chapter be expunged, and your lordship's titles, distinctions, arms and good actions, be placed at the front of the preceding chapter : all which from the words *De gustibus non est disputandum,* and whatever else in this book relates to Hobby-horses, but no more shall stand dedicated to your lordship. The rest I dedicate to the moon, who, by-the-by, of all the patrons or matrons I can think of, has most power to set my book a-going, and make the world run mad after it.

Bright Goddess,

If thou art not too busy with Candid and Miss Cunegund's affairs, take Tristram Shandy's under thy protection also.

Tristram Shandy.

THOMAS GRAY.

1716–1771.

JOURNAL FROM KESWICK TO KENDAL.

OCTOBER 8th.   Bid farewell to Keswick and took the Ambleside road in a gloomy morning ; wind east and afterwards north east ; about two miles from the town mounted an eminence called *Castle Rigg*, and the sun breaking out discovered the most beautiful view I have yet seen of the whole valley behind me, the two lakes, the river, the mountain, all in their glory ! had almost a mind to have gone back again.   The road in some little patches is not completed, but good country road through sound, but narrow and stony lanes, very safe in broad daylight.   This is the case about *Causeway-foot*, and among *Naddle-fells* to *Lanthwaite*.   The vale you go in has little breadth, the mountains are vast and rocky, the fields little and poor, and the inhabitants are now making hay, and see not the sun by two hours in a day so long as at Keswick.   Came to the foot of Helvellyn, along which runs an excellent road, looking down from a little height on Lee's-water, (called also Thirlmeer, or Wiborn-water) and soon descending on its margin. The lake from its depth looks black, (though really as clear as glass) and from the gloom of the vast crags, that scowl over it : it is narrow and about three miles long, resembling a river in its course ; little shining torrents hurry down the rocks to join it, with not a bush to overshadow them, or cover their march : all is rock and loose stones up to the very brow, which lies so near your way, that not above half the height of Helvellyn can be seen.   (To be continued, but now we have not franks.)

Past by the little chapel of *Wiborn*, out of which the Sunday congregation were then issuing.   Past a beck near *Dunmail-raise* and entered Westmoreland a second time, now begin to see *Helm-crag* distinguished from its rugged neighbours not

so much by its height, as by the strange broken outline of its
top, like some gigantic building demolished, and the stones
that composed it flung across each other in wild confusion.
Just beyond it opens one of the sweetest landscapes that art
ever attempted to imitate. The bosom of the mountains
spreading here into a broad bason discovers in the midst *Gras-
mere-water;* its margin is hollowed into small bays with
bold eminences : some of them rocks, some of soft turf
that half conceal and vary the figure of the little lake they
command.   From the shore a low promontory pushes itself far
into the water, and on it stands a white village with the parish-
church rising in the midst of it, hanging enclosures, corn-fields,
and meadows green as an emerald, with their trees and hedges,
and cattle fill up the whole space from the edge of the water.
Just opposite to you is a large farm-house at the bottom of
a steep smooth lawn embosomed in old woods, which climb
half way up the mountain's side, and discover above them a
broken line of crags, that crown the scene.   Not a single red
tile, no flaming gentleman's house, or garden walks break in upon
the repose of this little unsuspected paradise, but all is peace,
rusticity, and happy poverty in its neatest, most becoming attire.

The road winds here over *Grasmere-hill,* whose rocks soon
conceal the water from your sight, yet it is continued along
behind them, and contracting itself to a river communicates
with *Ridale-water,* another small lake, but of inferior size and
beauty ; it seems shallow too, for large patches of reeds appear
pretty far within it.   Into this vale the road descends : on the
opposite banks large and ancient woods mount up the hills, and
just to the left of our way stands *Ridale-hall,* the family seat of
Sir Mic. Fleming, but now a farm-house, a large old fashioned
fabric surrounded with wood, and not much too good for its
present destination.   Sir Michael is now on his travels, and all
this timber far and wide belongs to him, I tremble for it
when he returns.   Near the house rises a huge crag called
Ridale-head, which is said to command a full view of *Wynander-
mere,* and I doubt it not, for within a mile that great lake
is visible even from the road.   As to going up the crag, one
might as well go up Skiddaw.

Came to *Ambleside* eighteen miles from *Keswick,* meaning to
lie there, but on looking into the best bed-chamber dark and
damp as a cellar, grew delicate, gave up *Wynander-mere* in
despair, and resolved I would go on to *Kendal* directly, fourteen
miles farther ; the road in general fine turnpike but some parts
(about three miles in all) not made, yet without danger.

Unexpectedly was well rewarded for my determination. The afternoon was fine, and the road for full five miles runs along the side of *Wynander-mere*, with delicious views across it, and almost from one end to the other : it is ten miles in length and at most a mile over, resembling the course of some vast and magnificent river, but no flat marshy grounds, no osier beds, or patches of scrubby plantation on its banks : at the head two valleys open among the mountains, one, that by which we came down, the other Langsledale (Langdale) in which Wrynose and Hard-knot two great mountains rise above the rest. From thence the falls visibly sink and soften along its sides. Sometimes they run into it, (but with a gentle declivity) in their own dark and natural complexion, oftener they are green and cultivated with farms interspersed and round eminences on the border covered with trees : towards the South it seems to break into larger bays with several islands and a wider cultivation : the way rises continually till at a place called *Orresthead* it turns to South East losing sight of the water. Passed by *Ing's* chapel and *Stavely*, but I can say no farther for the dusk of the evening coming on I entered *Kendal* almost at dark, and could distinguish only a shadow of the castle on a hill, and tenter grounds spread far and wide round the town, which I mistook for houses. My inn promised sadly, having two wooden galleries (like Scotland) in front of it. It was indeed an old ill-contrived house, but kept by civil sensible people, so I stayed two nights with them, and fared and slept very comfortably.

Journal in the Lakes.

ADAM SMITH.

1723–1790.

OF THE ORIGIN AND USE OF MONEY.

WHEN the division of labour has been once thoroughly established, it is but a very small part of a man's wants, which the produce of his own labour can supply. He supplies the far greater part of them by exchanging that surplus part of the produce of his own labour, which is over and above his own consumption, for such parts of the produce of other men's labour as he has occasion for. Every man thus lives by exchanging, or becomes in some measure a merchant, and the society itself grows to be what is properly a commercial society.

But when the division of labour first began to take place, this power of exchanging must frequently have been very much clogged and embarrassed in its operations. One man, we shall suppose, has more of a certain commodity than he himself has occasion for, while another has less. The former consequently would be glad to dispose of, and the latter to purchase, a part of this superfluity. But if this latter should chance to have nothing that the former stands in need of, no exchange can be made between them (*). The butcher has more meat in his shop than he himself can consume, and the brewer and the baker would each of them be willing to purchase a part of it. But they have nothing to offer in exchange, except the different productions of their respective trades, and the butcher is already provided with all the bread and beer which he has immediate occasion for. No exchange can, in this case, be made between them. He cannot be their merchant, nor they his customers; and they are all of them thus mutually less

* This first gave rise to merchants who kept stores, and then to the invention of money; the middle-man must have preceded the invention of money.

serviceable to one another. In order to avoid the inconveniency of such situations, every prudent man in every period of society, after the first establishment of the division of labour, must naturally have endeavoured to manage his affairs in such a manner, as to have at all times by him, besides the peculiar produce of his own industry, a certain quantity of some one commodity or other, such as he imagined few people would be likely to refuse in exchange for the produce of their industry.

Many different commodities, it is probable, were successively both thought of and employed for this purpose. In the rude ages of society, cattle are said to have been the common instrument of commerce ; and, though they must have been a most inconvenient one, yet in old times we find things were frequently valued according to the number of cattle which had been given in exchange for them. The armour of Diomede, says Homer, cost only nine oxen ; but that of Glaucus cost an hundred oxen. Salt is said to be the common instrument of commerce and exchanges in Abyssinia ; a species of shells in some parts of the coast of India ; dried cod at Newfoundland ; tobacco in Virginia ; sugar in some of our West India colonies ; hides or dressed leather in some other countries : and there is at this day a village in Scotland where it is not uncommon, I am told, for a workman to carry nails instead of money to the baker's shop or the alehouse.

In all countries, however, men seem at last to have been determined by irresistible reasons to give the preference, for this employment, to metals above every other commodity. Metals can not only be kept with as little loss as any other commodity, scarce any thing being less perishable than they are ; but they can likewise, without any loss, be divided into any number of parts, as by fusion those parts can easily be re-united again ; a quality which no other equally durable commodities possess, and which more than any other quality renders them fit to be instruments of commerce and circulation. The man who wanted to buy salt, for example, and had nothing but cattle to give in exchange for it, must have been obliged to buy salt to the value of a whole ox, or a whole sheep, at a time. He could seldom buy less than this, because what he was to give for it could seldom be divided without loss ; and if he had a mind to buy more, he must, for the same reasons, have been obliged to buy double or triple the quantity, the value, to wit, of two or three oxen, or of two or three sheep. If, on the contrary, instead of sheep or oxen, he had metals to give in exchange for it, he could easily proportion the quantity of the metal to the precise quantity of the commodity which he had immediate occasion for.

Different metals have been made use of by different nations for this purpose. Iron was the common instrument of commerce among the ancient Spartans ; copper among the ancient Romans ; and gold and silver among all rich and commercial nations.

Those metals seem originally to have been made use of for this purpose in rude bars without any stamp or coinage. Thus we are told by Pliny, upon the authority of Timæus, an ancient historian, that, till the time of Servius Tullius, the Romans had no coined money, but made use of unstamped bars of copper, to purchase whatever they had occasion for. These rude bars, therefore, performed at this time the function of money.

The use of metals in this rude state was attended with two very considerable inconveniencies ; first, with the trouble of weighing ; and, secondly, with that of assaying them. In the precious metals, where a small difference in the quantity makes a great difference in the value, even the business of weighing, with proper exactness, requires at least very accurate weights and scales. The weighing of gold in particular is an operation of some nicety. In the coarser metals, indeed, where a small error would be of little consequence, less accuracy would, no doubt, be necessary. Yet we should find it excessively troublesome, if every time a poor man had occasion either to buy or sell a farthing's worth of goods, he was obliged to weigh the farthing. The operation of assaying is still more difficult, still more tedious ; and, unless a part of the metal is fairly melted in the crucible, with proper dissolvents, any conclusion that can be drawn from it, is extremely uncertain. Before the institution of coined money, however, unless they went through this tedious and difficult operation, people must always have been liable to the grossest frauds and impositions ; and instead of a pound weight of pure silver, or pure copper, might receive in exchange for their goods, an adulterated composition of the coarsest and cheapest materials, which had, however, in their outward appearance, been made to resemble those metals. To prevent such abuses, to facilitate exchanges, and thereby to encourage all sorts of industry and commerce, it has been found necessary, in all countries that have made any considerable advances towards improvement, to affix a public stamp upon certain quantities of such particular metals, as were in those countries commonly made use of to purchase goods. Hence the origin of coined money, and of those public offices called mints; institutions exactly of the same nature with those of the aulnagers and stampmasters of woollen and linen cloth. All of them are equally meant to ascertain, by means of a public stamp, the quantity and uniform goodness of those different commodities when brought to market.

The first public stamps of this kind that were affixed to the current metals, seem in many cases to have been intended to ascertain, what it was both most difficult and most important to ascertain, the goodness or fineness of the metal, and to have resembled the sterling mark which is at present affixed to plate and bars of silver, or the Spanish mark which is sometimes affixed to ingots of gold, and which being struck only upon one side of the piece, and not covering the whole surface, ascertains the fineness, but not the weight of the metal. Abraham weighs to Ephron the four hundred shekels of silver which he had agreed to pay for the field of Machpelah. They are said however to be the current money of the merchant, and yet are received by weight, and not by tale, in the same manner as ingots of gold and bars of silver are at present. The revenues of the antient Saxon kings of England are said to have been paid, not in money but in kind; that is, in victuals and provisions of all sorts. William the Conqueror introduced the custom of paying them in money. This money, however, was, for a long time, received at the exchequer, by weight, and not by tale.*

The inconveniency and difficulty of weighing those metals with exactness, gave occasion to the institution of coins, of which the stamp, covering entirely both sides of the piece, and sometimes the edges too, was supposed to ascertain not only the fineness, but the weight of the metal. Such coins, therefore, were received by tale as at present, without the trouble of weighing.

---

* So late as the 14th century, 20,000 sacks of wool were sent to Antwerp, to pay the expenses of the English army in the Netherlands.

In all countries where great payments are made in silver, they are till this day made by weight, and not by tale; though the weight is used to ascertain the tale, by which the value is reckoned. In France, before the revolution, when payments were made in silver crowns, they were made up into sacks of 1200 livres, or 6,000 livres, which were transferred by weight. The receiver might indeed count the money if he pleased; but the trouble was so great, that it was very seldom done. The bankers, money-brokers, and notaries, all had large and accurate scales and weights for this purpose; and any excess over the number of sacks wanted, was paid by counting so many pieces of money. The same practice prevailed all over the continent.

The denominations of those coins seem originally to have expressed the weight or quantity of metal contained in them. In the time of Servius Tullius, who first coined money at Rome, the Roman As or Pondo contained a Roman pound of good copper. It was divided in the same manner as our Troyes pound, into twelve ounces, each of which contained a real ounce of good copper. The English pound sterling in the time of Edward I. contained a pound Tower weight, of silver of a known fineness. The Tower pound seems to have been something more than the Roman pound, and something less than the Troyes pound. This last was not introduced into the Mint of England till the 18th of Henry VIII. The French livre contained in the time of Charlemagne a pound, Troyes weight, of silver of a known fineness. The fair of Troyes in Champaign was at that time frequented by all the nations of Europe, and the weights and measures of so famous a market were generally known and esteemed. The Scots money pound contained, from the time of Alexander the First to that of Robert Bruce, a pound of silver of the same weight and fineness with the English pound sterling. English, French, and Scots pennies too, contained all of them originally a real pennyweight of silver, the twentieth part of an ounce, and the two hundred-and-fortieth part of a pound. The shilling too, seems originally to have been the denomination of a weight. *When wheat is at twelve shillings the quarter*, says an antient statute of Henry III., *then wastel bread of a farthing shall weigh eleven shillings and four pence.* The proportion, however, between the shilling and either the penny on the one hand, or the pound on the other, seems not to have been so constant and uniform as that between the penny and the pound. During the first race of the kings of France, the French sou or shilling appears upon different occasions to have contained five, twelve, twenty, and forty pennies. Among the antient Saxons a shilling appears at one time to have contained only five pennies, and it is not improbable that it may have been as variable among them as among their neighbours, the antient Franks. From the time of Charlemagne among the French, and from that of William the Conqueror among the English, the proportion between the pound, the shilling, and the penny, seems to have been uniformly the same as at present, though the value of each has been very different. For in every country of the world, I believe, the avarice and injustice of princes and sovereign states, abusing the confidence of their subjects, have by degrees diminished the real quantity of metal, which had been originally contained in their coins. The Roman As, in the latter ages of the Republic, was reduced to the twenty-fourth part of its original value ; and, instead of weighing a pound, came to weigh only half an ounce. The English pound and penny contain at present about a third only ; the Scots pound and penny about a thirty-sixth ; and the French pound and penny about a sixty-sixth part of their original value. By means of those operations the princes and sovereign states which performed them, were enabled, in appearance, to pay their debts and fulfil their engagements with a smaller quantity of silver than would otherwise have been requisite. It was indeed in appearance only ; for their creditors were really defrauded of a part of what was due to them. All other debtors in the state were allowed the same privilege, and might pay with the same nominal sum of the new and debased coin whatever they had borrowed in the old. Such operations, therefore, have always proved favourable to the debtor, and ruinous to the creditor ; and have sometimes produced a greater and more universal revolution in the fortunes of private persons, than could have been occasioned by a very great public calamity.

It is in this manner that money has become in all civilized nations the universal instrument of commerce, by the intervention of which goods of all kinds are bought and sold, or exchanged for one another.

Of the Discouragement of Agriculture in the ancient State of Europe after the Fall of the Roman Empire.

WHEN the German and Scythian nations over-ran the western provinces of the Roman empire, the confusions which followed so great a revolution lasted for several centuries. The rapine and violence which the barbarians exercised against the ancient inhabitants, interrupted the commerce between the towns and the country. The towns were deserted, and the country was left uncultivated, and the western provinces of Europe, which had enjoyed a considerable degree of opulence under the Roman empire, sunk into the lowest state of poverty and barbarism. During the continuance of those confusions, the chiefs and principal leaders of those nations, acquired or usurped to themselves the greater part of the lands of those countries. A great part of them was uncultivated ; but no part of them, whether cultivated or uncultivated, was left without a proprietor. All of them were engrossed, and the greater part by a few great proprietors.

This original engrossing of uncultivated lands, though a great, might have been but a transitory evil. They might soon have been divided again, and broke into small parcels either by succession or by alienation. The law of primogeniture hindered them from being divided by succession ; the introduction of entails prevented their being broke into small parcels by alienation.

When land, like moveables, is considered as the means only of subsistence and enjoyment, the natural law of succession divides it, like them, among all the children of the family ; of all of whom the subsistence and enjoyment may be supposed equally dear to the father. This natural law of succession accordingly took place among the Romans, who made no more distinction between elder and younger, between male and female, in the inheritance of lands, than we do in the distribution of movables. But when land was considered as the means, not of subsistence merely, but of power and protection, it was thought better that it should descend undivided to one. In those disorderly times, every great landlord was a sort of petty prince. His tenants were his subjects. He was their judge, and in some respects their legislator in peace, and their leader in war. He made war according to his own discretion, frequently against his neighbours, and sometimes against his sovereign. The security of a landed estate, therefore, the protection which its owner could afford to those who dwelt on it, depended upon its greatness. To divide it was to ruin it, and to expose every part of it to be oppressed and swallowed up by the incursions of its neighbours. The law of primogeniture, therefore, came to take place, not immediately, indeed, but in process of time, in the succession of landed estates, for the same reason that it has generally taken place in that of monarchies, though not always at their first institution. That the power, and consequently the security of the monarchy, may not be weakened by division, it must descend entire to one of the children. To which of them so important a preference shall be given, must be determined by some general rule, founded not upon the doubtful distinctions of personal merit, but upon some plain and evident difference which can admit of no dispute. Among the children of the same family, there can be no indisputable difference but that of sex, and that of age. The male sex is universally preferred to the female ; and when all other things are equal, the elder every-where takes place of the younger. Hence the origin of the right of primogeniture, and of what is called lineal succession.

Laws frequently continue in force long after the circumstances, which first gave occasion to them, and which could alone render them reasonable, are no more.* In the present state of Europe the proprietor of a single acre of land is as perfectly secure of his possession as the proprietor of a hundred thousand. The right of primogeniture, however, still continues to be respected, and as of all institutions it is the fittest to support the pride of family distinctions, it is still likely to endure for many centuries. In every other respect, nothing can be more contrary to the real interest of a numerous family, than a right which, in order to enrich one, beggars all the rest of the children.

Entails are the natural consequences of the law of primogeniture. They were introduced to preserve a certain lineal succession, of which the law of primogeniture first gave the idea, and to hinder any part of the original estate from being carried out of the proposed line either by gift, or devise, or alienation ; either by the folly, or by the misfortune of any of its successive owners. They were altogether unknown to the Romans. Neither their substitutions, nor sideicommisses bear any resemblance to entails, though some French lawyers have thought proper to dress the modern institution in the language and garb of those ancient ones.

When great landed estates were a sort of principalities, entails might not be unreasonable. Like what are called the fundamental laws of some monarchies, they might frequently hinder the security of thousands from being endangered by the caprice or extravagance of one man. But in the present state of Europe, when small as well as great estates derive their security from the laws of their country, nothing can be more completely absurd. They are founded upon the most absurd of all suppositions, the supposition that every successive generation of men have not an equal right to the earth, and to all that it possesses ; but that the property of the present generation should be restrained and regulated according to the fancy of

---

* Had the French monarchical government attended to this truth, the revolution might perhaps have been avoided ; and indeed there is no nation that ought not to pay due attention to so well established, and so important a truth. Since the book was written, the possessors of land in many parts of Europe find they hold them by a tenure much less secure than that here expressed.

those who died perhaps five hundred years ago.* Entails, however, are still respected through the greater part of Europe, in those countries particularly in which noble birth is a necessary qualification for the enjoyment either of civil or military honours. Entails are thought necessary for maintaining this exclusive privilege of the nobility to the great offices and honours of their country; and that order having usurped one unjust advantage over the rest of their fellow-citizens, lest their poverty should render it ridiculous, it is thought reasonable that they should have another. The common law of England, indeed, is said to abhor perpetuities, and they are accordingly more restricted there than in any other European monarchy; though even England is not altogether without them. In Scotland more than one-fifth, perhaps more than one-third part of the whole lands of the country, are at present supposed to be under strict entail.

Great tracts of uncultivated land were, in this manner, not only engrossed by particular families, but the possibility of their being divided again was as much as possible precluded for ever. It seldom happens, however, that a great proprietor is a great improver. In the disorderly times which gave birth to those barbarous institutions, the great proprietor was sufficiently employed in defending his own territories, or in extending his jurisdiction and authority over those of his neighbours. He had no leisure to attend to the cultivation and improvement of land. When the establishment of law and order afforded him this leisure, he often wanted the inclination, and almost always the requisite abilities. If the expence of his house and person either equalled or exceeded his revenue, as it did very frequently, he had no stock to employ in this manner. If he was an œconomist, he generally found it more profitable to employ his annual savings in new purchases, than in the improvement of his old estate. To improve land with profit, like all other commercial projects, requires an exact attention to small savings and small gains, of which a man born to a great fortune, even though naturally frugal, is very seldom capable. The situation of such a person naturally disposes him to attend rather to ornament which pleases his fancy, than to profit for which he has so little occasion. The elegance of his dress, of his equipage, of his house, and household

---

* The observations on entails deserve the most strict attention from the legislature. They are abolished in some countries, and the advantage will in time be so felt as to afford a contrast, that will become very dangerous to the governments of those countries in which they are preserved.

furniture, are objects which from his infancy he has been accustomed to have some anxiety about. The turn of mind which this habit naturally forms, follows him when he comes to think of the improvement of land. He embellishes perhaps four or five hundred acres in the neighbourhood of his house, at ten times the expence which the land is worth after all his improvements ; and finds that if he was to improve his whole estate in the same manner, and he has little taste for any other, he would be a bankrupt before he had finished the tenth part of it. There still remain in both parts of the united kingdom some great estates which have continued without interruption in the hands of the same family since the times of feudal anarchy. Compare the present condition of those estates with the possessions of the small proprietors in their neighbourhood, and you will require no other argument to convince you how unfavourable such extensive property is to improvement.

If little improvement was to be expected from such great proprietors, still less was to be hoped for from those who occupied the land under them. In the antient state of Europe, the occupiers of land were all tenants at will. They were all or almost all slaves : but their slavery was of a milder kind than that known among the ancient Greeks and Romans, or even in our West Indian colonies. They were supposed to belong more directly to the land than to their master. They could, therefore, be sold with it, but not separately. They could marry, provided it was with the consent of their master ; and he could not afterwards dissolve the marriage by selling the man and wife to different persons. If he maimed or murdered any of them, he was liable to some penalty, though generally but to a small one. They were not, however, capable of acquiring property. Whatever they acquired was acquired to their master, and he could take it from them at pleasure. Whatever cultivation and improvement could be carried on by means of such slaves, was properly carried on by their master. It was at his expence. The seed, the cattle, and the instruments of husbandry were all his. It was for his benefit. Such slaves could acquire nothing but their daily maintenance. It was properly the proprietor himself, therefore, that, in this case, occupied his own lands, and cultivated them by his own bondmen. This species of slavery still subsists in Russia, Poland, Hungary, Bohemia, Moravia, and other parts of Germany. It is only in the western and south-western provinces of Europe, that it has gradually been abolished altogether.

But if great improvements are seldom to be expected from

great proprietors, they are least of all to be expected when they employ slaves for their workmen. The experience of all ages and nations, I believe, demonstrates that the work done by slaves, though it appears to cost only their maintenance, is in the end the dearest of any. A person who can acquire no property, can have no other interest but to eat as much, and to labour as little as possible. Whatever work he does beyond what is sufficient to purchase his own maintenance, can be squeezed out of him by violence only, and not by any interest of his own. In ancient Italy, how much the cultivation of corn degenerated, how unprofitable it became to the master when it fell under the management of slaves, is remarked by both Pliny and Columella. In the time of Aristotle it had not been much better in ancient Greece. Speaking of the ideal republic described in the laws of Plato, to maintain five thousand idle men (the number of warriors supposed necessary for its defence) together with their women and servants, would require, he says, a territory of boundless extent and fertility, like the plains of Babylon.

The pride of man makes him love to domineer, and nothing mortifies him so much as to be obliged to condescend to persuade his inferiors. Wherever the law allows it, and the nature of the work afford it, therefore, he will generally prefer the service of slaves to that of freemen.

Wealth of Nations.

SIR JOSHUA REYNOLDS.

1723–1792.

FROM DISCOURSE IV.

THE value and rank of every art is in proportion to the mental labour employed in it, or the mental pleasure produced by it. As this principle is observed or neglected, our profession becomes either a liberal art, or a mechanical trade. In the hands of one man it makes the highest pretensions, as it is addressed to the noblest faculties: in those of another it is reduced to a mere matter of ornament; and the painter has but the humble province of furnishing our apartments with elegance.

This exertion of mind, which is the only circumstance that truly ennobles our Art, makes the great distinction between the Roman and Venetian schools. I have formerly observed that perfect form is produced by leaving out particularities, and retaining only general ideas : I shall now endeavour to show that this principle, which I have proved to be metaphysically just, extends itself to every part of the Art ; that it gives what is called the *grand style*, to Invention, to Composition, to Expression, and even to Colouring and Drapery.

Invention in Painting does not imply the invention of the subject ; for that is commonly supplied by the Poet or His-torian. With respect to the choice, no subject can be proper that is not generally interesting. It ought to be either some eminent instance of heroick action, or heroick suffering. There must be something either in the action, or in the object, in which men are universally concerned, and which powerfully strikes upon the publick sympathy.

Strickly speaking, indeed, no subject can be of universal, hardly can it be of general, concern ; but there are events and characters so popularly known in those countries where our

Art is in request, that they may be considered as sufficiently general for all our purposes. Such are the great events of Greek and Roman fable and history, which early education, and the usual course of reading, have made familiar and interesting to all Europe, without being degraded by the vulgarism of ordinary life in any country. Such too are the capital subjects of scripture history, which, beside their general notoriety, become venerable by their connection with our religion.

As it is required that the subject selected should be a general one, it is no less necessary that it should be kept unembarrassed with whatever may any way serve to divide the attention of the spectator. Whenever a story is related, every man forms a picture in his mind of the action and expression of the persons employed. The power of representing this mental picture on canvass is what we call invention in a Painter. And as in the conception of this ideal picture, the mind does not enter into the minute peculiarities of the dress, furniture, or scene of action ; so when the Painter comes to represent it, he contrives those little necessary concomitant circumstances in such a manner, that they shall strike the spectator no more than they did himself in his first conception of the story.

I am very ready to allow, that some circumstances of minuteness and particularity frequently tend to give an air of truth to a piece, and to interest the spectator in an extraordinary manner. Such circumstances therefore cannot wholly be rejected : but if there be any thing in the Art which requires peculiar nicety of discernment, it is the disposition of these minute circumstantial parts ; which, according to the judgment employed in the choice, become so useful to truth, or so injurious to grandeur.

However, the usual and most dangerous error is on the side of minuteness ; and therefore I think caution most necessary where most have failed. The general idea constitutes real excellence. All smaller things, however perfect in their way, are to be sacrificed without mercy to the greater. The Painter will not inquire what things may be admitted without much censure ; he will not think it enough to show that they may be there ; he will show that they must be there ; that their absence would render his picture maimed and defective.

Thus, though to the principal group a second or third be added, and a second and third mass of light, care must be taken that these subordinate actions and lights, neither each in particular, nor all together, come into any degree of competition with the principal : they should merely make a part of that whole which would be imperfect without them. To every kind of painting this rule may be applied. Even in portraits, the grace, and, we may add, the likeness, consists more in taking the general air, than in observing the exact similitude of every feature.

Thus figures must have a ground whereon to stand ; they must be clothed ; there must be a back-ground ; there must be light and shadow ; but none of these ought to appear to have taken up any part of the artist's attention. They should be so managed as not even to catch that of the spectator. We know well enough, when we analyze a piece, the difficulty and the subtilty with which an artist adjusts the back-ground, drapery, and masses of light ; we know that a considerable part of the grace and effect of his picture depends upon them ; but this art is so much concealed, even to a judicious eye, that no remains of any of these subordinate parts occur to the memory when the picture is not present.

The great end of the art is to strike the imagination. The Painter therefore is to make no ostentation of the means by which this is done ; the spectator is only to feel the result in his bosom. An inferior artist is unwilling that any part of his industry should be lost upon the spectator. He takes as much pains to discover, as the greater artist does to conceal, the marks of his subordinate assiduity. In works of the lower kind, every thing appears studied, and encumbered ; it is all boastful art, and open affectation. The ignorant often part from such pictures with wonder in their mouths, and indifference in their hearts.

But it is not enough in Invention that the Artist should restrain and keep under all the inferior parts of his subject ; he must sometimes deviate from vulgar and strict historical truth, in pursuing the grandeur of his design.

How much the great style exacts from its professors to conceive and represent their subjects in a poetical manner, not confined to mere matter of fact, may be seen in the Cartoons of Raffaelle. In all the pictures in which the painter has represented the apostles, he has drawn them with great nobleness ; he has given them as much dignity as the human figure is capable of receiving ; yet we are expressly told in Scripture they had no such respectable appearance ; and of St. Paul in particular, we are told by himself, that his *bodily* presence was *mean.* Alexander is said to have been of a low stature : a Painter ought not so to represent him. Agesilaus was low, lame, and of a mean appearance : none of these defects ought to appear in a piece of which he is the hero. In conformity to custom, I call this part of the art History Painting ; it ought to be called Poetical, as in reality it is.

All this is not falsifying any fact ; it is taking an allowed poetical licence. A Painter of portraits, retains the individual likeness ; a Painter of history, shows the man by showing his actions. A Painter must compensate the natural deficiencies of his art. He has but one sentence to utter, but one moment to exhibit. He cannot, like the poet or historian, expatiate, and impress the mind with great veneration for the character of the hero or saint he represents, though he lets us know at the same time, that the saint was deformed, or the hero lame. The Painter has no other means of giving an idea of the dignity of the mind, but by that external appearance which grandeur of thought does generally, though not always, impress on the countenance ; and by that correspondence of figure to sentiment and situation, which all men wish, but cannot command. The Painter who may in this one particular attain with ease what others desire in vain, ought to give all that he possibly can, since there are so many circumstances of true greatness that he cannot give at all. He cannot make his hero talk like a great man ; he must make him look like one. For which reason, he ought to be well studied in the analysis of those circumstances which constitute dignity of appearance in real life.

As in Invention, so likewise in Expression, care must be taken not to run into particularities. Those expressions alone should be given to the figures which their respective situations generally produce. Nor is this enough ; each person should also have that expression which men of his rank generally exhibit. The joy, or the grief of a character of dignity is not to be expressed in the same manner as a similar passion in a vulgar face. Upon this principle, Bernini, perhaps, may be subject to censure. This sculptor, in many respects admirable, has given a very mean expression to his statue of David, who is represented as just going to throw the stone from the sling ; and in order to give it the expression of energy, he has made him bite his under-lip. This expression is far from being general, and still farther from being dignified. He might have seen it in an instance or two ; and he mistook accident for generality.

With respect to Colouring, though it may appear at first a part of painting merely mechanical, yet it still has its rules, and those grounded upon that presiding principle which regulates both the great and the little in the study of a Painter. By this, the first effect of the picture is produced ; and as this is performed, the spectator as he walks the gallery, will stop, or pass along. To give a general air of grandeur at first view, all trifling, or artful play of little lights, or an attention to a variety of tints is to be avoided ; a quietness and simplicity must reign over the whole work ; to which a breadth of uniform, and simple colour, will very much contribute. Grandeur of effect is produced by two different ways, which seem entirely opposed to each other. One is, by reducing the colours to little more than chiara oscuro, which was often the practice of the Bolognian schools ; and the other, by making the colours very distinct and forcible, such as we see in those of Rome and Florence ; but still, the presiding principle of both those manners is simplicity. Certainly, nothing can be more simple than monotony ; and the distinct blue, red, and yellow colours which are seen in the draperies of the Roman and Florentine schools, though they have not that kind of harmony which is produced by a variety of broken and transparent colours, have that effect of grandeur which was intended. Perhaps these distinct colours strike the mind more forcibly, from there not being any great union between them ; as martial music, which is intended to rouse the nobler passions, has its effect from the sudden and strongly marked transitions from one note to another, which that style of music requires ; whilst in that which is intended to move the softer passions, the notes imperceptibly melt into one another.

In the same manner as the historical Painter never enters into the detail of colours, so neither does he debase his conceptions with minute attention to the discriminations of Drapery. It is the inferior style that marks the variety of stuffs. With him, the cloathing is neither woollen, nor linen, nor silk, satin, or velvet ; it is drapery ; it is nothing more. The art of disposing the foldings of the drapery makes a very considerable part of the Painter's study. To make it merely natural, is a mechanical operation, to which neither genius nor taste are required ; whereas, it requires the nicest judgment to dispose the drapery, so that the folds shall have an easy communication, and gracefully follow each other, with such natural negligence as to look like the effect of chance, and at the same time show the figure under it to the utmost advantage.

Carlo Maratti was of opinion, that the disposition of drapery was a more difficult art than even that of drawing the human figure ; that a Student might be more easily taught the latter than the former ; as the rules of drapery, he said, could not be so well ascertained as those for delineating a correct form. This, perhaps, is a proof how willingly we favour our own peculiar excellence. Carlo Maratti is said to have valued himself particularly upon his skill in this part of his art ; yet in him, the disposition appears so ostentatiously artificial, that he is inferior to Raffaelle, even in that which gave him his best claim to reputation.

Such is the great principle by which we must be directed in the nobler branches of our art. Upon this principle, the Roman, the Florentine, the Bolognese schools, have formed their practice ; and by this they have deservedly obtained the highest praise. These are the three great schools of the world in the epic style. The best of the French school, Poussin, Le Sueur, and Le Brun, have formed themselves upon these models, and consequently may be said, though Frenchmen, to be a colony from the Roman school. Next to these, but in a very different style of excellence, we may rank the Venetian, together with the Flemish and the Dutch schools ; all professing to depart from the great purposes of painting, and catching at applause by inferior qualities.

I am not ignorant that some will censure me for placing the Venetians in this inferior class, and many of the warmest admirers of painting will think them unjustly degraded ; but I wish not to be misunderstood. Though I can by no means allow them to hold any rank with the nobler schools of painting, they accomplished perfectly the thing they attempted. But as mere elegance is their principal object, as they seem more willing to dazzle than to affect, it can be no injury to them to suppose that their practice is useful only to its proper end. But what may heighten the elegant may degrade the sublime. There is a simplicity, and I may add, severity, in the great manner, which is, I am afraid, almost incompatible with this comparatively sensual style.

FROM DISCOURSE VIII.

THE same just moderation must be observed in regard to ornaments ; nothing will contribute more to destroy repose than profusion, of whatever kind, whether it consists in the multiplicity of objects, or the variety and brightness of colours.

On the other hand, a work without ornament, instead of simplicity, to which it makes pretensions, has rather the appearance of poverty. The degree to which ornaments are admissable, must be regulated by the professed style of the work; but we may be sure of this truth,—that the most ornamental style requires repose to set off even its ornaments to advantage. I cannot avoid mentioning here an instance of repose, in that faithful and accurate painter of nature, Shakespeare; the short dialogue between Duncan and Banquo, whilst they are approaching the gates of Macbeth's castle. Their conversation very naturally turns upon the beauty of its situation, and the pleasantness of the air : and Banquo observing the martlets' nests in every recess of the cornice, remarks, that where those birds most breed and haunt, the air is delicate. The subject of this quiet and easy conversation gives that repose so necessary to the mind, after the tumultuous bustle of the preceding scenes, and perfectly contrasts the scene of horrour that immediately succeeds. It seems as if Shakespeare asked himself, What is a Prince likely to say to his attendants on such an occasion ? The modern writers seem, on the contrary, to be always searching for new thoughts, such as never could occur to men in the situation represented. This is also frequently the practice of Homer ; who, from the midst of battles and horrours, relieves and refreshes the mind of the reader, by introducing some quiet rural image, or picture of familiar domestic life. The writers of every age and country, where taste has begun to decline, paint and adorn every object they touch ; are always on the stretch ; never deviate or sink a moment from the pompous and the brilliant. Lucan, Statius, and Claudian, (as a learned critick has observed,) are examples of this bad taste and want of judgment ; they never soften their tones, or condescend to be natural ; all is exaggeration and perpetual splendour, without affording repose of any kind.

Discourses.

OLIVER GOLDSMITH.

1728–1774.

A COUNTRY PARSONAGE.

*A proof that even the humblest fortune may grant happiness,
which depends not on circumstances but constitution.*

THE place of our retreat was in a little neighbourhood,
consisting of farmers, who tilled their own grounds, and were
equal strangers to opulence and poverty. As they had almost
all the conveniences of life within themselves, they seldom
visited towns or cities, in search of superfluity. Remote from
the polite, they still retained the primæval simplicity of
manners ; and frugal by habit, they scarcely knew that temper-
ance was a virtue. They wrought with cheerfulness on days of
labour ; but observed festivals as intervals of idleness and
pleasure. They kept up the Christmas carol, sent true-love-
knots on Valentine morning, eat pancakes on Shrove-tide,
shewed their wit on the first of April, and religiously cracked
nuts on Michaelmas eve. Being apprized of our approach, the
whole neighbourhood came out to meet their minister, drest in
their finest cloaths, and preceded by a pipe and tabor : A feast
also was provided for our reception, at which we sate cheerfully
down ; and what the conversation wanted in wit, was made up
in laughter.

Our little habitation was situated at the foot of a sloping hill,
sheltered with a beautiful underwood behind, and a prattling
river before : on one side a meadow, on the other a green. My
farm consisted of about twenty acres of excellent land, having
given an hundred pound for my predecessor's goodwill.
Nothing could exceed the neatness of my little enclosures ; the
elms and hedge-rows appearing with inexpressible beauty. My
house consisted of but one story, and was covered with thatch,

which gave it an air of great snugness ; the walls on the inside were nicely white-washed, and my daughters undertook to adorn them with pictures of their own designing. Though the same room served us for parlour and kitchen, that only made it the warmer. Besides, as it was kept with the utmost neatness, the dishes, plates, and coppers being well scoured, and all disposed in bright rows on the shelves, the eye was agreeably relieved, and did not want richer furniture. There were three other apartments, one for my wife and me, another for our two daughters, within our own, and the third, with two beds, for the rest of the children.

The little republic to which I gave laws, was regulated in the following manner ; by sun-rise we all assembled in our common apartment ; the fire being previously kindled by the servant. After we had saluted each other with proper ceremony, for I always thought fit to keep up some mechanical forms of good breeding, without which freedom ever destroys friendship, we all bent in gratitude to that Being who gave us another day. This duty being performed, my son and I went to pursue our usual industry abroad, while my wife and daughters employed themselves in providing breakfast, which was always ready at a certain time. I allowed half an hour for this meal, and an hour for dinner ; which time was taken up in innocent mirth between my wife and daughters, and in philosophical arguments between my son and me.

As we rose with the sun, so we never pursued our labours after it was gone down, but returned home to the expecting family ; where smiling looks, a neat hearth, and pleasant fire were prepared for our reception. Nor were we without guests : sometimes farmer Flamborough, our talkative neighbour, and often the blind piper would pay us a visit, and taste our goose-berry wine ; for the making of which we had lost neither the receipt nor the reputation. These harmless people had several ways of being good company ; while one played, the other would sing some soothing ballad, Johnny Armstrong's last good night, or the cruelty of Barbary Allen. The night was con-cluded in the manner we began the morning, my youngest boys being appointed to read the lessons of the day, and he that read loudest, distinctest, and best, was to have an halfpenny on Sunday to put in the poor's box.

When Sunday came, it was indeed a day of finery, which all my sumptuary edicts could not restrain. How well soever I fancied my lectures against pride had conquered the vanity of my daughters ; yet I still found them secretly attached to all their former finery : they still loved laces, ribbands, bugles, and catgut ; my wife herself retained a passion for her crimson paduasoy, because I formerly happened to say it became her.

The first Sunday in particular their behaviour served to mortify me : I had desired my girls the preceding night to be drest early the next day ; for I always loved to be at church a good while before the rest of the congregation. They punctually obeyed my directions ; but when we were to assemble in the morning at breakfast, down came my wife and daughters, drest out all in their former splendour ; their hair plastered up with pomatum, their faces patched to taste, their trains bundled up in a heap behind, and rustling at every motion. I could not help smiling at their vanity, particularly that of my wife, from whom I expected more discretion. In this exigence, therefore, my only resource was to order my son, with an important air, to call our coach. The girls were amazed at the command ; but I repeated it with more solemnity than before.——"Surely, my "dear, you jest," cried my wife, "we can walk it perfectly well : "we want no coach to carry us now."—"You mistake, child," returned I, "we do want a coach ; for if we walk to church in "this trim, the very children in the parish will hoot after us." —"Indeed," replied my wife, "I always imagined that my "Charles was fond of seeing his children neat and handsome "about him."—"You may be as neat as you please," interrupted I, "and I shall love you the better for it ; but all this is not "neatness, but frippery. These rufflings, and pinkings, and "patchings will only make us hated by all the wives of all our "neighbours. No, my children," continued I more gravely, "those gowns may be altered into something of a plainer cut ; "for finery is very unbecoming in us, who want the means of "decency. I do not know whether such flouncing and "shredding is becoming even in the rich, if we consider, upon a "moderate calculation, that the nakedness of the indigent world "may be cloathed from the trimmings of the vain."

This remonstrance had the proper effect ; they went with great composure, that very instant, to change their dress ; and the next day I had the satisfaction of finding my daughters, at their own request, employed in cutting up their trains into Sunday waistcoats for Dick and Bill, the two little ones, and what was still more satisfactory, the gowns seemed improved by this curtailing.

Vicar of Wakefield.

EDMUND BURKE.

1730–1797.

SECOND SPEECH ON CONCILIATION.

I HOPE, Sir, that notwithstanding the austerity of the Chair, your good-nature will incline you to some degree of indulgence towards human frailty. You will not think it unnatural that those who have an object depending, which strongly engages their hopes and fears, should be somewhat inclined to superstition. As I came into the House full of anxiety about the event of my motion, I found, to my infinite surprise, that the grand penal Bill, by which we had passed sentence on the trade and sustenance of America, is to be returned to us from the other House. I do confess I could not help looking on this event as a fortunate omen. I look upon it as a sort of providential favour, by which we are put once more in possession of our deliberative capacity upon a business so very questionable in its nature, so very uncertain in its issue. By the return of this Bill, which seemed to have taken its flight for ever, we are at this very instant nearly as free to choose a plan for our American government as we were on the first day of the session. If, Sir, we incline to the side of conciliation, we are not at all embarrassed (unless we please to make ourselves so) by an incongruous mixture of coercion and restraint. We are therefore called upon, as it were by a superior warning voice, again to attend to America ; to attend to the whole of it together ; and to review the subject with an unusual degree of care and calmness.

Surely it is an awful subject ; or there is none so on this side of the grave. When I first had the honour of a seat in this House, the affairs of that continent pressed themselves upon us, as the most important and most delicate object of parliamentary attention. My little share in this great deliberation oppressed me. I found myself a partaker in a very high trust; and having no sort of reason to rely on the strength of my natural abilities for the proper execution of that trust, I was obliged to take more than common pains to instruct myself in everything which relates to our colonies. I was not less under the necessity of forming some fixed ideas concerning the general policy of the British empire. Something of this sort seemed to be indispensable; in order, amidst so vast a fluctuation of passions and opinions, to concentre my thoughts; to ballast my conduct; to preserve me from being blown about by every wind of fashionable doctrine. I really did not think it safe or manly to have fresh principles to seek upon every fresh mail which should arrive from America.

At that period I had the fortune to find myself in perfect concurrence with a large majority in this House. Bowing under that high authority, and penetrated with the sharpness and strength of that early impression, I have continued ever since, without the least deviation, in my original sentiments. Whether this be owing to an obstinate perseverance in error, or to a religious adherence to what appears to me truth and reason, it is in your equity to judge.

Sir, Parliament having an enlarged view of objects, made, during this interval, more frequent changes in their sentiments and their conduct, than could be justified in a particular person upon the contracted scale of private information. But though I do not hazard anything approaching to a censure on the motives of former Parliaments to all those alterations, one fact is undoubted—that under them the state of America has been kept in continual agitation. Everything administered as remedy to the public complaint, if it did not produce, was at least followed by a heightening of the distemper; until, by a variety of experiments, that important country has been brought into her present situation; a situation which I will not miscall, which I dare not name; which I scarcely know how to comprehend in the terms of any description.

In this posture, Sir, things stood at the beginning of the session. About that time, a worthy member of great parliamentary experience, who, in the year 1766, filled the chair of the American Committee with much ability, took me aside, and, lamenting the present aspect of our politics, told me things were come to such a pass, that our former methods of proceeding in the House would be no longer tolerated. That the public tribunal (never too indulgent to a long and unsuccessful opposition) would now scrutinize our conduct with unusual severity. That the very vicissitudes and shiftings of ministerial measures, instead of convicting their authors of inconstancy and want of system, would be taken as an occasion of charging us with a predetermined discontent, which nothing could satisfy; whilst we accused every measure of vigour as cruel, and every proposal of lenity as weak and irresolute. The public, he said, would not have patience to see us play the game out with our adversaries : we must produce our hand. It would be expected that those who for many years had been active in such affairs should show that they had formed some clear and decided idea of the principles of colony government ; and were capable of drawing out something like a platform of the ground which might be laid for future and permanent tranquillity.

I felt the truth of what my honourable friend represented ; but I felt my situation too. His application might have been made with far greater propriety to many other gentlemen. No man was indeed ever better disposed, or worse qualified, for such an undertaking, than myself. Though I gave so far into his opinion, that I immediately threw my thoughts into a sort of parliamentary form, I was by no means equally ready to produce them. It generally argues some degree of natural impotence of mind, or some want of knowledge of the world, to hazard plans of government, except from a seat of authority. Propositions are made, not only ineffectually, but somewhat disreputably, when the minds of men are not properly disposed for their reception ; and for my part, I am not ambitious of ridicule—not absolutely a candidate for disgrace.

Besides, Sir, to speak the plain truth, I have in general no very exalted opinion of the virtue of paper government ; nor of any politics in which the plan is to be wholly separated from the execution. But when I saw that anger and violence prevailed every day more and more, and that things were hastening towards an incurable alienation of our colonies, I confess my caution gave way. I felt this as one of those few moments in which decorum yields to higher duty. Public calamity is a mighty leveller ; and there are occasions when any, even the slightest, chance of doing good, must be laid hold on, even by the most inconsiderable person.

To restore order and repose to an empire so great and so distracted as ours, is, merely in the attempt, an undertaking that would ennoble the flights of the highest genius, and obtain pardon for the efforts of the meanest understanding. Struggling a good while with these thoughts, by degrees I felt myself more firm. I derived, at length, some confidence from what in other circumstances usually produces timidity. I grew less anxious, even from the idea of my own insignificance. For, judging of what you are by what you ought to be, I persuaded myself that you would not reject a reasonable proposition, because it had nothing but its reason to recommend it. On the other hand, being totally destitute of all shadow of influence, natural or adventitious, I was very sure that, if my proposition were futile or dangerous ; if it were weakly conceived, or improperly timed, there was nothing exterior to it, of power to awe, dazzle, or delude you. You will see it just as it is, and you will treat it just as it deserves.

The proposition is peace. Not peace through the medium of war ; not peace to be hunted through the labyrinth of intricate and endless negotiations ; not peace to arise out of universal discord, fomented, from principle, in all parts of the empire ; not peace to depend on the juridical determination of perplexing questions, or the precise marking the shadowy boundaries of a complex government. It is simple peace ; sought in its natural course and in its ordinary haunts. It is peace sought in the spirit of peace, and laid in principles purely pacific. I propose, by removing the ground of the difference, and by restoring the former unsuspecting confidence of the colonies in the mother country, to give permanent satisfaction to your people ; and (far from a scheme of ruling by discord) to reconcile them to each other in the same act, and by the bond of the very same interest which reconciles them to British government.

My idea is nothing more. Refined policy ever has been the parent of confusion, and ever will be so, as long as the world endures. Plain good intention, which is as easily discovered at the first view as fraud is surely detected at last, is, let me say, of no mean force in the government of mankind. Genuine simplicity of heart is a healing and cementing principle. My plan, therefore, being formed upon the most simple grounds imaginable, may disappoint some people when they hear it. It has nothing to recommend it to the pruriency of curious ears. There is nothing at all new and captivating in it. It has nothing of the splendour of the project which has been lately laid upon your table by the noble lord in the blue ribbon. It does not propose to fill your lobby with squabbling colony agents, who will require the interposition of your Mace at every instant to keep the peace amongst them. It does not institute a magnificent auction of finance, where captivated provinces come to general ransom by bidding against each other until you

knock down the hammer, and determine a proportion of payments beyond all the powers of algebra to equalize and settle.

The plan which I shall presume to suggest derives, however,
one great advantage from the proposition and registry of that
noble lord's project. The idea of conciliation is admissible.
First, the House, in accepting the resolution moved by the
noble lord, has admitted, notwithstanding the menacing front of
our Address, notwithstanding our heavy Bill of Pains and
Penalties, that we do not think ourselves precluded from all
ideas of free grace and bounty.

The House has gone farther: it has declared conciliation
admissible, previous to any submission on the part of America.
It has even shot a good deal beyond that mark, and has admitted
that the complaints of our former mode of exerting the right of
taxation were not wholly unfounded. That right thus exerted is
allowed to have something reprehensible in it, something unwise,
or something grievous, since, in the midst of our heat and
resentment, we, of ourselves, have proposed a capital alteration ;
and, in order to get rid of what seemed so very exceptionable,
have instituted a mode that is altogether new ; one that is,
indeed, wholly alien from all the ancient methods and forms of
Parliament.

The principle of this proceeding is large enough for my
purpose. The means proposed by the noble lord for carrying
his ideas into execution, I think, indeed are very indifferently
suited to the end ; and this I shall endeavour to show you
before I sit down. But, for the present, I take my ground on
the admitted principle. I mean to give peace. Peace implies
reconciliation ; and, where there has been a material dispute,
reconciliation does in a manner always imply concession on the
one part or on the other. In this state of things I make no
difficulty in affirming that the proposal ought to originate from
us. Great and acknowledged force is not impaired, either in
effect or in opinion, by an unwillingness to exert itself. The
superior power may offer peace with honour and with safety.
Such an offer from such a power will be attributed to magnanimity. But the concessions of the weak are the concessions
of fear. When such a one is disarmed, he is wholly at the
mercy of his superior ; and he loses for ever that time and those
chances, which, as they happen to all men, are the strength and
resources of all inferior power.

The capital leading questions on which you must this day
decide are these two: First, whether you ought to concede ; and
secondly, what your concession ought to be. On the first of

these questions we have gained (as I have just taken the liberty of observing to you) some ground. But I am sensible that a good deal more is still to be done. Indeed, Sir, to enable us to determine both on the one and the other of these great questions with a firm and precise judgment, I think it may be necessary to consider distinctly the true nature and the peculiar circumstances of the object which we have before us. Because after all our struggle, whether we will or not, we must govern America according to that nature and to those circumstances, and not according to our own imaginations, not according to abstract ideas of right; by no means according to mere general theories of government, the resort to which appears to me, in our present situation, no better than arrant trifling. . . . .

I am sensible, Sir, that all which I have asserted in my detail is admitted in the gross; but that quite a different conclusion is drawn from it. America, gentlemen say, is a noble object. It is an object well worth fighting for. Certainly it is, if fighting a people be the best way of gaining them. Gentlemen in this respect will be led to their choice of means by their complexions and their habits. Those who understand the military art will of course have some predilection for it. Those who wield the thunder of the State may have more confidence in the efficacy of arms. But I confess, possibly for want of this knowledge, my opinion is much more in favour of prudent management than of force; considering force not as an odious, but a feeble instrument, for preserving a people so numerous, so active, so growing, so spirited as this, in a profitable and subordinate connection with us.

First, Sir, permit me to observe that the use of force alone is but temporary. It may subdue for a moment, but is does not remove the necessity of subduing again; and a nation is not governed which is perpetually to be conquered.

My next objection is its uncertainty. Terror is not always the effect of force, and an armament is not a victory. If you do not succeed, you are without resource; for, conciliation failing, force remains; but, force failing, no further hope of reconciliation is left. Power and authority are sometimes bought by kindness; but they can never be begged as alms by an impoverished and defeated violence.

A further objection to force is, that you impair the object by your very endeavours to preserve it. The thing you fought for is not the thing which you recover; but depreciated, sunk, wasted, and consumed in the contest. Nothing less will content me than whole America. I do not choose to consume its strength along with our own ; because in all parts it is the British strength that I consume. I do not choose to be caught by a foreign enemy at the end of this exhausting conflict, and still less in the midst of it. I may escape ; but I can make no insurance against such an event. Let me add, that I do not choose wholly to break the American spirit ; because it is the spirit that has made the country.

Lastly, we have no sort of experience in favour of force as an instrument in the rule of our colonies. Their growth and their utility have been owing to methods altogether different. Our ancient indulgence has been said to be pursued to a fault. It may be so. But we know, if feeling is evidence, that our fault was more tolerable than our attempt to mend it ; and our sin far more salutary than our penitence.

These, Sir, are my reasons for not entertaining that high opinion of untried force, by which many gentlemen, for whose sentiments in other particulars I have great respect, seem to be so greatly captivated. But there is still behind a third consideration concerning this object, which serves to determine my opinion on the sort of policy which ought to be pursued in the management of America, even more than its population and its commerce, I mean its temper and character.

In this character of the Americans, a love of freedom is the predominating feature which marks and distinguishes the whole ; and as an ardent is always a jealous affection, your colonies become suspicious, restive, and untractable, whenever they see the least attempt to wrest from them by force or shuffle from them by chicane, what they think the only advantage worth living for. This fierce spirit of liberty is stronger in the English colonies probably than in any other people of the earth ; and this from a great variety of powerful causes ; which to understand the true temper of their minds, and the direction which this spirit takes, it will not be amiss to lay open somewhat more largely.

First, the people of the colonies are descendants of Englishmen. England, Sir, is a nation which still I hope respects, and formerly adored, her freedom. The colonists emigrated from you when this part of your character was most predominant ; and they took this bias and direction the moment they departed from your hands. They are therefore not only devoted to liberty, but to liberty according to English ideas, and on English principles. Abstract liberty, like other mere abstractions, is not to be found. Liberty inheres in some sensible object ; and every nation has formed to itself some favourite point, which by way of eminence becomes the criterion of their happiness. It happened, you know, Sir, that the great contests for freedom in this country were from the earliest times chiefly upon the question of taxing. Most of the contests in the ancient commonwealths turned primarily on the right of election of magistrates ; or on the balance among the several orders of the State. The question of money was not with them so immediate. But in England it was otherwise. On this point of taxes the ablest pens and most eloquent tongues have been exercised ; the greatest spirits have acted and suffered. In order to give the fullest satisfaction concerning the importance of this point, it was not only necessary for those who in argument defended the excellence of the English Constitution to insist on this privilege of granting money as a dry point of fact, and to prove that the right had been acknowledged in ancient parchments and blind usage to reside in a certain body called a House of Commons. They went much farther ; they attempted to prove, and they succeeded, that in theory it ought to be so, from the particular nature of a House of Commons as an immediate representative of the people, whether the old records had delivered this oracle or not. They took infinite pains to inculcate, as a fundamental principle, that in all monarchies the people must in effect themselves, mediately or immediately, possess the power of granting their own money, or no shadow of liberty could subsist. The colonies draw from you, as with their life blood, these ideas and principles. Their love of liberty, as with you, fixed and attached on this specific point of taxing. Liberty might be safe, or might be endangered, in twenty other particulars, without their being much pleased or alarmed. Here they felt its pulse ; and as they found that beat, they thought themselves sick or sound. I do not say whether they were right or wrong in applying your general arguments to their own case. It is not easy indeed to make a monopoly of theorems and corollaries. The fact is, that they did thus apply those general arguments ; and your mode of governing them, whether through lenity or indolence, through wisdom or mistake, confirmed them in the imagination, that they, as well as you, had an interest in these common principles.

They were further confirmed in this pleasing error by the form of their provincial legislative assemblies. Their governments are popular in a high degree ; some are merely popular ; in all, the popular representative is the most weighty ; and this share of the people in their ordinary government never fails to inspire them with lofty sentiments, and with a strong aversion from whatever tends to deprive them of their chief importance.

If anything were wanting to this necessary operation of the form of government, religion would have given it a complete effect. Religion, always a principle of energy, in this new people is no way worn out or impaired ; and their mode of professing it is also one main cause of this free spirit. The people are Protestants ; and of that kind which is the most adverse to all implicit submission of mind and opinion. This is a persuasion not only favourable to liberty, but built upon it. I do not think, Sir, that the reason of this averseness in the dissenting churches, from all that looks like absolute government, is so much to be sought in their religious tenets as in their history. Every one knows that the Roman Catholic religion is at least coeval with most of the governments where it prevails ; that it has generally gone hand in hand with them, and received great favour and every kind of support from authority. The Church of England too was formed from her cradle under the nursing care of regular government. But the dissenting interests have sprung up in direct opposition to all the ordinary powers of the world ; and could justify that opposition only on a strong claim to natural liberty. Their very existence depended on the powerful and unremitted assertion of that claim. All Protestantism, even the most cold and passive, is a sort of dissent. But the religion most prevalent in our northern colonies is a refinement on the principle of resistance ; it is the dissidence of dissent, and the Protestantism of the Protestant religion. This religion, under a variety of denominations agreeing in nothing but in the communion of the spirit of liberty, is predominant in most of the northern provinces, where the Church of England, notwithstanding its legal rights, is in reality no more than a sort of private sect, not composing most probably the tenth of the people. The colonists left England when this spirit was high, and in the emigrants was the highest of all, and even that stream of foreigners, which has been constantly flowing into these colonies, has, for the greatest part, been composed of dissenters from the establishments of their several countries, and have brought with them a temper and character far from alien to that of the people with whom they mixed. . . . . .

Perhaps, Sir, I am mistaken in my idea of an empire, as distinguished from a single State or kingdom. But my idea of it is this : that an empire is the aggregate of many States under one common head ; whether this head be a monarch, or a presiding republic. It does, in such constitutions, frequently happen (and nothing but the dismal, cold, dead uniformity of servitude can prevent its happening) that the subordinate parts have many local privileges and immunities. Between these privileges and the supreme common authority the line may be extremely nice. Of course, disputes, often, too, very bitter disputes, and much ill blood, will arise. But though every privilege is an exemption (in the case) from the ordinary exercise of the supreme authority, it is no denial of it. The claim of a privilege seems rather, *ex vi termina*, to imply a superior power. For to talk of the privileges of a State, or of a person, who has no superior, is hardly any better than speaking nonsense. Now, in such unfortunate quarrels among the component parts of a great political union of communities, I can scarcely conceive anything more completely imprudent than for the head of the empire to insist that, if any privilege is pleaded against his will, or his acts, his whole authority is denied ; instantly to proclaim rebellion, to beat to arms, and to put the offending provinces under the ban. Will not this, Sir, very soon teach the provinces to make no distinctions on their part ? Will it not teach them that the Government, against which a claim of liberty is tantamount to high treason, is a Government to which submission is equivalent to slavery ? It may not always be quite convenient to impress dependent communities with such an idea.

We are indeed, in all disputes with the colonies, by the necessity of things, the judge. It is true, Sir. But I confess that the character of judge in my own cause is a thing that frightens me. Instead of filling me with pride, I am exceedingly humbled by it. I cannot proceed with a stern, assured, judicial confidence, until I find myself in something more like a judicial character. I must have these hesitations as long as I am compelled to recollect that, in my little reading upon such contests as these, the sense of mankind has, at least, as often decided against the superior as the subordinate power. Sir, let me add too, that the opinion of my having some abstract right in my favour would not put me much at my ease in passing sentence, unless I could be sure that there were no rights which, in their exercise under certain circumstances, were not the most odious of all wrongs, and the most vexatious of all injustice. Sir, these considerations have great weight with me, when I find things so circumstanced, that I see the same party at once a civil litigant against me in point of right ; and a culprit before me, while I sit as a criminal judge on acts of his, whose moral quality is to be decided upon the merits of that very litigation. Men are every now and then put, by the complexity of human affairs, into strange situations ; but justice is the same, let the judge be in what situation he will.

There is, Sir, also a circumstance which convinces me that this mode of criminal proceeding is not (at least in the present stage of our contest) altogether expedient ; which is nothing less than the conduct of those very persons who have seemed to adopt that mode, by lately declaring a rebellion in Massachusetts Bay, as they had formerly addressed to have traitors brought hither, under an Act of Henry the Eighth, for trial. For though rebellion is declared, it is not proceeded against as such ; nor have any steps been taken towards the apprehension or conviction of any individual offender, either on our late or our former Address ; but modes of public coercion have been adopted, and such as have much more resemblance to a sort of qualified hostility towards an independent power than the punishment of rebellious subjects. All this seems rather inconsistent ; but it shows how difficult it is to apply these judicial ideas to our present case.

In this situation, let us seriously and coolly ponder. What is it we have got by all our menaces, which have been many and ferocious ? What advantage have we derived from the penal laws we have passed, and which, for the time, have been severe and numerous ? What advances have we made towards our object, by the sending of a force which, by land and sea, is no contemptible strength ? Has the disorder abated ? Nothing less. When I see things in this situation, after such confident hopes, bold promises, and active exertions, I cannot for my life avoid a suspicion that the plan itself is not correctly right.

If then the removal of the causes of this spirit of American liberty be, for the greater part, or rather entirely, impracticable ; if the ideas of criminal process be inapplicable, or if applicable, are in the highest degree inexpedient ; what way yet remains ? No way is open but the third and last—to comply with the American spirit as necessary ; or, if you please, to submit to it as a necessary evil.

If we adopt this mode ; if we mean to conciliate and concede ; let us see of what nature the concession ought to be : to ascertain the nature of our concession we must look at their complaint. The colonies complain that they have not the characteristic mark and seal of British freedom. They complain that they are taxed in a Parliament in which they are not represented. If you mean to satisfy them at all, you must satisfy them with regard to this complaint. If you mean to please any people, you must give them the boon which they ask ; not what you may think better for them, but of a kind totally different.   Such an act may be a wise regulation, but it is no concession ; whereas our present theme is the mode of giving satisfaction.

Sir, I think you must perceive that I am resolved this day to have nothing at all to do with the question of the right of taxation.   Some gentlemen startle—but it is true ; I put it totally out of the question.   It is less than nothing in my consideration.   I do not indeed wonder, nor will you, Sir, that gentlemen of profound learning are fond of displaying it on this profound subject.   But my consideration is narrow, confined, and wholly limited to the policy of the question.   I do not examine whether the giving away a man's money be a power excepted and reserved out of the general trust of government ; and how far all mankind, in all forms of polity, are entitled to an exercise of that right by the charter of Nature.   Or whether, on the contrary, a right of taxation is necessarily involved in the general principle of legislation, and inseparable from the ordinary supreme power.   These are deep questions, where great names militate against each other ; where reason is perplexed ; and an appeal to authorities only thickens the confusion.   For high and reverend authorities lift up their heads on both sides ; and there is no sure footing in the middle.   This point "is the great Serbonian bog, betwixt Damiata and Mount Casius old, where armies whole have sunk."   I do not intend to be overwhelmed in that bog, though in such respectable company.   The question with me is, not whether you have a right to render your people miserable, but whether it is not your interest to make them happy.   It is not what a lawyer tells me I may do, but what humanity, reason, and justice tell me I ought to do.   Is a politic act the worse for being a generous one !   Is no concession proper, but that which is made from your want of right to keep what you grant ?   Or does it lessen the grace or dignity of relaxing in the exercise of an odious claim, because you have your evidence-room full of titles, and your magazines stuffed with arms to enforce them ?   What signify all those titles and all those arms ?   Of what avail are they, when the reason of the thing tells me that the assertion of my title is the loss of my suit ; and that I could do nothing but wound myself by the use of my own weapons ?

Such is steadfastly my opinion of the absolute necessity of keeping up the concord of this empire by a unity of spirit, though in a diversity of operations, that, if I were sure the colonists had, at their leaving this country, sealed a regular compact of servitude ; that they had solemnly abjured all the rights of citizens ; that they had made a vow to renounce all ideas of liberty for them and their posterity to all generations ; yet I should hold myself obliged to conform to the temper I found universally prevalent in my own day, and to govern two millions of men, impatient of servitude, on the principles of freedom. I am not determining a point of law ; I am restoring tranquillity ; and the general character and situation of a people must determine what sort of government is fitted for them. That point nothing else can or ought to determine.

My idea, therefore, without considering whether we yield as matter of right, or grant as matter of favour, is to admit the people of our colonies into an interest in the constitution ; and, by recording that admission in the journals of Parliament, to give them as strong an assurance as the nature of the thing will admit, that we mean for ever to adhere to that solemn declaration of systematic indulgence. . . . .

But the colonies will go farther. Alas ! alas ! when will this speculation against fact and reason end ? What will quiet these panic fears which we entertain of the hostile effect of a conciliatory conduct ? Is it true that no case can exist in which it is proper for the Sovereign to accede to the desires of his discontented subjects ? Is there anything peculiar in this case to make a rule for itself ? Is all authority of course lost when it is not pushed to the extreme ? Is it a certain maxim, that the fewer causes of dissatisfaction are left by Government, the more the subject will be inclined to resist and rebel ?

All these objections being in fact no more than suspicions, conjectures, divinations, formed in defiance of fact and experience, they did not, Sir, discourage me from entertaining the idea of a conciliatory concession, founded on the principles which I have just stated.

In forming a plan for this purpose, I endeavoured to put myself in that frame of mind which was the most natural and the most reasonable, and which was certainly the most probable means of securing me from all error. I set out with a perfect distrust of my own abilities ; a total renunciation of every speculation of my own ; and with a profound reverence for the wisdom of our ancestors, who have left us the inheritance of so happy a constitution, and so flourishing an empire, and, what is a thousand times more valuable, the treasury of the maxims and principles which formed the one and obtained the other.

During the reigns of the kings of Spain of the Austrian family, whenever they were at a loss in the Spanish councils, it was common for their statesmen to say that they ought to consult the genius of Philip the Second. The genius of Philip the Second might mislead them; and the issue of their affairs showed that they had not chosen the most perfect standard. But, Sir, I am sure that I shall not be misled, when in a case of constitutional difficulty I consult the genius of the English Constitution. Consulting at that oracle (it was with all due humility and piety), I found four capital examples in a similar case before me; those of Ireland, Wales, Chester, and Durham.

Ireland, before the English conquest, though never governed by a despotic power, had no Parliament. How far the English Parliament itself was at that time modelled according to the present form, is disputed among antiquaries. But we have all the reason in the world to be assured that a form of Parliament such as England then enjoyed, she instantly communicated to Ireland; and we are equally sure that almost every successive improvement in constitutional liberty, as fast as it was made here, was transmitted thither. The feudal baronage and the feudal knighthood, the roots of our primitive constitution, were early transplanted into that soil; and grew and flourished there. Magna Charta, if it did not give us originally the House of Commons, gave us at least a House of Commons of weight and consequence. But your ancestors did not churlishly sit down alone to the feast of Magna Charta. Ireland was made immediately a partaker. This benefit of English laws and liberties, I confess, was not at first extended to all Ireland. Mark the consequence. English authority and English liberties had exactly the same boundaries. Your standard could never be advanced an inch before your privileges. Sir John Davis shows beyond a doubt that the refusal of a general communication of these rights was the true cause why Ireland was five hundred years in subduing; and after the vain projects of a military government, attempted in the reign of Queen Elizabeth, it was soon discovered that nothing could make that country English, in civility and allegiance, but your laws and your forms of legislature. It was not English arms, but the English Constitution, that conquered Ireland. From that time, Ireland has ever had a general Parliament, as she had before a partial Parliament. You changed the people; you altered the religion; but you never touched the form or the vital substance of free government in that kingdom. You deposed kings; you restored them; you altered the succession to theirs, as well as to your own Crown; but you never altered their constitution; the principle of which was respected by usurpation ; restored with the restoration of monarchy, and established, I trust, for ever, by the glorious revolution. This has made Ireland the great and flourishing kingdom that it is ; and from a disgrace and a burthen intolerable to this nation, has rendered her a principal part of our strength and ornament. This country cannot be said to have ever formally taxed her. The irregular things done in the confusion of mighty troubles, and on the hinge of great revolutions, even if all were done that is said to have been done, form no example. If they have any effect in argument, they make an exception to prove the rule. None of your own liberties could stand a moment if the casual deviations from them, at such times, were suffered to be used as proofs of their nullity. By the lucrative amount of such casual breaches in the constitution, judge what the stated and fixed rule of supply has been in that kingdom. Your Irish pensioners would starve if they had no other fund to live on than taxes granted by English authority. Turn your eyes to those popular grants from whence all your great supplies are come ; and learn to respect that only source of public wealth in the British empire.

My next example is Wales. This country was said to be reduced by Henry the Third. It was said more truly to be so by Edward the First. But though then conquered, it was not looked upon as any part of the realm of England. Its old constitution, whatever that might have been, was destroyed ; and no good one was substituted in its place. The care of that tract was put into the hands of Lord Marchers—a form of government of a very singular kind ; a strange heterogeneous monster, something between hostility and government ; perhaps it has a sort of resemblance, according to the modes of those times, to that of commander-in-chief at present, to whom all civil power is granted as secondary. The manners of the Welsh nation followed the genius of the Government ; the people were ferocious, restive, savage, and uncultivated ; sometimes composed, never pacified. Wales, within itself, was in perpetual disorder ; and it kept the frontier of England in perpetual alarm. Benefits from it to the State there were none. Wales was only known to England by incursion and invasion.

Sir, during that state of things, Parliament was not idle. They attempted to subdue the fierce spirit of the Welsh by all sorts of rigorous laws. They prohibited by statute the sending all sorts of arms into Wales, as you prohibit by proclamation (with something more of doubt on the legality) the sending arms to America. They disarmed the Welsh by statute, as you

attempted (but still with more question on the legality) to dis-
arm New England by an instruction. They made an Act to
drag offenders from Wales into England for trial, as you have
done (but with more hardship) with regard to America. By
another Act, where one of the parties was an Englishman, they
ordained that his trial should be always by English. They
made Acts to restrain trade, as you do ; and they prevented
the Welsh from the use of fairs and markets, as you do the
Americans from fisheries and foreign ports. In short, when the
Statute-book was not quite so much swelled as it is now, you
find no less than fifteen Acts of penal regulation on the subject
of Wales.

Here we rub our hands—a fine body of precedents for the
authority of Parliament and the use of it !—I admit it fully ;
and pray add likewise to these precedents, that all the while
Wales rid this kingdom like an *incubus ;* that it was an unprofitable and oppressive burthen ; and that an Englishman
travelling in that country could not go six yards from the high
road without being murdered.

The march of the human mind is slow. Sir, it was not, until
after two hundred years, discovered, that, by an eternal law,
Providence had decreed vexation to violence, and poverty to
rapine. Your ancestors did, however, at length open their eyes
to the ill husbandry of injustice. They found that the tyranny
of a free people could of all tyrannies the least be endured ;
and that laws made against a whole nation were not the most
effectual methods of securing its obedience. Accordingly, in
the twenty-seventh year of Henry the Eighth, the course was
entirely altered. With a preamble stating the entire and perfect rights of the Crown of England, it gave to the Welsh all
the rights and privileges of English subjects. A political order
was established ; the military power gave way to the civil ; the
marches were turned into counties. But that a nation should
have a right to English liberties, and yet no share at all in the
fundamental security of these liberties—the grant of their own
property—seemed a thing so incongruous, that, eight years
after—that is, in the thirty-fifth of that reign—a complete and
not ill-proportioned representation by counties and boroughs·
was bestowed upon Wales by Act of Parliament. From that
moment, as by a charm, the tumults subsided, obedience was
restored, peace, order, and civilization followed in the train of
liberty. When the day-star of the English Constitution
had arisen in their hearts, all was harmony within and
without—

> —simul alba nautis
> Stella refulsit,
> Defluit saxis agitatus humor ;
> Concidunt venti,, fugiuntque nubes,
> Et minax (quod sic voluere) ponto
> Unda recumbit.

The very same year the County Palatine of Chester received the same relief from its oppressions, and the same remedy to its disorders. Before this time Chester was little less distempered than Wales. The inhabitants, without rights themselves, were the fittest to destroy the rights of others ; and from thence Richard the Second drew the standing army of archers, with which for a time he oppressed England. The people of Chester applied to Parliament in a petition penned as I shall read to you :

> "To the King our Sovereign Lord, in most humble wise shewen unto your excellent Majesty the inhabitants of your Grace's County Palatine of Chester : (1). That where the said County Palatine of Chester is and hath been always hitherto exempt, excluded and separated out and from your High Court of Parliament, to have any Knights and Burgesses within the said Court ; by reason whereof the said inhabitants have hitherto sustained manifold disherisons, losses, and damages, as well as their lands, goods, and bodies, as in the good, civil, and politic governance and maintenance of the commonwealth of their said Country : (2). And forasmuch as the said inhabitants have always hitherto been bound by the Acts and Statutes made and ordained by your said Highness, and your most noble progenitors, by authority of the said Court, as far forth as other counties, cities, and boroughs have been, that have had their Knights and Burgesses within your said Court of Parliament, and yet have had neither Knight ne Burgess there for the said County Palatine ; the said inhabitants, for lack thereof, have been oftentimes touched and grieved with Acts and Statutes made within the said Court, as well derogatory unto the most ancient jurisdictions, liberties, and privileges of your said County Palatine, as prejudicial unto the commonwealth, quietness, rest, and peace of your Grace's most bounden subjects inhabiting within the same."

What did Parliament with this audacious address ?—Reject it as a libel ? Treat it as an affront to Government ? Spurn it as a derogation from the rights of legislature ? Did they toss it over the table? Did they burn it by the hands of the common hangman? They took the petition of grievance, all rugged as it was, without softening or temperament, unpurged of the original bitterness and indignation of complaint; they made it the very preamble to their Act of redress; and consecrated its principle to all ages in the sanctuary of legislation.

Here is my third example. It was attended with the success of the two former. Chester, civilized as well as Wales, has demonstrated that freedom, and not servitude, is the cure of anarchy; as religion, and not atheism, is the true remedy for superstition. Sir, this pattern of Chester was followed in the reign of Charles the Second with regard to the County Palatine of Durham, which is my fourth example. This county had long lain out of the pale of free legislation. So scrupulously was the example of Chester followed, that the style of the preamble is nearly the same with that of the Chester Act; and, without affecting the abstract extent of the authority of Parliament, it recognizes the equity of not suffering any considerable district, in which the British subjects may act as a body, to be taxed without their own voice in the grant.

Now, if the doctrines of policy continued in these preambles, and the force of these examples in the Acts of Parliaments avail anything, what can be said against applying them with regard to America? Are not the people of America as much Englishmen as the Welsh? The preamble of the Act of Henry the Eighth says the Welsh speak a language no way resembling that of his Majesty's English subjects. Are the Americans not as numerous? If we may trust the learned and accurate Judge Barrington's account of North Wales, and take that as a standard to measure the rest, there is no comparison. The people cannot amount to above 200,000, not a tenth part of the number in the colonies. Is America in rebellion? Wales was hardly ever free from it. Have you attempted to govern America by penal statutes? You made fifteen for Wales. But your legislative authority is perfect with regard to America; was it less perfect in Wales, Chester, and Durham? But America is virtually·represented. What! does the electric force of virtual representation more easily pass over the Atlantic than pervade Wales, which lies in your neighbourhood; or than Chester and Durham, surrounded by abundance of representation that is actual and palpable? But, Sir, your ancestors thought this sort of virtual representation, however ample, to be totally insufficient for the freedom of the inhabitants of territories that are so near and comparatively so inconsiderable. How then can I think it sufficient for those which are infinitely greater and infinitely more remote? . . . .

It is not fair to judge of the temper or dispositions of any man, or any set of men, when they are composed and at rest, from their conduct, or their expressions, in a state of disturbance and irritation. It is besides a very great mistake to imagine that mankind follow up practically any speculative principle, either of government or of freedom, as far as it will go in argument and logical illation. We Englishmen stop very short of the principles upon which we support any given part of our Constitution; or even the whole of it together. I could easily, if I had not already tired you, give you very striking and convincing instances of it. This is nothing but what is natural and proper. All government, indeed every human benefit and enjoyment, every virtue, and every prudent act, is founded on compromise and barter. We balance inconveniences; we give and take; we remit some rights, that we may enjoy others; and we choose rather to be happy citizens, than subtle disputants. As we must give away some natural liberty, to enjoy civil advantages; so we must sacrifice some civil liberties, for the advantages to be derived from the communion and fellowship of a great empire. But, in all fair dealings, the thing bought must bear some proportion to the purchase paid. None will barter away the immediate jewel of his soul. Though a great house is apt to make slaves haughty, yet it is purchasing a part of the artificial importance of a great empire too dear, to pay for it all essential rights, and all the intrinsic dignity of human nature. None of us who would not risk his life rather than fall under a government purely arbitrary. But although there are some amongst us who think our Constitution wants many improvements, to make it a complete system of liberty; perhaps none who are of that opinion would think it right to aim at such improvement by disturbing his country and risking everything that is dear to him. In every arduous enterprise, we consider what we are to lose, as well as what we are to gain; and the more and better stake of liberty every people possess, the less they will hazard in a vain attempt to make it more. These are the cords of man. Man acts from adequate motives relative to his interest; and not on metaphysical speculations. Aristotle, the great master of reasoning, cautions us, and with great weight and propriety, against this species of delusive geometrical accuracy in moral arguments, as the most fallacious of all sophistry.

The Americans will have no interest contrary to the grandeur and glory of England, when they are not oppressed by. the weight of it ; and they will rather be inclined to respect the acts of a superintending legislature ; when they see them the acts of that power which is itself the security, not the rival, of their secondary importance.　In this assurance my mind most perfectly acquiesces ; and I confess I feel not the least alarm from the discontents which are to arise from putting people at their ease ; nor do I apprehend the destruction of this empire, from giving, by an act of free grace and indulgence, to two millions of my fellow-citizens some share of those rights upon which I have always been taught to value myself.

It is said, indeed, that this power of granting, vested in American assemblies, would dissolve the unity of the empire ; which was preserved entire, although Wales, Chester, and Durham were added to it.　Truly, Mr. Speaker, I do not know what this unity means ; nor has it ever been heard of, that I know, in the constitutional policy of this country.　The very idea of subordination of parts excludes this notion of simple and undivided unity.　England is the head, but she is not the head and the members too.　Ireland has ever had from the beginning a separate, but not an independent, legislature, which, far from distracting, promoted the union of the whole. Everything was sweetly and harmoniously disposed through both islands for the conservation of English dominion, and the communication of English Liberties.　I do not see that the same principles might not be carried into twenty islands, and with the same good effect.　This is my model with regard to America, as far as the internal circumstances of the two countries are the same.　I know no other unity of this empire, than I can draw from its example during these periods, when it seemed to my poor understanding more united than it is now, or than it is likely to be by the present methods. . . . . .

Cannot you, in England ; cannot you, at this time of day ; cannot you, a House of Commons, trust to the principle which has raised so mighty a revenue, and accumulated a debt of near 140 millions in this country?　Is this principle to be true in England, and false everywhere else?　Is it not true in Ireland?　Has it not hitherto been true in the colonies?　Why should you presume that in any country a body duly constituted for any function will neglect to perform its duty, and abdicate its trust?　Such a presumption would go against all governments in all modes.　But, in truth, this dread of penury of supply, from a free assembly, has no foundation in Nature.

For first observe, that, besides the desire which all men have naturally of supporting the honour of their own government, that sense of dignity, and that security to property, which ever attends freedom, has a tendency to increase the stock of the free community. Most may be taken where most is accumulated. And what is the soil or climate where experience has not uniformly proved that the voluntary flow of heaped-up plenty, bursting from the weight of its own rich luxuriance, has ever run with a more copious stream of revenue than could be squeezed from the dry husks of oppressed indigence by the straining of all the politic machinery in the world?

Next, we know that parties must ever exist in a free country. We know, too, that the emulations of such parties, their contradictions, their reciprocal necessities, their hopes, and their fears, must send them all in their turns to him that holds the balance of the State. The parties are the gamesters; but Government keeps the table, and is sure to be the winner in the end. When this game is played, I really think it is more to be feared that the people will be exhausted, than that Government will not be supplied. Whereas, whatever is got by acts of absolute power, ill obeyed, because odious, or by contracts ill kept, because constrained, will be narrow, feeble, uncertain, and precarious. "Ease would retract vows made in pain, as violent and void."

I, for one, protest against compounding our demands : I declare against compounding, for a poor limited sum, the immense, ever-growing, eternal debt, which is due to generous government from protected freedom. And so may I speed in the great object I propose to you, as I think it would not only be an act of injustice, but would be the worst economy in the world, to compel the colonies to a sum certain, either in the way of ransom, or in the way of compulsory compact.

But to clear my ideas on this subject—a revenue from America transmitted hither—do not delude yourselves : you never can receive it—no, not a shilling. We have experience that from remote countries it is not to be expected. If, when you attempted to extract revenue from Bengal, you were obliged to return in loan what you had taken in imposition, what can you expect from North America? For certainly, if ever there was a country qualified to produce wealth, it is India ; or an institution for the transmission, it is the East India Company. America has none of these aptitudes. If America gives you taxable objects, on which you lay your duties here, and gives you, at the same time, a surplus by a foreign sale of her commodities to pay the duties on these objects, which you tax at home, she has performed her part to the British revenue. But with regard to her own internal establishments, she may—I doubt not she will—contribute in moderation. I say in moderation ; for she ought not to be permitted to exhaust herself. She ought to be reserved to a war ; the weight of which, with the enemies that we are most likely to have, must be considerable in her quarter of the globe. There she may serve you, and serve you essentially.

For that service, for all service, whether of revenue, trade, or empire, my trust is in her interest in the British Constitution. My hold of the colonies is in the close affection which grows from common names, from kindred blood, from similar privileges, and equal protection. These are the ties which, though light as air, are as strong as links of iron. Let the colonies always keep the idea of their civil rights associated with your government ; they will cling and grapple to you, and no force under heaven will be of power to tear them from their allegiance. But let it be once understood that your government may be one thing and their privileges another ; that these two things may exist without any mutual relation ; the cement is gone, the cohesion is loosened, and everything hastens to decay and dissolution. As long as you have the wisdom to keep the sovereign authority of this country as the sanctuary of liberty, the sacred temple consecrated to our common faith, wherever the chosen race and sons of England worship freedom, they will turn their faces towards you. The more they multiply, the more friends you will have ; the more ardently they love liberty, the more perfect will be their obedience. Slavery they can have anywhere. It is a weed that grows in every soil. They may have it from Spain, they may have it from Prussia. But, until you become lost to all feeling of your true interest and your natural dignity, freedom they can have from none but you. This is the commodity of price, of which you have the monopoly. This is the true Act of Navigation which binds to you the commerce of the colonies, and through them secures to you the wealth of the world. Deny them this participation of freedom, and you break that sole bond which originally made and must still preserve the unity of the empire. Do not entertain so weak an imagination as that your registers and your bonds, your affidavits and your sufferances, your cockets and your clearances, are what form the great securities of your commerce. Do not dream that your letters of office, and your instructions, and your suspending clauses are the things that hold together the great contexture of the mysterious whole. These things do not make your government. Dead instruments, passive tools as they are, it is the spirit of the English communion that gives all their life and efficacy to them. It is the spirit of the English Constitution, which, infused through the mighty mass, pervades, feeds, unites, invigorates, vivifies every part of the empire, even down to the minutest member.

It is not the same virtue which does everything for us here in England? Do you imagine, then, that it is the Land Tax Act which raises your revenue? that it is the annual vote in the Committee of Supply which gives you your army? or that it is the Mutiny Bill which inspires it with bravery and discipline? No! surely no! It is the love of the people : it is their attachment to their Government, from the sense of the deep stake they have in such a glorious institution, which gives you your army and your navy, and infuses into both that liberal obedience without which your army would be a base rabble, and your navy nothing but rotten timber.

All this, I know well enough, will sound wild and chimerical to the profane herd of those vulgar and mechanical politicians who have no place among us ; a sort of people who think that nothing exists but what is gross and material ; and who, therefore, far from being qualified to be directors of the great movement of empire, are not fit to turn a wheel in the machine. But to men truly initiated and rightly taught, these ruling and master principles, which in the opinion of such men as I have mentioned have no substantial existence, are in truth everything and all in all. Magnanimity in politicians is not seldom the truest wisdom ; and a great empire and little minds go ill together. If we are conscious of our station, and glow with zeal to fill our places as becomes our situation and ourselves, we ought to auspicate all our public proceedings on America with the old warning of the church, *Surdum corda!* We ought to elevate our minds to the greatness of that trust to which the order of Providence has called us. By adverting to the dignity of this high calling, our ancestors have turned a savage wilderness into a glorious empire ; and have made the most extensive, and the only honourable conquests, not by destroying, but by promoting the wealth, the number, the happiness of the human race. English privileges have made it all that it is ; English privileges alone will make it all it can be.

Works.

EDWARD GIBBON.

1737–1794.

THE ANTONINES.

As soon as Hadrian's passion was either gratified or disappointed, he resolved to deserve the thanks of posterity, by placing the most exalted merit on the Roman throne. His discerning eye easily discovered a senator about fifty years of age, blameless in all the offices of life ; and a youth of about seventeen, whose riper years opened a fair prospect of every virtue ; the elder of these was declared the son and successor of Hadrian, on condition, however, that he himself should immediately adopt the younger. The two Antonines (for it is of them we are now speaking) governed the Roman world forty-two years, with the same invariable spirit of wisdom and virtue. Although Pius had two sons, he preferred the welfare of Rome to the interest of his family, gave his daughter Faustina in marriage to the young Marcus, obtained from the Senate the tribunitian and proconsular powers, and with a noble disdain, or rather ignorance of jealousy, associated him to all the labours of government. Marcus, on the other hand, revered the character of his benefactor, loved him as a parent, obeyed him as his sovereign, and, after he was no more, regulated his own administration by the example and maxims of his predecessor. Their united reigns are possibly the only period of history in which the happiness of a great people was the sole object of government.

Titus Antoninus Pius has been justly denominated a second Numa. The same love of religion, justice, and peace, was the distinguishing characteristic of both princes. But the situation of the latter opened a much larger field for the exercise of those virtues. Numa could only prevent a few neighbouring villages from plundering each other's harvests.

Antoninus diffused order and tranquillity over the greatest part of the earth. His reign is marked by the rare advantage of furnishing very few materials for history; which is, indeed, little more than the register of the crimes, follies, and misfortunes of mankind. In private life, he was an amiable as well as a good man. The native simplicity of his virtue was a stranger to vanity and affectation. He enjoyed with moderation the conveniences of his fortune, and the innocent pleasures of society; and the benevolence of his soul displayed itself in a cheerful serenity of temper.

The virtue of Marcus Aurelius Antoninus was of a severer and more laborious kind. It was the well-earned harvest of many a learned conference, of many a patient lecture, and many a midnight lucubration. At the age of twelve years, he embraced the rigid system of the stoics, which taught him to submit his body to his mind, his passions to his reason; to consider virtue as the only good, vice as the only evil, all things external as things indifferent. His meditations, composed in the tumult of a camp, are still extant; and he even condescended to give lessons of philosophy, in a more public manner than was perhaps consistent with the modesty of a sage, or the dignity of an emperor. But his life was the noblest commentary on the precepts of Zeno. He was severe to himself, indulgent to the imperfections of others, just and beneficent to all mankind. He regretted that Avidius Cassius, who excited a rebellion in Syria, had disappointed him by a voluntary death, of the pleasure of converting an enemy into a friend; and he justified the sincerity of that sentiment, by moderating the zeal of the Senate against the adherents of the traitor. War he detested, as the disgrace and calamity of human nature; but when the necessity of a just defence called upon him to take up arms, he readily exposed his person to eight winter campaigns on the frozen banks of the Danube, the severity of which was at last fatal to the weakness of his constitution. His memory was revered by a grateful posterity; and above a century after his death, many persons preserved the image of Marcus Antoninus among those of their household gods.

If a man were called to fix a period in the history of the world during which the condition of the human race was most happy and prosperous, he would without hesitation, name that which elapsed from the death of Domitian to the accession of Commodus. The vast extent of the Roman empire was governed by absolute power, under the guidance of virtue and wisdom. The armies were restrained by the firm but gentle hand of four successive emperors, whose characters and authority commanded involuntary respect. The forms of the civil administration were carefully preserved by Nerva, Trojan, Hadrian, and the Antonines, who delighted in the image of liberty, and were pleased with considering themselves as the accountable ministers of the laws. Such princes deserved the honour of restoring the republic, had the Romans of their days been capable of enjoying a rational freedom.

POPE JOHN XII.

THE Roman pontiffs, of the ninth and tenth centuries, were insulted, imprisoned, and murdered, by their tyrants ; and such was their indigence after the loss and usurpation of the ecclesiastical patrimonies, that they could neither support the state of a prince, nor exercise the charity of a priest. The influence of two sister prostitutes, Marozia and Theodora, was founded on their wealth and beauty, their political and amorous intrigues : the most strenuous of their lovers were rewarded with the Roman mitre, and their reign may have suggested to the darker ages the fable of a female pope. The bastard son, the grandson, and the great grandson of Marozia, a rare genealogy, were seated in the chair of Saint Peter, and it was at the age of nineteen years that the second of these became the head of the Latin church. His youth and manhood were of a suitable complexion ; and the nations of pilgrims could bear testimony to the charges that were urged against him in a Roman synod, and in the presence of Otho the great. As John XII. had renounced the dress and the decencies of his profession, the *soldier* may not perhaps be dishonoured by the wine which he drank, the blood that he spilt, the flames that he kindled, or the licentious pursuits of gaming and hunting. His open simony might be the consequence of distress ; and his blasphemous invocation of Jupiter and Venus, if it be true, could not possibly be serious. But we read with some surprise, that the worthy grandson of Marozia lived in public adultery with the matrons of Rome ; that the Lateran palace was turned into a school for prostitution, and that his rapes of virgins and widows had deterred the female pilgrims from visiting the tomb of St. Peter, lest, in the devout act, they should be violated by his successor. The protestants have dwelt with malicious pleasure on these characters of anti-christ ; but to a philosophic eye, the vices of the clergy are far less dangerous than their virtues. After a long series of scandal, the apostolic see was reformed and exalted by the austerity and zeal of Gregory VII. That ambitious monk devoted his life to the execution of two projects. I. To fix in the college of cardinals the freedom and independence of election, and for ever to abolish the right or usurpation of the emperors and the Roman people. II. To bestow or resume the western empire as a fief or benefice of the church, and to extend his temporal dominion over the kings and kingdoms of the earth. After a contest of fifty years, the first of these designs was accomplished by the firm support of the ecclesiastical order, whose liberty was connected with that of their chief. But the second attempt, though it was crowned with some partial and apparent success, has been vigorously resisted by the secular power, and finally extinguished by the improvement of human reason.

A GERMAN KAISER AND A GENUINE CÆSAR.

IT is in the fourteenth century that we may view in the strongest light the state and contrast of the Roman empire of Germany, which no longer held, except on the borders of the Rhine and Danube, a single province of Trojan or Constantine. Their unworthy successors were the counts of Hapsburgh, of Nassau, of Luxemburgh, and of Schwartzenburgh : the Emperor Henry VII. procured for his son the crown of Bohemia, and his grandson Charles IV. was born among a people, strange and barbarous in the estimation of the Germans themselves. After the excommunication of Lewis of Bavaria, he received the gift or promise of the vacant empire from the Roman pontiffs, who, in the exile and captivity of Avignon, affected the dominion of the earth. The death of his competitors united the electoral college, and Charles was unanimously saluted king of the Romans, and future emperor : a title which in the same age was prostituted to the Cæsars of Germany and Greece. The German emperor was no more than the elective and impotent magistrate of an aristocracy of princes, who had not left him a village that he might call his own. His best prerogative was the right of presiding and proposing in the national senate, which was convened at his summons ; and his native kingdom of Bohemia, less opulent than the adjacent city of Nuremburgh, was the firmest seat of his power and the richest source of his revenue. The army with which he passed the Alps consisted of three hundred horse. In the cathedral of St. Ambrose, Charles was crowned with the *iron* crown, which tradition assigned to the Lombard monarchy : but he was admitted only with a peaceful train ; the gates of the city were shut upon him ; and the King of Italy was held a captive by the arms of the Visconti, whom he confirmed in the sovereignty of Milan. In the Vatican he was again crowned with the *golden* crown of the empire ; but, in obedience to a secret treaty, the Roman emperor immediately withdrew, without reposing a single night within the walls of Rome. The eloquent Petrarch, whose fancy revived the visionary glories of the Capitol, deplores and upbraids the ignominious flight of the Bohemian ; and even his contemporaries could observe, that the sole exercise of his authority was in the lucrative sale of privileges and titles. The gold of Italy secured the election of his son ; but such was the shameful poverty of the Roman emperor, that his person was arrested by a butcher in the streets of Worms, and was detained in the public inn, as a pledge or hostage for the payment of his expences.

From this humiliating scene, let us turn to the apparent majesty of the same Charles in the diets of the empire. The golden bull which fixes the Germanic constitution, is promulgated in the style of a sovereign and legislator. An hundred princes bowed before his throne, and exalted their own dignity by the voluntary honours which they yielded to their prince or minister. At the royal banquet, the hereditary great officers, the seven electors, who in rank and title were equal to kings, performed their solemn and domestic service of the palace. The seals of the triple kingdom were borne in state by the archbishops of Mentz, Cologne, and Treves, the perpetual arch-chancellors of Germany, Italy, and Arles. The great marshall, on horseback, exercised his function with a silver measure of oats, which he emptied on the ground, and immediately dismounted to regulate the order of the guests. The great steward, the court palatine of the Rhine, placed the dishes on the table. The great chamberlain, the margave of Branden-burgh, presented, after the repast, the golden ewer and bason, to wash. The king of Bohemia, as great cup-bearer, was represented by the emperor's brother, the duke of Luxemburgh and Brabant ; and the procession was closed by the great huntsmen, who introduced a boar and a stag, with a loud

chorus of horns and hounds. Nor was the supremacy of the
emperor confined to Germany alone ; the hereditary monarchs
of Europe confessed the pre-eminence of his rank and dignity ;
he was the first of the Christian princes, the temporal head of
the great republic of the West : to his person the title of
majesty was long appropriated ; and he disputed with the
pope the sublime prerogative of creating kings and assembling
councils. The oracle of civil law, the learned Bartolm, was a
pensioner of Charles IV. ; and his school resounded with the
doctrine, that the Roman emperor was the rightful sovereign of
the earth, from the rising to the setting sun. The contrary
opinion was condemned, not as an error, but as an heresy,
since even the gospel had pronounced, "And then went forth
"a decree from Cæsar Augustus, that *all the world* should be
"taxed."

If we annihilate the interval of time and space between
Augustus and Charles, strong and striking will be the contrast
between the two Cæsars ; the Bohemian, who concealed his
weakness under the mask of ostentation, and the Roman, who
disguised his strength under the semblance of modesty. At
the head of his victorious legions, in his reign over the sea and
land, from the Nile and Euphrates to the Atlantic ocean,
Augustus professed himself the servant of the senate and the
equal of his fellow citizens. The conqueror of Rome and her
provinces assumed the popular and legal form of the censor, a
consul, and a tribune. His will was the law of mankind, but in
the declaration of his laws he borrowed the voice of the senate
and people ; and, from their decrees, their master accepted and
received his temporary commission to administer to the republic. In his dress, his domestics, his titles, in all the offices
of social life, Augustus maintained the character of a private
Roman ; and his most artful flatterers respected the secret of
absolute and perpetual monarchy.

Decline and Fall.

SIR WALTER SCOTT.

1771–1832.

THE ANTIQUARY'S TREASURES.

MR. OLDBUCK had by this time attained the top of the winding stair which led to his own apartment, and opening a door, and pushing aside a piece of tapestry with which it was covered, his first exclamation was, "What are you about here, you sluts?" A dirty barefooted chambermaid threw down her duster, detected in the heinous fact of arranging the *sanctum sanctorum*, and fled out of an opposite door from the face of her incensed master. A genteel-looking young woman, who was superintending the operation, stood her ground, but with some timidity.

"Indeed, uncle, your room was not fit to be seen, and I just came to see that Jenny laid everything down where she took it up."

"And how dare you, or Jenny either, presume to meddle with my private matters?" (Mr. Oldbuck hated *putting to rights* as much as Dr. Orkborne, or any other professed student.) "Go sew your sampler, you monkey, and do not let me find you here again, as you value your ears.—I assure you, Mr. Lovel, that the last inroad of these pretended friends to cleanliness was almost as fatal to my collection as Hudibras's visit to that of Sidrophel ; and I have ever since missed

> ' My copperplate, with almanacks
> Engraved upon't, and other knacks ;
> My moon-dial, with Napier's bones,
> And several constellation stones ;
> My flea, my morepeon, and punaise,
> I purchased for my proper ease.'

And so forth, as old Butler has it."

The young lady, after curtseying to Lovel, had taken the
opportunity to make her escape during this enumeration of
losses. "You'll be poisoned here with the volumes of dust
they have raised," continued the Antiquary ; "but I assure you
the dust was very ancient, peaceful, quiet dust, about an hour
ago, and would have remained so for a hundred years, had not
these gipsies disturbed it, as they do everything else in the
world."

It was indeed some time before Lovel could, through the
thick atmosphere, perceive in what sort of den his friend had
constructed his retreat. It was a lofty room, of middling size,
obscurely lighted by high narrow latticed windows. One end
was entirely occupied by book-shelves, greatly too limited in
space for the number of volumes placed upon them, which
were, therefore, drawn up in ranks of two or three files deep,
while numberless others littered the floor and the tables, amid a
chaos of maps, engravings, scraps of parchment, bundles of
papers, pieces of old armour, swords, dirks, helmets, and Highland targets. Behind Mr. Oldbuck's seat (which was an ancient
leathern-covered easy-chair, worn smooth by constant use), was
a huge oaken cabinet, decorated at each corner with Dutch
cherubs, having their little duck-wings displayed, and great
jolter-headed visages placed between them. The top of this
cabinet was covered with busts, and Roman lamps and pateræ,
intermingled with one or two bronze figures. The walls of the
apartment were partly clothed with grim old tapestry, representing the memorable story of Sir Gawaine's wedding, in
which full justice was done to the ugliness of the Lothely Lady ;
although, to judge from his own looks, the gentle knight had
less reason to be disgusted with the match on account of
disparity of outward favour, than the romancer has given us to
understand. The rest of the room was panelled, or wain-
scotted, with black oak, against which hung two or three portraits in armour, being characters in Scottish history, favourites
of Mr. Oldbuck, and as many in tie-wigs and laced coats, staring representatives of his own ancestors. A large old-fashioned
oaken table was covered with a profusion of papers, parchments,
books, and nondescript trinkets and gew-gaws, which seemed
to have little to recommend them, besides rust and the antiquity which it indicates. In the midst of this wreck of ancient
books and utensils, with a gravity equal to Marius among the
ruins of Carthage, sat a large black cat, which, to a superstitious eye, might have presented the *genus loci*, the tutelar
demon of the apartment. The floor, as well as the table

and chairs, was overflowed by the same *mare magnum* of miscellaneous trumpery, where it would have been as impossible to find any individual article wanted, as to put it to any use when discovered.

Amid this medley, it was no easy matter to find one's way to a chair, without stumbling over a prostrate folio, or the still more awkward mischance of overturning some piece of Roman or ancient British pottery. And, when the chair was attained, it had to be disencumbered, with a careful hand, of engravings which might have received damage, and of antique spurs and buckles, which would certainly have occasioned it to any sudden occupant. Of this the Antiquary made Lovel particularly aware, adding, that his friend, the Rev. Doctor Heavysterne from the Low Countries, had sustained much injury by sitting down suddenly and incautiously on three ancient calthrops, or *craw-taes*, which had been lately dug up in the bog near Bannock-burn, and which, dispersed by Robert Bruce to lacerate the feet of the English chargers, came thus in process of time to endamage the sitting part of a learned professor of Utrecht.

Having at length fairly settled himself, and being nothing loath to make inquiry concerning the strange objects around him, which his host was equally ready, as far as possible, to explain, Lovel was introduced to a large club, or bludgeon, with an iron spike at the end of it, which, it seems, had been lately found in a field on the Monkbarns property, adjacent to an old burying ground. It had mightily the air of such a stick as the Highland reapers use to walk with on their annual perigrina-tions from their mountains ; but Mr. Oldbuck was strongly tempted to believe, that, as its shape was singular, it might have been one of the clubs with which the monks armed their peasants in lieu of more martial weapons,—whence, he observed, the villains were called *Colve-carles*, or *Kolb-kerls*, that is, *Clavigeri*, or club-bearers. For the truth of this custom, he, quoted the chronicle of Antwerp and that of St. Martin ; against which authorities Lovel had nothing to oppose, having never heard of them till that moment.

Mr. Oldbuck next exhibited thumb-screws, which had given the Covenanters of former days the cramp in their joints, and a collar with the name of a fellow convicted of theft, whose services, as the inscription bore, had been adjudged to a neighbouring baron, in lieu of the modern Scottish punishment, which, as Oldbuck said, sends such culprits to enrich England by their labour, and themselves by their dexterity. Many and various were the other curiosities which he showed ;—but it was chiefly upon his books that he prided himself, repeating, with a complacent air, as he led the way to the crowded and dusty shelves, the verses of old Chaucer—

> " For he would rather have, at his bed-head,
> A twenty books, clothed in black or red,
> Of Aristotle, or his philosophy,
> Than robes rich, rebeck, or saltery."

This pithy motto he delivered, shaking his head, and giving each guttural the true Anglo-Saxon enunciation, which is now forgotten in the southern parts of this realm.

The collection was indeed a curious one, and might well be envied by an amateur. Yet it was not collected at the enormous prices of modern times, which are sufficient to have appalled the most determined as well as earliest bibliomaniac upon record, whom we take to have been none else than the renowned Don Quixote de la Mancha, as, among other slight indications of an infirm understanding, he is stated, by his veracious historian, Cid Hamet Benengeli, to have exchanged fields and farms for folios and quartos of chivalry. In this species of exploit, the good knight-errant has been imitated by lords, knights, and squires of our own day, though we have not yet heard of any that has mistaken an inn for a castle, or laid his lance in rest against a windmill. Mr. Oldbuck did not follow these collectors in such excess of expenditure ; but, taking a pleasure in the personal labour of forming his library, saved his purse at the expense of his time and toil. He was no encourager of that ingenious race of peripatetic middle-men, who, trafficking between the obscure keeper of a stall and the eager amateur, make their profit at once of the ignorance of the former, and the dear-bought skill and taste of the latter. When such were mentioned in his hearing, he seldom failed to point out how necessary it was to arrest the object of your curiosity in its first transit, and to tell his favourite story of Snuffy Davie and Caxton's Game at Chess.—" Davy Wilson," he said, "commonly called Snuffy Davy, from his inveterate addiction to black rappee, was the very prince of scouts for searching blind alleys, cellars, and stalls, for rare volumes. He had the scent of a slow-hound, sir, and the snap of a bull-dog. He would detect you an old black-letter ballad among the leaves of a law-paper, and find an *editio princeps* under the mask of a school Corderius. Snuffy Davie bought the 'Game of Chess, 1474,' the first book ever printed in England, from a stall in Holland, for about two groschen, or twopence of our money. He sold it to Osborne for twenty pounds, and as many books as came to twenty pounds more. Osborne resold this inimitable windfall to Dr. Askew for sixty guineas. At Dr. Askew's sale," continued the old gentleman, kindling as he spoke, "this inestimable treasure blazed forth in its full value, and was purchased by Royalty itself, for one hundred and seventy pounds !—Could a copy now occur, Lord only knows," he ejaculated, with a deep sigh and lifted-up hands—"Lord only knows what would be its ransom ; and yet it was originally secured, by skill and research, for the easy equivalent of two-pence sterling. Happy, thrice happy, Snuffy Davie !—and blessed were the times when thy industry could be so rewarded !

"Even I, sir," he went on, "though far inferior in industry and discernment and presence of mind, to that great man, can show you a few—a very few things, which I have collected, not by force of money, as any wealthy man might,—although, as my friend Lucian says, he might chance to throw away his coin only to illustrate his ignorance,—but gained in a manner that shows I know something of the matter. See this bundle of ballads, not one of them later than 1700, and some of them an hundred years older. I wheedled an old woman out of these, who loved them better than her psalm-book. Tobacco, sir, snuff, and the Complete Syren, were the equivalent ! For that mutilated copy of the Complaynt of Scotland, I sat out the drinking of two dozen bottles of strong ale with the late learned proprietor, who, in gratitude, bequeathed it to me by his last will. These little Elzevirs are the memoranda and trophies of many a walk by night and morning through the Cowgate, the Cannongate, the Bow, Saint Mary's Wynd,—wherever, in fine, there were to be found brokers and trokers, those miscellaneous dealers in things rare and curious. How often have I stood haggling on a halfpenny, lest, by a too ready acquiescence in the dealer's first price, he should be led to suspect the value I set upon the article !—how have I trembled, lest some passing stranger should chop in between me and the prize, and regarded each poor student of divinity that stopped to turn over the books at the stall, as a rival amateur, or prowling bookseller in disguise !—And then, Mr. Lovel, the sly satisfaction with which one pays the consideration, and pockets the article, affecting a cold indifference, while the hand is trembling with pleasure !—Then to dazzle the eyes of our wealthier and emulous rivals by showing them such a treasure as this" (displaying a little black smoked book about the size of a

primer ;) "to enjoy their surprise and envy, shrouding meanwhile, under a veil of mysterious consciences, our own
superior knowledge and dexterity ;—these, my young friend,
these are the white moments of life, that repay the toil, and
pains, and sedulous attention, which our profession, above all
others, so peculiarly demands ! "

Lovel was not a little amused at hearing the old gentleman
run on in this manner, and, however incapable of entering into
the full merits of what he beheld, he admired, as much as could
have been expected, the various treasures which Oldbuck
exhibited. Here were editions esteemed as being the first,
and there stood those scarcely less regarded as being the last
and best ; here was a book valued because it had the author's
final improvements, and there another which (strange to tell !)
was in request because it had them not. One was precious
because it was a folio, another because it was a duodecimo ;
some because they were tall, some because they were short ;
the merit of this lay in the title-page—of that in the arrangement of the letters in the word Finis. There was, it seemed,
no peculiar distinction, however trifling or minute, which might
not give value to a volume, providing the indispensable quality
of scarcity, or rare occurrence was attached to it.

The Antiquary.

SAMUEL TAYLOR COLERIDGE.

1772–1834.

TWO VISITS.

So ended my first canvass : from causes that I shall presently mention, I made but one other application in person. This took place at Manchester to a stately and opulent wholesale dealer in cottons. He took my letter of introduction, and, having perused it, measured me from head to foot and again from foot to head, and then asked if I had any bill or invoice of the thing. I presented my prospectus to him. He rapidly skimmed and hummed over the first side, and still more rapidly the second and concluding page ; crushed it with his fingers and the palm of his hand ; then most deliberately and significantly rubbed and smoothed one part against the other ; and lastly putting it into his pocket turned his back on me with an "*over-run* with these articles !" and so without another syllable retired into his counting-house. And, I can truly say, to my unspeakable amusement.

This, I have said, was my second and last attempt. On returning baffled from the first, in which I had vainly essayed to repeat the mircle of Orpheus with the Brummagem patriot, I dined with the tradesman who had introduced him to me. After dinner he importuned me to smoke a pipe with him, and two or three other *illuminati* of the same rank. I objected, both because I was engaged to spend the evening with a minister and his friends, and because I had never·smoked except once or twice in my life-time, and then it was herb tobacco mixed with Oronooko. On the assurance, however, that the tobacco was equally mild, and seeing too that it was of a yellow colour ;—not forgetting the lamentable difficulty, I have always experienced in saying, "No," and in abstaining from what the people about me were doing,—I took half a pipe, filling the lower half of the bowl with salt. I was soon however compelled to resign it, in consequence of a giddiness and a distressful feeling in my eyes, which, as I had drunk but a single glass of ale, must, I knew, have been the effect of the tobacco. Soon after, deeming myself recovered, I sallied forth to my engagement ; but the walk and the fresh air brought on all the symptoms again, and, I had scarcely entered the minister's drawing-room, and opened a small pacquet of letters, which he had received from Bristol for me ; ere I sank back on the sofa in a sort of swoon rather than sleep. Fortunately I had found just time enough to inform him of the confused state of my feelings, and of the occasion. For here and thus I lay, my face like a wall that is white-washing, deathly pale and with the cold drops of perspiration running down it from my fore-head, while one after another there dropped in the different gentlemen, who had been invited to meet, and spend the evening with me, to the number of from fifteen to twenty. As the poison of tobacco acts but for a short time, I at length awoke from insensibility, and looked round on the party, my eyes dazzled by the candles which had been lighted in the interim. By way of relieving my embarrassment one of the gentlemen began the conversation, with " Have you seen a paper to-day, Mr. Coleridge ?" " Sir ! " I replied, rubbing my eyes, " I am far from convinced, that a Christian is permitted to read either newspapers or any other works of merely political and temporary interest." This remark, so ludicrously inapposite to, or rather, incongruous with, the purpose, for which I was known to have visited Birmingham, and to assist me in which they were all then met, produced an involuntary and general burst of laughter ; and seldom indeed have I passed so many delightful hours, as I enjoyed in that room from the moment of that laugh till an early hour the next morning. Never, perhaps, in so mixed and numerous a party have I since heard conversa-tion sustained with such animation, enriched with such variety of information and enlivened with such a flow of anecdote. Both then and afterwards they all joined in dissuading me from proceeding with my scheme ; assured me in the most friendly and yet most flattering expressions, that neither was the employ-ment fit for me, nor I fit for the employment.

Biographia Literaria.

ON READERS.

READERS may be divided into four classes :

1. Sponges, who absorb all they read, and return it nearly in the same state, only a little dirtied.

2. Sand-glasses, who retain nothing, and are content to get through a book for the sake of getting through the time.

3. Strange-bags, who retain merely the dregs of what they read.

4. Mogul diamonds, equally rare and valuable, who profit by what they read, and enable others to profit by it also.

I adverted in my last lecture to the prevailing laxity in the use of terms : this is the principal complaint to which the moderns are exposed ; but it is a grievous one, inasmuch as it inevitably tends to the misapplication of words, and to the corruption of language. I mentioned the word "taste," but the remark applies not merely to substantives and adjectives, to things and their epithets, but to verbs : thus, how frequently is the verb "indorsed" strained from its true signification, as given by Milton in the expression—"And elephants endorsed with towers." Again "virtue" has been equally perverted : originally it signified merely strength ; then it became strength of mind and valour, and it has now been changed to the class term for moral excellence in all its various species. I only introduce these as instances by the way, and nothing could be easier than to multiply them.

At the same time, while I recommend precision both of thought and expression, I am far from advocating a pedantic niceness in the choice of language : such a course would only render conversation stiff and stilted. Dr. Johnson used to say that in the most unrestrained discourse he always sought for the properest word,—that which best and most exactly conveyed his meaning : to a certain point he was right, but because he carried it too far, he was often laborious where he ought to have been light, and formal where he ought to have been familiar. Men ought to endeavour to distinguish subtly, that they may be able afterwards to assimilate truly.

I have often heard the question put whether Pope is a great poet, and it has been warmly debated on both sides, some positively maintaining the affirmative, and others dogmatically insisting upon the negative ; but it never occurred to either parties to make the necessary preliminary inquiry—What is meant by the words "poet" and "poetry?" Poetry is not merely invention ; if it were, Gulliver's Travels would be poetry ; and before you can arrive at a decision of the question, as to Pope's claim, it is absolutely necessary to ascertain what people intend by the words they use. Harmonious versification no more makes poetry than mere invention makes a poet ; and to both these requisites there is much besides to be added. In morals, politics, and philosophy no useful discussion can be entered upon, unless we begin by explaining and understanding the terms we employ. It is therefore requisite that I should state to you what I mean by the word " poetry," before I commence any consideration of the comparative merits of those who are popularly called " poets."

Words are used in two ways :—

1. In a sense that comprises everything called by that name. For instance, the words " poetry " and " sense " are employed in this manner, when we say that such a line is bad poetry or bad sense, when in truth it is neither poetry nor sense. If it be bad poetry, it is not poetry ; if it be bad sense, it is not sense. The same of " metre :" bad metre is not metre.

2. In a philosophic sense, which must include a definition of what is essential to the thing. Nobody means mere metre by poetry ; so, mere rhyme is not poetry. Something more is required, and what is that something? It is not wit, because we may have wit where we never dream of poetry. Is it the just observation of human life? Is it a peculiar and a felicitous selection of words? This, indeed, would come nearer to the taste of the present age, when sound is preferred to sense ; but I am happy to think that this taste is not likely to last long.

The Greeks and Romans, in the best period of their literature, knew nothing of any such taste. High-flown epithets and violent metaphors, conveyed in inflated language, is not poetry. Simplicity is indispensable, and in Catullus it is often impossible that more simple language could be used ; there is scarcely a word or a line, which a lamenting mother in a cottage might not have employed. That I may be clearly understood, I will venture to give the following definition of poetry.

Lectures on Shakespeare.

ROBERT SOUTHEY.

1774–1843.

NELSON.

THE total British loss in the battle of Trafalgar amounted to 1,587. Twenty of the enemy struck : unhappily, the fleet did not anchor, as Nelson, almost with his dying breath, had enjoined. A gale came on from the south-west : some of the prizes went down, some went on shore ; one effected its escape into Cadiz ; others were destroyed ; four only were saved, and those by the greatest exertions. The wounded Spaniards were sent ashore, an assurance being given that they should not serve till regularly exchanged ; and the Spaniards, with a generous feeling, which would not perhaps have been found in any other people, offered the use of their hospitals for our wounded, pledging the honour of Spain that they should be carefully attended there. When the storm, after the action, drove some of the prizes upon the coast, they declared that the English, who were thus thrown into their hands, should not be considered as prisoners of war ; and the Spanish soldiers gave up their own beds to their shipwrecked enemies. The Spanish vice-admiral, Alva, died of his wounds. Villeneuve was sent to England, and permitted to return to France. The French Government say that he destroyed himself on the way to Paris, dreading the consequences of a court-martial ; but there is every reason to believe that the tyrant, who never acknow-ledged the loss of the battle of Trafalgar, added Villeneuve to the numerous victims of his murderous policy.

It is almost superfluous to add that all the honours which a grateful country could bestow were heaped upon the memory of Nelson. His brother was made an Earl, with a grant of £6,000 a year ; £10,000 were voted to each of his sisters, and £100,000 for the purchase of an estate. A public funeral was decreed, and a public monument. Statues and monuments also were voted by most of our principal cities. The leaden coffin in which he was brought home was cut in pieces, which were distributed as relics of St. Nelson—so the gunner of the *Victory* called them ; and when at his interment his flag was about to be lowered into the grave, the sailors who assisted at the ceremony with one accord rent it in pieces, that each might preserve a fragment while he lived.

The death of Nelson was felt in England as something more than a public calamity ; men started at the intelligence and turned pale, as if they had heard of the loss of a dear friend. An object of our admiration and affection, of our pride and of our hopes, was suddenly taken from us ; and it seemed as if we had never till then known how deeply we loved and reverenced him. What the country had lost in its great naval hero—the greatest of our own and of all former times—was scarcely taken into the account of grief. So perfectly indeed had he performed his part, that the maritime war after the battle of Trafalgar was considered at an end : the fleets of the enemy were not merely defeated, but destroyed ; new navies must be built, and a new race of seamen reared for them, before the possibility of their invading our shores could again be contemplated. It was not, therefore, from any selfish reflection upon the magnitude of our loss that we mourned for him ; the general sorrow was of a higher character. The people of England grieved that funeral ceremonies, and public monuments, and posthumous rewards were all which they could now bestow upon him whom the King, the Legislature, and the nation would have alike delighted to honour ; whom every tongue would have blessed ; whose presence in every village through which he might have passed would have waked the church bells, have given school-boys a holiday, have drawn children from their sports to gaze upon him, and "old men from the chimney corner" to look upon Nelson ere they died. The victory of Trafalgar was celebrated, indeed, with the usual forms of rejoicing, but they were without joy ; for such already was the glory of the British navy through Nelson's surpassing genius, that it scarcely seemed to receive any addition from the most signal victory that ever was achieved upon the seas ; and the destruction of this mighty fleet, by which all the maritime schemes of France were totally frustrated, hardly appeared to add to our security or strength, for while Nelson was living to watch the combined squadrons of the enemy we felt ourselves as secure as now, when they were no longer in existence.

There was reason to suppose, from the appearances upon opening the body, that in the course of nature he might have attained, like his father, to a good old age. Yet he cannot be said to have fallen prematurely whose work was done, nor ought he to be lamented who died so full of honours and at the height of human fame. The most triumphant death is that of the martyr ; the most awful that of the martyred patriot ; the most splendid that of the hero in the hour of victory ; and if the chariot and the horses of fire had been vouchsafed for Nelson's translation, he could scarcely have departed in a brighter blaze of glory. He has left us, not indeed his mantle of inspiration, but a name and an example which are at this hour inspiring thousands of the youth of England—a name which is our pride, and an example which will continue to be our shield and our strength. Thus it is that the spirits of the great and the wise continue to live and to act after them, verifying in this sense the language of the old mythologist :—

Τοὶ μὲν δαίμονές εἰσι, Διὸς μέγαλου διὰ βουλὰς
᾿Εσθλοὶ, ἐπιχθόνιοι, φύλακες θνητῶν ἀνθρώπων.

Life of Nelson.

CHARLES LAMB.

1775-1834.

A DISSERTATION UPON ROAST PIG.

MANKIND, says a Chinese manuscript, which my friend M. was obliging enough to read and explain to me, for the first seventy thousand ages ate their meat raw, clawing it or biting it from the living animal, just as they do in Abyssinia to this day. This period is not obscurely hinted at by their great Confucius in the second chapter of his Mundane Mutations, where he designates a kind of golden age by the term Cho-fang, literally the Cook's holiday. The manuscript goes on to say, that the art of roasting, or rather broiling (which I take to be the elder brother) was accidentally discovered in the manner following. The swine-herd, Ho-ti, having gone out into the woods one morning, as his manner was, to collect mast for his hogs, left his cottage in the care of his eldest son Bo-bo, a great lubberly boy, who being fond of playing with fire, as younkers of his age commonly are, let some sparks escape into a bundle of straw, which kindling quickly, spread the conflagration over every part of their poor mansion, till it was reduced to ashes. Together with the cottage (a sorry antediluvian make-shift of a building, you may think it), what was of much more importance, a fine litter of new-farrowed pigs, no less than nine in number, perished. China pigs have been esteemed a luxury all over the East from the remotest periods that we read of. Bo-bo was in the utmost consternation, as you may think, not so much for the sake of the tenement, which his father and he could easily build up again with a few dry branches, and the labour of an hour or two, at any time, as for the loss of the pigs. While he was thinking what he should say to his father, and wringing his hands over the smoking remnants of one of those untimely sufferers, an odour assailed his nostrils, unlike any scent which

he had before experienced. What could it proceed from ?—
not from the burnt cottage—he had smelt that smell before—
indeed this was by no means the first accident of the kind
which had occurred through the negligence of this unlucky young
firebrand. Much less did it resemble that of any known herb,
weed, or flower. A premonitory moistening at the same time
overflowed his nether lip. He knew not what to think. He
next stooped down to feel the pig, if there were any signs of
life in it. He burnt his fingers, and to cool them he applied
them in his booby fashion to his mouth. Some of the crumbs
of the scorched skin had come away with his fingers, and for
the first time in his life (in the world's life indeed, for before
him no man had known it) he tasted—*crackling !* Again he
felt and fumbled at the pig. It did not burn him so much now,
still he licked his fingers from a sort of habit. The truth at
length broke into his slow understanding, that it was the pig
that smelt so, and the pig that tasted so delicious ; and,
surrendering himself to the new-born pleasure, he fell to tearing
whole handfuls of the scorched skin with the flesh next it, and
was cramming it down his throat in his beastly fashion, when
his sire entered amid the smoking rafters, armed with retribu-
tory cudgel, and finding how affairs stood, began to rain blows
upon the young rogue's shoulders, as thick as hail-stones, which
Bo-bo heeded not any more than if they had been flies. The
tickling pleasure, which he experienced in his lower regions,
had rendered him quite callous to any inconveniences he might
feel in those remote quarters. His father might lay on, but he
could not beat him from his pig, till he had fairly made an end
of it, when, becoming a little more sensible of his situation,
something like the following dialogue ensued :

"You graceless whelp, what have you got there devouring ?
Is it not enough that you have burnt me down three houses
with your dog's tricks, and be hanged to you, but you must be
eating fire, and I know not what—what have you got there, I
say ?"

"O father, the pig, the pig, do come and taste how nice the
burnt pig eats."

The ears of Ho-ti tingled with horror. He cursed his son,
and he cursed himself that ever he should beget a son that
should eat burnt pig.

Bo-bo, whose scent was wonderfully sharpened since morning,
soon raked out another pig, and fairly rending it asunder, thrust
the lesser half by main force into the fists of Ho-ti, still shouting
out, "Eat, eat, eat the burnt pig, father, only taste,—O Lord,"—

with such-like barbarous ejaculations, cramming all the while as if he would choke.

Ho-ti trembled every joint while he grasped the abominable thing, wavering whether he should not put his son to death for an unnatural young monster, when the crackling scorching his fingers, as it had done his son's, and applying the same remedy to them, he in his turn tasted some of its flavour, which, make what sour mouths he would for a pretence, proved not altogether displeasing to him. In conclusion (for the manuscript here is a little tedious) both father and son fairly sat down to the mess, and never left off till they had despatched all that remained of the litter.

Bo-bo was strictly enjoined not to let the secret escape, for the neighbours would certainly have stoned them for a couple of abominable wretches, who could think of improving upon the good meat which God had sent them. Nevertheless, strange stories got about. It was observed that Ho-ti's cottage was burnt down now more frequently than ever. Nothing but fires from this time forward. Some would break out in broad day, others in the night time. As often as the sow farrowed, so sure was the house of Ho-ti to be in a blaze; and Ho-ti himself, which was the more remarkable, instead of chastising his son, seemed to grow more indulgent to him than ever. At length they were watched, the terrible mystery discovered, and father and son summoned to take their trial at Pekin, then an inconsiderable assize town. Evidence was given, the obnoxious food itself produced in court, and verdict about to be pronounced, when the foreman of the jury begged that some of the burnt pig, of which the culprits stood accused, might be handed into the box. He handled it, and they all handled it, and burning their fingers, as Bo-bo and his father had done before them, and nature prompting to each of them the same remedy, against the face of all the facts, and the clearest charge which the judge had ever given,—to the surprise of the whole court, townsfolk, strangers, reporters, and all present—without leaving the box, or any manner of consultation whatever, they brought in a simultaneous verdict of Not Guilty.

The judge, who was a shrewd fellow, winked at the manifest iniquity of the decision; and, when the court was dismissed, went privily, and bought up all the pigs that could be had for love or money. In a few days his Lordship's town house was observed to be on fire. The thing took wing, and now there was nothing to be seen but fires in every direction. Fuel and pigs grew enormously dear all over the districts. The insurance offices one and all shut up shop. People built slighter and slighter every day, until it was feared that the very science of architecture would in no long time be lost to the world. Thus this custom of firing houses continued, till in process of time, says my manuscript, a sage arose, like our Locke, who made a discovery, that the flesh of swine, or indeed of any other animal, might be cooked (*burnt*, as they called it) without the necessity of consuming a whole house to dress it. Then first began the rude form of a gridiron. Roasting by the string, or spit, came in a century or two later, I forget in whose dynasty. By such slow degrees, concludes the manuscript, do the most useful, and seemingly the most obvious arts, make their way among mankind.—

Without placing too implicit faith in the account above given, it must be agreed, that if a worthy pretext for so dangerous an experiment as setting houses on fire (especially in these days) could be assigned in favour of any culinary object, that pretext and excuse might be found in ROAST PIG.

Of all the delicacies in the whole *mundus edibilis*, I will maintain it to be the most delicate—*princeps obsoniorum.*

I speak not of your grown porkers—things between pig and pork—those hobbydehoys—but a young and tender suckling—under a moon old—guiltless as yet of the sty—with no original speck of the *amor immunditiæ*, the hereditary failing of the first parent, yet manifest—his voice as yet not broken, but something between a childish treble, and a grumble—the mild forerunner, or *præludium*, of a grunt.

He must be roasted. I am not ignorant that our ancestors ate them seethed, or boiled—but what a sacrifice of the exterior tegument !

There is no flavour comparable, I will contend, to that of the crisp, tawny, well-watched, not over-roasted, *crackling*, as it is well called—the very teeth are invited to their share of the pleasure at this banquet in overcoming the coy, brittle resistance —with the adhesive oleaginous—O call it not fat—but an indefinable sweetness growing up to it—the tender blossoming of fat—fat cropped in the bud—taken in the shoot—in the first innocence—the cream and quintessence of the child-pig's yet pure food—the lean, no lean, but a kind of animal manna,—or, rather, fat and lean (if it must be so) so blended and running into each other, that both together make but one ambrosian result, or common substance.

Behold him while he is doing—it seemeth rather a refreshing warmth, than a scorching heat, that he is so passive to. How equably he twirleth round the string!—Now he is just done. To see the extreme sensibility of that tender age, he hath wept out his pretty eyes—radiant jellies—shooting stars—

See him in the dish, his second cradle, how meek he lieth!—wouldst thou have had this innocent grow up to the grossness and indocility which too often accompany maturer swinehood? Ten to one he would have proved a glutton, a sloven, an obstinate, disagreeable animal—wallowing in all manner of filthy conversation—from these sins he is happily snatched away—

> Ere sin could blight, or sorrow fade,
> Death came with timely care—

his memory is odoriferous—no clown curseth, while his stomach half rejecteth, the rank bacon—no coalheaver bolteth him in reeking sausages—he hath a fair sepulchre in the grateful stomach of the judicious epicure—and for such a tomb might be content to die.

He is the best of sapors. Pine-apple is great. She is indeed almost too transcendent—a delight, if not sinful, yet so like to sinning, that really a tender-conscienced person would do well to pause—too ravishing for mortal taste, she woundeth and excoriateth the lips that approach her—like lovers' kisses, she biteth—she is a pleasure bordering on pain from the fierceness and insanity of her relish—but she stoppeth at the palate—she meddleth not with the appetite—and the coarsest hunger might barter her consistently for a mutton chop.

Pig—let me speak his praise—is no less provocative of the appetite, than he is satisfactory to the criticalness of the censorious palate. The strong man may batten on him, and the weakling refuseth not his mild juices.

Unlike to mankind's mixed characters, a bundle of virtues and vices, inexplicably intertwisted, and not to be unravelled without hazard, he is—good throughout. No part of him is better or worse than another. He helpeth, as far as his little means extend, all around. He is the least envious of banquets. He is all neighbours' fare.

I am one of those, who freely and ungrudgingly impart a share of the good things of this life which fall to their lot (few as mine are in this kind) to a friend. I protest I take as great an interest in my friend's pleasures, his relishes, and proper satisfactions, as in mine own. "Presents," I often say, "endear Absents." Hares, pheasants, partridges, snipes, barn-door chickens (those "tame villatic fowl"), capons, plovers, brawn, barrels of oysters, I dispense as freely as I receive them. I love to taste them, as it were, upon the tongue of my friend. But a stop must be put somewhere. One would not, like Lear, "give everything." I make my stand upon pig. Methinks it is an ingratitude to the Giver of all good flavours, to extra-domiciliate, or send out of the house, slightingly (under pretext of friendship, or I know not what), a blessing so particularly adapted, predestined, I may say, to my individual palate.—It argues an insensibility.

I remember a touch of conscience in this kind at school. My good old aunt, who never parted from me at the end of a holiday without stuffing a sweetmeat, or some nice thing into my pocket, had dismissed me one evening with a smoking plum-cake, fresh from the oven. In my way to school (it was over London Bridge) a gray-headed old beggar saluted me (I have no doubt at this time of day that he was a counterfeit). I had no pence to console him with, and in the vanity of self-denial, and the very coxcombry of charity, school-boy-like, I made him a present of—the whole cake ! I walked on a little, buoyed up, as one is on such occasions, with a sweet soothing of self-satis-faction ; but before I had got to the end of the bridge, my better feelings returned, and I burst into tears, thinking how ungrateful I had been to my good aunt, to go and give her good gift away to a stranger, that I had never seen before, and who might be a bad man for ought I knew ; and then I thought of the pleasure my aunt would be taking in thinking that I—I myself, and not another—would eat her nice cake—and what should I say to her the next time I saw her—how naughty I was to part with her pretty present—and the odour of that spicy cake came back upon my recollection, and the pleasure and the curiosity I had taken in seeing her make it, and her joy when she sent it to the oven, and how disappointed she would feel that I had never had a bit of it in my mouth at last—and I blamed my impertinent spirit of alms-giving, and out-of-place hypocrisy of goodness, and above all I wished never to see the face again of that insidious, good-for-nothing, old gray impostor.

Our ancestors were nice in their method of sacrificing these tender victims. We read of pigs whipt to death with something of a shock, as we hear of any other obsolete custom. The age of discipline is gone by, or it would be curious to inquire (in a philosophical light merely) what effect this process might have towards intenerating and dulcifying a substance, naturally so mild and dulcet as the flesh of young pigs. It looks like refin-ing a violet. Yet we should be cautious, while we condemn the inhumanity, how we censure the wisdom of the practice. It might impart a gusto—

I remember an hypothesis, argued upon by the young students, when I was at St. Omer's, and maintained with much learning and pleasantry on both sides, "Whether, supposing that the flavour of a pig who obtained his death by whipping (*per flagellationem extremam*) superadded a pleasure upon the palate of a man more intense than any possible suffering we can conceive in the animal, is man justified in using that method of putting the animal to death?" I forget the decision.

His sauce should be considered. Decidedly a few bread crumbs, done up with his liver and brains, and a dash of mild sage. But, banish, dear Mrs. Cook, I beseech you, the whole onion tribe. Barbecue your whole hogs to your palate, steep them in shalots, stuff them out with plantations of the rank and guilty garlic; you cannot poison them, or make them stronger than they are—but consider, he is a weakling—a flower.

Essays of Elia.

OLD CHINA.

I HAVE an almost feminine partiality for old china. When I go to see any great house, I inquire for the china-closet, and next for the picture-gallery. I cannot defend the order of preference, but by saying, that we have all some taste or other, of too ancient a date to admit of our remembering distinctly that it was an acquired one. I can call to mind the first play and the first exhibition, that I was taken to; but I am not conscious of a time when china jars and saucers were introduced into my imagination.

I had no repugnance then—why should I now have?—to those little lawless, azure-tinctured grotesques, that under the notion of men and women, float about, uncircumscribed by any element, in that world before perspective—a china tea-cup.

I like to see my old friends—whom distance cannot diminish —figuring up in the air (so they appear to our optics), yet on *terra firma* still—for so we must in courtesy interpret that speck of deep blue, which the decorous artist, to prevent absurdity, has made to spring up beneath their sandals.

I love the men with women's faces, and the women, if possible, with still more womanish expressions.

Here is a young and courtly Mandarin, handing tea to a lady

from a salver—two miles off. See how distance seems to set
off respect ! And here the same lady, or another—for likeness
is identity on tea-cups—is stepping into a little fairy-boat,
moored on the other side of this calm garden river, with a
dainty mincing foot, which in a right angle of incidence (as
angles go in our world) must infallibly land her in the midst of
a flowery mead—a furlong off on the other side of the same
strange stream !

Farther on—if far or near can be predicated of their world—
see horses, trees, pagodas, dancing the hays.

Here—a cow and a rabbit couchant, and co-extensive—so
objects show, seen through the lucid atmosphere of fine Cathay.

I was pointing out to my cousin last evening, over our Hyson
(which we are old-fashioned enough to drink unmixed still of an
afternoon), some of these *speciosa miracula* upon a set of extraordinary old blue china (a recent purchase) which we were now
for the first time using ; and could not help remarking, how
favourable circumstances had been to us of late years, that we
could afford to please the eye sometimes with trifles of this sort
—when a passing sentiment seemed to over-shade the brows
of my companion. I am quick at detecting these summer clouds
in Bridget.

"I wish the good old times would come again," she said,
"when we were not quite so rich. I do not mean, that I want
to be poor ; but there was a middle state ;"—so she was pleased
to ramble on—"in which I am sure we were a great deal
happier. A purchase is but a purchase, now that you have
money enough and to spare. Formerly it used to be a triumph.
When we coveted a cheap luxury (and, O ! how much ado I
had to get you to consent in those times !) we were used to
have a debate two or three days before, and to weigh the *for*
and *against*, and think what we might spare it out of, and what
saving we could hit upon, that should be an equivalent. A
thing was worth buying then, when we felt the money that we
paid for it.

"Do you remember the brown suit, which you made to hang
upon you, till all your friends cried shame upon you, it grew so
threadbare—and all because of that folio Beaumont and
Fletcher, which you dragged home late at night from Barker's
in Covent Garden ? Do you remember how we eyed it for
weeks before we could make up our minds to the purchase, and
had not come to a determination till it was near ten o'clock of
the Saturday night, when you off from Islington, fearing you
should be too late—and when the old bookseller with some

grumbling opened his shop, and by the twinkling taper (for he was setting bedwards) lighted out the relic from his dusty treasures —and when you lugged it home, wishing it were twice as cumbersome—and when you presented it to me—and when we were exploring the perfectness of it (*collating* you called it)—and while I was repairing some of the loose leaves with paste, which your impatience would not suffer to be left till daybreak—was there no pleasure in being a poor man? or can those neat black clothes which you wear now, and are so careful to keep brushed, since we have become rich and finical, give you half the honest vanity, with which you flaunted it about in that over-worn suit— your old corbeau—for four or five weeks longer than you should have done, to pacify your conscience for the mighty sum of fifteen—or sixteen shillings was it?—a great affair we thought it then—which you had lavished on the old folio. Now you can afford to buy any book that pleases you, but I do not see that you ever bring me home any nice old purchases now.

"When you came home with twenty apologies for laying out a less number of shillings upon that print after Leonardo, which we christened the 'Lady Blanche;' when you looked at the purchase, and thought of the money—and thought of the money, and looked again at the picture—was there no pleasure in being a poor man? Now, you have nothing to do but to walk into Colnaghi's, and buy a wilderness of Leonardos. Yet do you?

"Then, do you remember our pleasant walks to Enfield, and Potter's Bar, and Waltham, when we had a holiday—holidays, and all other fun, are gone, now we are rich—and the little hand-basket in which I used to deposit our day's fare of savoury cold lamb and salad—and how you would pry about at noontide for some decent house, where we might go in, and produce our store—only paying for the ale that you must call for—and speculate upon the looks of the landlady, and whether she was likely to allow us a table-cloth—and wish for such another honest hostess, as Izaak Walton has described many a one on the pleasant banks of the Lea, when he went a-fishing—and sometimes they would prove obliging enough, and sometimes they would look grudgingly upon us—but we had cheerful looks still for one another, and would eat our plain food savourily, scarcely grudging Piscator his Trout Hall? Now, when we go out a day's pleasuring, which is seldom moreover, we *ride* part of the way—and go into a fine inn, and order the best of dinners, never debating the expense—which, after all, never has half the relish of those chance country snaps, when we were at the mercy of uncertain usage, and a precarious welcome.

" You are too proud to see a play anywhere now but in the pit.
Do you remember where it was we used to sit, when we saw the
Battle of Hexham, and the Surrender of Calais, and Bannister
and Mrs. Bland in the Children in the Wood—when we
squeezed out our shillings a-piece to sit three or four times in a
season in the one-shilling gallery—where you felt all the time
that you ought not to have brought me—and more strongly I
felt obligation to you for having brought me—and the pleasure
was the better for a little shame—and when the curtain drew up,
what cared we for our place in the house, or what mattered it
where we were sitting, when our thoughts were with Rosalind in
Arden, or with Viola at the Court of Illyria? You used to say,
that the gallery was the best place of all for enjoying a play
socially—that the relish of such exhibitions must be in proportion to the infrequency of going—that the company we met
there, not being in general readers of plays, were obliged to
attend the more, and did attend, to what was going on, on the
stage—because a word lost would have been a chasm, which it
was impossible for them to fill up. With such reflections we
consoled our pride then—and I appeal to you, whether, as a
woman, I met generally with less attention and accommodation,
than I have done since in more expensive situations in the
house? The getting in indeed, and the crowding up those
inconvenient staircases, was bad enough,—but there was still a
law of civility to women recognized to quite as great an extent
as we ever found in the other passages—and how a little
difficulty overcome heightened the snug seat, and the play
afterwards ! Now we can only pay our money, and walk in.
You cannot see, you say, in the galleries now. I am sure we saw,
and heard too, well enough then—but sight, and all, I think, is
gone with our poverty.

" There was pleasure in eating strawberries, before they
became quite common—in the first dish of peas, while they
were yet dear—to have them for a nice supper, a treat. What
treat can we have now? If we were to treat ourselves now—
that is, to have dainties a little above our means, it would be
selfish and wicked. It is the very little more that we allow
ourselves beyond what the actual poor can get at, that makes
what I call a treat—when two people living together, as we
have done, now and then indulge themselves in a cheap luxury,
which both like ; while each apologizes, and is willing to take
both halves of the blame to his single share. I see no harm in
people making much of themselves in that sense of the word.
It may give them a hint how to make much of others. But

now—what I mean by the word—we never do make much of ourselves. None but the poor can do it. I do not mean the veriest poor of all, but persons as we were, just above poverty.

"I know what you were going to say, that it is mighty pleasant at the end of the year to make all meet—and much ado we used to have every Thirty-first night of December to account for our exceedings—many a long face did you make over your puzzled accounts, and in contriving to make it out how we had spent so much—or that we had not spent so much —or that it was impossible we should spend so much next year —and still we found our slender capital decreasing—but then, betwixt ways, and projects, and compromises of one sort or another, and talk of curtailing this charge, and doing without that for the future—and the hope that youth brings, and laughing spirits (in which you were never poor till now), we pocketed up our loss, and in conclusion, with 'lusty brimmers' (as you used to quote it out of *hearty cheerful Mr. Cotton*, as you called him), we used to welcome in the 'coming guest.' Now we have no reckoning at all at the end of the old year— no flattering promises about the new year doing better for us."

Bridget is so sparing of her speech on most occasions, that when she gets into a rhetorical vein, I am careful how I interrupt it. I could not help, however, smiling at the phantom of wealth which her dear imagination had conjured up out of a clear income of poor—hundred pounds a year. "It is true we were happier when we were poorer, but we were also younger, my cousin. I am afraid we must put up with the excess, for if we were to shake the superflux into the sea, we should not much mend ourselves. That we had much to struggle with, as we grew up together, we have reason to be most thankful. It strengthened, and knit our compact closer. We could never have been what we have been to each other, if we had always had the sufficiency which you now complain of. The resisting power—those natural dilations of the youthful spirit, which circumstances cannot straiten—with us are long since passed away. Competence to age is supplementary youth ; a sorry supplement indeed, but I fear the best that is to be had. We must ride where we formerly walked : live better and lie softer—and shall be wise to do so—than we had means to do in those good old days you speak of. Yet could those days return—could you and I once more walk our thirty miles a-day —could Bannister and Mrs. Bland again be young, and you and I be young to see them—could the good old one-shilling gallery days return—they are dreams, my cousin, now—but could you and I at this moment, instead of this quiet argument, by our well-carpeted fireside, sitting on this luxurious sofa—be once more struggling up those inconvenient staircases, pushed about, and squeezed, and elbowed by the poorest rabble of poor gallery scramblers—could I once more hear those anxious shrieks of yours—and the delicious *Thank God, we are safe,* which always followed when the topmost stair, conquered, let in the first light of the whole cheerful theatre down beneath us—I know not the fathom line that ever touched a descent so deep as I would be willing to bury more wealth in than Crœsus had, or the great Jew R—— is supposed to have, to purchase it. And now do just look at that merry little Chinese waiter holding an umbrella, big enough for a bed-tester, over the head of that pretty insipid half-Madonna-ish chit of a lady in that very blue summer-house."

Last Essays of Elia.

WALTER SAVAGE LANDOR.

1775-1864.

OPINIONS ON CÆSAR AND MILTON.

No person has a better right than Lord Brougham to speak contemptuously of Cæsar, and of Milton. Cæsar was the purest and most Attic writer of his country, and there is no trace of intemperance, in thought or expression, throughout the whole series of his hostilities. He was the most generous friend, he was the most placable enemy ; he rose with moderation, and he fell with dignity. Can we wonder then at Lord Brougham's unfeigned antipathy and assumed contempt? Few well educated men are less able to deliver a sound opinion of style than his lordship ; and perhaps there are not many of our contemporaries who place a just value on Cæsar's, dissimilar as it is in all its qualities to what they turn over on the sofa-table. There is calmness, there is precision, there is a perspicuity which shows objects in their proper size and position ; there is strength without strain, and superiority without assertion. I acknowledge my preference of his styles, and he must permit me to add Cicero's, to that which he considers the best of all, namely his own ; and he must pardon me if I entertain an early predilection for easy humour over hard vulgarity, and for graceful irony over intractable distortion. I was never an admirer, even in youth, of those abrupt and splintery sentences, which like many coarse substances, sparkle only when they are broken, and are looked at only for their sharpnesses and inequalities. Lord Brougham will not allow us to contemplate greatness at our leisure : he will not allow us indeed to look at it for a moment. Cæsar must be stript of all his laurels and left bald, or some rude soldier, with bemocking gestures, must be thrust before his triumph. If he fights, he does not know how to hold his sword ; if he speaks, he speaks vile Latin. I wonder that Cromwell fares no better; if, signal as were his earlier services to his country, he lived a hypocrite and died a traitor. Milton is indeed less pardonable. He adhered through good report and through evil report (and there was enough of both) to those who had asserted liberty of conscience, and who alone were able to maintain it.

But an angry cracked voice is now raised against that eloquence,

> "Of which all Europe rang from side to side."

I shall only make a few remarks on his English, and a few preliminary on the importance of style in general, which none understood better than he. The greater part of those who are most ambitious of it are unaware of all its value. Thought does not separate man from the brutes; for the brutes think: but man alone thinks beyond the moment and beyond himself. Speech does not separate them; for speech is common to all perhaps, more or less articulate, and conveyed or received through different organs in the lower and more inert. Man's thought, which seems imperishable, loses its form, and runs along from proprietor to impropriator, like any other transitory thing, unless it is invested so becomingly and nobly that no successor can improve upon it, by any new fashion or combination. For want of dignity or beauty, many good things are passed and forgotten; and much ancient wisdom is overrun and hidden by a rampant verdure, succulent but unsubstantial. It would be invidious to bring forward proofs of this out of authors in poetry and prose, now living or lately dead. A distinction must, however, be made between what falls upon many, like rain, and what is purloined from a cistern or a conduit belonging to another man's house. There are things which were another's before they were ours, and are not less ours for that; not less than my estate is mine because it was my grandfather's. There are features, there are voices, there are thoughts, very similar in many; and when ideas strike the same chord in any two with the same intensity, the expression must be nearly the same. Let those who look upon style as unworthy of much attention, ask themselves how many, in proportion to men of genius, have excelled in it. In all languages, ancient and modern, are there ten prose writers at once harmonious, correct, and energetic? Harmony and correctness are not uncommon separately, and force is occasionally with each; but when, excepting in Milton, where, among all

the moderns, is energy to be found always in the right place?
Even Cicero is defective here, and sometimes in the most
elaborate of his orations. In the time of Milton it was not
customary for men of abilities to address to the people at large
what might inflame their passions. The appeal was made to
the serious, to the well-informed, to the learned, and was made
in the language of their studies. The phraseology of our Bible,
on which no subsequent age has improved, was thought to
carry with it solemnity and authority; and even when popular
feelings were to be aroused to popular interests, the language
of the prophets was preferred to the language of the vulgar.
Hence, amid the complicated antagonisms of war there was
more austerity than ferocity. The gentlemen who attended the
court avoided the speech as they avoided the manners of their
adversaries. Waller, Cowley, and South, were resolved to
refine what was already pure gold, and inadvertently threw into
the crucible many old family jewels, deeply enchased within it.
Eliot, Pym, Selden, and Milton, reverenced their father's house,
and retained its rich language unmodified. Lord Brougham
would make us believe that scarcely a sentence in Milton is
easy, natural, and vernacular. Nevertheless, in all his disserta-
tions, there are many which might appear to have been written
in our days, if indeed any writer in our days were endowed
with the same might and majesty. Even in his *Treatise on
Divorce*, when the Bible was most open to him for quotations,
and when he might be the most expected to recur to the grave
and antiquated, he has often employed, in the midst of theo-
logical questions and juridical formularies, the plainest terms
of his contemporaries. Even his arguments against prelacy,
when he rises into poetry like the old prophets, and when his
ardent words assume in their periphery the rounded form of
verse, there is nothing stiff or constrained. I remember a
glorious proof of this remark, which I believe I have quoted
before, but no time is lost by reading it twice.

> " . . . But when God commands to take the trumpet,
>   And blow a dolorous or thrilling blast,
>   It rests not with man's will what he shall say,
>   Or what he shall conceal."

Was ever anything more like the inspiration it refers to?
Where is the harshness in it? Where is the inversion?
The style usually follows the conformation of the mind.
Solemnity and stateliness are Milton's chief characteristics.

Nothing is less solemn, less stately, less composed, or less
equable, than Lord Brougham's. When he is most vivacious,
he shows it by twitches of sarcasm ; and when he springs
highest it is from agony.   He might have improved his manner
by recurring to Shaftesbury and Bolingbroke, equally discontented politicians : but there was something of high breeding in
their attacks, and more of the rapier than of the bludgeon.   He
found their society uncongenial to him, and trundled home in
preference the sour quarter-cask of Smollett.   Many acrid
plants throw out specious and showy flowers ; few of these are
to be found in his garden.   What then has he ?   I will tell you
what he has : more various and greater talents than any other
man ever was adorned with, who had nothing of genius and
little of discretion.   He has exhibited a clear compendious
proof, that a work of extraordinary fiction may be elaborated in
the utter penury of all those qualities which we usually assign
to imagination.   Between the language of Milton and Brougham
there is as much difference as between an organ and a bagpipe.
One of these instruments fills, and makes to vibrate, the amplest,
loftiest, and most venerable edifices, and accords with all that
is magnificent and holy ; the other is followed by vile animals
in fantastical dresses and antic gestures, and surrounded by the
clamorous and disorderly.

Works.

THOMAS DE QUINCEY.

1785–1859.

THE CÆSARS.

THE majesty of the Roman Cæsar Semper Augustus has never yet been fully appreciated ; nor has any man explained sufficiently in what respects this title and this office were absolutely unique. There was but one Rome : no other city, as we are satisfied by the collation of many facts, has ever rivalled this astonishing metropolis in the grandeur of magnitude ; and not many—perhaps if we except the cities built under Grecian auspices along the line of three thousand miles, from Western Capua or Syracuse to the Euphrates and oriental Palmyra, none at all—in the grandeur of architectural display. Speaking even of London, we ought in all reason to say—the *Nation of London*, and not the city of London ; but of Rome in her meridian hours, nothing else could be said in the naked rigour of logic. A million and a half of souls—that population, apart from any other distinction—is *per se* for London a justifying ground for such a classification ; *a fortiori*, then, will it belong to a city which counted from one horn to the other of its mighty suburbs not less than four millions of inhabitants at the very least, as we resolutely maintain after reviewing all that has been written on that much-vexed theme, and not impossibly half as many more. Republican Rome had her *prerogative* tribe ; the earth has its *prerogative* city ; and that city was Rome.

As was the city, such was its prince—mysterious, solitary, unique. Each was to the other an adequate counterpart, each reciprocally that perfect mirror which reflected, as *in alia materia*, those incommunicable attributes of grandeur, that under the same shape and denomination never upon this earth were destined to be revived. Rome has not been repeated ; neither has Cæsar. *Ubi Cæsar, ibi Roma*, was a maxim of

Roman Jurisprudence. And the same maxim may be translated into a wider meaning ; in which it becomes true also for our historical experience. Cæsar and Rome have flourished and expired together. Each reciprocally was essential to the other. Even the Olympian Pantheon needed Rome for its full glorification ; and Jove himself first knew his own grandeur when robed and shrined as Jupiter Capitolinus. The illimitable attributes of the Roman prince boundless and comprehensive as the universal air—like that also bright and apprehensible to the most vagrant eye, yet in parts (and those not far removed) unfathomable as outer darkness (for no chamber in a dungeon could shroud in more impenetrable concealment a deed of murder than the upper chambers of the air)—these attributes so impressive to the imagination, and which all the subtilty of the Roman wit could as little fathom as the fleets of Cæsar could traverse the Polar basin, or unlock the gates of the Pacific, are best symbolized, and find their most appropriate exponent, in the illimitable city itself—that Rome, whose centre, the Capitol, was immovable as Teneriffe or Atlas, but whose circumference was shadowy, uncertain, restless, and advancing as the frontiers of her all-conquering empire. It is false to say that with Cæsar came the destruction of Roman greatness. Peace, hollow rhetoricians ! until Cæsar came, Rome was a minor ; by him she attained her majority, and fulfilled her destiny. Caius Julius, you say, deflowered the virgin purity of her civil liberties. Doubtless, then, Rome had risen immaculate from the arms of Sylla and of Marius. But, if it were Caius Julius that deflowered Rome, if under him she forfeited her dowry of civic purity, if to him she first unloosed her maiden zone, then be it affirmed boldly—that she reserved her greatest favours for the noblest of her wooers ; and we may plead the justification of Falconbridge for his mother's transgression with the lion-hearted king—such a sin was self-ennobled. Did Julius deflower Rome? Then, by that consummation, he caused her to fulfil the functions of her nature ; he compelled her to exchange the imperfect and inchoate character of a mere *fæmina* for the perfections of a *mulier*. And, metaphor apart, we maintain that Rome lost no liberties by the mighty Julius. That which in tendency, and by the spirit of her institutions—that which, by her very corruptions and abuses cooperating with her laws, Rome promised and involved in the germ—even that, and nothing less or different, did Rome unfold and accomplish under this Julian violence. The rape [if such it were] of Cæsar, her final Romulus, completed for Rome that which the rape under Romulus, her initial or inaugurating Cæsar, had prosperously begun. And thus by one supreme man was a nation-city matured ; and from the everlasting and *nameless city was a man produced—capable of taming her indomitable nature, and of forcing her to immolate her wild virginity to the state best fitted for the destined " Mother of Empires." Peace, then, rhetoricians, false threnodists of false liberty ! hollow chanters over the ashes of a hollow republic ! Without Cæsar, we affirm a thousand times, that there would have been no perfect Rome ; and, but for Rome, there could have been no such man as Cæsar.

Both then were immortal ; each worthy of each. And the *Cui viget nihil simile aut secundum* of the poet was as true of one as of the other. For, if by comparison with Rome other cities were but villages, with even more propriety it may be asserted, that after the Roman Cæsars all modern kings, kaisers, or emperors, are mere phantoms of royalty. The Cæsar of Western Rome—he only of all earthly potentates, past or to come, could be said to reign as a *monarch*, that is, as a solitary king. He was not the greatest of princes, simply because there was no other but himself. There were doubtless a few outlying rulers, of unknown names and titles, upon the margin of his empire, there were tributary lieutenants and barbarous *regali*, the obscure vassals of his sceptre, whose homage was offered on the lowest step of his throne, and scarcely known to him but as objects of disdain. But these feudatories could no more break the unity of his empire, which embraced the whole οἰκουμένη—the total habitable world as then known to geography, or recognised by the muse of history—than at this day the British empire on the sea can be brought into question or made conditional, because some chief of Owyhee or Tongataboo should proclaim a momentary independence of the British trident, or should even offer a transient outrage to her sovereign flag. Such a *tempestas in matula* might raise a brief uproar in his little native archipelago, but too feeble to reach the shores of Europe by an echo—or to ascend by so much as an infantine *susuorus* to the ears of the British Neptune. Parthia, it is true, might pretend to the dignity of an empire. But her sovereigns, though sitting in the seat of the great king (ὁ βασιλεύς), were no longer the rulers of a

---

* " *Nameless* city : " The true name of Rome it was a point of religion to conceal ; and, in fact, it never was revealed.

vast and polished nation.   They were regarded as barbarians—
potent only by their standing army, not upon the larger basis of
civic strength ; and, even under this limitation, they were supposed to owe more to the circumstances of their position—their
climate, their remoteness, and their inaccessibility except
through arid and sultry deserts—than to intrinsic resources,
such as could be prominently relied on in a serious trial of
strength between the two powers.   The kings of Parthia, therefore, were far enough from being regarded in the light of
antagonistic forces to the majesty of Rome.   And, these with-
drawn from the comparison, who else was there—what prince,
what king, what potentate of any denomination, to break the
universal calm, that through centuries continued to lave, as
with the quiet undulations of summer lakes, the sacred footsteps
of the Cæsarean throne?

The Cæsars.

SIR WILLIAM NAPIER.

1785–1860.

SIR JOHN MOORE.

SIR JOHN MOORE, while earnestly watching the result of the fight about the village of Elvina, was struck on the left breast by a cannon shot; the shock threw him from his horse with violence; he rose again in a sitting posture; his countenance unchanged, and his steadfast eye still fixed upon the regiments engaged in his front; no sigh betrayed a sensation of pain; but in a few moments when he was satisfied that the troops were gaining ground, his countenance brightened, and he suffered himself to be taken to the rear. Then was seen the dreadful nature of his hurt; the shoulder was shattered to pieces, the arm was hanging by a piece of skin, the ribs over the heart broken, and bared of flesh, and the muscles of the breast torn into long strips, which were interlaced by their recoil from the dragging of the shot. As the soldiers placed him in a blanket his sword got entangled, and the hilt entered the wound. Captain Hardinge, a staff officer, who was near, attempted to take it off, but the dying man stopped him, saying, "*It is as* "*well as it is. I had rather it should go out of the field with* "*me.*" And in that manner, so becoming to a soldier, Moore was borne from the fight.

During this time the army was rapidly gaining ground. The reserve, overthrowing everything in the valley, and obliging La Housraye's dragoons (who had dismounted) to retire, turned the enemy's left, and even approached the eminence upon which the great battery was posted. On the left, Colonel Nicholls, at the head of some companies of the fourteenth, carried Palavio Abaxo (which general Foy defended but feebly), and in the centre, the obstinate dispute for Elvina terminated in favour of the British; so that when the night set in their line was considerably advanced beyond the original position of the morning, and the French were falling back in confusion.

.... From the spot where he fell, the general who had conducted it [the retreat to Coruña] was carried to the town by a party of soldiers. The blood flowed fast, and the torture of his wound increased ; but such was the unshaken firmness of his mind, that those about him judging from the resolution of his countenance that his hurt was not mortal, expressed a hope of his recovery. Hearing this, he looked stedfastly at the injury for a moment, and then said, "*No, I feel that to be* "*impossible.*" Several times he caused his attendants to stop and turn him round, that he might behold the field of battle, and when the firing indicated the advance of the British he discovered his satisfaction, and permitted the bearers to proceed. Being brought to his lodgings the surgeons examined his wound, but there was no hope ; the pain increased, and he spoke with great difficulty. At intervals he asked if the French were beaten, and addressing his old friend colonel Anderson, he said, "*You know that I always wished to die this way.*" Again he asked if the enemy were defeated, and being told they were, observed, "*It is a great satisfaction to me to know we* "*have beaten the French.*" His countenance continued firm, and his thoughts clear ; once only, when he spoke of his mother, he became agitated. He inquired after the safety of his friends, and the officers of his staff, and he did not even in this moment forget to recommend those whose merit had given them claims to promotion. His strength was failing fast, and life was just extinct, when, with an unsubdued spirit, as if anticipating the baseness of his posthumous calumniators, he exclaimed, "*I* "*hope the people of England will be satisfied! I hope the country* "*will do me justice!*" The battle was scarcely ended, when his corpse wrapped in a military cloak, was interred by the officers of his staff in the citadel of Coruña. The guns of the enemy paid his funeral honours, and Soult, with a noble feeling of respect for his valour, raised a monument to his memory.

Thus ended the career of Sir John Moore, a man whose uncommon capacity was sustained by the purest virtue, and governed by a disinterested patriotism more in keeping with the primitive than the luxurious age of a great nation. His tall graceful person, his dark searching eyes, strongly defined forehead, a singularly expressive mouth, indicated a noble disposition and a refined understanding. The lofty sentiments of honour habitual to his mind, adorned by a subtle playful wit, gave him in conversation an ascendency that he could well preserve by the decisive vigour of his actions.   He maintained the right with a vehemence bordering upon fierceness, and every important transaction in which he was engaged increased his reputation for talent, and confirmed his character as a stern enemy to vice, a stedfast friend to merit, a just and faithful servant of his country.   The honest loved him, the dishonest feared him ; for while he lived, he did not shun but scorned and spurned the base, and, with characteristic propriety, they spurned at him when he was dead.

A soldier from his earliest youth, he thirsted for the honours of his profession, and feeling that he was worthy to lead a British army, hailed the fortune that placed him at the head of the troops destined for Spain.   The stream of time passed rapidly, and the inspiring hopes of triumph disappeared, but the austerer glory of suffering remained ; with a firm heart he accepted that gift of a severe fate, and confiding in the strength of his genius, disregarded the clamours of presumptuous ignorance ; opposing sound military views to the foolish projects so insolently thrust upon him by the ambassador, he conducted a long and arduous retreat with sagacity, intelligence, and fortitude.   No insult could disturb, no falsehood deceive him, no remonstrance shake his determination ; fortune frowned without subduing his constancy ; death struck, and the spirit of the man remained unbroken when his shattered body scarcely afforded it a habitation.   Having done all that was just towards others, he remembered what was due to himself.   Neither the shock of the mortal blow, nor the lingering hours of acute pain which preceded his dissolution, could quell the pride of his gallant heart, or lower the dignified feeling with which (conscious of merit) he asserted his right to the gratitude of the country he had served so truly.

If glory be a distinction, for such a man death is not a leveller !

Peninsular War.

PERCY BYSSHE SHELLEY.

1792–1822.

A DEFENCE OF POETRY.

POETRY, in a general sense, may be defined to be "the expression of the imagination : " and poetry is connate with the origin of man. Man is an instrument over which a series of external and internal impressions are driven, like the alternations of an ever-changing wind over an Æolian lyre, which move it by their motion to ever-changing melody. But there is a principle within the human being, and perhaps within all sentient beings, which acts otherwise than in the lyre, and produces not melody alone, but harmony, by an internal adjustment of the sounds or motions thus excited to the impressions which excite them. It is as if the lyre could accommodate its chords to the motions of that which strikes them, in a determined proportion of sound ; even as the musician can accommodate his voice to the sound of the lyre. A child at play by itself will express its delight by its voice and motions ; and every inflexion of tone and every gesture will bear exact relation to a corresponding antitype in the pleasurable impressions which awakened it ; it will be the reflected image of that impression ; and as the lyre trembles and sounds after the wind has died away, so the child seeks, by prolonging in its voice and motions the duration of the effect, to prolong also a consciousness of the cause. In relation to the objects which delight a child, these expressions are, what poetry is to higher objects. The savage (for the savage is to ages what the child is to years) expresses the emotions produced in him by surrounding objects in a similar manner ; and language and gesture, together plastic or pictorial imitation, become the image of the combined effect of those objects, and of his apprehension of them. Man in society, with all his passions and his pleasures,

next becomes the object of the passions and pleasures of man ;
an additional class of emotions produces an augumented
treasure of expressions ; and language, gesture, and the
imitative arts, become at once the representation and the
medium, the pencil and the picture, the chisel and the statue,
the chord and the harmony. The social sympathies, or those
laws from which, as from its elements, society results, begin to
develop themselves from the moment that two human beings
co exist ; the future is contained within the present, as the
plant within the seed ; and equality, diversity, unity, contrast,
mutual dependence, become the principles alone capable of
affording the motives according to which the will of a social
being is determined to action, inasmuch as he is social ; and
constitute pleasure in sensation, virtue in sentiment, beauty in
art, truth in reasoning, and love in the intercourse of kind.
Hence men, even in the infancy of society, observe a certain
order in their words and actions, distinct from that of the
objects and the impressions represented by them, all expression
being subject to the laws of that from which it proceeds. But
let us dismiss those more general considerations which might
involve an inquiry into the principles of society itself, and
restrict our view to the manner in which the imagination is
expressed upon its forms.

In the youth of the world, men dance and sing and imitate
natural objects, observing in these actions, as in all others, a
certain rhythm or order. And, although all men observe a
similar, they observe not the same order, in the motions of the
dance, in the melody of the song, in the combinations of
language, in the series of their imitations of natural objects.
For there is a certain order or rhythm belonging to each of
these classes of mimetic representation, from which the hearer
and the spectator receive an intenser and purer pleasure than
from any other : the sense of an approximation to this order
has been called taste by modern writers. Every man in the
infancy of art, observes an order which approximates more or
less closely to that from which this highest delight results : but
the diversity is not sufficiently marked, as that its gradations
should be sensible, except in those instances where the pre-
dominance of this faculty of approximation to the beautiful (for
so we may be permitted to name the relation between this
highest pleasure and its cause) is very great. Those in whom
it exists in excess are poets, in the most universal sense of the
word ; and the pleasure resulting from the manner in which
they express the influence of society or nature upon their own

minds, communicate itself to others, and gathers a sort of
reduplication from that community. Their language is vitally
metaphorical : that is, it marks the before unapprehended relations of things and perpetuates their apprehension, until the
words which represent them, become, through time, signs for
portions or classes of thoughts instead of pictures of integral
thoughts : and then if no new poets should arise to create
afresh the associations which have been thus disorganised,
language will be dead to all the nobler purposes of human
intercourse. These similitudes or relations are finely said by
Lord Bacon to be "the same footsteps of nature impressed
upon the various subjects of the world"*—and he considers the
faculty which perceives them as the storehouse of axioms
common to all knowledge. In the infancy of society every
author is necessarily a poet, because language itself is poetry ;
and to be a poet is to apprehend the true and the beautiful, in
a word, the good which exists in the relation, subsisting, first
between existence and perception, and secondly between perception and expression. Every original language near to its
source is in itself the chaos of a cyclic poem : the copiousness
of lexicography and the distinctions of grammar are the works
of a later age, and are merely the catalogue and the form of the
creations of poetry.

But poets, or those who imagine and express this indestruc-
tible order, are not only the authors of language and of music,
of the dance, and architecture, and statuary, and painting :
they are the institutors of laws, and the founders of civil society,
and the inventors of the arts of life, and the teachers, who draw
into a certain propinquity with the beautiful and the true, that
partial apprehension of the agencies of the invisible world which
is called religion. Hence all original religions are allegorical,
or susceptible of allegory, and, like Janus, have a double face of
false and true. Poets, according to the circumstances of the
age and nation in which they appeared, were called, in the
earlier epochs of the world, legislators, or prophets : a poet
essentially comprises and unites both these characters. For
he not only beholds intensely the present as it is, and discovers
those laws according to which present things ought to be
ordered, but he beholds the future in the present, and his
thoughts are the germs of the flower and fruit of the latest time.
Not that I assert poets to be prophets in the gross sense of the
word, or that they can foretell the form as surely as they

* De Augment. Scient., cap. 1, lib. iii.

know the spirit of events : such is the pretence of superstition, which would make poetry an attribute to prophecy, rather than prophecy an attribute to poetry. A poet participates in the eternal, the infinite, and the one ; as far as relates to his conceptions, time and place and number are not. The grammatical forms which express the moods of time, and the difference of persons, and the distinction of place, are convertible with respect to the highest poetry without injuring it as poetry ; and the choruses of Æschylus, and the book of Job, and Dante's Paradise, would afford, more than any other writings, examples of this fact, if the limits of this essay did not forbid citation. The creations of sculpture, painting, and music are illustrations still more decisive.

Language, colour, form, and religious and civil habits of action, are all the instruments and materials of poetry ; they may be called poetry by that figure of speech which considers the effect as a synonyme of the cause. But poetry in a more restricted sense expresses those arrangements of language, and especially metrical language, which are created by that imperial faculty, whose throne is curtained within the invisible nature of man. And this springs from the nature itself of language, which is a more direct representation of the actions and passions of our internal being, and is susceptible of more various and delicate combinations, than colour, form, or motion, and is more plastic and obedient to the control of that faculty of which it is the creation. For language is arbitrarily produced by the imagination, and has relation to thoughts alone ; but all other materials, instruments, and conditions of art have relations among each other, which limit and interpose between conception and expression. The former is as a mirror which reflects, the latter as a cloud which enfeebles, the light of which both are mediums of communication. Hence the fame of sculptors, painters, and musicians, although the intrinsic powers of the great masters of these arts may yield in no degree to that of those who have employed language as the hieroglyphic of their thoughts, has never equalled that of poets in the restricted sense of the term ; as two performers of equal skill will produce unequal effects from a guitar and a harp. The fame of legislators and founders of religions, so long as their institutions last, alone seems to exceed that of poets in the restricted sense ; but it can scarcely be a question, whether, if we deduct the celebrity which their flattery of the gross opinions of the vulgar usually conciliates, together with that which belonged to them in their higher character of poets, any excess will remain.

We have thus circumscribed the word poetry within the limits of that art which is the most familiar and the most perfect expression of the faculty itself. It is necessary, however, to make the circle still narrower, and to determine the distinction between measured and unmeasured language; for the popular division into prose and verse is inadmissible in accurate philosophy.

Sounds as well as thoughts have relation both between each other and towards that which they represent, and a perception of the order of those relations has always been found connected with a perception of the order of the relations of thoughts. Hence the language of poets has ever affected a certain uniform and harmonious recurrence of sound, without which it were not poetry, and which is scarcely less indispensable to the communication of its influence, than the words themselves, without reference to that peculiar order. Hence the vanity of translation; it were as wise to cast a violet into a crucible that you might discover the formal principle of its colour and odour, as seek to transfuse from one language into another the creations of a poet. The plant must spring again from its seed, or it will bear no flower—and this is the burthen of the curse of Babel.

Essays.

THOMAS CARLYLE.

1795–1881.

THE EPIDEMIC OF "DESCRIPTION."

'To Peace, however, in this vortex of existence, can the Son
'of Time not pretend : still less if some Spectre haunt him from
'the Past ; and the Future is wholly a Stygian Darkness,
'spectre-bearing. Reasonably might the Wanderer exclaim to
'himself : Are not the gates of this world's Happiness inexorably
'shut against thee ; hast thou a hope that is not mad ? Never-
'theless, one may still murmur audibly, or in the original Greek
'if that suit thee better "Whoso can work on Death will start
'" at no shadows."
   'From such meditations is the Wanderer's attention called
'outwards ; for now the Valley closes-in abruptly, intersected
'by a huge mountain mass, the stony water-worn ascent of
'which is not to be accomplished on horse-back. Arrived
'aloft, he finds himself again lifted into the evening sunset
'light ; and cannot but pause, and gaze round him, some
'moments there. An upland irregular expanse of wold, when
'valleys in complex branchings are suddenly or slowly arranging
'their descent towards every quarter of the sky. The moun-
'tain-ranges are beneath four feet, and folded together : only
'the loftier summits look down here and there as on a second
'plain ; lakes also lie clear and earnest in their solitude. No
'trace of man now visible ; unless indeed it was he who
'fashioned that little visible link of Highway, here, as would
'seem, scaling the inaccessible, to unite Province with Province.
'But sun-wards, lo you ! how its towers sheer up, a world of
'Mountains, the diadem and centre of the mountain region.
'A hundred and a hundred savage peaks, in the last light of
'Day ; all glowing, of gold and amethyst, like giant spirits
'of the wilderness ; there in silence, in their solitude, even as

'on the night when Noah's Deluge first dried !   Beautiful, nay
'solemn, was the sudden aspect to our wanderer. He gazed
'over those stupendous masses with wonder, almost with
'longing desire ; never till this hour had he known Nature,
'that she was One, that she was his Mother and divine. And
'as the ruddy glow was fading into clearness in the sky, and
'the Sun had now departed, a murmur of Eternity and
'Immensity, of Death and of Life, stole through his soul ;
'and he felt as if death and life were one, as if the Earth were
'not dead, as if the Spirit of the Earth had its throne in
'that splendour, and his own spirit were therewith holding
'communion.
  'The spell was broken by a sound of carriage-wheels.
'Emerging from the hidden Northward, to sink soon into the
'hidden Southward, came a gay Barouche-and-four : it was
'open ; servants and postillions wore wedding favours : that
'happy pair, then, had found each other, it was their marriage
'evening !   Few moments brought them near : *Du Himmel !*
'It was Herr Towgood and——Blumine !   With slight unrecog-
'nising salutation they passed me ; plunged down among
'the neighbouring thickets, onwards, to Heaven, and to Eng-
'land ; and I, in my friend Richter's words, *I remained alone,*
'*behind them, with the Night.'*
  Were it not cruel in these circumstance, here might be the
place to insert an observation, gleaned long ago from the great
Clothes-Volume, where it stands with quite other intent : 'Some
'time before Small-pox was extirpated,' says the Professor,
'there came a new malady of the spiritual sort on Europe : I
'mean the epidemic, now endemical, of View-hunting. Poets of
'old date, being privileged with Senses, had also enjoyed external
'Nature ; but chiefly as we enjoy the crystal cup which holds
'good or bad liquor for us ; that is to say, in silence, or with
'slight incidental commentary : never, as I compute, till after
'the *Sorrows of Werter*, was there man found who would say :
'Come let us make a Description !   Having drunk the liquor,
'come let us eat the glass !   Of which endemic the Jenner is
'unhappily still to seek.'   Too true.

Sartor Resartus.

DANTE.

ETERNITY : thither, of a truth, not elsewhither, art thou and all things bound ! The great soul of Dante, homeless on earth, made its home more and more in that awful other world. Naturally his thoughts brooded on that, as the one fact important for him. Bodied or bodiless, it is the one fact important for all men :—but to Dante, in that age, it was bodied in fixed certainty of scientific shape ; he no more doubted of that *Malebogle* Pool, that it all lay there with its gloomy circles, with *alti guai*, and that he himself should see it, than we doubt that we should see Constantinople if we went thither. Dante's heart, long filled with this, brooding over it in speechless thought and awe, bursts forth at length into 'mystic unfathomable song ;' this his *Divine Comedy*, the most remarkable of all modern Books, is the result.

It must have been a great solacement to Dante, and was, as we can see, a proud thought for him at times, that he, here in exile, could do this work ; that no Florence, nor no man or men, could hinder him from doing it, or even much help him in doing it. He knew too, partly, that it was great ; the greatest a man could do. 'If thou follow thy star, *Se tu segui tua stella*,—so could the Hero, in his forsakenness, in his extreme need, still say to himself : "Follow thou thy star, thou shalt not "fail of a glorious haven !"' The labour of writing, we find, and indeed could know otherwise, was great and painful for him ; he says, 'This Book, which has made me lean for many years.' Ah yes, it was won, all of it, with pain and sore toil,—not in sport, but in grim earnest. His Book, as indeed most good Books are, has been written, in many senses, in his heart's blood. It was his whole history, this Book. He died after finishing it ; not yet very old, at the age of fifty-six ;—broken-hearted rather, as is said. He lies buried in his death-city Ravenna : *Hic claudor Dantes patriis extorris ab oris.* The Florentines begged back his body, in a century after ; the Ravenna people would not give it. "Here am I Dante laid, "shut out from my native shores."

I said, Dante's Poem was a Song : it is Tieck who calls it 'a 'mystic unfathomable Song ;' and such is literally the character of it. Coleridge remarks very pertinently somewhere, that wherever you find a sentence musically worded, of true rhythm and melody in the words, there is something deep and good in the meaning too. For body and soul, word and idea, go strangely together here as everywhere. Song : we said before, it was the Heroic of speech ! All *old*, Homer's and the rest, are authentically Songs. I would say, in strictness, that all right Poems are ; that whatsoever is not *sung* is properly no Poem, but a piece of Prose cramped into jingling lines, to the great injury of the grammar, to the great grief of the reader, for most part ! What we want to get at is the *thought* the man had, if he had any : why should he twist it into jingle, if he *could* speak it out plainly? It is only when the heart of him is rapt into true passion of melody, and the very tones of him, according to Coleridge's remark, become musical by the greatness, depth and music of his thoughts, that we can give him right to rhyme and sing ; that we call him a Poet, and listen to him as the Heroic of Speaking,—whose speech *is* Song. Pretenders to this are many ; and to an earnest reader, I doubt, it is for the most part a very melancholy, not to say insupportable business, that of reading rhyme ! Rhyme that had no inward necessity to be rhymed ;—it ought to have told us plainly, without any jingle, what it was aiming at. I would advise all men who *can* speak their thought, not to sing it ; to understand that, in a serious time, among serious men, there is no vocation in them for singing it. Precisely as we love the true song, and are charmed by it as something divine, so shall we hate the false song, and account it a mere wooden noise, a thing hollow, superfluous, altogether an insincere and offensive thing.

I give Dante my highest praise when I say of his *Divine Comedy* that it is, in all senses, genuinely a Song. In the very sound of it there is a *canto firmo* ; it proceeds as by a chant. The language, his simple *terza rima*, doubtless helped him in this. One reads along naturally with a sort of *lilt*. But I add, that it could not be otherwise ; for the essence and material of the work are themselves rythmic. Its depth, and rapt passion and sincerity, makes it musical ; go *deep* enough, there is music everywhere. A true inward symmetry, what one calls an architectural harmony, reigns in it, proportionates it all: architectural ; which also partakes of the character of music. The three kingdoms, *Inferno*, *Purgatorio*, *Paradiso*, look-out on one another like compartments of a great edifice ; a great supernatural world-cathedral, piled-up there, stern, solemn, awful ; Dante's World of Souls ! It is, at bottom, the *sincerest* of all Poems ; sincerity, here too, we find to be the measure of worth. It came deep out of the author's heart of hearts ; and it goes deep, and through long generations, into ours. The people of

Verona, when they saw him in the streets, used to say, "*Eccovi*
"*l'uom ch' è stato all' Inferno*," "See, there is the man that was
"in Hell!" Ah yes, he had been in Hell;—in Hell enough, in
long severe sorrow and struggle; as the like of him is pretty
sure to have been. Commedius that come-out *divine* are not
accomplished otherwise. Thought, true labour of any kind,
highest virtue itself, is it not the daughter of Pain? Born as
out of the black whirlwind;—true *effort*, in fact, as of a captive
struggling to free himself: that is Thought. In all ways we are
"to become perfect through *suffering*."—But, as I say, no work
known to me is so elaborated as this of Dante's. It has all
been as if molten, in the hottest furnace of his soul. It made
him 'lean' for many years. Not the general whole only;
every compartment of it is worked-out, with intense earnestness,
into truth, into clear visuality. Each answers to the other;
each fits in its place, like a marble stone accurately hewn and
polished. It is the soul of Dante, and in this the soul of the
middle ages, rendered for ever rhythmically visible there. No
light task; a right intense one: but a task which is *done*.

Perhaps one would say, *intensity*, with the much which
depends on it, is the prevailing character of Dante's genius.
Dante does not come before us as a large catholic mind;
rather as a narrow, and even sectarian mind: it is partly the
fruit of his age and position, but partly the fruit of his own
nature. His greatness has, in all senses, concentred itself
into fiery emphasis and depth. He is world-great not because
he is world-wide, but because he is world deep. Through all
objects he pierces as it were down into the heart of Being.
I know nothing so intense as Dante. Consider, for example,
to begin with the outermost development of his intensity,
consider how he paints. He has a great power of vision;
seizes the very type of a thing; presents that and nothing
more. You remember the first view he gets of the Hall of
Dite: *red* pinnacle, redhot cone of iron glowing through the
dim immensity of gloom;—so vivid, so distinct, visible at once
and forever! It is an emblem of the whole genius of Dante.
There is a brevity, an abrupt precision in him: Tacitus is not
briefer, more condensed; and then in Dante it seems a natural
condensation, spontaneous to the man. One smiting word;
and then there is silence, nothing more said. His silence is
more eloquent than words. It is strange with what a sharp
decisive grace he snatches the true likeness of a matter: cuts
into the matter as with a pen of fire. Plutus, the blustering
giant, collapses at Virgil's rebuke it is 'as the sails sink, the

'mast being suddenly broken.' Or that poor Brunetto Latini, with the *cotto aspetto*, the 'face *baked*,' parched brown and lean ; and the 'fiery snow' that falls on them there, a 'fiery 'snow without wind,' slow, deliberate, never-ending ! Or the lids of those Tombs ; square sarcophaguses, in that silent dim-burning Hall, each with its Soul in torment ; the lids laid open there ; they are to be shut at the Day of Judgment, through Eternity. And how Farinata rises ; and how Cavalcante falls—at the hearing of his son, and the past tense '*fue !*' The very movements in Dante have something brief ; swift, decisive, almost military. It is of the inmost essence of his genius this sort of painting. The fiery, swift Italian nature of the man, so silent, passionate, with its quick abrupt movements, its silent 'pale rages,' speaks itself in these things.

For though this of painting is one of the outermost developments of a man, it comes like all else from the essential faculty of him ; it is physiognomical of the whole man. Find a man whose words paint you a likeness, you have found a man worth something ; mark his manner of doing it, as very characteristic of him. In the first place, he could not have discerned the object at all, or seen the vital type of it, unless he had, what we may call, *sympathised* with it,—had sympathy in him to bestow on objects. He must have been *sincere* about it too ; sincere and sympathetic : a man without worth cannot give you the likeness of any object ; he dwells in vague outwardness, fallacy, and trivial hearsay, about all objects. And, indeed, may we not say that intellect altogether expresses itself in this power of discerning what an object is? Whatsoever of faculty a man's mind may have will come out here. It is even of business a matter to be done? The gifted man is he who *sees* the essential point, and leaves all the rest aside as surplusage : it is his faculty too, the man of business's faculty, that he discern the true likeness, not the false superficial one, of the thing he has got to work in. And how much of *morality* is in the kind of insight we get of anything ; 'the eye seeing in all 'things what it brought with it the faculty of seeing !' To the mean eye all things are trivial, as certainly as to the jaundiced they are yellow. Raphael, the Painters tell us, is the best of all portrait painters withal. No most gifted eye can exhaust the significance of any object. In the commonest human face there lies more than Raphael will take away with him.

The Hero as Poet.

LORD MACAULAY.

1800–1859.

THE ROMAN CHURCH.

THERE is not, and there never was on this earth, a work of human policy so well deserving of examination as the Roman Catholic Church. The history of that Church joins together with two great ages of human civilisation. No other institution is left standing which carries the mind back to the times when the smoke of sacrifice rose from the Pantheon, and when camelopards and tigers bounded in the Flavian amphitheatre. The proudest royal houses are but of yesterday, when compared with the line of the Supreme Pontiffs. That line we trace back in an unbroken series, from the Pope who crowned Napoleon in the nineteenth century to the Pope who crowned Pepin in the eighth; and far beyond the time of Pepin the august dynasty extends, till it is lost in the twilight of fable. The republic of Venice came next in antiquity. But the republic of Venice was modern when compared with the Papacy; and the republic of Venice is gone, and the Papacy remains. The Papacy remains, not in decay, not a mere antique, but full of life and youthful vigour. The Catholic Church is still sending forth to the farthest ends of the world missionaries as zealous as those who landed in Kent with Augustin, and still confronting hostile kings with the same spirit with which she confronted Attila. The number of her children is greater than in any former age. Her acquisitions in the New World have more than compensated for what she has lost in the Old. Her spiritual ascendancy extends over the vast countries which lie beween the plains of the Missouri and Cape Horn, countries which, a century hence, may not improbably contain a population as large as that which now inhabits Europe. The members of her communion are certainly not fewer than a hundred and fifty millions ; and it will be difficult to show that all other Christian sects united amount to a hundred and twenty millions. Nor do we see any sign which indicates that the term of her long dominion is approaching. She saw the commencement of all the governments and of all the ecclesiastical establishments that now exist in the world ; and we feel no assurance that she is not destined to see the end of them all. She was great and respected before the Saxon had set foot on Britain, before the Frank had passed the Rhine, when Grecian eloquence still flourished at Antioch, when idols were still worshipped in the temple ot Mecca. And she may still exist in undiminished vigour when some traveller from New Zealand shall, in the midst of a vast solitude, take his stand on a broken arch of London Bridge to sketch the ruins of St. Paul's.

WM. MAKEPEACE THACKERAY.

1811–1863.

BECKY SHARP.

Miss Sharp's father was an artist, and in that quality had given lessons of drawing at Miss Pinkerton's school. He was a clever man ; a pleasant companion ; a careless student ; with a great propensity for running into debt, and a partiality for the tavern. When he was drunk, he used to beat his wife and daughter ; and the next morning, with a headache, he would rail at the world for its neglect of his genius, and abuse, with a good deal of cleverness, and sometimes with perfect reason, the fools, his brother painters. As it was with the utmost difficulty that he could keep himself, and as he owed money for a mild round Soho, where he lived, he thought to better his circumstances by marrying a young woman of the French nation, who was by profession an opera-girl. The humble calling of her female parent, Miss Sharp never alluded to, but used to state subsequently that the Entrechats were a noble family of Gascony, and took great pride in her descent from them. And curious it is, that as she advanced in life this young lady's ancestors increased in rank and splendour.

Rebecca's mother had had some education somewhere, and her daughter spoke French with purity and a Parisian accent. It was in those days rather a rare accomplishment, and led to her engagement with the orthodox Miss Pinkerton. For her mother being dead, her father, finding himself not likely to recover, after his third attack of *delirium tremens*, wrote a manly and pathetic letter to Miss Pinkerton, recommending the orphan child to her protection, and so descended to the grave, after two bailiffs had quarrelled over his corpse. Rebecca was seventeen when she came to Chiswick, and was bound over as an articled pupil ; her duties being to talk French, as we have seen; and her privileges to live cost free, and, with a few guineas a year, to gather scraps of knowledge from the professors who attended the school.

She was small and slight in person; pale, sandy-haired, and with eyes habitually cast down: when they looked up they were very large, odd, and attractive; so attractive, that the Reverend Mr. Crisp, fresh from Oxford, and curate to the Vicar of Chiswick, the Reverend Mr. Flowerdew, fell in love with Miss Sharp; being shot dead by a glance of her eyes which was fired all the way across Chiswick Church from the school-pew to the reading-desk. This infatuated young man used sometimes to take tea with Miss Pinkerton, to whom he had been presented by his mamma, and actually proposed something like marriage in an intercepted note, which the one-eyed apple-woman was charged to deliver. Mrs. Crisp was summoned from Buxton, and abruptly carried off her darling boy; but the idea, even, of such an eagle in the Chiswick dovecot caused a great flutter in the breast of Miss Pinkerton, who would have sent away Miss Sharp, but that she was bound to her under a forfeit, and who never could thoroughly believe the young lady's protestations that she had never exchanged a single word with Mr. Crisp, except under her own eyes on the two occasions when she had met him at tea.

By the side of many tall and bouncing young ladies in the establishment, Rebecca Sharp looked like a child. But she had the dismal precocity of poverty. Many a dun had she talked to, and turned away from her father's door; many a tradesman had she coaxed and wheedled into good-humour, and into the granting of one meal more. She sate commonly with her father, who was very proud of her wit, and heard the talk of many of his wild companions—often but ill-suited for a girl to hear. But she never had been a girl, she said; she had been a woman since she was eight years old. O why did Miss Pinkerton let such a dangerous bird into her cage?

The fact is, the old lady believed Rebecca to be the meekest creature in the world, so admirably, on the occasions when her father brought her to Chiswick, used Rebecca to perform the part of the *ingénue;* and only a year before the arrangement by which Rebecca had been admitted into the house, and when Rebecca was sixteen years old, Miss Pinkerton majestically, and with a little speech, made her a present of a doll—which was, by the way, the confiscated property of Miss Swindle, discovered surreptitiously nursing it in school-hours. How the father and

daughter laughed as they trudged home together after the
evening party, (it was on the occasion of the speeches, when all
the professors were invited,) and how Miss Pinkerton would
have raged had she seen the caricature of herself which the
little mimic, Rebecca, managed to make out of her doll.
Becky used to go through dialogues with it; it formed the
delight of Newman Street, Gerard Street, and the artists'
quarter: and the young painters, when they came to take their
gin and water with their lazy, dissolute, clever, jovial senior, used
regularly to ask Rebecca if Miss Pinkerton was at home: she was
well known to them, poor soul! as Mr. Lawrence or President
West. Once Rebecca had the honour to pass a few days at
Chiswick; after which she brought back Jemima, and erected
another doll as Miss Jemmy: for though that honest creature
had made and given her jelly and cake enough for three
children, and a seven-shilling piece at parting, the girl's sense
of ridicule was far stronger than her gratitude, and she sacrificed
Miss Jemmy quite as pitilessly as her sister.

The catastrophe came, and she was brought to the Mall as to
her home. The rigid formality of the place suffocated her: the
prayers and the meals, the lessons and the walks, which were
arranged with a conventual regularity, oppressed her almost
beyond endurance; and she looked back to the freedom and
the beggary of the old studio in Soho with so much regret, that
everybody, herself included, fancied she was consumed with
grief for her father. She had a little room in the garret, where
the maids heard her walking and sobbing at night; but it was
with rage, and not with grief. She had not been much of a
dissembler, until now her loneliness taught her to feign. She
had never mingled in the society of women: her father,
reprobate as he was, was a man of talent; his conversation was
a thousand times more agreeable to her than the talk of such of
her own sex as she now encountered. The pompous vanity of
the old schoolmistress, the foolish good-humour of her sister,
the silly chat and scandal of the elder girls, and the frigid
correctness of the governesses equally annoyed her; and she
had no soft maternal heart, this unlucky girl, otherwise the
prattle and talk of the younger children, with whose care she
was chiefly intrusted, might have soothed and interested her;
but she lived among them two years, and not one was sorry that
she went away. The gentle tender-hearted Amelia Sedley was
the only person to whom she could attach herself in the least;
and who could help attaching herself to Amelia?

The happiness—the superior advantages of the young women

round about her, gave Rebecca inexpressible pangs of envy. "What airs that girl gives herself, because she is an Earl's grand-daughter," she said of one. "How they cringe and bow to that Creole, because of her hundred thousand pounds! I am a thousand times cleverer and more charming than that creature, for all her wealth. I am as well bred as the Earl's grand-daughter, for all her fine pedigree ; and yet every one passes me by here. And yet, when I was at my father's, did not the men give up their gayest balls and parties in order to pass the evening with me?" She determined at any rate to get free from the prison in which she found herself, and now began to act for herself, and for the first time to make connected plans for the future.

She took advantage, therefore, of the means of study the place offered her ; and as she was already a musician and a good linguist, she speedily went through the little course of study which was considered necessary for ladies in those days. Her music she practised incessantly, and one day, when the girls were out, and she had remained at home, she was overheard to play a piece so well, that Minerva thought wisely, she could spare herself the expense of a master for the juniors, and intimated to Miss Sharp that she was to instruct them in music for the future.

The girl refused ; and for the first time, and to the astonishment of the majestic mistress of the school. "I am here to speak French with the children," Rebecca said abruptly, "not to teach them music, and save money for you. Give me money, and I will teach them."

Minerva was obliged to yield, and, of course, disliked her from that day. "For five-and-thirty years," she said, and with great justice, "I never have seen the individual who had dared in my own house to question my authority. I have nourished a viper in my bosom."

"A viper—a fiddlestick," said Miss Sharp to the old lady, almost fainting with astonishment. "You took me because I was useful. There is no question of gratitude between us. I hate this place, and want to leave it. I will do nothing here but what I am obliged to do."

It was in vain that the old lady asked her if she was aware she was speaking to Miss Pinkerton? Rebecca laughed in her face, with a horrid sarcastic demoniacal laughter, that almost sent the schoolmistress into fits. "Give me a sum of money," said the girl, "and get rid of me—or, if you like better, get me a good place as governess in a nobleman's family—you can do so if you please." And in their further disputes she always returned to this point, "Get me a situation—we hate each other, and I am ready to go."

Worthy Miss Pinkerton, although she had a Roman nose and a turban, and was as tall as a grenadier, and had been up to this time an irresistible princess, had no will or strength like that of her little apprentice, and in vain did battle against her, and tried to overawe her. Attempting once to scold her in public, Rebecca hit upon the before-mentioned plan of answering her in French, which quite routed the old woman. In order to maintain authority in her school, it became necessary to remove this rebel, this monster, this serpent, this firebrand ; and hearing about this time that Sir Pitt Crawley's family was in want of a governess, she actually recommended Miss Sharp for the situation, firebrand and serpent as she was. " I cannot, certainly," she said, " find fault with Miss Sharp's conduct, except to myself ; and must allow that her talents and accomplishments are of a high order. As far as the head goes, at least, she does credit to the educational system pursued at my establishment."

And so the schoolmistress reconciled the recommendation to her conscience, and the indentures were cancelled, and the apprentice was free. The battle here described in a few lines, of course, lasted for some months. And as Miss Sedley, being now in her seventeenth year, was about to leave school, and had a friendship for Miss Sharp ("'tis the only point in Amelia's behaviour," said Minerva, " which has not been satisfactory to her mistress,") Miss Sharp was invited by her friend to pass a week with her at home, before she entered upon her duties as governess in a private family.

Thus the world began for these two young ladies. For Amelia it was quite a new, fresh, brilliant world, with all the bloom upon it. It was not quite a new one for Rebecca— (indeed, if the truth must be told with respect to the Crisp affair, the tart-woman hinted to somebody, who took an affidavit of the fact to somebody else, that there was a great deal more than was made public regarding Mr. Crisp and Miss Sharp, and that his letter was *in answer* to another letter). But who can tell you the real truth of the matter ? At all events, if Rebecca was not beginning the world, she was beginning it over again.

Vanity Fair.

9 783337 282424